D1510141

# CELESTIAL
# MATTERS

# CELESTIAL MATTERS

# RICHARD GARFINKLE

**TOR®**

A TOM DOHERTY ASSOCIATES BOOK

NEW YORK

CELESTIAL MATTERS

This book is printed on acid-free paper.

Edited by David G. Hartwell

Design by Lynn Newmark

A Tor Book
Published by Tom Doherty Associates, Inc.
175 Fifth Avenue
New York, N.Y. 10010

Tor Books on the World Wide Web:
http://www.tor.com

Tor® is a registered trademark of Tom Doherty Associates, Inc.

Library of Congress Cataloging-in-Publication Data

Garfinkle, Richard.
    Celestial matters / Richard Garfinkle. —1st ed.
        p.    cm.
    "A Tom Doherty Associates book."
    ISBN 0–312–85934–1 (acid-free paper)
    I. Title.
PS3557.A71536C4    1996
813'.54—dc20                                    95–29998

First edition: April 1996

Printed in the United States of America

0 9 8 7 6 5 4 3 2 1

To my wife, Alessandra

# α

I supplicate myself before Apollo of the poets and before the Muses. I ask them to fill me, a weak-voiced scientist, with their gifts so that I may in their honor adorn the tale I must tell with beauty, yet in it say nothing but the truth.

But forgive me, O gods, it is not right that I honor Apollo with my voice and dishonor his father Zeus, god of guests, with my anonymity. Therefore, I tell you that my name is Aias; that I was born in the city of Tyre in the 935th year since the founding of the Delian League; that my antecedents are honorable, since my mother was a child of a great Phoenician merchant house and my father a Spartan general who in his youth commanded armies and in his maturity served as military governor of many city-states within the League.

As for my personal honors, I graduated at the age of twenty from the Athenian Akademe and in the twenty-three years since then I served the League as a scholar in the fields of Pyrology and Ouranology. Most recently I held the post of Scientific commander of the celestial ship *Chandra's Tear*, and on that vessel I oversaw the researching, creation, and operation of Project

Sunthief. It is because of my actions in that capacity that I am now called and do freely submit myself and my story to the gods for judgment.

Once again I bow before Phoibos and the Nine who follow him, and offer prayers for their assistance. With their help and your indulgence, therefore, permit me to begin my tale during the last peaceful period in my life, that final stretch of pleasant time the Fates gave me before they snarled the thread of my existence.

For three years I had been in command of *Chandra's Tear*, during which time I and my subordinates had by the labor of our minds and the experiments of our hands brought Project Sunthief from a theoretical possibility to an incipient reality. At the end of those three years, we were actually capable of spinning celestial matter mined from the inner planets into a sun net. We believed and hoped that we would be able to use such a net to capture a portion of 'Elios's celestial fire.

But the exact specifications of the sun net still required a great deal of patient calculation and experimentation that could only be performed by Mihradarius, my chief Ouranologist. No other progress could be made until he finished that part of the project. When I put the matter to him Mihradarius passed a few minutes in silent contemplation, then confidently declared that he would be able to complete the work in a month.

So, much to our surprise, I and my other two primary subordinates, Kleon, chief Celestial Navigator of *Chandra's Tear*, and Ramonojon, the Chief Dynamicist, found ourselves with nothing to do for thirty days. We each decided to take advantage of this unexpected gift of time to take leave from the ship.

Of the thousand days that had passed since my crew had first assembled on *Chandra's Tear* not one of us had spent more than ten on the earth. I do not know how the others felt, but I had come to dream of once again walking across Gaea's stationary ground, and laying my motion-wracked body on her peaceful grassy surface, and enjoying the stillness of that static globe that lay at the center of the endlessly moving cosmos.

I sent messages down to Earth requesting permission from the Athenian bureaucracy, the Spartan military high command, and the Archons on Delos for a month's vacation for the three of us. Both of the Archons approved without comment. The Spartans had no objection since *Chandra's Tear* would still be guided by its Military Commander, my friend and partner, Aeson. They knew, as I did, that the firm hand of that wise officer would ensure that the project proceeded smoothly and securely. But the bureaucrats in Athens were another matter. They had no problem with Kleon and Ramonojon taking time off, but to their pedantic minds a ship's commander belonged on his ship.

For four days message capsules flew back and forth between *Chandra's Tear* and Athens conveying my arguments and their counterarguments. They finally gave in when I threatened to lodge protests with the Archons and the provost of the Akademe. I hinted at dire consequences to careers, and implied a level of influence with those in power that I was not sure I had. My bluff worked, but out of spite the bureaucrats insisted I find some way to pay for my absence. I grudgingly offered to make a lecture tour of some of the city-states around the Mediterranean to offset the minute costs of my month's rest.

That matter settled, Kleon, Ramonojon, and I cleared our desks of paperwork and prepared to depart. We arranged to disembark from the ship at the sky dock on Crete and come aboard again one month later from the port in Athens. I considered having a formal ceremony of departure, during which I would explicitly hand over scientific command of *Chandra's Tear* to Mihradarius, who was my second-in-command. But on reflection I decided that a formal ceremony of leave-taking with the requisite prayers, sacrifice, and taking of omens would make the crew too conscious of my absence and worry them unduly. However, neither did I want to simply vanish from my own ship like a thief in the night, so, the night before I was to go back down to Earth, I had a celebratory feast laid on in the ship's commissary.

The slave cooks did a marvelous job of preparing the meal, which centered around a whole roasted lamb marinated liberally in olive oil and oregano, served with barley bread fresh from the ship's ovens; there were also fresh vegetables from all across the world and little honey cakes dotted with dates. To add to the celebration, Mihradarius himself brought out some jars of Persian wine that had aged for many years in his family estates near Persepolis. He broke the seal on a dark red vintage and let the heady smell waft deliciously from the clay clask; then he poured and mixed the wine with water and toasted me with fulsome congratulations for having brought Sunthief this close to final success.

The whole scene is engraved in my heart with perfect clarity; I remember Mihradarius's aristocratic, upright stance, his flowing Athenian scholar's robes, and the sight of his right hand as he raised up the plate of wine. The last rays of sunlight glinted off the deep crimson liquid while the silvery glow that came up from the ship's deck set off the black figure painting of Mithras on the underside of the drinking vessel.

"To Aias of Athens," Mihradarius said, his voice carrying clearly though the crisp air of five hundred miles up. "Commander, may you well enjoy your rest after long labors."

I bowed my head in thanks and the two hundred crewmen of *Chandra's Tear*, both my own scientific staff and Aeson's soldiers, raised their plates of wine and drank to my triumph from which their own triumphs would flow.

As the sun set, I raised my plate and drank to my crew in the mingled silver light of moon and stars and ship. That dark purple draft of Dionysos flowed down my throat and elated me with thoughts of my soon-to-be-completed achievement. All around me my crew were drinking and laughing, praising me and delighting in their own efforts. O gods, how easy it is for man to fall into hubris. O Prometheus, maker of man, why did you bless us with so little of your divine forethought?

Basking in the warmth of wine and praise, I took a plate of lamb and wandered for a while through the party, graciously accepting the congratulations of all about me and complimenting each crewman in turn upon his work. In one corner of the commissary, seated on two adjacent couches, I came upon Mihradarius and Ramonojon in animated discussion. They formed a strange contrast, the tall, intense young Persian genius, keen and clear with his ideas, and the old Indian man cautiously rounding off the sharp corners of concepts, smoothing the way for Mihradarius's notions to be put into actual practice. In the three years we had worked together they had fallen into a secure practice of continual wrangling from which had emerged the designs for the sun net and the mechanism that would secure it to the ship

"Commander," Mihradarius said as I walked up to them.

"Aias," Ramonojon said, greeting me as friend to friend instead of subordinate to leader.

"Ramonojon, you have no work for the next month," I said. "Why are you sitting here arguing with Mihradarius?"

"There was a matter of the net specifications," he said.

"I did not ask what you were arguing about," I said. "But why were you arguing?"

Ramonojon bit his thumbnail in contemplation. He sat for a few moments thinking intensely. "Habit," he said at last. "Just habit."

Ramonojon lowered his head in mock shame and ate a little of the lamb on his plate. Mihradarius and I laughed lightly at Ramonojon's self-mockery.

"Do not worry about the sun net, Chief Dynamicist," Mihradarius said to Ramonojon. "I shall keep all your concerns in mind while you are gone."

"Thank you, Senior Ouranologist," Ramonojon said. He smiled for a moment, but then it seemed as if a heaviness settled briefly on his shoulders before being dispelled by a shake of his head. "But only I can keep all my concerns in mind."

I wondered what was troubling him, and was about to ask, but at that point Kleon darted out of the crowd and flitted over to us. He was carrying a small plate of olives and sweet wheat cakes, one of which he was in the process of devouring. True to his Pythagorean vows, my Chief Celestial Navigator never ate meat, but that had never stopped him from relishing his food.

"Mihradarius," Kleon said, wiping the last few crumbs of cake from his thin, scraggly beard. "I hope you will keep my ship safe while I am down on Earth."

The navigator's musical voice held an air of joking amusement, but underneath that tone lay a clear note of real concern. It was hard for Kleon to leave the ship he had been piloting for three years; he knew his second navigator to be a competent pilot but not divinely gifted as Kleon had become through years of Pythagorean mathematical contemplation.

Mihradarius nodded patiently to Kleon. "Tell me what you think I should do," he said.

Kleon and Mihradarius settled down to a discussion of the ship's routine, including flight schedules, maintenance work that needed to be done, and so on. Mihradarius was remarkably indulgent of Kleon; usually my second-in-command had little or no patience for such things. I noted it in my mind as further evidence that Mihradarius would one day be an excellent scientific commander.

While Kleon and Mihradarius were going over the rotation schedule for the junior navigators, Ramonojon stood up quietly and faded into the crowd, not wanting to be drawn into such a lackluster conversation.

For similar reasons I also slipped off, ducking through the throng of scientists and soldiers sharing idle talk and grandiose hopes, and made my way to the aft end of the commissary, where the slave cooks waited with more food and wine.

My co-commander Aeson was seated on a couch next to the serving table. Between small bites of plain bread he swept his glance over the crowd, studying his soldiers and officers with an appraising eye. His Spartan spirit kept the men from indulging in excess, and made them remember that they were the crew of a celestial ship of the Delian League.

While I could inspire my scientists with the vision of Sunthief, it was Aeson who kept the whole crew, civilian and soldier alike, aware of the military importance of our work. Watching him, I became keenly aware of the central tenet of Delian rulership: two leaders for every command. There was a pang in my heart, an instant of worry about my absence. Would the ship run as smoothly with one full commander and one second-in-command? But that brief touch of wise caution was swept out of me by the spirit of surety that reigned over my ship.

Aeson nodded to me and handed me a plate of wine. "Enjoy your rest, Aias," he said. "I will keep watch over our command."

I drank the wine to the last drop, put down the plate, and gripped Aeson's elbow as friend to friend. "I have no doubt of that," I said.

Aeson returned the gesture, his scarred, strong warrior's hand giving my arm a gentle clutch of reassurance. The two of us together raised a toast to our crew and to Sunthief and then with the hurrahs of my men still ringing in my ears, I retired to pack my traveling satchel and sleep off the heady wine of confidence.

The next morning *Chandra's Tear* docked above Crete to take on supplies. Kleon, Ramonojon, and I bade farewell to our comrades and underlings, then disembarked to enjoy once again the pleasures that only Earth could provide. Kleon remained in Crete at the celestial navigators guild to obtain some new impellers for our ship and to catch up on the latest advances in mathematics with his fellow Pythagoreans. Ramonojon and I shared a light breakfast of bread and olives at a small restaurant on the coast; then he boarded a fast ocean ship bound for his home in India. Alone and at peace, I reacquainted my body with the sensations of immobility before setting out to refamiliarize my mind with the luxurious life to be found around the central sea of the Delian League.

My first stop was Memphis in Egypt; there I walked along the banks of the Nile, watched slaves harvest papyrus reeds to be pressed into scrolls, and saw the steamships ferrying gold and exotic foods from the heart of Africa into the Mediterranean basin. I paid due homage to Thoth-'Ermes at the temple in Memphis and gave a ten-year-old lecture on the properties of light-gathering materials to the schoolmasters and junior scholars of that city.

From there I passed on to 'Ierusalem and enjoyed a lively debate with the Pyrology staff at the rabbinical college on the exact motive properties of different forms of fire. We argued for seven hours without a pause and only stopped because night was about to fall and the 'Ebreu holy day of rest began that evening. The next day I and a few other visitors wandered the nearly deserted streets of the city while the inhabitants stayed in their homes praying with their families or went to their temple to worship their god.

The next day I traveled by underground evac tube to the port of Gaza and boarded a Spartan warship traveling to Rome in order to pick up soldiers needed for the war in North Atlantea. The Forum in Rome buzzed with the latest battle news; merchants and aristocrats argued cogently about what strategies the Spartan high command would use to capture the plains of that continent and what means the army of the Middle Kingdom would use to try and stop our armies. Of all the peoples in the Delian League the Romans come closest to the Spartans in their fascination with war.

As I was leaving the Forum, I was accosted by an old veteran who had when a much younger man served under my father's command. I bought the retired soldier a bowl of wine and listened respectfully as he told me of the campaigns of his youth and the battles he had fought to take the river Mississipp.

He was particularly vehement about how easy today's soldiers had it, since he had been in the army before the invention of celestial ships. In those days the enemy ruled the skies with their battle kites and our troops had only the artillery to defend themselves with. Before I left, he asked me how my father was. I smiled and shrugged, not wanting to tell this loyal old man that my father and I had not spoken in over two decades.

Not surprisingly, my lecture to the Roman college was poorly attended as I refused to speak about weapons research. The Spartans would have had my head if I had actually given out any details about an important military project like Sunthief. The night before I left I attended the New Orphic mysteries in the catacombs beneath the Pantheon, then I paid my respects to Zeus of the Capital and sailed away.

From Rome I went to Syrakuse, where I offered the traditional sacrifice of the blood from a black-wooled sheep to the heroscientist Archimedes, one of the first great weapon makers. Few ask for his intercession, but I needed all the divine assistance I could muster for the completion of my work. In the bustling port of Syrakuse I took ship to the Pillars of 'Erakles; from there I traveled on land in the sweltering steel box of a military fire chariot eastward across the north coast of Africa. The soldiers driving the steam-powered wagon asked me if I had ever been in anything this hot. I, who was planning to capture a fragment of the sun itself, had no choice but to laugh all the way to Carthage.

The citizens of that part of the world are very traditional people. Of all the cities on the Mediterranean, Carthage is the only one to have no modern conveniences. Their tallest buildings are three stories high, there is no sky dock, no evac tubes for intracity transport, no weather-filtering grids of air-silver above their houses. They even refuse to grow animals in spontaneous generation farms.

Some people, no doubt, derive contentment from that primitive existence, but I had come back to Earth to enjoy myself. After giving a very abbreviated lecture and taking as few questions as possible, I fled on the first ship I could find bound for Tyre, the city of my birth.

I reached Tyre four days before my vacation was due to end. The moment I stepped off the boat, I was mobbed by two dozen of my maternal relatives. Young cousins pulled at the blue fringe on my scholar's robe and asked me all sorts of questions about life on a celestial ship. Uncles offered me advice on how to keep my subordinates in line, and my aunts presented me with the names of several eligible women I might wish to marry; after all, I was forty-three and not getting any younger.

To drive home this point my aunt Philida insisted I attend my niece's wedding the next day. She had me on prominent display, holding one of the two-foot-tall red candles in front of Ishtar's altar. Looking down on me from a gallery near the waist of the huge gilded statue of the goddess of love were two dozen young women my aunt had assembled to look me over. By keeping my mind on the solemnity of the occasion, I think I managed to look distant and bewildered enough to disinterest them. Whether that is the case or not, I passed through the ceremony without becoming affianced.

At the wedding feast I indulged like a sybarite in the wonders of Phoenician cooking, supping on lamb with dates and figs, chickens potted with Atlantean tubers, wine aged in cedar casks, and fragrant honey-nut cakes. When my mouth was not full, I fended off the moneymaking schemes of my merchant cousins. To them science was neither a pure pursuit of knowledge, nor a vital factor in the prosecution of the war between the Delian League and the Middle Kingdom. No, to them science was a source of new devices they could sell. I enjoyed immensely ducking their attempts to inveigle me into complex deals that revolved around my inventing something for them, their selling it, and all of us making a fortune.

I stayed with my mother's family for one more day before taking ship to Athens, where I was to give one last lecture, meet Kleon and Ramonojon, and be picked up at the city's sky dock by *Chandra's Tear*.

At the marina in Tyre I looked over the Spartan high-speed priority transport ship that had been assigned to take me to Athens. The sleek steel craft, its long fire-gold impellers bristling like spines off its bow, would reach the city of knowledge in half an hour's time. But I did not want my vacation to end that quickly; I wanted to savor the past month's pleasures for a little longer before immersing myself in the rigor of the Athenian Akademe. So I told the captain I would find other transportation. A few piers away I came across a Phoenician merchantman that was bound for Athens but would take a leisurely twelve hours to reach that queen of all cities. My identification scroll marked with the seal of the Archons and a few obols from my purse bought me passage.

And that is how I came to be lounging on the open deck of an unarmed antique steamship rather than under the steel aegis of a cannonaded naval vessel when the Middler battle kite swooped out of the peaceful afternoon sky and tried to kill me.

At first the attacking aircraft was just a spot against the brazen disk of the sun; I thought it was a celestial ship, hundreds of miles above the earth, but as it drove down on us it grew larger much too quickly for something that distant. It darted away from the sun and I made out its silhouette against a lone cloud. A coiled serpentine form twenty feet long with broad translucent wings half the length of its body. I knew then what it was, a silk dragon with a human pilot and enough Taoist armament to easily sink this ship.

The dragon looped above the cloud, then furled its wings and plunged straight down toward the merchantman. On the tips of the aircraft's wings its twin silver Xi lances vibrated, roiling the ocean with waves of invisible fury. My fragile merchant vessel pitched back and forth, toppling me onto the foredeck. The rough grain of the oak flooring scraped my face. At the same moment a surge of water came over the side; it drenched my robes, stung my eyes, and diluted the flow of blood from my scratched cheeks.

I pressed my salty robe against my face to stop the bleeding, wincing at the sting of brine. My lungs coughed out a spume of seawater. Again the silver lances shimmered; the realm of Poseidon heeded their silent command and waves rose up fifty feet from the formerly calm seas and slammed into our hull. The ship turned on its side, narrowly avoiding capsizing. Amid the angry rocking, I clawed my way across the boat, hoping to reach the navigation tower amidships before we were swamped.

Hand over hand I crawled across the slippery deck, spewing water and maledictions from my throat. First I spat oaths of condemnation against the shoddy old ship, against its antique engine, so slow that the ship did not even have restraining straps. Then I laid my curses where they belonged, against myself for taking civilian transport. But even as I scrambled and swore, my mind focused on the impossibility of the situation: I was on the Mediterranean Sea, not the front lines in Atlantea. How, in Athena's name, had an enemy aircraft reached the center of the Delian League, and where was the Spartan navy when you needed it?

The dragon's shadow rippled in multicolored grace as it soared upward and coiled into a loop, a serpent biting its own tail. It held that posture for a moment, then unfurled and swooped down over the steamer's paddle wheel. It passed directly over me, blotting out the sun with its shimmering body. I could see the pilot, a small man in a black silk gi, pulling guide wires, turning the Xi lances to bear on our starboard side. I sucked in air and offered silent prayers for my life to Poseidon and Amphitrite, sure that the next blast would sink us.

My ears had been numbed by the hum of the Xi lances, so I

didn't hear the shot that saved us, but, O gods, I saw it. On the horizon a thin corridor of air pointing from sea to sky shimmered into sharp clarity. A trickle of hope entered my heart at the sight; that line of rarified air meant that just beyond my field of vision an evac cannon was prepared to fire. My hopes were realized; a steel tetrahedron the size of a man's head flew skyward up that line of thin air. My practiced eyes followed the brightly outlined projectile, and I knew the gunner had done his job well. The twenty-degree incline of trajectory would carry the tetrahedron to a spot directly over our heads at the exact second when the projectile ran out of impetus.

The equations that governed the movement for an object of that shape and material swam through my mind, offering reassurance of our salvation, but they were drowned out by memories of my boyhood self standing up in classrooms and reciting the simplified forms of Aristotle's laws of motion.

*A terrestrial object under forced motion travels in a straight line, slowing until it stops.*

The tetrahedron ceased its forward flight five hundred feet directly above the dragon. In the clear air I could see the gleam of sunlight reflecting off the pyramid's four faces and six knife-sharp edges.

*A terrestrial object under natural motion moves in a straight line forever . . .*

The tetrahedron plummeted down into the kite, tearing silk and bamboo, flesh and bone like a scythe through papyrus reeds.

*unless stopped by some force.*

The projectile, spattered with blood and festooned with strips of torn silk, struck the steamship's deck, gouging grooves into the thick wooden planks. Jagged splinters flew out from the impact, but the tetrahedron did not break through the thick slats of oak. The tetra teetered on one of its vertices for a moment, then fell over and sat still as if it had been eternally fixed into the ship like the pyramids into the sands of Giza.

The shattered corpse of the dragon lost control of the winds that were carrying it and crashed into our paddle wheel, wedging shards of silk and splinters of bamboo between the turning planks.

The wheel stopped spinning, raising a wail of protest from the steam engine as it labored fruitlessly to give impetus to the ship.

That clamor cleared the numbness from my ears and filled my heart with fear. I ran aft, slipping several times on the tilting, sodden deck. Sailors ran past me. Cries of "Abandon ship!" resounded from the navigation tower. Some of the men dived overboard, desperate to get away before the archaic engine exploded.

The Xi lances, still protruding like claws from the broken wings of the dragon, shattered under the strain of the angry wheel. Silver shards rained down on the deck, biting into the loinclothed sailors. I threw my arm across my face and a dozen needles stabbed into my forearm instead of putting out my eyes.

The deck careened to port then starboard then port again as the ocean's currents, free from the power of Middler science, yoked themselves again to the natural flow of the tides. Amid the chaos I kept running until I reached the steam engine.

Twin jets of steam spurted out from the nozzles on either side of the huge bronze sphere that held the boiling water. The streams of hot vapor tried to spin the sphere; the belt of leather that tied the brazen ball to the paddle wheel wanted to be turned by that spinning; the paddle wheel wanted to receive that turning and so turn itself in the ocean and make the ship go. But the paddle wheel was chained by the corpse of the kite and could not accept this gift of movement. This rejection was passed on to the leather loop, which could not move across its pulleys and so passed its stasis back to the engine, which was locked into place by this chain of refusals.

But the steam kept coming out of the pipes, stubbornly trying to imitate the Prime Mover and set all things in motion. Cracks appeared in the ball, rivets popped out, and a dozen little hisses joined the great blasts of boiled water.

I ducked below the sphere, wrapped the hem of my robe around my hand, and yanked open the door in the side of the fire box that boiled the water. Gouts of no-longer-contained fire rushed up into the sky. I rolled to the aft railing just fast enough to avoid being scorched.

The steam from the orb turned into heavy mist as the flame

that had kept it boiling rose upward, forming an ascending pillar of fire, a flare that could be seen for miles. The blaze continued to rise until, pushed upon by the air, the atoms of fire dispersed, joining their fellows in the glow of daylight.

I collapsed onto the deck, my seared throat choking on the sodden air. I coughed phlegm into my drenched robes, then lay still, sweating like a Marathon runner. The cloud of steam gradually condensed into dribbles of water. The paddle wheel, freed from the chains of impetus, rolled gently backward, pushed by the Mediterranean tides, and the broken battle kite and its broken pilot fell gracefully into the wine dark sea.

A cheer rose from the crew; I struggled to my feet to acknowledge the accolade, but it wasn't me they were lauding. From the east a two-hundred-foot-long steel ship, bristling from prow to stern with evac cannons and armored soldiers, bore down on us. I sank back in exhaustion and thanked Ares and Athena for our salvation. The navy had arrived.

With Spartan efficiency, the battleship *Lysander* heaved alongside the damaged merchantman, pulled the formerly panicked, now cheering sailors from the water, and laid a gangplank between the two vessels. During these unhurried maneuvers, I propped myself against the empty fire box, stanched the blood dripping from my cheek with my robe, and watched. The *Lysander*'s presence and bearing restored my sense of safety. She was a long, sleek ship, covered from stem to stern with a canopy of steel to protect her from aerial bombardment. Her steel hull had been painted a utilitarian iron gray. The only adornment on the entire ship was the figurehead on her prow, 'Era, patron goddess of Sparta, arms crossed in front of her, eyes scanning the horizon for anyone who would dare offend against her people.

I bowed my head to the image of heaven's queen, then turned to gaze with personal pride at the onyx pyramid that covered the sternmost twenty feet of the ship. My 'Eliophile engine, my only claim to glory until Sunthief. It had been twenty years since I discovered how to attract and catch the atoms of fire that danced in the sunlight and use them to power ships. Since then every ocean-going vessel built in the navy's shipyards had been fitted with one of my engines. They had become so common that few people even remembered that I had invented them, such are the vagaries of the goddess Fame.

A cough interrupted my reverie. A lightly bearded young Aethiopean wearing the black-fringed tunic and professionally concerned expression of a naval doctor was standing over me with an open satchel of instruments.

"I am not seriously injured, Doctor. Attend to the sailors," I said, knowing exactly what his response would be.

"Let me be the judge of that," the young man said with solemnity that belied his years. Doctors always said the same thing in the same tone of voice and they always had the same casual disregard for orders; the Oath of 'Ippokrates is much stronger than the discipline of armies.

"No great injuries," he said after looking down my throat, rubbing a light metal probe over my cheek, and feeling my limbs for fractures. "Just some scratches and a parched throat."

He pulled a brown glass bottle with the Egyptian hieroglyph for blood incised on it and a clean goose quill out of his leather bag, filled the quill with red liquid from the bottle, and jabbed it into my arm. "Just an injection of Sanguine Humour to speed the healing process," he said, as if I hadn't known that. "Apart from that all you need is some rest," as if I hadn't been resting when he came along.

The doctor turned to go and snapped off a quick salute to a young woman in armor just crossing the gangplank from the *Lysander* to the merchantman. I almost ignored her; after all, many of the battleship's crew had come over to secure the smaller ship. But she was not wearing a naval uniform. She was caparisoned in the thick steel breastplate, hoplite sword, and two-foot-long bronze evac thrower of an army officer. But what particularly caught my eye was the horsehair-crested helmet and the iron brassard only worn by graduates of the Spartan military college. What was she doing on a naval vessel?

She stepped onto the Phoenician ship and strode briskly toward me. As she neared, I began to make out the person under the steel. Her skin had the terra-cotta coloring that identifies the native of North Atlantea and her long, braided black hair, sharp features, and wiry, athletic build told me she was from the Xeroki city-states. But her eyes were a color I had never seen, golden like 'Elios, but with a glint that I thought at the time was coldness, as if the gates of her soul were two wards of frozen fire.

"Commander Aias?" she asked in a voice that perfectly melded Xeroki syllabling with 'Ellenic enunciation.

I nodded, unable to look away from her cold-gold eyes.

"You must come with me," she said like a judge passing sentence.

"What?"

She opened a thin leather pouch strapped to her belt and handed me a sheet of papyrus. It bore a few lines of mechanical block printing, two signatures, and the seal of the Delian League: two circles interlocked, the left one containing Athena's owl, the right one 'Era's peacock.

The message read:

> The scholar Aias of Athens, scientific commander of the celestial ship *Chandra's Tear*, is ordered to accept Captain Yellow Hare of Sparta as his bodyguard and obey any commands she deems necessary for the protection of his life.
>
> > By order of
> > Kroisos, Archon of Athens
> > Miltiades, Archon of Sparta

I read the letter thrice, hoping to make some sense of it. The idea of a Spartan captain assigned the lowly task of bodyguard was ludicrous; if the Archons had ever set my father such a menial job he'd have boiled into a rage, but this Yellow Hare seemed to accept it like a stoic. And why after three years did I suddenly need a bodyguard? Had the Archons somehow known about the battle kite? No, impossible!

"What does this mean?" I asked her. "What's happened?"

"My orders had no explanation. I was called, I came."

"Do you know how that battle kite reached here?"

"No."

"Do you know why it attacked this merchantman?"

"It must have been sent to kill you," she said. "Now come with me to the *Lysander* so I can prevent the next attempt."

"To kill me?" I said. "Of all the military targets in the Mediterranean why would the Middlers send a battle kite to kill me?"

"I do not know," she said. "But I was told that attempts would be made on your life. Commander Aias, I must insist that you come with me."

I found myself momentarily unable to move; my mind, honed by long years of Akademe training, needed to understand what was happening before I acted. And to leave the fragile Tyrian merchantman for the safety of the battleship would be to give in to ignorance. But I couldn't defy the orders of the Archons or the Spartan confidence in Captain Yellow Hare's voice; I gathered my traveling bag and followed her onto the *Lysander*. All the while my heart was churning up possible explanations for this impossible attack.

My soft leather sandals slapped harshly against the steel deck of the warship, but my new bodyguard's bronze leggings made no noise at all, as if the clash of metal against metal was a sacrilege she was too holy to commit.

Leather-armored seamen stopped their work, leaving guns unloaded and decks unswabbed to salute her as we walked down the steel-canopied foredeck toward the battleship's prow. But though they saluted, the sailors gave Captain Yellow Hare a wide berth, as if unsure how to treat the high-ranked landlubber.

We passed by an open hatch in which I saw a ladder that led down to the crew's quarters. Below there would be baths and a place to rid myself of my itchy, salt-stained robes. "I would like to change my clothes," I said.

Captain Yellow Hare shook her head. "The spaces below are too confined. An assassin might be hiding there."

"On a Spartan warship? That's impossible."

"No more impossible than a battle kite reaching the heartlands of the League."

"But—"

She chopped the air between us with her right arm, cutting off my argument. "Your safety is more important than your convenience. You will be able to bathe when we reach Athens."

We marched to the bow, stopping just a few feet in back of the 'Era figurehead. My bodyguard looked out from under the steel canopy and swept her gaze across the sea and the sky. I followed her eyes, wondering what she was looking for; then for just a moment the military lessons my father beat into me came forth and I saw as she did.

There were half a dozen ships within sight; four were merchant ships plying the many trade paths of the Mediterranean, one was a passenger steamer carrying civilians from city to city, and the last was a naval messenger boat, just twenty feet long, only one gun, but fast enough to sail rings around the *Lysander*. Above us there were half a dozen specks that were most likely celestial ships or moon sleds flying high over the few clouds strewn about the sky. But suppose they weren't. Suppose one of those ships was carrying a Middler assassin. Suppose one of the dots circling overhead was another battle kite. If the first impossible attack had come, how many more could follow it?

"You are right, Captain," I said. "My apologies. I have served too long in positions of safety. I will defer to your judgment."

She nodded curtly, then shifted her attention to the ship's armament, scrutinizing the evac cannons set in drum-shaped swivel mounts every five feet along the port and starboard rails. They looked like twin rows of phalloi at a Dionysiac festival. One by one the tops of the long cannons described circles in the air as the gunners greased and tested the aiming gears. My bodyguard nodded curt approval and returned her unreadable gaze to me.

I began to wonder if this assignment was some sort of punishment for her. The idea gave me a perverse sense of relief since it reduced the likelihood that I was in real danger. But two facts glared down this comforting hypothesis: First, Spartan officers who made mistakes were either forgiven or executed depending on the seriousness of the crime.

Second, and more compelling: that battle kite had attacked a ship carrying merchants, wool, and purple dye. The only thing on it of any great value to the Delian League was an important scientist. But I was by no means the most important target in the heart of the League. Unless the Middle Kingdom had found out about Sunthief.

My thoughts were interrupted by the boatswain shouting, "Brace for speed!"

I reflexively grabbed and held on to the support rail that ran the length of the deck and braced my feet against the corrugated flooring.

He shouted, "Deploy impellers!" and a line of golden wedges sprouted on the prow's fluted waterline. A fiery gleam washed under the canopy, limning 'Era's statue with a divine light. The aura of Zeus's bride flowed backward, suffusing Yellow Hare's armor with a fiery brightness. She stood so still and looked so majestic in the light that I thought, forgive the impiety, that there were two statues of goddesses in front of me.

My eyes grew accustomed to the glow and the moment of inspiration passed. I took a deep sniff of the rarified water that wafted like a bracing mist from the impellers. The fire-impregnated metal thinned the ocean, so the ship could sail swiftly without being slowed by the sluggishly heavy waters.

As the ship sped toward Athens on a carpet of unresisting ocean, I gripped the railing hard to brace myself against the backpush. But Captain Yellow Hare's only precaution against the sudden speed was to lean slightly forward and tense her legs. And that little action stopped her from sliding across the deck or tumbling over the side. Immobile as the earth, she let the cosmos shift around her, heaving Spartan defiance in the face of physics.

The ocean spray leaped into the sky in front of us, rushing onto the deck. It stung my face a little, but my cuts had mostly healed and I relished the sharp touch of speeding droplets. I closed my eyes and inhaled the tangy melange of salt and rarified air; then I cleared my head with a deep breath and started to sort through the strange things that had happened since I left Tyre.

Two facts appeared instantly in my thoughts: Ramonojon and Kleon. Had they also been assigned bodyguards? They were in my estimation more valuable to the League than I was. Kleon was universally regarded as the ablest celestial navigator ever to graduate from the school on Crete. And Ramonojon, despite not being an Akademe graduate, was the most skilled dynamicist from India to Atlantea. If the Middle Kingdom wanted to set the Delian League's celestial ship design work back five years, they only had to kill him.

And Ramonojon was vacationing in India, so near the Middle Kingdom border. If they could get a kite to me here . . . O Athena, I prayed, bearer of the Aigis, keep my friend safe.

I turned to Captain Yellow Hare and shouted over the noise of the waves breaking against the ship, "Have guards been assigned to Kleon and Ramonojon?"

"I do not know," she said. "My orders were rushed to me from Delos without explanation."

Athena struck me with a sudden revelation. Whatever had prompted Captain Yellow Hare's presence had to have happened within the last few hours. The Athenian bureaucracy knew my entire itinerary; they would have been able to reach me with a message or with bodyguards at any time in the last month. What could have happened in a few hours to bring about this response?

The boatswain called, "Retract impellers," snapping me from my reverie.

*Lysander* slowed as we neared port. My heart lifted; If there was any place in the world where I could find answers it was in Athens, the city of knowledge.

I stared with wide welcoming eyes at the chaotic jumble of buildings that comprised my adopted city. Towers twenty stories high, built within the last century, made the city appear to be a forest of bronze and steel, and at their bases like newly grown mushrooms around ancient trees were clusters of one-story stone *oikoi* built millennia ago by the founders of Athens. Most of the citizens wandered through that jumbled thicket of stone, metal, and time unsure of where or when they were.

My gaze wandered upward, beyond the tall metal trees to the spire that dwarfed them all: the sky dock of Athens, the one building at the harbor that stood aloof from the ceaseless clanking of daily life. The tapering steel cylinder towered a mile above the clifflike buildings of the harbor. The uppermost quarter mile of the sky dock was covered with flares and lamps to illuminate the way for approaching ships. Once the vessels were over Athens, those same bright beacons guided the celestial ships in to dock at the top of the tower; the vessels came bearing news and raw materials from the inner spheres, then left again laden with commands from the earth to the heavens.

As *Lysander* joined the throng of ocean ships entering port, a four-hundred-foot-long gleaming silver arrow, its sides studded with cannonades, detached itself from atop the sky dock, rose into the air, and flew off westward, a warship dispatched to Atlantea to clear the skies of battle kites. No doubt there were on that ship green soldiers being granted their first glimpse of Athens from the air and being amazed at the orderliness that lay hidden in the chaos of buildings below them.

It had been a quarter of a century since I had first been blessed with that vision of unity arising from discord like Aphrodite from the roiling ocean. At that time I was still a student at the Akademe, and my Ouranology class was being taken to the moon so that we pupils, our heads stuffed with theory, might have our first practical experience of the celestial. We traveled on one of the school's celestial ships, a decommissioned early military model without any of the conveniences a modern craft like *Chandra's Tear* enjoyed.

Most of my fellow students had stared up at the heavens, eager for their first close-up view of the spheres, but I looked down over the railing on the ship's rim at the place we were leaving behind and made sense of the city of the goddess of wisdom.

The narrow twisty streets and the brightly painted buildings, both old and new, were clumped around three hubs of activity: the harbor, the Acropolis, and the Akademe. The city was a pendant comprised of three huge gems surrounded by clusters of smaller stones. I wondered then whether in her idle moments Athena sometimes opened her jewelry box and studied this most beautiful of her ornaments, knowing that none of the other gods had its equal among their jewels.

I had wanted to continue staring over the silvery edge at that cluster of gems, but my teacher pulled me back and strapped me down on a couch as we set off on the ten-thousand-mile journey to the moon.

I shook away my remembrances as the *Lysander* steered slowly into the harbor of Athens. The piers were, as always, jammed with packet ships from all corners of the Delian League. Egyptian barges rubbed gunwales with Persian triremes, Indian frigates, Atlantean longships, and so many others. And everywhere there were Spartan warships, sending up signal flares to welcome a brother combatant home.

I had heard many captains complain about using ships of the line as messengers between Sparta and Athens. They bitterly resented being stationed in the Mediterranean when they could have been off battling the Middle Kingdom's navies in the Pacific Islands or off the coast of Atlantea. *Lysander*'s captain would have a story of combat that would give his comrades in dull duty hope for battle, though I doubted anyone else would be happy to hear it.

Lonely but confident in this crowd of bullying athletes was a single Phoenician merchant ship, much like the one we had left behind. A clumsy gang of hulking Norse slaves was hoisting a pile of tan bales from her hold: papyrus, the lifeblood of the city's bureaucrats.

The paper was trundled on float carts into the bureaucracy's office buildings, which clustered around the harbor like manmade cliffs, anthills filled with thousands of workers sucking in and spewing out the paperwork that kept the League alive. A web of evac tubes connected the cliffs to one another. The port was alive with hums and clanks as message capsules rushed through the tubes from one building to the next.

*Lysander* drew parallel to a long stone pier, and ropes were tossed from her deck and tied to the mooring anchors. Then the warship rolled out its gangway, which met the dock with an audible clang. Harbor slaves started to come aboard but Captain Yellow Hare ordered them back.

"No one is to come within thirty feet of the gangway," she said. Soldiers, sailors, and slaves moved quickly away. The orders of a Spartan were not lightly ignored. Only when there was room enough around the plank for her to keep track of every person nearby did she permit me to debark.

So it was that with aching muscles, scratched skin, itchy robe, and a bewildered mind, I set foot for the last time in the city of Athens.

# β

ommander Aias?" A thin-lipped man of indeterminate middle age stepped from the dockside crowd into the space Yellow Hare had cleared. As he approached, he reached his right hand into a fold of his plain brown robe, but before he could remove whatever was concealed there Captain Yellow Hare had leaped on him, pulled him several yards from me, and pressed the edge of her sword against his throat.

"Commander Aias," he croaked. "What is the meaning of this?"

"I told everyone to stay back," my bodyguard said. "Why did you disobey?"

"I thought you meant the slaves and sailors," the man said, peering nervously at the cleanly honed sword blade. "I was sent to request Commander Aias's presence."

"Where is he wanted?" she asked.

The man raised his left hand slowly and pointed up at one of the whitewashed stone buildings that housed the bureaucracy. "There's some paperwork waiting for him."

A laugh rose up unbidden in my throat and burst out at the absurd banality. "Please let him go, Captain," I said. "I recognize him; he is a clerk from the budgetary bureaucracy."

Yellow Hare sheathed her sword and released the bureaucrat. He straightened up, trying to regain some of his dignity before the crowd of smirking onlookers who, no doubt, were enjoying the rare sight of a humiliated clerk. He tried again to approach me, but Captain Yellow Hare placed herself between us, forming with her wiry body a barrier more imposing than any wall of stone or steel.

"Commander," he said, "I really must protest your officer's actions. I will lodge a formal complaint with the Archons."

"There is no need for that," I said. "I apologize for my bodyguard's zealousness, but she was just doing her duty." I was not overly concerned about the effect the protests of a clerk would have on me, but I did not, at the time, know whether Yellow Hare's record would be immune to such a complaint.

"And I was doing my duty," he said, puffing himself up, to the amusement of the now larger crowd of harbor slaves who had gathered to watch the fracas. "Now will you come with me and do your duty?"

"Of course," I said; I bowed my head slightly as if accepting the clerk's reprimand. There seemed no point in continuing a dispute with a man whose view of the world was confined to bureaucratic procedure and an inflated sense of his own dignity.

"Then come this way please," the man said. I followed him across the cement dock; Captain Yellow Hare kept between us while sweeping a corridor through the mingling crowd of slaves and sailors. As we passed, whispered rumors rose around and behind us. Clerks, Athenian scholars, and Spartan captains were everyday sights to the denizens of the harbor, but my bodyguard's demands for security while we walked were unknown in the supposedly safe heart of the League.

The clerk led us through the bustling dockyard, where priority cargo ships were being repaired and refitted with new engines, keels, and impellers by crews of slaves overseen by dynamicists, past the green-and-white granite warehouses stuffed with the produce of half the world, and into the steamy interior of a bureaucratic anthill.

We climbed seven flights of stairs, and of the three of us only I was short of breath when we stopped. The clerk pointed me into one of the innumerable cramped offices honeycombing the blocky edifice. "Wait in here, sir."

"No," Captain Yellow Hare said. "A larger room."

"But Captain," the clerk started to protest. She silenced his objections with a single look.

"Very well. Please wait one moment." He stepped into the tiny chamber, pulled a pile of papyrus scrolls from atop the pine-wood table that filled half the room, then led us down the hall to a larger office. "Will this suffice for your needs, Captain?"

Captain Yellow Hare appraised the room with a sweep of her eyes. The granite walls were lined from floor to ceiling with wooden scroll shelves. There were half a dozen writing tables littered with scraps of papyrus; each table also had two snap-down scroll readers, endlessly unrolling and rerolling papers that no one was reading. The open ends of evac tubes stuck out of every wall, waiting hungrily to suck message capsules into neighboring buildings. The only seating was provided by six unupholstered pine benches. The room reeked of that pseudo-Spartan scrimping beloved of those who affect rather than practice austerity.

"It will do," my bodyguard said.

"If you will excuse me, Commander, Captain," the clerk said nodding to each of us in turn. "I will find Senior Clerk Phrynis."

He dropped the pile of scrolls on one of the tables and disappeared into the hall, while I went in and sat down on one of the uncomfortable benches. As I leaned back against the hard wall, I could feel the strain from my efforts during the attack.

"Is there a problem, Commander?" my bodyguard asked.

"A month of leisure followed by five minutes of battle," I said. "I should not have indulged myself so much during my vacation."

Captain Yellow Hare nodded but said nothing more. She stationed herself beside the uncurtained doorway and again became perfectly still.

After a few minutes, a pinch-faced Corinthian official wandered in and sat down in front of the imposing heap of rolled papyrus.

"Good day, Commander," he said. "I am Senior Clerk Phrynis. Thank you for making time for this meeting."

"It was no problem," I lied. "I assume you want an accounting of my expenses for the last month."

"No, Commander." He pulled a thick scroll off the top and unrolled it.

"This is a list of all the cost overruns and staffing requests you have made since the inception of Project Sunthief, three years ago. We decided to take advantage of your presence in Athens to go over them with you."

I should have known that they would do something like this. I quashed a momentary desire to fight their pettiness with a petty display of temper. Instead, I nodded magnanimously and said, "Very well, Phrynis, but please be quick about it."

"As quick as I can," he said as he studied the scroll with a leisurely eye. I should have guessed that some form of petty revenge would be taken for my having outmaneuvered the bureaucracy. It may seem strange that after having been attacked I would sit still for a two-hour interrogation about the petty details of my work, but those two hours comforted me like the waters of Lethe; they let me forget, for a while, the true madness of that day.

So, secure in that womb of stone and triviality, I listened and I answered. "Why did you ask for five tons of aluminum, Commander Aias? Couldn't you have made the tracks from silver?"

"Aluminum requires less water to maintain its atomic integrity. There is no water in the celestial realms."

"Why did you request Aerologist Ptolemy's analyses of solar wind, Commander Aias? Wouldn't a lesser-known scholar have done?"

"The success of Sunthief depends on my navigator being able to keep control of the ship only two miles from 'Elios. We needed to know exactly how strong the winds are that close to the sun."

"Why have you reconfigured the dynamics of your ship four times, Commander Aias? Surely Dynamicist Ramonojon could have done it correctly the first time and saved the League considerable expense?"

"Are you questioning Dynamicist Ramonojon's competence or decisions?"

The man hesitated. "No, Commander," he said finally.

And on and on. He wrote down every word I said, filed it, and moved on without comment.

When this labor of paperwork and pointless argument finally ended, the Corinthian rolled up the scroll of answers, sealed it into a capsule, and pushed it into an evac tube. "Thank you for your assistance, Commander Aias."

I nodded to him and walked stiffly out of the granite-and-papyrus confines of the bureaucratic world onto the streets of Athens. The sun was halfway down the western sky, casting the long shadows of the anthills into those ancient avenues, only a few hours until nightfall. I wanted to be home before darkness came.

Captain Yellow Hare pointed toward a tube-capsule station. The sign over the entrance said: To the Akademe. I walked down the long tunnel and boarded an empty capsule, eager to return to the sanity of the scientific world.


Nine-foot-high statues of Athena and Aristotle stood on the left and right flanks of the Akademe's ivory gate. I made obeisance to both, bowing first to the gilded bronze goddess who looked down beneficently with her owl eyes, then to the blue marble hero who stared up at the heavens searching for the divine knowledge Pallas already possessed. Captain Yellow Hare ignored Aristotle, but she saluted Athena like a soldier reporting to a superior officer. Athena seemed to nod her approval to the captain.

We walked past the hero and the goddess and entered the mile-wide circle of red marble laboratories, green lecture halls, and blue apartments that surrounded the grove of Akademe itself. Home at last, I thought, even if it's only for one day.

The sweet smell of artificial spring air cleared my brine-encrusted nostrils as I stepped through the inner gate. Overhead, the huge cage of air-silver bars that regulated temperature inside the Akademe sparkled in the late afternoon sun. Outside this mesh the seasons passed in their unchanging cycle, covering the streets of Athens with the myriad discomforts of weather, heat, rain, fog, and cold, but the Akademe was kept warm and dry by its silver armor.

One of the horde of young Akademe slaves who cared for the welfare of students and scholars alike saw me enter and darted up to greet me.

"Scholar Aias?" the pale young man asked, bowing his red head.

"Yes?"

"May I conduct you to the visiting scholar's quarters?"

The question startled me for a moment, but of course, my former rooms would have been given to some other scholar when I left for *Chandra's Tear*. Not as much home as I would have liked, I thought; nevertheless, a place of comfort.

"Please do," I said to the slave.

He took us to a nearby blue building colonnaded with subtly carved Korai, almost lifelike figures of young maidens. Inside, another slave was waiting to attend me. She took my traveling bag and placed my clothes in a cedar chest. She drew me a bath, filling the round brass tub with water and pouring a thin layer of lavender oil on top. Another slave brought me bread and wine. Captain Yellow Hare inspected the room and the tub, and made the slave taste the food before she let me eat it.

"Everything seems safe," my bodyguard said, and stationed herself in a shadowed corner that commanded an excellent view of the bath and the curtained entryway.

I stripped and washed the blood and brine from my body in the hot lavender water. Then I leaned back in the tub, ate a bit of honey bread, sipped from the bowl of Aethiopian wine, and let the tension leak out of me into the bath.

After an hour of blissful inaction and thoughtless freedom from all cares and fears, I left the bath. I stepped into the rarified-air cabinet next to the tub. The last lingering drops of bathwater vanished into the artificially thirsty air, making my skin tingle and reawakening my lethargic mind. The slave dressed me in the formal blue-fringed white robes of a scholar, and I was ready to face the Akademe.

"Would it be safe for me to wander around?" I asked Captain Yellow Hare.

"If I go with you," she said.

My sandals slapped familiarly against the smooth marble floor as I strolled into the pristine white corridors that linked the entrances to labs, lecture halls, dormitories, and scholars' quarters. Those corridors were kept simple; the floors were scrubbed to a gleam, the ceilings and walls painted a bland undecorated white— all this to enhance the presence of the statues of scientist-heroes that stood in arching alcoves along the hallway. Each had been deified for some great contribution to the knowledge of the Akademe and the power of the Delian League.

If Sunthief succeeds, I thought as I bowed to each hero in turn, there will be a statue of me here. My mind filled for a moment with visions of the Elysian fields, of receiving sacrifices of blood and wine, of a blissful afterlife free from the gloom of 'Ades. Forgive my hubris, O ye gods.

I turned my thoughts back to Earth, to drink in the welcoming Akademic sounds of debate and experiment that echoed through the hallways. A knot of students, disarrayed in their red-fringed robes, hurried past me at a gait that said, "I'm not running, sir. I'm maintaining the proper dignified pace for a young scholar, sir."

I strolled on through the corridors, only stopping when I saw a whiff of smoke coiling out from under a familiar soot-spattered curtain. I peeked through the stained tapestry into the students' pyrology lab, a room I had spent a great deal of time learning and teaching in.

Inside the four-foot-thick concrete-and-steel walls of the scarred room a score of young men and women were seated on stone stools. Each youth leaned intently over a small bronze cauldron mounted on a tripod.

Smoke rose from some of the pots; others produced nothing. I hid a smile behind my hand. They were trying to stabilize fire, to keep a single flame burning forever. It was an exercise essential to the study of pyrology, but it had struck terror into many a neo-phyte scholar unused to the vagaries of this most volatile of the four elements.

The smiling middle-aged woman standing on the lecturer's stage caught my eye and invited me in with a crooked finger. Polianara of Carthage was older, a little stouter; her hair was much grayer than when I left three years before; but her brown eyes still twinkled with amusement as they had since we were students together, twenty-five years ago.

Captain Yellow Hare preceded me through the curtain. Polianara's eyes widened at the sight of this Spartan officer in the middle of the Akademe.

"What is going on?" Polianara whispered after I joined her.

"Don't ask! It's complicated and unpleasant. Talk to me about anything but that."

"Such as?"

I shrugged and looked around the familiar room, renewing my acquaintance with each burn mark on the walls. "Tell me about your class."

Curiosity was written in her gleaming eyes, but she respected my wishes and regaled me with the usual problems of teaching a first-year Pyrology class; the naïveté of the students, their nervousness around fire, the inevitable explosions.

"But there is the joy of teaching," Polianara said. "Watch the boy in the corner." She pointed to a young man with black hair, deep red skin, a chiseled Olmek face, and a large gold collar around his neck. He was laying thin rods of fire-gold in a criss-cross pattern over the top of his cauldron and studying the effect with a careful eye.

I hid my smile behind the blue fringe of my sleeve. This boy obviously understood the first lesson that every Pyrology teacher had to beat into his or her students' heads: Fire naturally moves upward.

And he had also clearly learned to apply that piece of theory to the real-world problem before him. If the fire is covered with a heavy material such as earth or water, that material will move downward to replace the flame and extinguish it. If covered with a light material such as fire or air the flame will leap up into the sky and disperse. But if the fire is covered with heavy material that has been previously saturated with fire, such as fire-gold, then the flame will remain where it is, burning forever.

The Olmek boy seemed fascinated by what he had done, but hadn't called attention to his success.

"I wish I'd been that calm when I succeeded," I whispered to Polianara.

She snorted, "As I recall, you shouted, 'Eureka! Eureka!' in that barbarous accent you had."

I laughed out loud. Several of the students looked up, but a glare from Polianara returned them to their work. My provincial accent had been the curse of my student years. I had spent more time working to rid myself of it than I had studying science. "You grow up in Tyre, North Atlantea, and India and see how your voice sounds," I said.

"No thank you," she replied. "Besides, I didn't have it any easier coming from a backwater like Carthage."

"Oh yes," I said, enjoying the teasing privileges of an old school friend. "I remember how you gawked at Athens's tall buildings and refused to board a celestial ship for fear of falling off."

We traded a few more reminiscences, but gradually we fell silent as our thoughts drifted back to our school days. At first I remembered the joys of school, learning, arguing, reading more than I had ever done before. But in the midst of my nostalgia some spirit—demon, hero, or god, I could not say—replaced those memories with recollections of the unpleasant aspects of the Akademe that I had blotted out in my three-year absence.

Memories welled up: of the Athenian provincialism of the scholars, the assumption that only in the city of wisdom was there any true understanding of anything. Of the scientific provincialism, the belief that the understanding of nature was the only worthwhile understanding. And of the militarist provincialism, the belief that only the science that aided the nine-hundred-year-long war was worthwhile science.

The spirit filled the mirror of my mind with a blasphemous

image. I saw the Akademe not as a nurturing mother to whom I, her wandering son, had returned, but rather as a 'etaira, beautiful in appearance, learned in speech, but fundamentally a whore.

"Tell me about the lecture you're going to give us this evening," Polianara said, breaking the silence and forcing the image into a dark corner of my thoughts, where something snatched it away. "Everyone is waiting to hear about your secret research."

I laughed, trying to return myself to the mood of joyous homecoming, but the laugh was hollow. Secret, what a joke. The Akademe is the only place in the world where "secret" means "we'll discuss it quietly," and "most secret" means "let me whisper it to you."

But Captain Yellow Hare was glaring at me; to a Spartan, secret meant secret. I did not wish to explain the attitudes of the Akademe on this matter to Captain Yellow Hare or to the Spartan general staff if she reported me for a breach of security.

"Sorry," I said to Polianara, a bit too loudly, "it's most secret."

She offered her ear for me to whisper in. I cupped my hand over the side of my mouth and spoke at normal volume. "It's really secret."

She crossed her arms in front of her and looked at me like a stern elder sister. "Listen, Aias, rumors about this lecture have been running around the Akademe for the last month. All the senior scholars will be waiting in the main lecture clearing tonight. If you don't have something interesting to say, your reputation will be ruined. Again."

Now that was a problem. My reputation in certain circles of the Akademe was not good. Normally I would have been happy to tell those detractors of mine that the Archons had found a speculative paper I had once written on possible methods for capturing celestial fire and had given me the task of turning theory into reality. But I did not care to do so with Captain Yellow Hare listening.

But I had to tell the Akademe something in the lecture that evening, and I had to tell Polianara something now. "I'll give it some thought."

"Really?" Polianara's voice turned dry, bringing out that penchant for sarcasm Carthaginians are famous for. "You have three whole hours to make up your mind."

"That should be more than enough," I said as I left the lab followed by my silent bodyguard.

I considered returning to my quarters, reviewing my notes, and cobbling together a talk that alluded to my work on Project Sunthief without being indiscreet.

Under pressure I did what scholars at the Akademe have done since Plato first bought this suburban orchard and transformed it into a college. I passed through the inner gates and wandered through the carefully manicured woods, hoping to draw inspiration from nature.

The leaves crunched pleasantly under my sandals. The aroma of a thousand trees, brought to the Akademe from all parts of the League, mingled with the bright scent of spring to sharpen my thoughts. Many of the more visionary scholars had seen Athena herself come down from Olympos to sample that heady mixture of fruit smells, spicy nut scents, and the cloy of sweet sap. Was it hubris on the part of scholars to imagine her wandering through our grove, letting that melange of odors tingle her divine nose and excite her matchless mind?

Hoping Athena would stop and touch me with her presence, I sat down under a chestnut tree and idly cracked some of the fallen nuts against the bark. I noticed Captain Yellow Hare dip her finger into the running sap of a maple and taste the sweet libation of her native land.

I was about to speak to her, but my voice froze in my throat; something bright and large danced into my mind accompanied by a chorus of praising singers. A goddess had descended to grip my thoughts with holy inspiration. But it was not Athena, mistress of that orchard. The radiance and the music clarified into a familiar image and voice. Kleio, the Muse of history, stood on the plane of my thoughts, calling me back to her.

At first I was afraid, afraid that she had come to chastise me for abandoning her service. For years I had been one of the few devotees of her disregarded field of study, but when her sister Ourania had called me to work on Sunthief I had given Kleio up for the sake of my reputation. Now she had returned.

I humbled myself before her and begged forgiveness for my apostasy. Her countenance was stormy but her eyes were loving. She was angry with me for neglecting her worship these last three years, but I could see she wanted me back. In her hands she cradled a scroll that I knew contained the lecture I would give to the Akademe that night. I held out my hands to receive her gift, but Kleio withheld it. Before she would grant me this favor, she would remind me why I had first entered her service.

Kleio cast me into the arms of Memory, pulling me back over the years to the time of my despair, when Fame had blessed me with a year's glory for inventing the 'Eliophile engine and then abandoned me for not following it with any further triumphs.

My thoughts had run dry, my lectures were barely attended, and I had been relegated by the provost of the Akademe to teaching introductory Ouranology. In a fit of confusion, I had decided to visit my father in Sparta; my hope was that his completely different view of the world might pull me from the clutches of despair. Instead, he greeted me with silence and aloofness and gave me over to the care of his servants.

After two days of watching him stalk by me without a word of greeting, I retreated into his meager library, hoping for something to take my thoughts away from both Athens and Sparta. Among the numerous tracts on strategy I found a chronicle of battles written by a Persian general six and a half centuries before my birth. It was a rambling discourse by a bitter old man who, like me, had been abandoned by the fickle goddess Fame.

The man's morose words reached across the centuries and filled me with black bile. But when I put the scroll down and his anger left me, I realized I had learned a great deal about the time in which he had lived. I found myself wanting to know more, to drown my sorrows in the lives of dead men. It was then that Kleio first appeared to me and unrolled the scroll of time for my mind's eye to read.

In the years that followed I snooped through the dusty archives of every city in the Delian League. I read chronicles and ship manifests, scholarly arguments and legal disputes. I stuck my nose into every faded piece of paper from India to Atlantea. I even managed to acquire some documents from the Middle Kingdom, though they taught me little. I tried to organize this knowledge, to formulate theories of the past that I might offer to Kleio as the fruits of my scientific training. But since the Akademe did not consider history a true field of study, my papers were not published, and my lectures were orated before an audience of empty benches.

When the Archons gave me command of *Chandra's Tear*, I gave up Kleio's worship in order to conform to the proper image of a research scientist; sharp-eyed, clean of mind, lacking in eccentricities. Now the Muse was back to reclaim me and use me for what she had originally intended. Tonight, the entire Akademe would hear me speak, and Kleio, whose voice had been unheeded since Aristotle's day, would speak through me.

The Muse pulled me to my feet and made me walk through the orchard. As I passed each tree, Kleio showed me a different part of the world, a different component of the past out of which she had assembled the present.

Here was a cedar from my homeland, where trade was born and from which the 'Ellenic hand had stretched out across the Mediterranean. Here were incense trees from India, where Alexander united a thousand warring Razas and pointed them eastward toward the Middle Kingdom. Here was a baobab from Africa, where the gold that powered our weapons was found, and a maple from North Atlantea, where the nine-centuries' war against the Middlers still raged. And throughout the grove grew the olives of Athens, the source of Delian technology.

The divine grip grew stronger as I leaned against one of those olives to compose my speech from Kleio's divine words.

The sun set over the Acropolis, scattering red light through the silver bars of the Akademe's cage and bloodying Captain Yellow Hare's armor. I brushed leaves from my robes as I stood up and stretched the kinks of inaction out of my muscles. To calm my stomach I ate an apple off a nearby tree before striding through the orchard to the lecture clearing.

Redheaded slaves, stomping around with northern European gracelessness, uncovered sustained-fire lamps. In the clean blue light I saw dozens of students and scholars milling about between the low stage on which I would speak and the ring of marble benches on which my peers would sit to judge me.

The blue-fringed scholars chirped like crickets as they argued the esoterica of their fields while red-fringed students listened respectfully. Occasionally, a brave youngster would interject a question into the rarified discussion. Most such interruptions would be dismissed with a succinct sharp answer calculated to instill in the student an awareness of his own foolishness. Rarely, the question would be one of those strokes of juvenile brilliance, and neither query nor querier would be berated. Instead, the sages would debate the matter, growing the fruits of implications from the callow seed of youthful inquiry. The student who had spoken would listen with parental pride, drinking in the envy of his friends.

The time for my speech approached and the senior kerux of the Akademe strode onto the stage and banged his wooden speaker's staff three times. The noise of the crowd dulled to a murmur. The kerux waited a moment, gathering all eyes to him before speaking. "Aias of Tyre will now address the Akademe."

I stepped into the light, and the knots of talking people drifted apart as I passed among them. Captain Yellow Hare faded into the shadows as silence came to the meadow.

The students seated themselves cross-legged on the ground in attentive rows, while the scholars perched on the marble benches. The young had come to hear what it was like to command a League project, to develop weapons for the good of the state. The old wanted to know what that weapon was. With Kleio's aid I planned to disappoint all of them.

"May Athena and Aristotle bless this assemblage with wisdom and knowledge," I said. The assemblage made the obligatory response. The students leaned forward like grass before the wind; the scholars steepled their hands and sat straight backed. "Tonight, my subject is history; my thesis is that nine centuries ago the Akademe abandoned the study of philosophy for that of science, and that abandonment was done not for the glory of Athena but for political reasons."

"What is this nonsense?" a querulous voice warbled from the back bench. Pisistratos, one of my teachers in Ouranology, forced himself to his feet, fighting the natural tendency of ninety-year-old bones to remain seated. "What are you babbling about, Aias?"

I flinched slightly; harsh words from a hated teacher could still cut deep. Pisistratos had been particularly vicious to me in my youth; he had confidently asserted that I would never be a scientist, he had sulked when I flirted with fame, and he had gloated when I had faded away for two decades. No doubt he resented my recent return to glory, and no doubt he was pleased at the folly of my topic.

"This is a lecture on the history and purpose of the Akademe," I said. "You need not stay if you do not wish to learn."

Several scholars stood up and left, not even following the common practice of slinking quietly into the orchard to escape dull lectures. But most remained as if chained to their benches by my celebrity. Pisistratos stayed as well; I knew he was waiting for a chance to challenge me publicly and remind the Akademe that Aias the commander had for a long time been Aias, "that fool dabbling in history."

I kept silence until the last straggler had left. "Does anyone know why Athenians, of all the peoples of the League, developed science to explain the mysteries of nature?"

I waited, but the only sound in the grove was the chittering of Egyptian scarabs warring over nuts and fruits with European squirrels.

"What is the cornerstone of science?" I asked, needing some response from them before my talk could go forward.

Chorus of students: "Experimentation!"

Now I had them. "Who discovered experimentation?"

The students looked at me as if I were speaking a foreign language. I could almost hear their thoughts. Experimentation is the way things are done. One might as well ask who discovered breathing or pouring libations to the gods.

Pisistratos narrowed his eyes and leaned forward into a hunter's posture. When I had made a complete fool of myself, he would spring and gut me with a well-placed aphorism.

A Cretan boy with matted black hair and a straggly beard spoke up from the fourth row of students. His harsh Minoan accent and his uncertain speech reminded me of myself at his age. "Aristotle was the first to perform an experiment."

"Why?"

The boy's comrades looked at him with sober frowns, but the gleam in their eyes was all too familiar to me. They were happy to watch one of their own make a fool of himself. "Sir," he asked, "what do you mean why?"

I leaned back, clasped my hands behind my head, and gazed up at the pockmarked moon. "What motive did Aristotle have to do something no one had ever done before?"

"Um . . . uh . . ." The boy stammered into silence. He glanced around like a hunted deer seeking escape from pursuing hounds. Then he looked at Pisistratos and pleaded silently for help.

The old man gathered up his dignity and the hem of his robe and strode forward to battle me. The students parted for him like wheat before the wind. "Aias, why do you waste our time? This is an institute of science. That is all we study."

"That is precisely my point. Why is science all we study?"

He threw up his hands in melodramatic disgust. "Would you rather we wasted our time with Platonist dithering on the nature of ideal forms while the Middle Kingdom conquered us with their impossible Taoist science?"

I knew that dirty word "Platonist" would come out eventually. "No, Pisistratos, I do not want to waste our time on that nonsense. But I do want the students to know how we came to study science and nothing else."

He let out an exaggerated sigh. "What else is worth studying?"

Pisistratos was finally debating me, giving me a chance to make my case. But I didn't let my happiness blind me to the Sokratic trap he'd laid. I framed my counterquestion carefully. "Can science be studied without knowing anything else?"

Pisistratos sidestepped like a bull dancer. "What other subject do you need? Philosophy? Theology? Ethics? Perhaps drama and comedy are used in your secret research, but I have never needed them."

"History is needed in my work."

He lowered an eyebrow, twisting his lined face into a frown. All eyes fixed on him. Watching scholars debate has been the favorite sport of students ever since Sokrates faced off against the Sophists.

"History. What can history tell you?"

I offered a prayer of thanks to Kleio for guiding me and felt her breath on my back filling me with divine strength. "Tell me, Pisistratos, would you ever impregnate fertile earth with fire?"

He glared at me, adding wrinkles of annoyance to the map of his face. "Of course not; it would explode."

"How do you know that?"

He snorted majestically, a sacred bull ready for sacrifice. "Every educated person knows that."

I leaned forward and pointed toward his emaciated stomach. "But how do you know it?"

He waved airily toward the north edge of the orchard. "Because, one hundred and fifty years ago the hero Kofites blew himself to pieces trying to do exactly that."

I bowed my head as if acknowledging his mastery. The moonlight shimmered down through the silver cage, casting a checkered pattern on his sneering face.

"Then you use history to avoid past mistakes," I said quietly.

"But—"

I cut him off. The knowledge I had gathered through years spent in the neglected archives of the Akademe poured out of my lips, overwhelming him with an epic tale of the labor thousands of scholars had performed in the last nine centuries of painful research to determine the myriad facts every educated person knew.

"Everyone in the world knows something of the past," I said. "Family history, the history of their particular fields of science. Some, like the best Spartans, know military history. But the Akademe does not want its students to know its own history. Why?"

The audience looked eagerly at Pisistratos. They wanted an answer to my question. But he didn't know it, so their heads turned back to face me. And Pisistratos walked in stiff-necked stubbornness back to his seat.

I paused to gather my thoughts and drink again the wine of Kleio's inspiration. Then I began to speak.

"The Akademe," I said, "is not primarily a place of knowledge, but of war."

Silence.

"The supposedly equal partnership between Athens and Sparta that has ruled the Delian League since its founding is dominated by Spartan thinking."

A questioning rustle.

"To prove this, I will lay out three examples from the history of science; I will start with the most recent and progress backward to the time of Aristotle and Alexander."

The wind stilled and even the scarabs and squirrels quieted at the mention of those heroes.

"The first event I will discuss happened only forty years ago."

The eyes of the assembled students brightened. They knew what I would speak about: the first voyage to the moon.

At that time the classical school of Ouranology said such a journey would be impossible because there was a Sphere of Fire between Earth and Selene and there was no air beyond that sphere, only unbreathable ether. But the modern school denied the existence of the Sphere of Fire and claimed that air extended all through the universe out to the Sphere of Fixed Stars.

I told my audience how the modern school was proved right when Kroisos and Miltiades crashed the first celestial ship, *Selene's Chariot*, on the moon, and returned in triumph, flying on a piece of celestial matter they had carved out of the moon itself. The wonders of the spheres became available for study, and the science of Ouranology flourished because of their efforts. The students would have cheered, but that would have been contrary to Akademe etiquette.

"But," I said, "It was not for the sake of Ouranology that those two great men risked their lives. They went to Selene because

Sparta wanted flying weapons, platforms to seize the skies from the domination of the Middle Kingdom."

The divine voice rushed through me, filling my thoughts. I could no longer see my audience; I could only speak Kleio's words.

I vaulted back three centuries for my second instance. At that time the Middle Kingdom had just invented battle kites and our ground troops had no defenses against them. To counter this advantage Sparta needed thousands of huge evac cannons to shoot them down. The generals demanded that the scholars produce the vast supply of fire-gold needed to rarify the air inside these cannons.

The Akedeme dragooned all its pyrologists and geologists, their task to turn the production of fire-enriched metals from a slow, dangerous, complex task to a simple, safe, easy one. Ten years and ten million obols later, they succeeded. In the process two fields of science were advanced, and float carts, capsule tubes, and a thousand other modern conveniences based on fire-metals were made practical, but again those were side effects of military demands.

To complete my trinity of examples, I looked back six hundred years to a time when the League's armies were too large to be fed on their extended campaigns. Sparta called on Athens for help and spontaneous-generation research became the most important subject at the Akademe. Seven years of work led the hero Aigistos to discover the formula for producing cows from garbage. Armies could now travel where they wanted for as long as they needed.

"As an afterthought he eliminated hunger throughout the League," I said, "and he sparked the First Indian Rebellion."

I had made clear the dominance of Sparta over Athens; now I had to show that that dominance came about through political machination. I went backward nine centuries to speak about the two heroes who had chained the Akademe to the battlefield: Alexander and Aristotle.

The scarred moon had fallen behind the heads of the students, limning the grove of varied trees in a ghostly aura. I imagined Alexander and Aristotle standing on this very spot under a moon untouched by man. The young general asked the old philosopher-turned-scientist for help in remaking the Delian League into a force that could conquer the Middle Kingdom. Legend said they worked under a divine vision of the future, but the dusty chronicles in the cellars of the Akademe said otherwise.

I paused to catch my breath for a moment; Kleio also paused, pulling away from my mind so that I might recover from the throes of her epistasy.

I looked at my audience for the first time in an hour. The scholars weren't bored anymore. They leaned forward, their hands were knotted in their robes, their eyes were bright with interest. The students rocked back and forth on their crossed legs. Their faces were rapt like maenads about to tear apart a goat for the glory of Dionysos.

Before Kleio would take my mind again, Athena stepped in and stopped my voice with sudden wisdom. Pallas made me look at the scholars and students and understand that they had not heard what I had said. I had told them the bloody history of the Akademe, and they were proud of it. If I told them the truth about Alexander and Aristotle, they'd ignore me. Crazy Aias, they'd think, hope the Archons don't expect much from his work.

The pressure of their attention washed over me with a wave of fatiguing realization. It would make no difference to them if I told this assemblage that Aristotle had connived with Alexander to purge the Platonists from the Akademe by force.

If I proved to them that the founder of modern science had sacrificed his philosophy to make weapons for a boy who thought he was a god long before his death and apotheosis, it would not matter. These pursuers of truth would not care that Aristotle gave up his vision of uniting all knowledge so he could become master of the school founded by Plato, the teacher he hated.

I stood poised between two goddesses, both of whom claimed my allegiance. I did not know then why Athena counseled the speaking of falsehoods in her home, though I believe I do now. I begged Kleio's forgiveness and opened my mouth to pour forth in thunderous rendition the legend of two heroes and their divine vision of science and military working together for the good of all.

When I ceased my oration, the scholars and students rose as one and thanked me for showing them the value of history. Even old Pisistratos apologized for his earlier behavior.

I turned away from them, and from the shadowed woods I saw Captain Yellow Hare glaring at me with the look of disgust Spartans reserved for cowards. But then something settled on her shoulders and her expression softened to one of puzzlement. Did she know I had betrayed the goddess I had promised to serve, and what spirit spoke to her and removed her anger? Never having dared to ask, I still do not know the answer to that; I can only guess that she too saw history's Muse in Athena's grove and shared something of my inspiration.

Yellow Hare led me back to the visiting scholars' quarters and stalked out of the room to stand guard.

A slave brought me a bowl of wine which I poured out on the marble floor, a libation to Kleio. Then I lay down on the couch, and as I fell asleep I fancied I heard the two goddesses conferring. Both sounded pleased. Why? I wondered as 'Upnos clutched me. Why were neither Wisdom nor History angry?

# γ

I was pulled from a welter of unrecalled dreams by the undertones of a whispered argument that drifted through the curtains of my quarters like the first late autumn breeze that hinted of winter.

"What is going on here?" demanded a voice with an Indian accent. It took me a moment to recognize it: Ramonojon! Thank the gods, he was safe. "Where is Aias?"

"Commander Aias is inside," I heard Captain Yellow Hare say. "You may not go in."

I sat upright on my sleeping couch, tossed the linen blanket to the floor, threw on the robes I had worn the night before, and stepped through the curtain. Yellow Hare instantly placed herself between me and Ramonojon and waved her hand to keep me from coming too close.

"Aias," Ramonojon said. "What is all this? Why are you under guard?"

Ramonojon had become much thinner during his month's absence; his short Indian tunic and skirt hung very loosely on his wiry frame. There was a haggard look in his eyes, as if he hadn't slept in ages. His skin had become hard, as if he had been put through a tannery. And his voice and face had a strange placidity, as if he had not spent every one of the fifty years of life in constant thought.

"It's all right, Captain," I said to Yellow Hare. "I vouch for Senior Dynamicist Ramonojon." I turned to my Indian friend. "Come into my quarters and I'll explain."

My bodyguard stood to the side and ushered Ramonojon past me through the hanging draperies. She followed us in, keeping her piercing golden gaze fixed on my friend.

Ramonojon tilted his head and looked at me expectantly.

"I was attacked on the way back to Athens."

His eyes widened and his face took on the look of startlement that had made many a superficial judge of character think him simple. Then he blinked as if he realized what his face looked like; he took four slow, deep breaths and his expression melted back into this mysterious new passivity.

"Attacked?" he asked, as if I had just told him a snippet of innocuous gossip.

"A battle kite appeared in the Mediterranean skies and tried to sink the merchantman I was traveling on."

"A battle kite? Here? That's—" He cut himself off and took four more breaths. "How can that be?" he said.

I could not muster up an answer. The distance he was trying to maintain between us was hard to fathom. All I could do was study his face going through its cycles of astonishment, breath, and control. It was like watching an actor prepare for a role he was not yet comfortable with.

"Has something happened to you?" I asked. "Did you have any trouble on the way back from India?"

"No, Aias," he said, "my journey was uneventful. Tell me more about the attack on you."

As I told the tale, I watched his eyes and mouth grow wide with disbelief. I drew comfort from the normality of those reactions, but, just as *Lysander* was about to shatter the enemy aircraft with one perfect shot, Ramonojon's stunned expression vanished into a now perfect expression of disconcerting blankness, as if the actor now knew his part and had donned the mask of a serene demon.

Unnerved, I tried to dislodge the expression by drawing out the details of the danger, lingering on the near explosion of the steam engine and soaring to unaccustomed heights of oratory as I described my reckless actions to save the ship. But Ramonojon seemed unmoved. My narrative dripped into silence after the point when Captain Yellow Hare took me aboard *Lysander*.

Ramonojon was silent for a little while; then in carefully controlled tones he asked, "How long until we can get you back to the safety of our ship?"

Yellow Hare answered him. "*Chandra's Tear* will arrive at the sky dock of Athens one hour after noon."

I looked over at the water clock in the northeast corner of the room. We had five hours to wait. The idea of spending that time in the Akademe, being visited by colleagues come to offer congratulations for my "triumph" of the night before, twisted my stomach. I wanted to be gone before anyone else awoke.

But where to go? A memory wafted through my mind, a delicious smell of flour and honey enticing me back to one of my favorite places in all of Athens.

There was a bakery on a curving little side street half a mile from the Akademe, hidden from the crush of traffic. The baker was an old man whose family had been baking bread and selling it for twelve hundred years. The stone walls were impregnated with the sweet scent of barley bread, baked from a recipe unchanged for centuries. The only difference between that baker and his many-times-great-grandfather was that he used an oven of self-heating metal rather than one of brick and ash.

I could think of no place I wanted to be more than in that shop, eating fresh bread drizzled with sweet olive oil and discussing the Athens of centuries past with that baker, in that piece of living history.

I told Captain Yellow Hare that I wanted to walk the streets of the real Athens, not the city of self-important bureaucrats and self-deluding scientists, but Athena's blessed city of real people living the same real lives their ancestors had led since the Mykenaeans had ruled the Peloponnese.

"No, Commander," Yellow Hare said with the finality of Zeus rendering judgment. "I cannot allow you to take any risks."

I heard noises in the corridors, slaves mopping the floors, polishing the statues. Soon the students would awake for their morning exercises, and then the scholars would rise to teach and argue. The Akademe was stirring, and I wanted to be gone before it blinked its sleepy eyes and saw me.

Athena tapped me gently on the shoulder and told me the way out. Though my bodyguard denied me the heart of the city, she could not keep me from its soul. I turned to Captain Yellow Hare. "May we go to the Acropolis? I wish to make amends to Kleio."

"Of course," she said, and in the gleam of her golden eyes I saw the hint of approval. "Even the Middlers would not attack a sanctuary of the gods."

I splashed cold water and rubbed warm oil over my body, changed into my sturdy traveling robes, and grabbed two apples and a piece of nut bread from the heavy-laden breakfast tray a slave brought in, and then Yellow Hare, Ramonojon, and I left the Akademe. I did not even glance backward at the halls and grove I was abandoning.

Captain Yellow Hare commandeered a tube capsule for us and prevented anyone else from using it. The men who guarded the tube stations grumbled about that, but no ordinary soldier would dispute the orders of a Spartan officer. The trip from the suburbs to the center of Athens passed quietly and uneventfully. I was wrapped up in my thoughts, contemplating how best to frame my prayers. Ramonojon leaned back on the bench and twisted the leather straps tightly around his hands. His eyes were shut and he seemed to be whispering to himself, though I could not hear the words he was saying. Captain Yellow Hare sat next to me, straight backed, alert eyed, one arm poised next to the hilt of her sword, the other touching the ammunition bag at the butt of her evac thrower. Like the lightning before a storm she brooded, waiting to strike at the first clash of thunder.

We emerged from the terminus station into the long morning shadow near the western base of the Acropolis, and climbed the stairway carved into the side of that holy hill. There was already a throng of worshipers passing through the gaily colored gate of the propylaea. Citizens of Athens come to pay their respects and ask the gods for fortune, love, or glory rubbed shoulders with visitors from the provinces come to see the original statue of Athena Parthenos from which myriad copies had been made and placed in temples throughout the League.

Once inside the holy enclosure, Captain Yellow Hare apparently felt we were safe enough to leave Ramonojon and me to our own devices for an hour while she went to the small temple of Athena Nike, just south of the gateway. I presumed she had gone to ask the victorious goddess for aid in her duties.

Ramonojon and I went over the top of the hill, bypassing the red-and-blue-columned Parthenon itself; we walked over the flagstoned path down the other side of the Acropolis into the Erektheon, where most of the gods were housed. We passed the statue of Athena, Protectress of the City, and descended the short staircase to the gallery of lesser gods on the lower level.

I approached the niche that held the Muses hesitantly, head bowed, arms outstretched with a bowl of wine in my hands that I offered in libation to Kleio before I whispered to her. "Goddess who took me from despair and gave me life, who offered me words of truth to speak when my own voice was dumb. Forgive me that I did not speak your oracle to the Akademe. But they would not have heard me. I offer myself again to you and swear by Zeus in the heavens, Poseidon in the waters, and 'Ades below the earth to do all that I can in your service from this day forth."

I turned away from the smooth-hewn alcove and saw Ramonojon bowing perfunctorily to the gods with a startling look of indifference, almost distaste, on his face. I could not understand what had happened to him. He had always been a very religious man, enthusiastic in his prayers and sacrifices to the huge array of Hindu deities, nor had he ever been lax in offering obeisance to the 'Ellenic gods. I wanted to challenge his actions, but I could not bring myself to question his devotion in the presence of a goddess I had blasphemed and whose favor I was trying to regain.

When I had poured a final libation to the Muse and was about to leave, Ramonojon held up a hand to stop me. He waved me away from the dozen or so other worshipers pouring their offerings out to the deities.

In a dark corner, Ramonojon reached into his tunic, pulled out a scroll, and slipped it into the sleeve of my robes.

The scroll was not papyrus, but had the soft fragility of rice paper, which meant it had to come from the Middle Kingdom. I unrolled the beginning of it and saw the complex ideographs that the Middlers use for writing. The title said: *Records of the Historian* by Ssu-ma X'ien.

I nearly tore the paper in my excitement. Here was a document I had only heard rumors of. It was written by the greatest historian the Middle Kingdom had ever produced, and was said to detail Alexander's attack on the Middlers and the political upheaval it caused in the Middle Kingdom.

"I knew how much you've wanted to read it," Ramonojon said, a thin smile cracking his demeanor.

"Thank you," I whispered, unsure if I was speaking to my friend or to the goddess of history, who perhaps had just given me a sign of her forgiveness.

"How did you get this?" I asked Ramonojon.

"I chanced upon it in India," he said vaguely. And I knew he would not tell me any more.

I hid the document carefully in the folds of my robes, not wanting my bodyguard to see me perusing a Middle Kingdom document. Spartans have a habitual distrust of those who show too much interest in the ways of the enemy.

We met Captain Yellow Hare in the Parthenon and joined the crowd offering general prayers to the gilded statue of Athena. We wandered the temple complex watching the crowds, looking over the city from its second-highest structure, and so on until 'Elios had climbed to the highest point in his journey through the sky.

Then we commandeered another tube capsule and took a quick trip under the city to meet *Chandra's Tear*.

Security at the sky dock was tighter than I had ever seen it. Four guards instead of the usual two were stationed at the thick steel gates that led into the complex of warehouses, bureaucratic office buildings, and slave quarters around the mile-high steel pillar. These guards looked over my identity scroll three times, feeling the seal for signs of forgery or tampering, making sure I matched the written description down to the last detail. Ramonojon was even more carefully scrutinized, and I was required to swear over water, earth, and fire that he was who his documents said he was. Captain Yellow Hare of course was passed without comment. There was no way to counterfeit that Spartan air she had, and no common soldier would question the integrity of a Spartan officer.

We threaded our way through the crowd of slaves loading huge wooden crates onto large bronze float carts which hovered a few inches above the ground, clerks checking written manifests and directing the slaves to drive this load of lunar matter into that warehouse, pull out that crate full of newly manufactured evac throwers and prepare it for loading, watch where you're going with that box of gold. Be careful you lackwitted northerners don't you know that shipment of onyx is fragile? Careful you, oh I beg your pardon, Commander, Captain. The inner gates are this way.

We passed through the security procedure again outside the basalt gates to the inner courtyard that surrounded the dock itself. As we waited to pass through this checkpoint, *Chandra's Tear* hove into view, floating over the horizon from the east. My ship was a mile-long piece of the moon, carved by Ramonojon's crews into a perfect silver teardrop. She floated majestically over the city, at first just a gleaming disk in the sky no larger than an obol. A dozen tiny black spots appeared on her underside, the water-filled ballast balls that controlled the ship's descent. *Chandra's Tear* grew larger as it came closer to the earth. The silvery light it shed grew brighter until it washed out the gold of the sun. A mile above the ground my ship connected with the top of the sky dock. There was a clang of steel and a pure, high-pitched tone like the ringing of a stone bell carved by a master; it was the pure harmonic of the moon, one of the seven notes of the music of the spheres.

I looked up longingly and all I could think was that I would soon be home aboard her at last.

We were let through the final gate into the central courtyard. Slaves and soldiers filled the compound. The soldiers were systematically checking the contents of crates before giving them to the slaves. The slaves in turn would pack the boxes into hemispheric cargo capsules, then push the capsules into the hollow up-tube of the sky dock. The huge steam engines next to the pillar would whine as they pulled the air out of the tube. Then the ground would throb as the pusher plate buried beneath the tube would spring out of the ground, shooting the capsules up through the thin air into *Chandra's Tear*'s docking bay.

In the compound we immediately spotted the one man dressed neither as a soldier nor as a slave. Kleon was a welcome sight in a short Cretan tunic, a bright blue skirt, and sandals so neatly tied they looked woven.

He was running around the courtyard like a frightened chicken, pointing out one pile of huge boxes and demanding they be sent up next. I grinned at Ramonojon, and he responded with a half smile that he quickly suppressed.

"Kleon, what is all this?" I shouted, so as to be heard above the hissing and banging of the steam engines.

"Aias!" he shrieked in delight. "You'll never believe what happened! I—" He spun around and shouted at a soldier routing through a long thin box. "Careful with that. You could buy half of Persia with what's in there." He turned back to me. "I got the Ares impellers. They'll cut weeks off our travel time."

"You did what?" I shook my head, hoping the noise was playing tricks on my ears. The Ares impellers were the longest air-rarifiers ever built; when assembled, there would be forty rods of solid fire-gold, each half a mile long. They had been created for a survey mission of the fifth planet, not for *Chandra's Tear*. I cringed to think about how much of our budget Kleon had spent on these things, and how many favors Aeson and I now owed to commanders of other projects.

"To the crows with you, Kleon! I sent you to Crete to replace some broken impellers, not steal the most expensive project ever to come out of the Akademe. And what did you say to make the celestial navigators give them to you?"

Kleon smiled maniacally. His teeth shone out from his dark brown face, and his brown eyes sparkled in the silver light. "I showed them your authorization from Kroisos."

I clutched my head in disbelief. The Archon of Athens could have my head for this misuse of authority.

Kleon patted my hand like a consoling aunt. "Don't worry about it. The Ares designers sent a messenger to Delos before giving me the impellers. Kroisos personally authorized the transfer. The Celestial Navigator's Guild is so angry at me for snatching this prize from them, they might even expel me."

I couldn't believe he was happy about that. "Those impellers were designed for the *Spear of Ares*. Do you realize how much carving we'll have to do on *Chandra's Tear* so she'll be able to fly right after they're installed?"

"That's no problem." He started humming happily and turned to Ramonojon. "It'll be easy to reconfigure the dynamics, won't it?"

Ramonojon blinked as if he hadn't been listening to the conversation. "Hmm. Yes, I suppose so."

Had all of my subordinates lost their minds? For two years Ramonojon had been carefully sculpting *Chandra's Tear* so she'd be able to fly to 'Elios and back with and without the sun fragment. Now Kleon had undone all that work in one stroke, and Ramonojon acted as if it were a minor problem.

"Come on," Kleon said. "We'll take the next capsule up. I can't wait to start recalculating our flight path."

He ran to the nearest passenger capsule and climbed in.

Ramonojon shrugged and followed Kleon into the fire-gold–studded steel hemisphere. I strode after them, shadowed by Captain Yellow Hare.

We four strapped ourselves down on the capsule's steel floor, heavily padded with a carpet of cotton under a layer of thick leather, and with enough pillows to keep an Indian rani comfortable. I felt a small bump under us; through one of the tiny square windows in the side of the capsule I saw slaves push a float cart under our conveyance and trundle us into the sky dock's up tube.

Through the clear quartz roof, I looked up through the mile of darkness dotted with little glowing nodules of fire-gold. A pillar of stars, all sharply visible in the rarified air through which we would travel like a tetra out of a cannon.

The steam engines whined as they evacuated the tube, making the air as thin as humanly possible. We waited. Ramonojon breathed evenly. Kleon sang to himself, working out flight paths between the celestial spheres in the musical mathematics of Pythagoras. Captain Yellow Hare lay still as a corpse. I gripped the soft down pillows and counted backward from one hundred.

At sixty-four, the pusher plate slammed into the base of the capsule and we shot skyward. The breath rushed from my lungs as we flew up past the artificial stars toward the real ones.

A minute later there was a deafening clang as our hemispheric capsule hit the hemispheric dome at the top of the column. The leather straps dug into my chest and legs as my body tried to fly further up. After a moment's midair hesitation, the capsule gave up the notion of ascent and fell, but just a few feet. The floor rang like a muffled gong, sending shivers through my bones as we hit the catching plate that my ship's docking bay had automatically thrust between us and the mile-long drop down to Earth.

I caught my breath and slowly unstrapped myself. My muscles felt as fragile as dry reeds. A door opened in the side of the tube, letting in a rush of air and light. Two of the ship's slaves removed the capsule from the up tube and resealed the door so that the tube could be reevacuated for the next load of cargo.

The capsule door was opened, and, led by Captain Yellow Hare, we walked out quickly onto the glowing silver landscape of my ship. The cold, clear air of a mile up caressed my skin, sucking the accumulated dew of the earth from my body. The ship's surface pushed against my feet; I knew it was only the natural circular motion of lunar matter giving impetus to my terrestrial body's native linearity, but it felt like an affectionate welcome.

A man in black-painted bronze armor strode forward through the silver glare and snapped a brief salute at me. Anaxamander, security chief of *Chandra's Tear*, looked the same as when I'd left a month before: tall, olive-skinned, muscular, the perfect model of a Spartan officer, except, to his obvious shame, he was not a Spartan, not one of those who had been taught at the greatest military school in the world. His dignified bearing and haughtily stoic face concealed his well-known anger at having risen as high as he would be permitted in the Delian League's army.

"Commander Aeson has ordered a staff meeting for one hour from now," he said without a hint of greeting.

I nodded. So did Ramonojon. Kleon looked crestfallen. "I have to install the impellers."

"No time," Anaxamander growled. "My men," he said, and his voice rose with his pride at having others under his command. "My men will have to check the capsule's crates before the equipment is unpacked." He paused and looked down from his six feet of height to Kleon's diminutive five. "It is a matter of security."

Anaxamander turned back to address me, but when he looked over my shoulder at Captain Yellow Hare his well-practiced arrogance faltered. The perfection of her Spartanness overwhelmed his carefully honed pose as the light of the sun would the gleam of a lamp.

"Meeting in one hour," he mumbled to her behind the stiffest salute I'd ever seen him give.

Kleon saw an opportunity to argue with the security chief, but Ramonojon stopped him with a gentle hand on his shoulder. "There will be plenty of time for work. Commander Aeson has good reason to want to see us."

Ramonojon cast a glance at me, and I shook my head. Apart from his casually fearless style of piloting, Kleon was basically a high-strung, excitable person. I did not want to be the one to tell him about the attack.

Kleon glowered at all of us, then fixed his attention on Anaxamander. "How long until the last of the supplies are loaded?"

"Twenty minutes."

"Then I'll make sure we are under way before the meeting starts."

Kleon picked up his traveling bag and lyre case, nodded to all of us, then turned toward the bow of the ship and walked off with as much dignity as his grasshopperlike gait could lend him. I watched him walk-hop-walk across the open stretches of my ship's surface as he crossed the quarter mile between the docking bay and the navigation tower, where he lived and worked. I lost sight of him when he disappeared around the blue marble amphitheater that lay just aft of that glowing tower of granite and moon rock where he lived.

Ramonojon nodded to me and walked unsteadily aftward, passing around the large hill in the center of *Chandra's Tear*, presumably on his way to his underground laboratory in the stern of my ship.

A dozen of Anaxamander's security guards had assembled and were waiting patiently in front of the sealed cargo capsules. Behind them were about twenty large male slaves, lolling around in that pretense of interest that passes for discipline among northerners. I had been away from command for so long that it took me a moment to realize they were awaiting my permission before they began the inspection.

"Proceed, Security Chief," I said to Anaxamander. He saluted as I turned to leave, and set his men to work inspecting crates.

Captain Yellow Hare followed me as I slowly walked to port and a little astern. It took us a good ten minutes of ambling across bare moon rock to reach the steel dome that served as dormitory for my junior scientists. I thought about poking my head in and giving a general greeting to my subordinates, but decided to wait until after the staff meeting. Instead I walked fifty yards aft to the small, square marble building that squatted above my cave. As one of the ship's senior staff, I had the privacy of a home; most of the crew lived either in the port dormitory or the starboard barracks, depending on whether they were my scientists or Aeson's soldiers.

I passed between the green and red Doric columns of my home into the bare chamber that held only a spiral staircase cut downward into *Chandra's Tear*. I walked down those shallow silver stairs, into the body of my ship.

My hand grazed along the smooth cut wall of shimmering silver as I descended into my darkened quarters. Darkened? The slaves must have left the night blankets in place along the walls, ceiling, and floor; those blankets were a necessary precaution if one wanted to sleep in a cave carved from everglowing rock. Crewmen on some of the celestial ships had gone mad trying to shut their eyes against the constant moonlight.

I stopped to get my bearings before plowing into the darkness. There was always a chance that the slaves had rearranged some of the furniture, and I did not want to trip. But as I stepped into my cave, someone reached out and grabbed my arm, twisted me around, and threw me to the floor. A hand reached round to cover my mouth before I could cry out. I tried to roll out from under him, but he held me tight. A voice whispered in my ear in broken 'Ellenic, "Don't struggle. Or you die painful."

The voice was halting but there was an almost Spartan confidence in it.

Then I heard a dull thud, and the hand fell from my face. For a moment I was pressed harder against the ground, and then my attacker was gone from my back. I rolled away and jumped up. I couldn't see what was happening, but I knew Captain Yellow Hare was fighting for my life in the darkness.

I ran over to the wall and fumbled around until I felt the heavy cotton cord. I yanked it and the port wall night blanket rolled up like scroll into the ceiling. Silver light washed into the room, illuminating two struggling figures. Yellow Hare was locked corps-a-corps and sword to sword with a man in a grey silk gi. A Middler was on my ship!

I ran to my desk, cradled in the narrow aft end of the oval cave, picked up my heavy mahogany stool, and threw it at the Middler's back. He turned to duck and Yellow Hare stabbed him through the chest, steel puncturing silk, then skin, then heart. He crumpled soundlessly to the floor.

The Spartan leaned down to make sure he was dead, then walked over to me.

"Don't you ever put yourself at risk again!" she snarled, her divine stoniness breaking into human anger. "I am here to protect you, not you to protect me. Do you understand?"

I nodded. "Are you all right?" I asked.

"No injuries," she said. "Listen to me carefully, Commander. You are not a soldier; your presence makes it harder for me to fight, since I have to keep track of where you are. The next time this happens, I want you to find a hiding place and stay in it."

"Next time?"

"Yes, Commander, next time. Until I know how an enemy assassin got on board a supposedly secure ship, we must assume that there will be further attempts on your life."

"I understand, Captain," I said.

"And will you do what I feel is necessary for your safety, Commander?"

"As long as it does not interfere with my duties," I replied.

She nodded and then turned to look around the room, making sure everything was safe, then turned to examine the body. "A Nipponian commando. The Middlers don't use them very often."

She picked up the body with casual ease and walked up the staircase. "I will have a word with your security chief about this breach while you ready yourself for that meeting."

Alone in my home, where an assassin had been lying in wait for me. In my cave, on my ship.

I dropped into a seated position on the floor and gripped the black wool blanket with unsteady hands. My eyes drifted over to the starboard wall and the rows of scroll-filled cubbyholes that lined it. For several minutes I found myself wishing I could pull one of the scrolls out of its hole and lose myself in science or history. Anything to rid my mind of assassins and bodyguards.

Athena roused me from my stupor; she held the Aigis in front of my mind's eye, showing me the head of Medusa, sliced off by Perseus. The choice implicit in the goddess's gesture was clear. I could sit on the floor like a stone statue or stand up like a man. I thanked the goddess for her challenging presence as I rose from the ground.

I took off my sweat-stained traveling robes and threw them on the floor near my sleeping couch in the bow end of the cave. Then I opened the large cedar trunk near the head of the couch. The smell of fresh camphor and myrrh told me my clothes had been well cared for during my absence.

There was a jar of fresh oil next to my sleeping couch, so I rubbed some on my face and arms. I took a deep breath to clear my head and inhaled the pungent scent of spilled blood.

Eager to get out of the room, I donned clean scholar's robes and affixed the golden owl badge of scientific command to my left shoulder, just under the blue fringe. I laced on thin walking sandals with soles roughened for waking on *Chandra's Tear*, and secreted the copy of Ssu-ma X'ien's history in the bottom of the chest.

Dignity restored, I marched out of the cave and up the stairs to the surface of my ship. The ground hummed slightly and jerked a bit under my feet; the wind had picked up and the air was crisp, cold, and much drier than it had been. We had left the dock and were now circling perhaps forty miles above the earth and still climbing. I could feel the pure air separating my jumbled thoughts into clear, bright strands as the excess atoms of water and earth drifted out of my body with each deep breath I took. Every scholar knows that the heaviness of terrestrial Pneuma can fog a man's mind, tying his ideas into unreasoned knots; few realize the consequences of this, that the farther you go from the earth, the clearer your thoughts become.

*Chandra's Tear* continued to orbit the earth at her natural speed, the same pace as Selene herself kept in her daily circuit around the globe. The prow of the ship was tilted slightly upward, so my ship continued to gently rise. All to the good since this was the region of the sky most often patrolled by Middler battle kites. Once we were above three hundred miles, common belief held, we would be safe.

Captain Yellow Hare was waiting for me outside the anteroom. The assassin's body was nowhere to be seen.

She followed me closely as we hurried amidships toward the hill which Aeson and I used as meeting area and command center. Five minutes before the meeting was to start Yellow Hare and I reached the staircase carved into the port side of the hill and climbed the steep steps until we reached the colonnaded court-yard that crowned the highest point on my ship.

The port-side entry into the quadrangle, like its counterparts to fore and starboard, was blessed with a fifteen-foot-high statue of Athena and guarded by two of Aeson's soldiers. The three-sided symmetry of the gates was violated by the aft end of the courtyard. That was occupied by three square blue buildings: my office, the ship's library, and Aeson's office.

Yellow Hare and I passed through the port-side portal; the guards saluted us while we bowed to the red-and-gold statue of the goddess. Spear and Aigis upraised, this image of Pallas was armed for war; her piercing glance continually blessed *Chandra's Tear* and its crew with her battle skills while the chalcedony owl on her shoulder looked inward to the courtyard, blessing the ship's commanders with her wisdom.

We walked toward the center of the courtyard, where a pair of nine-foot-tall statues stood on four-foot-high pedestals. One was of Aristotle, painted in differing shades of blue. The great scientist held aloft in his right hand a glass model of the universe that moved in perfect imitation of the eternal movement begun by the Prime Mover. The model glinted in the sunlight, showing in intricate detail the seven planets held in their concentric crystal spheres, orbiting in their divine dance of cycles and epicycles around Earth.

Across from Aristotle was a statue of Alexander. It was carved from obsidian in the graceful Toltek style. The famous general carried a sword in one hand, pointed downward toward the earth, and a spear in the other, pointed up as if to challenge the gods. Both statues were of the heroes in the glory of their last years. Aristotle was stooped over at eighty, but his eyes still shone with genius. And Alexander at seventy-seven showed the long beard and craggy face of experience, but his muscles still held the tone and power Spartan training had imparted to the native grace of a young Makedonian prince.

Yellow Hare and I reached the circle of marble couches be-tween the statues where meetings were held. The rest of the senior staff—Kleon, Ramonojon, Mihradarius, Anaxamander, and of course Aeson—were already present, leaving only the couch nearest Aristotle, my seat, unoccupied. Aeson stood up from the couch closest to Alexander and walked toward me. The others quickly stood as well.

Aeson reached out for me and we grasped arms at the elbow. There was sadness in his gray eyes, and a twitch at his mouth that betrayed a nervousness that neither he nor any other Spartan would ever admit to.

I smiled at him, glad to once again feel his friendship. I released his arm and looked around the circle.

Anaxamander stood as he always did. His chest was puffed out and his gaze was tilted slightly upward, as if he were posing for a hero's statue. Ramonojon was next to him. He hadn't changed out of his traveling clothes. Kleon was next to him, shuffling his feet nervously. He alternated between eyeing the navigation tower and glaring at Anaxamander.

I turned to Mihradarius. He was dressed as I was, in the Athenian style. "Commander Aias," he said formally. "I return your ship to you."

"Thank you Senior Ouranologist," I said. Mihradarius seemed neither relieved nor saddened by the loss of command, as if it had been neither burden nor blessing, just another problem for his matchless intellect to solve.

Aeson nodded to me. We walked to the table in the center of the couches and picked up from it two gold goblets full of dark purple wine. We turned away from each other and walked out of the circle, I toward Aristotle, Aeson toward Alexander.

We stopped at precisely the same moment and poured libations at the feet of the heroes.

"Bless this assembly," we said.

"Avert the dangers of battle," Aeson said.

"Avert the dangers of folly," I said.

"Keep us safe in body and mind," we said.

"Bless this assembly."

The wine flowed over the statues into the heavy silver bowls in front of them. Aeson and I turned in unison, replaced the goblets on the table, and walked back to our couches. I sat down and nodded to Aeson, giving him full authority over the meeting.

"Two days ago," he said, "this ship was docked in South Atlantea when we received an emergency message capsule relayed from Delos through Tenoktiklan. It concerned Project Manmaker. . . ."

That surprised me. We rarely received any information about the other two branches of the Prometheus Projects.

"The message said that Aristogaros of Athens, Scientific Commander of Project Manmaker, had been killed by two Nipponian commandoes in his supposedly secret laboratory in the desert of Sudan. The message commanded us to tighten security and assign a bodyguard to our Scientific Commander."

He turned to me and his voice took on tones of elder-brotherly irony. "Our Scientific Commander, however, had been unwise enough to be on vacation."

Two days of worry were chiseled into his face, but his voice still held its Spartan calmness.

Aeson continued. "I sent a message to Sparta requesting Captain Yellow Hare as a bodyguard." He nodded to her. "She is the best commando in the League's army. The two attacks on Aias make it clear that I acted just in time."

"Attacks!?" Kleon shrieked. "What attacks?"

Aeson nodded to Yellow Hare, who gave a terse account of the battle kite and the assassin. "Commander, Aeson," she concluded. "I have already questioned your Security Chief as to how the Nipponian got on board this vessel."

"What was your answer, Security Chief?" Aeson said to Anaxamander.

"Sir," Anaxamander said, trying to remain stoic in the face of two displeased Spartans, "this ship has too many scientists in her crew for proper discipline to be maintained."

"Nevertheless," Aeson said, "this must not happen again. I am giving Captain Yellow Hare full authority to do whatever she thinks necessary to protect Commander Aias. You and your men are to obey her orders without question."

The Security Chief saluted without saying a word, but I could see anger brewing in him like thunder in the brows of Zeus.

Aeson went on. "From this point until we leave for 'Elios, contact between this ship and Earth will be minimized. We will make as few cargo stops as possible and there will be no more leave."

Mihradarius started to protest, but Aeson cut him off with a look. "Security will be tightened, all incoming capsules will be searched, and all senior staff members will let the guards know where they are at all times. Only Aias has been ordered to have a bodyguard, but any senior scientist who wants one will be given one."

Mihradarius and Ramonojon looked at each other for a moment, then shook their heads. Mihradarius looked annoyed at the suggestion; Ramonojon seemed sad.

Kleon, however, wanted one and an increased detail of soldiers at the entrance to the navigation tower.

Aeson coughed and looked at me expectantly. I had to say something to avoid dampening the morale of my subordinates. No muse came to inspire me with words to rally my people, so I said what I always said when the military needed to do something that my staff did not like. "For the sake of the project, I expect everyone to cooperate with the army on this matter."

They grumbled but accepted. Aeson nodded, encouraging me to take control of the meeting. I cocked my head toward my brilliant Persian underling. "Progress report."

Mihradarius stood up and walked over to the statue of Aristotle. "During the month you were gone, I completed my tests on the four sun net prototypes. My conclusion was that model Delta is the only design that can stand the stress of our return journey."

Ramonojon looked up, blinking in momentary surprise. "Might I see your calculations?"

"If you insist," Mihradarius said, "but, no offense to your intellect, Chief Dynamicist, I doubt you could follow my mathematics."

Oh no, I thought, not another argument.

"I am merely curious," Ramonojon said.

Mihradarius glared at him, then shrugged. "You can see the logs of the experiments if you want."

Ramonojon nodded and lapsed into silence. I breathed a sigh of relief that Ramonojon had not brought about another flare-up in Mihradarius's temper.

The Persian continued. "To build net Delta, we need twenty cubic feet of Aphroditean matter as well as seventy cubic feet of 'Ermean matter."

I swore under my breath. Getting material from 'Ermes was expensive enough, but at least the Delian League had a base there. To get the rock from Aphrodite a special expedition would have to be sent. That, combined with Kleon's acquisition of the Ares impellers, would cripple our budget. I could already hear Kroisos shouting at me about wasting the League's funds. But Mihradarius said we needed it, so I would have to get it.

"Build as much of the net as you can," I said. "We'll send a requisition to Delos and hope they approve it. If not we may have to stop at Aphrodite on our way out, mine the material ourselves, and weave the net as we go."

I turned to Kleon. "How long to install the impellers?"

He hummed and tapped his left foot while he calculated. "A week, two at the most."

"Ramonojon, how much reshaping will the ship need?"

He looked up suddenly. "I'm sorry, what was that?"

What was the matter with him? "How long will it take to alter the ship's dynamics to work with the new impellers?"

"Hmm. A month."

"That little time?" I would have thought he would need six weeks or even two months to do that large a reconfiguration.

He seemed surprised at the question. "Yes, I expect so."

"Anything else?" I asked. "Anyone?"

No one spoke. Through the silence of the meeting, the winds of the upper air touched my ears with the rumblings of my crew's life. From the forward part of the ship I heard Aeson's troops drilling. From under the hill came the noise of slaves working in the storage caves and the grunts of half-formed animals from the spontaneous-generation farm. And from aft there warbled the high-pitched arguments of junior scientists making minor alterations to the sun net apparatus.

I looked up to at 'Elios, rising above us in his fiery majesty. In the gleam of daylight, I felt the touch of Apollo in my voice. "Man and Nature conspire to halt us," I said. "But we will yet touch the sun."

"This meeting is ended," I said, returning my gaze to the assembly. "May the gods bless our work."

δ

I should have known something else was wrong; Zeus, it was my duty to know. However the rest of my actions are judged, however my doxa comes to be seen, let all know that I indict myself, that I was derelict in my command during those first three weeks back on *Chandra's Tear*.

I should never have accepted the excessive gifts of consideration the crew laid before me. In order to keep me safe from further assassination attempts, everybody—my crew, my bodyguard, my co-commander, even the slaves—rearranged the working procedures of my ship so that I never had to be anywhere except my home cave or my office.

Reports from all quarters of the ship were brought to my office desk, carrying with them the calm reassurance that everything was going smoothly. Meals were brought by the slaves so I never had to go to the commissary. Any questions I had were relayed by Yellow Hare to messenger slaves, who would find whomever I wanted to query, get an answer, and bring it back to me. All I had to do was sit at my desk, go over requisition forms, perform calculations, and let Captain Yellow Hare do whatever was necessary for my safety.

Truth to tell, I found it easy to convince myself that I was doing my duty. After all, it was not as if my days were spent in idleness. I had to solve a considerable number of logistical and supply problems caused by our reduced schedule of dockings. Maps of half the world with shipping lanes carefully marked were strewn across my desk in order that I might determine the best routes for consignments of supplies to take in order to meet us. At one point I actually ordered a machine-milled half-pound icosahedron of fire-bronze that the net-spinning device required to be sent by courier from the factory in Korinthos all the way to the southern tip of Africa; there it joined a shipment of gold we needed to make replacement parts for the impellers; then that joint requisition was transported to South Atlantea, where the obsidian lenses for our sun goggles were being ground. Three packages that we could have picked up ourselves on three simple stops were consolidated at great expense and confusion just for my safety.

And that was simple compared to the needs of the spontaneous-generation farmers. Papers were constantly crossing my desk about their need to stockpile more materials if they were going to keep making food animals for us. I don't know how many requests I routed for bat dung or crushed violets or who knows what obscure effluvia they needed to create cows, pigs, and chickens.

And I had my own scientific work to do. Ramonojon was building the ship, Kleon was installing the impellers, Mihradarius was working on the net, but the sun fragment itself was my responsibility. Celestial fire is a unique substance, existing in the body of the sun. It burns a million times hotter than terrestrial fire, it destroys and consumes matter like its earthly counterpart, but unlike normal flame it is eternal, indestructible, as are all things of the heavens. In sum, it is a fire that does not dissipate after it burns—the perfect weapon against terrestrial foes.

The nature of celestial fire is such that once a fragment of it was pulled away from 'Elios, the piece would form a sphere and hold together just as the body of the sun does. The natural motion of celestial fire, like all celestial matters, is circular, orbiting the earth at a set speed. The sun net would harness that circular movement, turning the sun fragment into a tiny planet orbiting *Chandra's Tear*. All well and good, and theoretically simple to control. But there was a gap of experience in our theories. We really only knew how celestial fire behaved in the region of 'Elios. I had to calculate how it would behave in the denser air of the lower spheres, in the water-laden atmosphere just above the earth, and in the solid body of Gaea herself. I had, of course, done most of this work during the previous three years, but theories can always be refined, and answers made more exact, particularly when the lives of my crew and the utility of Sunthief as a weapon depended on it.

But, despite all I was doing, my work was not the center of my life during those three weeks; security was, and Yellow Hare was the heart of that security. Every morning, I would wake up in my home cave, pull the cords that rolled up the night blankets, and see her, sitting cross-legged on the floor, awake, clean, oiled, and armored. I knew that she slept on the carpeting because she told me that she did, but she always waited until I was asleep before taking her own rest, and I knew she would waken before me and silently prepare herself for the day's work. Once I was awake she would send for slaves to wash me, dress me, and bring my breakfast, which she always made a slave taste before permitting me to dine. Then she would dismiss the slaves and make sure we were alone before preceding me out onto the surface of the ship.

During the walk to my office, she would carry her evac thrower drawn in her left hand and her sword in her right. She would permit no one to approach except Aeson or a soldier she personally trusted. When we would reach the courtyard at the top of the hill, she would leave me in Aeson's care while she prowled through my office like a sniffing jaguar.

Only when she was satisfied as to its safety would she let me into my own office. She would see me to my desk, then take up guard position next to the doorway, still as a statue. She remained like that until someone came to the door. Then she would take one step back and put one hand on the hilt of her sword and the other on the evac thrower slung across her back.

She always heard my visitors before I did. No matter how noisy the ship was, with the whine of the impellers, the rush of the wind, the clear bell-like clanging from the reshaping work, she was still able to hear people clear across the courtyard. She could also distinguish who they were by the sound of their footsteps. If she knew who the person was she would tell me before he arrived. But if she did not know, she would ask me to get up from my desk and stand behind her as she crouched beside the door, ready to spring if need be.

But though I became comfortable, grateful actually, for the care Yellow Hare showed for me during those three weeks, I found myself increasingly dissatisfied with the silence that lay between us. I resolved to find something to talk to her about, anything that would bridge the gap between us. But I had always had trouble finding common ground with Spartans. Aeson and I had become friends only after I found out that though he had been filled from birth with battles, strategies, and the marching of armies, still in a corner of his heart he harbored a romantic desire to journey to the outer planets. Anything I told him about the heavens affected him like wine, and his unschooled adoration of the wondrous spheres had many times during the course of Sunthief's development reminded me of the glories of Ouranian existence, which my training had reduced to mere calculations.

But Captain Yellow Hare had no such romanticisms. She soaked up all the details of the ship's layout, learned the names, descriptions, and duties of every member of the crew, interrogated Clovix, our chief slave, about his underlings, and so on, until she knew *Chandra's Tear* as well as Aeson and I did. But nothing any of us was doing mattered to her except as it threatened or aided the performance of her duty.

Near the end of the third week, there came a night when I tried to bridge the gap between us. I had been working late in my office, clearing away the last of the requisition forms. Clovix had brought us dinner: lab-grown venison roasted with olive oil, oregano, and basil. We also had two loaves of fresh-baked barley bread. For drink we had a large bowl of Babylonian wine and water to mix it with. Yellow Hare drank the water straight; Atlanteans have no tolerance for wine. And they smoke tobakou instead of Indian hemp. For all my years in Atlantea, I could never understand why. Tobakou does nothing for me. Hemp at least is relaxing.

I reclined on my couch and took a large bite of venison and bread, wiping a trickle of oil off my cheek with my sleeve. Yellow Hare sat cross-legged on the floor in the exact center of the room. It amused me that in seeking the most militarily useful position she had achieved perfect mathematical harmony with all the objects in my office. The desk was to her right; if an attack came she could roll under it and fire from cover. I reclined on the couch in front of her, and she could leap up in an instant and throw her body between me and any assailants. The wooden door was behind her, barred with a grate of iron she had ordered installed; she could spin to face it before anyone could break through. The walls, lined with cubbyholes, were to her left and right. If disarmed she could pull out heavy ivory scroll cases and lay them about her. The moon rock floor gave enough light for her to fight with, so the fixed fire-torches in the sconces along the rear wall could be picked up and used as weapons with impunity.

Perfectly placed, with no need to look around, she fixed her eyes firmly on me. Even when she was eating, her gaze never left me. She seemed to have an unerring ability to find her food without looking at it. She took rapid, small bites of bread and swallowed them instantly, like a bird pecking at a plate of seeds.

I poured wine into a small flat bowl, mixed in some water, and took a long swallow before trying to engage her in conversation.

"Which of the Xeroki city-states are you from?" I asked.

She stood up, walked over to my cubbyholes, and pulled out a map. I didn't know that she even knew what was there; my shelves were not labeled. She unrolled it and pointed to a small town on a river two-thirds of the way down the east coast of North Atlantea.

"I spent a lot of time in Atlantea as a child," I said, gamely trying to keep the conversation going.

"Hmm," she grunted.

"My father was Military Governor of Eto'ua for several years."

"Hmm."

I stopped speaking 'Ellenic and switched to Xeroki. "I'm very familiar with your homeland."

"Sparta is my homeland," she said.

"And the Xeroki?"

"Made me capable of being Spartan."

I nodded and fell silent. Not a long conversation, but enough to give me some understanding of her. Most of those who attended the Spartan military college retained a closeness to their native land. But some sucked inside them the communal living, dining, suffering, and training and became members of a different people. They became warriors not of their homelands, of the Delian League, or even of the city of Sparta, but of Nike, Ares, and Athena, the gods of war.

It is said that when Alexander entered the military college as a young boy, one of the first nonnative Spartans to be educated there, he carried his father Philip's dreams of learning the ways of the Delian League so that it and the third of Persia it controlled could be placed under Makedonian rule. King Philip had been surprised, to say the least, when the Delian army came instead to conquer his land, and stunned at the face of young Captain Alexander, who led the charge into his own palace.

The morning after my talk with Yellow Hare, I found out what had been happening on the rest of the ship while I had been protected from it. Two junior scientists tried to barge unannounced into my office shouting an impressive array of multilingual blasphemies at each other.

The twenty-five-year-old dressed in the red tunic and skirt of a Skythian was a young celestial navigator named Pandos. He was a normally pleasant-voiced young man with a reputation as a gregarious socializer. One would not have thought that about him given the way he was screaming insults in his native language and gesticulating menacingly with a rod of fire-gold. Yellow Hare grabbed his arm and twisted the two-foot-long, four-inch-thick club out of his hand. He kept swearing at the other man. My bodyguard laid the rod on my desk. I took a quick look at it. The top was rounded into a hemisphere with machine precision, but the bottom was ragged like a broken tree branch. The air grew clear and thin around it, distorting our voices into obnoxious squeaks.

Pandos bellowed like an angry mouse. "This oaf broke off one of the tertiary impellers."

I looked at his companion, a morose, well-muscled Egyptian dressed in nothing but a loincloth and a leather tool belt. I did not remember his name, but I knew he was one of the heavy-equipment operators who worked under Ramonojon. He was equally frenetic and angrily waved a sander in the air. The rough stone block noisily dripped water on my floor. "These twittering birdbrains won't even wait for us to finish beveling the prow before they install their impellers. We won't be held responsible if they turn *Chandra's Tear* into a lumbering hulk."

I held up a hand to silence them.

"Now, tell me what is happening," I said sternly. "One at a time." I pointed at the Egyptian. "You first."

Their accounts were decidedly laden with partisan anger, but I managed to piece together what was happening. Ramonojon's dynamic reshaping was taking longer than expected, and Kleon was impatient to get the Ares system emplaced, so their underlings were getting into fights over who should be working where.

And while this had been going on, all the reports that had crossed my desk had spoken of amicable progress.

The rage of Ares boiled up in my heart. "Return to your duties. I'll see to this matter myself."

I slipped a woolen cloak over my shoulders to keep the wind off and, followed by Captain Yellow Hare, stalked outside.

The sky at five hundred miles up was perfectly clear, and 'Elios blessed us with streams of his clean gold light. We walked down the hill and across the starboard side of the ship. I was impatient to reach the navigation tower, but Yellow Hare insisted on maintaining proper security procedures. We walked for a cautious half an hour and with each slow step my anger at being deceived festered and grew in my heart. Aeson's soldiers saluted as we passed their barracks, as did the gunners manning the starboard evac cannon battery, but none of them approached us. I don't know if it was Yellow Hare's orders or the fact that my countenance must have made me look like one of the Furies.

We were just passing the amphitheater when Athena tapped me on the shoulder. She reminded me that if I wanted answers, I would have to be calm, firm but calm. I stepped through the actors' entrance in the rear of the open-to-the-sky auditorium. Tiers of solid moonstone seats were set in a half-circle around a stage carved from terrestrial granite. It had been a long time since the crew had put on any amateur dramatics. Aeson and I planned to remedy that situation once we began the long journey to the sun, but if things were not settled between Kleon and Ramonojon that trip would never begin.

I walked around the low platform where the chorus would stand and climbed onto the stage to face my audience of one.

"Fool! to think that I would brook with blood to stain me from my throat." I quoted the *Orestes* of Euripides, hoping to expend my wrath in oratory.

"That is no way to contain your anger," Yellow Hare said from the center bottom seat.

"Then how?" I asked, surprised but pleased at her solicitude.

"Keep hold of it in your heart," she said, and I could almost see 'Ermes and Athena sitting on her shoulders, lending her eloquence and wisdom. "Let it give force to your words like the strength of your arm, but do not let it guide your words. At the Spartan college they say anger is fire; contain it with wisdom and it will give you strength forever; let it out and it will blow away, leaving only ashes."

"Thank you," I said. "Fire is something I understand."

We left the theater and climbed over the small rise bowward of it. The sight that greeted my eyes from the top of that hillock fed the fire in my heart like a forest of dry wood. Across the sharp prow of my ship, dynamicists and celestial navigation engineering crews swarmed like two tribes of warring ants.

Water-spraying bevelers came perilously close to fire-belching road graders. Cranes with heavy loads of stone and metal wavered perilously over the crowd. The forward cannon battery was being pulled back on float carts by teams of slaves under the direction of some dynamicists. Scant yards away, engineers lowered the Ares impellers over the bow on other cranes whose lines threatened to tangle with their rival machines.

"Stop!" I shouted.

There was too much noise for most of them to hear me, but the ones in the rear did, and they relayed the order from man to man until there was silence across the fore part of my ship.

"Work crew leaders come up here."

Kleon's and Ramonojon's senior deputies stepped up to the hill. They were about to open their mouths and complain but I raised my fist for silence. "I don't want to hear any explanations. I'll talk to your seniors about that. Clear everything carefully out of the way. Don't interrupt, I don't care how far behind schedule that will put you. I want this area to be safe before any more work is done."

"Yes, Commander," they said in uncomfortable unison.

"You will then work in alternate six-hour shifts, dynamicists first. Is that clear?"

"But, commander—"

"I asked if that was clear."

"Yes, sir," they said, and returned to their crews.

Yellow Hare and I went to the navigation tower while the cowed workers disentangled themselves. Yellow Hare spoke briefly to the guards stationed at the base of the moonstone spire, then preceded me through the thin blue curtain at the entrance and up the spiral stairs to Kleon's control room.

My chief navigator was hunched in front of a writing desk, strumming his lyre with one hand and drawing lines with charcoal on papyrus with the other. The panel that actually controlled the ship was being manned by one of Kleon's junior navigators, a young Theban woman named 'Ekuba, who was staring out through the square quartz window in front of the controls.

"Kleon!" I said, pulling slowly on the fire in my heart like Yellow Hare drawing on her pipe. "We need to talk."

His hands jumped, raising a harsh discord from his lyre. "I nearly had it. I could have cut three days off our travel time, and now I've lost the chords."

Then he looked up and saw who had interrupted him. "Aias? What are you doing out of your office?"

I ignored his question and pointed at the window. "Have you looked out there recently?"

Kleon leaned over to brush charcoal from the paper. The black dust fell slowly to the floor, then skittered trails across the hard stone as the ship's circular motion forced the powder into unnatural perambulations.

"It's not my fault," he said. "I'm following the schedule."

He picked up his lyre and pointed to a sheet of paper glued to the wall. It was in Ramonojon's meticulous handwriting and gave specific times and dates when his dynamicists would be working on each part of the ship. From the state of work outside, it appeared that they were two weeks behind. This was the first time in three years that Ramonojon's crews had been anything but punctual.

Kleon picked up his lyre and strummed the Pythagorean chords of the seven spheres. "My people are doing their jobs. I've tried to talk to Ramonojon about his workers, but he just says he'll look into it and then returns to whatever it is he's experimenting on."

"Why didn't you tell me this was happening?"

"I am sorry," he mumbled. "I did not mean to offend you, Commander, but with the danger and your own work . . . We thought it would be better to work things out among ourselves, but Ramonojon hasn't been doing his work."

"Ramonojon?"

"Yes, Aias. He said he would keep his men to the schedule but he hasn't been out here once to oversee them."

"Then you should have told me weeks ago."

"Yes, Aias."

"I'll speak to Ramonojon right away," I said, trying to keep my anger under control. "And as for you, the next time something like this happens I expect to see you in my office telling me about it."

"Yes, Commander," he said.

I stalked out of the tower and proceeded aft toward Ramonojon's laboratory. The fury rose in me; all I could think about was that my friend who had always supported me was now ignoring his duty both to the project and to me.

"Commander," Yellow Hare said quietly. "Settle yourself before you speak to him. Contain your anger."

"What do you suggest I do?"

"You have dealt with the immediate emergency. You have the time to settle yourself and think through what you want to say."

We came around the starboard side of the central hill and saw the bright yellow colonnade of the commissary.

"Food and wine to settle the balance of my humours," I said.

"Yes, Commander," she replied.

The commissary courtyard was nearly empty; only a tenth of the hundred eating couches were occupied. Most of the diners were junior scientific staff, but a few off-duty soldiers were present. These snapped to attention when Yellow Hare entered. I walked to the squat granite kitchen at the aft end and ordered a small loaf of bread and half a roast chicken from the chief cooking slave. Yellow Hare made the nervous old Norsewoman taste the food before letting me settle down to eat.

I had just cut off the drumstick when one of my staff approached me, a Theban woman named Phaedra; she was a good Ouranologist, but her student years at the Akademe had made her too cautious in proposing her own ideas. "Excuse me, Commander. I know how busy you are, but something strange came up and I didn't know if I should disturb you with it."

"Too many people have been trying to not disturb me, Phaedra." I took a bite of the chicken, concentrating on the taste to control my anger. It was fresh and hot; the skin slipped down my throat just right, leaving a tang of Indian pepper on my tongue. "Tell me."

"Chief Dynamicist Ramonojon came to the file room last

week and asked to see the archive report on the first 'Elios probe. I gave it to him. The next day, Security Chief Anaxamander reprimanded me. He said that report was restricted to the Ouranology staff."

"I'll look into it," I said. I finished the chicken and returned the bones to the kitchen so the spon-gen labs could use them in growing more birds. What would Ramonojon want with ten-year-old data on the sun? I wondered. And didn't Anaxamander have more important things to do than checking on my files?

Aft of the commissary we walked onto a square, open plain of gleaming moonstone that extended in for a quarter mile from the starboard edge of the ship. The area was flatter than the rest of *Chandra's Tear*, but with rougher ground. It was the place where ceremonial games were held and funerals performed. We had had no deaths so far, but both Aeson and I knew that we could not rob the sun without some loss of life. The corners of the plain were each marked with a 'Erm, a small head of 'Ermes Psychopompos set on a three-foot-high marble pillar. None of the crew knew that when Sunthief had begun, Aeson and I had gone to these statues and offered sacrifices of wine and blood to the god of thieves and guide of the dead.

Past the open enclosure at the ship's widest point lay the lab caverns, where my subordinates did their work. The surface entrances to these caves were hemispherical mounds with curtained openings behind which lay straight stairways down into the ship. We entered Ramonojon's lab through the starboardmost hillock.

Yellow Hare and I walked down two dozen steps and entered the dynamicist's moonlit underworld. The cave was a demicylinder, like an eastern Atlantean longhouse. Its long edge ran from fore to aft and we had entered from the lone door in its fore end. The center of the cave was empty, though the flat floor and high arched ceiling bore as much soot and scarring as the pyrology lab at the Akademe. Drawing tables, stores of pen and ink, and stacks of paper lined the port wall, but no one was in that side of the lab. The starboard wall was covered with stacks of thick steel cases, each containing a sample of some terrestrial or celestial material.

Ramonojon sat at a workbench near the cases, hunched over something. Yellow Hare gave the room a good eyeing, then nodded for me to enter.

Ramonojon looked up with a lined, haggard face. He coughed and rubbed his hands against his cheeks. "Aias, what are you doing here?"

"Trying to keep my ship from falling apart. Your people and Kleon's are practically at war."

He cocked his head. "What about?"

"The resculpting."

"Oh, that's my fault."

"Is that all you can say?"

"I thought I could leave that work to my juniors. I suppose I had better take care of it."

The rage began to spread from my heart into my blood. I could feel black bile rising to color my thoughts. Then I grasped the anger and did as Yellow Hare had advised. I placed my fury in the timbre of my voice. "Senior Dynamicist Ramonojon," I said, casting my words like the spear of Ares. "Why have you not been doing your duty?"

But my anger did not strike him. He reacted to my rebuke as if it were a simple question.

"Because of this," he said, and waved us over to his table.

On an oil-smudged cloth lay a scale model of *Chandra's Tear* carved from Selenean matter. It was chained to the table by bands of iron to keep it from spinning off under its natural motion. The model was a foot-long teardrop, carved in so much detail that I could not only make out large features like the hill and the amphitheater, but small ones like the entrance to my cave. Dynamicists only made such models when they needed to study the unique motive characteristics of a particular object.

Twenty small weights depended from the bottom, representing our ballast spheres, and ten small fire-gold balls, miniatures of our lift orbs, floated above it, secured to the model ship by steel rods. A groove had been cut in the aft end of the model where we'd planned to put the sun net. Also on the table was a four-inch-wide fire-containment box. Something inside it was making a steady thumping noise. A gossamer net about two inches long waved jerkily in the air, pulling in three different directions at three different rates. The net connected the model to whatever was in the box.

"What's this?"

"This is a model of sun net design Delta. I constructed it according to Mihradarius's specifications."

"I'm impressed. Mihradarius's work is so abstruse I doubt any Ouranologist could duplicate it. I know I couldn't. How did you do it?"

Ramonojon said nothing. He opened the fire box and scooped out a little glowing ball with a pair of tongs.

"This," he said, "is a model of the sun fragment. It is a mixture of rarified fire and 'Ermean and Selenean matter. I made it according to your formula for simulating the motive properties of celestial fire. I checked your figures against the 'Elios probe data."

I took a heat meter from the table and held it over the sphere. The water in the glass tube boiled in exactly the right amount of time. My formula was unstable since it used terrestrial fire and celestial solids to simulate celestial fire, but if kept in a fire box it would remain accurate for several days before the celestial matter drifted out of it.

Ramonojon wrapped the ball in the net, unchained the model of *Chandra's Tear*, and hooked the net to the model. The net started spinning around the ship, chained to a little wheel that rolled along the groove. The full-size net would be tied to a trolley, but on that scale, a wheel would suffice.

Ramonojon walked to the center of the room, released the model into the air, then ran as fast as he could back to us. The little *Chandra's Tear* flew straight forward for a few yards as the real ship normally did when its native circular motion was counterbalanced by the terrestrial pulls of the ballast spheres and lift orbs. As the ship cut through the air, the pseudo sun fragment orbited it in a perfect circle, once, twice, thrice.

But as it orbited, the net that tethered it to the ship began to drag a little, its lines twisting through the flame. The fireball tried to make a fourth orbit, but it was fouled in the nets; it began to thrash and pull the ship like a whale hauling a fishing boat half its size. The model began to vibrate as the fragment darted this way and that. A crack developed in the groove. The bottom weights snapped off. There was a spray of silver moondust, a noise of breaking stone, and the fragment broke away, carrying the net and the back end of the *Tear* with it.

The rest of the ship, no longer moored to a straight flight path, arced upward and shattered against the ceiling, shrieking the Pythagorean chord of Selene. I covered my ears to dampen the echoes of that pure scream.

Moondust floated gently around the room, congealing gracefully into a circling ring of silver.

"I have tested this three times already," Ramonojon said, trying unsuccessfully to conceal his distress in a dispassionate monotone. "The first time, the model ship floated around the room, spiraling randomly; the second time it crashed into the floor; the third time the result was the same as this test. The conclusion is inescapable. Mihradarius is using the wrong net."

I nodded slowly, and asked for his calculations. Ramonojon showed me Mihradarius's Ouranological formulas and what he had done with them to derive the dynamics for his model. Ramonojon knew nothing of Ouranology, but he was certainly capable of taking someone else's calculations of impetus and discerning the dynamics of an object subjected to those forces.

I went back to my cave and spent three hours going over my friend's work. It was compelling, but not convincing. There were so many places where he could have been incorrectly interpreting Mihradarius's theories that I was tempted to dismiss his fears out of hand. Also, he had been acting so strangely since our vacation. Perhaps something had happened to him. . . . But what if he was right? . . .

I returned to the dynamics lab and found Ramonojon seated cross-legged on the floor. He looked up when we came in. "Well?"

I sighed. "One of you is making a mistake," I said. "But I don't know which one."

"I do not envy you your position." A half smile cracked his

facade, then vanished, but not before I could smile in acknowledgment.

"See to the restructuring," I said. "I'll talk to Mihradarius and find a solution to this dilemma."

Yellow Hare and I walked out of the dynamics lab and through the field of mounds toward the Ouranology labs.

"I do not trust Senior Dynamicist Ramonojon," Yellow Hare said.

"Because he's Indian, I suppose," I said, annoyed at her seeming prejudice. "When will you Spartans forget the rebellions?"

"That is not the reason," she said.

"What, then?"

"Because you who are his friend are beginning to doubt him."

I rounded on her. "What concern is it of yours, Captain?"

"It is my duty to guard you," she said, touching her sword hilt. "From friends and enemies alike."

I held my temper. "And that gives you the power to discern my thoughts?"

"No," she said. "Athena bade me watch your face as you examined Ramonojon's work. Your expression was not one of concentrated effort but of friendly concern mixed with bewilderment."

At that point we reached the entrance to Mihradarius's laboratory, and the conversation ended for a time.

My chief Ouranologist's lab was in the center of the research warren. It was a cube six yards on a side buried deep down in the body of the ship. A much smaller working space than Ramonojon's, but Mihradarius was a theoretician; there was no risk of colliding with exploding models in his underground den.

With the safety of theory came the luxury of decoration; carved on Mihradarius's walls were friezes of the two events beloved of most 'Ellenized Persians. The richly sculpted images depicted first Xerxes' surrender of the western third of Persia to Athens and Sparta at the end of the Persian war. This took up only one of the three walls; the rest were occupied with Alexander's conquest of the rest of Persia and his capture of the emperor Darius. The scene was carved in the moon rock and colored with bright, transparent paint that gave a supernatural glow to that great triumph.

One of Mihradarius's assistants met us as we came down and conducted us to him. My genius subordinate was poring over a page of stress and balance formulas for arrangements of 'Ermean and Aphroditean matter so complex it would have taken me days to check them for accuracy.

He looked up as we approached. "Aias?" He looked over at Yellow Hare. "Is it safe for the commander to be wandering around?"

"No," she said. "But it is necessary."

"Ramonojon has some problems with your net design," I said slowly.

He narrowed his eyes into a glare. "What problems?"

I described Ramonojon's demonstration.

Mihradarius scowled, and his eyes lost their focus as they always did when he was in the depths of thought. I waited.

"The net design is perfect," he said at last. "Ramonojon must have made a mistake."

"One of you has," I said. "How do I judge between the most skilled dynamicist and the most brilliant Ouranologist in the League?"

"You do have a problem," he said stiffly.

"I could go over your calculations with you."

"With respect, Commander, your knowledge of Ouranology is too specialized for such a review. You know too much about the celestial fire and too little about the celestial solids."

"Do you have a better idea?"

Mihradarius stroked his beard thoughtfully and stared at me. I could almost feel his mind working, racing through possible options, looking for one that would satisfy me. A moment later he clapped his hands and smiled broadly. "I have it. I will work out a demonstration of my own using *Chandra's Tear* itself."

"You will not put my ship at risk!"

"Not to worry, Commander," he said, raising a hand to calm me. "I will build a net one-quarter the size of net Delta. If Ramonojon is right, a net on that scale would cause us some flight problems, but nothing Kleon could not handle. But if my calculations are correct, we will suffer no difficulties at all."

It sounded like a good idea at the time. After all, I rationalized, such an experiment would conclusively demonstrate the truth to my satisfaction and that of my subordinates.

"How long will you need to set up such a demonstration?"

He tapped his fingers together excitedly. "Three weeks, since I assume you want me to be careful."

"Very careful," I said, and walked out of the cave.

Four days later, I had a few hours away from the rigors of command and the constant presence of Captain Yellow Hare when the monthly meeting of the new Orphic mysteries was held. I had been invited to join the exclusive mystery twenty years ago during my first fling with Fame, and it had been a comfort and an assurance during the lean times that followed. Of the three-hundred-some soldiers and scientists on *Chandra's Tear*, there were only eight New Orphics, including myself, Aeson, and Kleon.

Yellow Hare waited for me outside while the eight of us marched carrying torches down the black-painted tunnel carved into the side of the hill that led into the black-painted, naturalistically carved cave which the various mystery cults took turns using. In that artistically cut, pseudo earthly cavern, it did not take much imagination to believe that we were deep in Gaea's umbral womb rather than flying five hundred miles above her.

The mystery began with each member taking an assigned role in the story of Orpheus. This time I wore the mask of 'Ades. Phaedra played Persephone. Aeson had the unrewarding role of Kerberus, and Kleon wore the mantle of Orpheus. He was too nervous and excitable for the role, but he could play the lyre, which lent verisimilitude to his overly frenetic performance.

The mystery play closely follows the myth of the divine musician. Orpheus's wife, Eurydice, dies, and the heroic musician goes down to 'Ades to rescue her. His music charms 'Ades, and the god of the dead promises to give Orpheus his wife if he follows a certain condition. In the mystery the condition laid on him and the ending of the myth are different from the normal telling of the tale. Initiation in the mystery requires that one swear never to reveal this version of the story. That I subsequently broke this oath should be taken into account in your judgment of me, but I will come to that event in due course.

After the ceremony we put away the masks and robes and settled down in our torchlit privacy to drink and talk. In the cities of the League many important political deals are made at such meetings, but there were so few of us on *Chandra's Tear* that we usually took the opportunity to relax in pleasant company.

As the player of Orpheus, Kleon had the duty to pour and mix the wine, since no slaves were permitted in the mystery cave.

Aeson and I settled on adjacent couches to talk.

"I need to ask you about Captain Yellow Hare."

He sipped thin wine from a dish and shrugged his broad shoulders. "What do you want to know?"

"Why is a Spartan officer serving as a bodyguard?" I said, finally voicing the question that had been troubling me for weeks. I had not been willing to ask this in Yellow Hare's presence in case the assignment involved some disgrace on her part. I had not yet learned that nothing could disgrace that perfect Spartan.

Aeson studied my face for a few minutes. He had that look of serious concentration that all Spartans have when deliberating. I once asked him, facetiously, if there was a course in frowning at the war college. He in turn inquired if there was one in sarcasm at the Akademe.

"I met Yellow Hare at the Olympics five years ago," he said. "She took the laurel in pankration."

I nearly spilled my wine in shock. I did not pay much attention to the Olympics. My father's constant prodding at me had taken away any interest I might have had in athletics. But I knew about pankration; it was unarmed fighting with no rules. The participants could use any style of combat, any tricks, any deceptions they liked. Deaths were not uncommon in those contests. I remembered vaguely hearing that for the first time in several centuries a woman had won that competition. Having seen her fight, I was not surprised that Yellow Hare was that victor, but that did not answer my question.

"But why was she assigned as my bodyguard?"

"The order to protect you said I could choose anyone. I chose the best."

"My father would never have accepted such a lowly assignment."

Aeson stared for a few moments into the flickering torchlight. "Aias, your father's name is entered in the Spartan rolls of honor. His advice is heeded by several members of the general staff. He was a great warrior and an able governor. . . ."

"But?" I said, hearing the lingering absence of completion in his words.

"But he only had half of the Spartan spirit. Captain Yellow Hare has all of it."

"I don't understand."

"I'm sorry," he said. "But I can't explain it better than that."

Kleon brought me a fresh bowl of wine, which I drank in silence, waiting for some god to explain Aeson's words to me. But no divinity came to fill my needs.

"Thank you for trying," I said to Aeson.

My co-commander smiled at me. "Any further questions?"

"Yes. Why did the Archons allow you such discretion in picking a bodyguard?"

"I don't know," he said. "I have had a few hints from the general staff that the Archons now consider the Prometheus Projects vital to the security of the League."

"That's crazy. Sunthief and Manmaker could be of great benefit to the war effort, if they work, but that's a very large if, and as for Forethought, that project's a complete waste of time."

He nodded and sipped a little more wine. "That's what I've heard, Aias. I did not say I believed it."

I chuckled at the dryness of his Spartan humor and handed him a plate of figs. "Has Anaxamander had any success tracking down the source of that commando?"

Aeson's face darkened and he waved away the fruits. "No, he

has not. I am beginning to wonder if we need a new Security Chief."

"Is there any reason not to replace him?" I said.

"Yes," Aeson replied, studying his reflection in the bowl of wine. "Anaxamander knows this ship and its crew. A new Security Chief would need months to learn what he knows. I have given Yellow Hare authority over him, and I have recently been watching his actions carefully. That should suffice."

"Did you know that he was interfering in the scientific side of this command?"

"That I did not," Aeson said.

I told Aeson about Phaedra's encounter with Anaxamander.

"I will ask him about it," he said, and I could feel the full weight of Spartan disapproval poised to fall on the Security Chief's shoulders.

"Thank you," I said, and I leaned back on my couch to drink down the bounty of Dionysos.

Two hours later I said good night to all and walked carefully up the dark tunnel. I had drunk much wine, and much of that fermented honey the northerners brew.

Captain Yellow Hare was waiting for me outside. I stumbled and she gently took my arm to steady me. Despite her strength her grip was no heavier than a feather's touch. I leaned against her for support, and nearly recoiled; her skin was like ice. She had stood out in the cold, whipping air while I was down drinking in the warm cave. I felt angry at myself for treating her as an inconvenience. As I looked up to offer an apology, I heard the telltale whoosh of evac cannons firing.

"Down!" she said, pushing me flat against the moon rock. Yellow Hare stood over me, gripping her evac thrower in her right hand and her sword in her left.

Over to port something huge and bat-shaped blotted out the stars: a high-altitude battle kite flying straight toward us. The port-side cannonade shot a dozen huge tetras straight through the body of the bat. It hovered for an instant, then crashed.

Two more kites dove in low, getting past the gunners before they could aim again. These were one-man kites, supposedly too small to survive that high in the air, and they should not have been that fast. Skimming low across our glistening surface, they flew toward the mystery cave; then they must have spotted me because they turned swiftly and darted toward where I was lying.

Yellow Hare slammed the back of her sword hand into the butt of her thrower, forcing a spray of tetras out through the rarified air of the tube. The silk wing of one kite shredded. The pilot leaped off to avoid the crash and was met by a second volley from Yellow Hare's thrower. His broken body fell, staining the silver *Tear* with blood.

Aeson's soldiers poured out of the starboard barracks, evac throwers already aimed and shooting at the final kite, but they were not fast enough. The silken bat flew right over me; its pilot jumped out, letting his aircraft splinter against the hill. He fell toward Yellow Hare. She thrust her sword up to meet him. He speared himself on it, but just before his spirit left his body he pointed something metal at me. There was a momentary gleam of silver and gold in my eyes. Then the object fell from the pilot's hand as he joined his ancestors.

His blood dripped on me from Yellow Hare's blade. A wave of nausea rose from my stomach. But it wasn't the blood making me sick, or the wine. My head was hot from sudden fever. My legs were like brittle stone; I could neither feel them nor move them. Mead and bile rose in my throat, and I threw up on my gleaming ship.

I tried to say something to Yellow Hare but no words came out. She reached down for me; I tried to take her hand but night and xaos claimed me first.

# E

The sun beat down on me. In his hands he held a fiery spear as long as the distance between the earth and his sphere; he stabbed me through the chest every time my heart tried to beat.

"Thief!" 'Elios shouted; his flaming breath seared my face. "Steal my cattle, will you?"

I tried to explain to him that it was Odysseus who had stolen the kine of the sun, and that I was merely Aias. But his spear thrusts kept cutting me off, tearing the breath from my lungs so I could not get the words out. Worse, each time he withdrew the fire-gold barb, my heart and lungs would draw life from the rest of my body to heal themselves. Like Prometheus chained to the mountain, I had pain without death.

'Erakles wandered up to the crystal peak where I was shackled; the hero carried a large bronze club and was dressed in the skin of the Nemean lion. He waved to 'Elios, who nodded a friendly greeting in return but continued to methodically stab me. 'Erakles looked me up and down, said, "This one's not worth rescuing," and wandered away.

A coyote strolled around from the far side of the mountain. He sauntered over to me and watched 'Elios spear me a few more times. The animal scratched itself under its chin; then, coming to a decision, it skinned itself, unrolling its mangy hide like a roman toga. The coyote's muscles and veins were exposed, showing the life pulsing in his arteries. He leaned over me and whispered in my ear, "Put on my skin if you want to escape."

The Atlantean tribes that knew of him said never to trust Coyote, but seeing no other option I slipped out of my fetters and put on the skin. Freed from my chains of silver, I ran away from the Sun on my four paws. I fled across crystal, across air, across water, and finally across stone until I came to the Akademe.

Aristotle was discoursing in the lecture grove. Sokrates looked on with amused condescension. Plato had turned his back on his teacher and his student and was yelling to the audience of scholars that they should to listen to him. But wanting science, not philosophy, the teachers and students of his Akademe paid their founder no mind.

I ran up to Aristotle, yipping for attention. He looked down on me with the condescension only divine reason can give and said, "Men are distinct from animals."

From his own heart, he drew out an obsidian knife that glinted like the statue of Alexander and flayed the coyote skin from my body. My blood poured onto the altar, and the crowd of philosopher-scientists ran forward to drink it.

Human once more, I tried to stand on my two feet, but the grassy ground of the Akademe dissolved into a field of cushions. My feet could find no purchase on the shifting pillows, so I fell over. My head struck something hard, the stone leg of a statue. I looked up and found myself staring into the huge, languid eyes of Morpheus of the Forms. The god of dreams towered over me, standing between the gates of horn and ivory, his pale lips gently curled into a knowing smile.

"Will you have a true dream or a false dream?" he asked, stroking each pillar in turn. No words came out of my mouth, but the god nodded as if I had answered him.

I was on the fields of Troy, staring up at her spiraling towers.

Their marble pinnacles cut through the thunderclouds massed above the battlefield. A thousand sky docks piercing the air, a thousand arrows aimed toward Olympos, poised to rain up death on the deathless gods.

Heroes were killing and dying all around me. 'Ektor slew Patrokles thinking he was Akhilleus, Akhilleus slew 'Ektor and dragged his body around the city walls, Paris shot Akhilleus with one of the arrows of Apollo. I ran through the 'Ellene battle lines, ducking arrows and spears, dodging between the mountainous wheels of the chariots, keeping low to the ground in order not to attract the notice of the heaven-gazing heroes around me.

I nearly made it to the line of burning ships hauled up on the beach, but I was stopped by an ox-hide shield seven feet tall.

A tall man, broad of shoulder and angry of visage, looked over the top of the shield, while a small wiry man armed with a bow looked around the side. Tall exchanged glances with small, then both looked down at me.

"Well, Aias the Lesser," said the large one to the small. "This is our namesake."

The small man's mouth twisted into a smile. "I see him, Aias the Greater. What should we give him with our inheritance of our name. My drowning? Your madness?"

"No, Aias the Lesser," said the giant. "Not the mercy of a hero's death. Give him the pain of a hero's life."

Aias the Lesser nodded his agreement. He drew back his bow, pulled a goose-fletched arrow back to his cheek, and released, piercing my arm with his shot. I yelped like a coyote and sat up in sudden startlement at the tickling pain. Then I fell back shivering onto the couch and gathered the blankets around myself.

Couch? Blankets? I blinked my eyes to clear away the crust. The green blur around me resolved into the green-painted cave that served as private ward in the ship's hospital caverns. And the white blob leaning over me became my ship's chief doctor, Euripos, a sixty-year-old Roman who had once been my father's battlefield physician. He had just removed a goose-feather quill from the spot on my arm where the arrow of Aias the Lesser had shot me, and was placing it on the mahogany instrument table behind him.

Captain Yellow Hare loomed over me and peered down into my eyes with a golden gaze of worry and anger.

Aeson stood directly behind the table, watching me with the stoic face Spartans used when staring directly into the eyes of death. Anaxamander stood at attention just inside the curtained entryway that led up to the rest of the hospital.

"Talk fast," Euripos said to Aeson. "I don't know how long he'll be coherent."

"Aias," Aeson said, "you're suffering the effect of some new unknown Taoist weapon. The doctors don't know how to fix what it did to you."

I nodded and smiled, completely undisturbed by the news that I was incurable. In fact, I found the idea funny, so funny I started to giggle.

"What's the matter with him?" Yellow Hare asked.

Euripos picked up a needle and a thin sheet of papyrus. He took a little blood from my finger and spread it on the paper. A purple stain appeared and spread quickly, impregnating the papyrus with a royal color my Phoenician cousins would have given anything to be able to sell. "His body's producing incredible amounts of Jovial Humour. I told you the balance of his fluids was fluctuating uncontrollably. The injection of Sanguine I gave him won't keep him stable for long."

I nodded sympathetically. The whole room suddenly smelled like a tomb. I began to moan loudly as if I were a paid mourner at my own funeral.

A jaguar's growl jumped from Yellow Hare's mouth. "If you can't cure him, find someone who can!"

Aeson shook his head. "No one in the League understands Taoist medicine."

My bodyguard turned to face him, Spartan to Spartan. "Commander, you must obtain a Middler doctor from a prison camp."

Must? Through the foggy gloom in my heart, I found comfort in that imperative.

Aeson looked questioningly at Euripos.

The old Roman nodded his stiff neck slowly. I could see he didn't like the idea, but knew he had no choice.

"Commander," Anaxamander said. "We cannot compromise Sunthief's security by letting a Middler on board this ship."

Aeson turned on his lieutenant. "Without Aias there is no Sunthief."

"You're a real friend, Aeson," I said, suddenly elated. "That's so nice of you." I coughed out a huge gob of phlegm. "I mean it. It's honestly wonderful of you." I couldn't stop talking.

Euripos put a cold compress on my head and made me lie down again. My eyes shut and I started to drift off, but an argument broke out.

"As chief of security, I can't allow this," Anaxamander said.

"As Military Commander I'm overruling you!" Metal-soled feet tramped noisily off.

I collapsed into a pool of pain.

A man stabbed a many-barbed spear straight toward my eyes. I was paralyzed, not from pain or fear, but from not knowing whether to jump left or right, front or back. The spear stopped an inch away from my face.

"This one thinks too much," the old Spartan trainer said. He waved me over to his left, where all the other failed applicants to the war college were assembled. We looked over sullenly at those on his right, who were lining up at attention, waiting to be taken inside the iron walls and transformed into Spartans.

Thinks too much! After two weeks of torturous tests during which nine out of ten dropped out, I had persevered. All that had remained was the Test of the Spear, and I had failed with the single explanation that I thought too much.

At seven years of age, I had to return to face my eager father and had to tell him that I would never be a Spartan because I thought too much. He said nothing, just handed me over to my mother and returned to his governmental duties.

Tears ran down my cheeks. I reached up to wipe them away, but my arms and legs had been tied down. I blinked grit out of my eyes, expecting the blur in front of me to become Euripos, but instead I saw an old, lined face, parchment yellow in color, framing two almond eyes red from lack of sleep.

I panicked, struggling against the ropes that tied my limbs. Had I been captured? Had the Middlers taken over my ship? Then I saw that Captain Yellow Hare was standing behind him, holding her unsheathed sword over his head.

"He should be well now," the Middler said in 'Ellenic thickly accented with the 'Unan dialect of his native land. He leaned forward, tapped my wrist, and smelled my breath. "I'm amazed I could cure him," he muttered in his native language. "How do these barbarians survive without real medicine?"

"Do not move," he said to me, switching back to my language, not knowing I understood his. "Your Xi flow needs time to stabilize."

"What does that mean?" I snapped, feeling that flash of irritation every scholar in the League felt when confronted with the enemy's nonsensical but frustratingly real science.

"You must keep still," he said. "And do not let this man"—he indicated Euripos with the tilt of his head—"use any of his counterfeit medicines on you. Now, permit me to finish your healing."

The Middler picked up a bowl full of red paint and a brush and drew a line across my forehead. As soon as he finished the stroke, I was asleep. This time 'Upnos and Morpheus blessed me with dreamlessness.

When I woke again, Euripos and Yellow Hare were on the opposite side of the room, near the large, glass-fronted medicine cabinet etched with the intertwining snakes of Asklepios. My bodyguard was whispering to my doctor and I could not make out the words, but the tone of concern was clearly audible. I sat up slowly. There was a numbness in my muscles, and my skin was tingling as if I were in a cool rushing stream.

"Could I see a mirror?" I asked through a painfully rough throat that gave my voice a sound like charcoal scratching on slate. Euripos walked over and handed me one of those little round mirrors doctors use to see if their patients are dead. My face was haggard and worn, and my whole body was covered with a tracery of strange red lines, as if my skin had been dyed. "What is all this?"

Euripos shrugged. "I wish I knew. When they brought that Middler in, he asked for twenty silver needles, twenty gold needles, a horsehair brush, and a pot of vermilion paint. Aeson had all the slaves on the ship search the storage cave until they found what he needed.

"When he had his supplies, that crazy Middler stuck the needles all over you. I wanted to stop him, but she wouldn't let me." He cocked his head to indicate Yellow Hare. "He painted lines all over you, connecting one pin to the next. Then he sat down in that chair, and just watched you for a day."

Euripos stopped for a moment; his face clouded over with a mixture of annoyance and bewilderment. I recognized that look. Every Academic who ever had to describe something Middler science had accomplished had that look on his face.

"It was like magic," Euripos said. "The paint migrated across your body, twisting into new patterns. For the next two days he kept painting new lines and twisting the needles until yesterday the lines stopped moving and he said you were cured."

I sighed, and coughed a little. My lungs felt a little congested, but apart from that, and the dryness in my throat, I felt much better. I offered my doctor the standard Akademe excuse on the incomprehensibility of Taoist science, but the words sounded hollow, the vain protestations of someone railing against fate. "Don't bother trying to understand it. Once the Middlers have been conquered we'll have all the time in the world to divine their secrets."

The old Roman's eyes lit up with the thought of conquest.

"How long have I been unconscious?" I asked.

"Ten days," Captain Yellow Hare said matter-of-factly.

"When can I get back to work?" I asked Euripos.

"According to that Middler, all we have to do is clean the paint off and you'll be fit for duty."

"Well then, send for a slave to wash me. I'm anxious to return to work."

Yellow Hare stepped forward and put her hand on the hilt of her sword. I realized she was about to offer it to me as an acknowledgment of her failure to protect me.

I had to make clear to her that I still had confidence in her. No one could have anticipated an attack at that time and place against an enemy using new weapons, and no one could have done a better job defending me, or been more zealous to revive me when I was injured. But I could not say those things; Spartans do not listen to excuses, particularly about their own failings.

A different approach was needed and, all praises to you, lady of wisdom, Athena provided me with the words I needed. "Captain, make sure the path back to the hill is safe."

"Commander . . . perhaps . . ."

"That is an order, Captain."

"Yes, Commander," she said, taking her hand from her sword.

By the time she returned from scouting out my route, I had been cleaned and dressed. Yellow Hare took my arm and helped me walk stiffly and slowly up through the hospital caverns and out onto the surface.

Dawn was breaking as I emerged and *Chandra's Tear* was flying eastward into it. 'Elios glowed a warm yellow-orange that welcomed me back into his light. He seemed no longer angry with me, assuming he ever had been.

"Do you need to rest?" Yellow Hare asked.

"No," I said, and turned my gaze toward the hill. "Lead on."

Yellow Hare escorted me bowward around the hill and up to the courtyard. Just as we ascended the final step and reached the starboard statue of Athena a cry rose up from a hundred voices assembled on the apex of the hill. "Hail Aias! Hail Commander!"

All the science staff had come together to welcome me back to the living.

"Hail to you all, and thank you," I said.

My three senior subordinates stepped forward.

"The reshaping of *Chandra's Tear* is completed, Commander," Ramonojon said, eyes slightly downcast. "I'm glad you're alive."

"The Ares impellers are installed, Commander," Kleon said. "And we've risen to eight hundred miles above the earth. We should be safe from attack here."

"Preparations for the demonstration are proceeding as scheduled," Mihradarius said.

"Well done," I said to them.

I stepped out to face the arrayed ranks of my subordinates.

"Forgive me," I said to that sea of anxious faces. "I cannot stay and drink my health with you because I have fallen several days behind in my work."

There was a scattering of relieved laughter. "But I want you all to go to the commissary and eat and drink your fill. And perhaps spill a little wine to Apollo and Asklepios to insure my continued health."

"Hail, Aias!" they said again, and left me alone with Yellow Hare and Aeson, who had emerged from his office when the speeches were done.

"Welcome back, Aias," he said, gripping my elbow gently.

"Thank you, Aeson," I said, returning the gesture.

He leaned over and whispered in my ear. "Yellow Hare asked to be replaced. I told her she'd have to talk to you about that. I advise you not to do it; there is no better soldier in all the League."

"The matter's been dealt with," I said. "I managed to stop her from asking."

"Good."

We straightened up and our voices resumed their normal volume.

"How did you arrange to get a Middler doctor?" I asked.

"I sent a message directly to the Archons and they had one shipped by moon sled from a prison camp in eastern India."

"No problems? No protests from either Athens or Sparta?" I could hardly believe that neither the bureaucracy nor the high command would complain about something this unorthodox.

"Interesting," I said.

"You have an explanation?" he said, divining my thoughts from the expression on my face.

"Clearly, Sunthief has grown in importance, yes?"

"Yes."

"I think that increase may have to do with the recent improvements in Middler technology."

"That makes sense," he said, "but I do not like it."

"Neither do I," I said. "But if the Archons wish to lavish their confidence on us, we had better not disappoint them."

He smiled and squeezed my elbow again. Then we broke our grips and separated, each going to his own office.

My accustomed workplace was a welcome sight, but the huge pile of scrolls waiting for me on my desk was not. By late afternoon I'd managed to sort through them and bring myself up-to-date on the present state of things aboard ship. I had my lunch brought to me, and ate far too much of it trying to make up for my enforced ten-day fast.

Near the bottom of the pile, I found more evidence of Sunthief's greater importance. It was an official scroll bearing the seal of the Delian League and the signature of Croesus, the Archon of Athens. It stated that we would be provided with the Aphroditean and 'Ermean matter Mihradarius had requested. I read it three times to make sure they were not demanding some budget cut to compensate, nor requiring that the requisition forms be filled out in triplicate and countersigned by the Athenian bureaucracy.

That added weight to my hypothesis, but made me feel even more uncomfortable. Sunthief was a military gamble. We couldn't guarantee it would work or that if it did work we would be able to reach 'AngXou, let alone drop the sun fragment on it.

I looked up at Yellow Hare. "I need the opinion of a Spartan," I said.

She beckoned with an open hand, as if to say, "Go on."

I outlined the situation.

"Should you not ask Commander Aeson about this?"

I shook my head. "I need an outside opinion. What do you think?"

"That the success of your project relies greatly on Fortune, an untrustworthy goddess. . . ." She paused.

"Go on," I said.

"Both of the Archons have been blessed by Fortune."

I chuckled. Considering that in their youth Kroisos and Miltiades had flown to the moon in a wicker basket suspended under a sphere of fire-gold, I had to agree with her.

"But," she said, "since their election to the office of Archon, neither has been inclined to gamble the safety of the League on that blessing."

"Then why are they doing so now?"

"I do not know the cause," she said, "but it must be a very grave one."

I nodded and we both fell into silent contemplation.

When evening came, Yellow Hare insisted we return to my cave so I could dine and rest. Dinner consisted of roast lamb, curried chicken, and fresh fruits from India. There was also a great deal of wheat bread. Yellow Hare ate very little, but that seemed less like Spartan fastidiousness than the distraction of deep thought. She spent most of the meal gnawing at a bit of lamb and methodically cutting an orange up into smaller and smaller pieces.

At the end of the meal she took a long wooden pipe out of her pack, filled its bowl with tobakou, and lit it with the flame from a small fire box.

"Are you thinking about the Archons?" I asked.

She flicked her eyes toward me and licked orange juice from her lips before taking a deep draw of smoke from the pipe. "No, I am trying to determine which of your crewmen is the spy."

"Spy? What spy?"

"The one who's telling the Middlers where and when to attack you."

"Why do you assume the Middlers knew?"

She focused her eyes on me like a teacher about to give careful instructions. "First, they clearly know what you look like. Second, they attacked when the ship's forward cannon battery was being moved for the reshaping. And third, they flew straight for the mystery cave, where you would be on only one day each month."

I nodded. Succinct and sensible. A small, hopeful thought appeared in my mind. If she was right, and the spy could be found, then the attempts on my life would end and Sunthief could be carried through. "Who do you suspect?"

"Ramonojon, the Indian." She made his nationality sound like an insult.

I took a deep breath to contain my outrage at her distrust, but instead of clarifying, pure air, I sucked in a lungful of earth-heavy smoke. "Why him?" I said with a cough.

She exhaled a billow of gray which gleamed in the moonlight. "Because he is exhibiting the first sign of treason."

"And what is that?"

"An abrupt change in behavior," she said. "Sometimes the change is obvious. Sometimes new traitors try to conceal it, but there are ways to penetrate such disguises."

"How do you know Ramonojon's acting differently? You only met him a few weeks ago."

"Because of the concern you have shown about his behavior. The reactions of a man's friends tell you a great deal about that man."

I had not realized my distress was that obvious. Certainly Ramonojon had changed, become distant and distracted, but I couldn't believe my friend would set an assassin on me. I decided to go on the attack. "Do you have any substantial proof?"

She shook her head.

"Then I suggest you find some before you accuse him."

"I will," she said, and I could feel Zeus of the thunders fill her voice with confidence.


Two days later Ramonojon came to see me in my office. Yellow Hare announced his approach half a minute before I heard his unsure knock on my door.

"Please let him in," I said, and my bodyguard did so with the confident stride of a tiger welcoming a deer.

He entered hesitantly. "Do you have some time, Aias?" he asked. "I need to talk to you."

I looked at the five scrolls on my desk, all that remained from the pile that had accumulated in my absence. "I always have time for you," I said, gently reminding him of our neglected friendship.

Ramonojon sat on the stool in front of my desk, hunched slightly over, making it impossible to see his expression. "I would like to speak to you alone," he said.

"No," Yellow Hare said; her eyes bored into his back like spears of celestial flame.

"Aias?" he said, and I thought I detected a twinge of pleading.

"I'm sorry, Ramonojon. I have to do what Yellow Hare thinks necessary for my safety."

"I see," he said, and then fell silent.

"Is this about Mihradarius's demonstration?" I asked after two minutes of strained quiet.

"Not really, no." He hesitated, as if he wanted to say more, then fell back into stillness.

I tried another safe option. "Are you having more problems with Kleon?"

He shook his head. I ate a fig from the bowl I kept on my desk and offered him one. He picked it up and studied it intently, as if he had never seen a fruit before, then put it back. Finally he spoke. "Aias, have you ever given any thought to the ethics of what we're doing?"

A strange question, to say the least. Ramonojon and I had talked many times about history, theology, politics, and many other topics the Akademe considered fruitless, but never ethics. My face must have suddenly put on the mask of my surprise. Yellow Hare's statue visage hardened into a look of condemning confidence, and I could almost see Dike, goddess of justice, glaring out from behind her eyes.

I concentrated on Ramonojon, knowing that I would never be able to make it through the discussion if I had to consider Yellow Hare's reactions to everything I said. And it seemed to me most important to find out what was really disturbing him and do what I could to help.

"Do you mean," I asked him, "have I thought about how Sunthief serves the Good? If so, I think the answer is obvious. Serving the state helps the people, hence it aids the Good."

"No, that is not the ethical matter I am concerned with," he said, enunciating each syllable carefully. He was clearly straining to control some weighty feeling.

"Is it then a question of which of our personal virtues we are increasing by this work?"

"Increasing?" His mask of calm cracked. "We're working to destroy a city of two million people. How can that aid virtue? How can that be good?"

Yellow Hare growled. "Innocent people always die in war."

He turned to look at her; I could not see his face, but whatever was written on it caused Yellow Hare to narrow her eyes to predatory slits.

"Should two million noncombatants die?" Ramonojon said.

I stood, walked around the desk, and stepped between them, forcing both my friend and my bodyguard to look at me. "The Son of Heaven," I said, "the Middle Kingdom bureaucracy, and the central military establishment are all headquartered in 'AngXou. It is the opinion of the Archons that destroying that city will cripple the enemy."

"Cripple?" he said. "I wonder how many Spartan generals, how many Archons have made that same claim during the course of this futile war."

"Futile?" Yellow Hare gripped the hilt of her sword at the insult to Sparta. "Are you accusing the general staff of incompetence?"

Ramonojon ignored this burst of heat from Yellow Hare. He seemed to draw calmness from some well deep within him as he steepled his hands together. "No, I am accusing them of ignoring the history of this war."

I was about to speak, but Kleio grabbed my throat and stilled my voice.

"Nine hundred years ago," Ramonojon said, "Alexander took the province of Xin from the Middle Kingdom. In response, the Middlers promptly ended the civil war they'd been fighting for some two centuries and put the first 'An emperor on the throne. He in turn forced the independent Taoist alchemists to become state scientists, and ordered them to provide his armies with weapons to counter the ones Aristotle had made for Alexander's troops. After Alexander's death, the Middle Kingdom armies used their new armament to push the League out of Xin back to their earlier border of India."

Yellow Hare looked at me for confirmation. I nodded, still unable to speak.

"Since that time," Ramonojon continued, "the Middle Kingdom has captured and in turn lost India and north Persia; the Spartan army has captured and lost Tibet and Xin. At this very moment, the armies of the League and the Kingdom are battling on the outskirts of Xin. Some soldier is fighting on the exact spot where Alexander himself stood nine centuries ago. How has any of this served the Good?"

Kleio released me and I answered. "It spurred us to expand and add Africa, the lands of the Russoi, and half of Atlantea to the League," I said. "Furthermore, the war forced the Delian League to become a strong, stable government rather than a group of arguing city-states."

"Was the stability worth the bloodshed?" Ramonojon challenged.

"How can you ask that?" I said. "Remember the history of your own country. When Alexander first reached India, he found a mass of warring kingdoms; each Raza had marshaled his own armies in order to try and to conquer his neighbors. Thanks to the League, India is united. A mere handful of your people die in battle each year compared to the vast numbers that used to fall in the internecine warfare."

Yellow Hare broke in at that moment. "And more of our warriors have died defending the League against Indian rebellions than India has lost in the war against the Middlers."

At that moment, I decided to change the line of discussion. Yellow Hare is one of the purest warriors ever born on Earth, but even she was not free of the Spartan grudge against the Indians for the ancient cow rebellion and the more recent Buddhist pacifist rebellion.

"Is there anything more?" I asked.

"What about the corruption of science and philosophy?" Ramonojon said.

I blushed out of shame. How could I deny that the war had been responsible for that? Yellow Hare too fell silent; I could feel her golden eyes upon me waiting for an answer, but I had none to give.

"Well?" Ramonojon asked.

"The war did not do that," I said. "Alexander and Aristotle did. Had Alexander conquered all of the Middle Kingdom in his lifetime and ended the war there and then, the Akademe would not have been turned back into the school it was under Plato."

Ramonojon shook his head sadly, stood up, and walked uncaring past Captain Yellow Hare.

He opened the door, but turned to face me just before leaving. "Remember Sokrates' final words in the *Apology*," he said; then he walked out.

I lapsed into silence, unsure of what to think about that strange discussion. After a few minutes, Yellow Hare cleared her throat and said, "What is the *Apology?*"

"Plato's final dialogue, published posthumously." She still looked interested, which surprised me. "I assume you have not read Plato," I said.

She shook her head; hardly surprising—few Akademics ever read him, let alone Spartans.

I felt a sudden wave of tiredness, so I walked over and lay down on my couch, staring up at the steel beams that reinforced my office's granite ceiling. "*The Apology* is a fictional trial, in which Sokrates is charged with being hopelessly old-fashioned and unable to appreciate modern philosophy; his accusers are those Plato called the 'younger generation of philosophers,' in other words, scientists.

"The trial as presented could hardly be called a model of justice; the jury plugs their ears or pounds the floor whenever Sokrates speaks. His questions are left unanswered, the judge refuses to let him call witnesses, and when the guilty verdict and sentence of death or exile is delivered, they blindfold the statue of Dike.

"At the end Sokrates drinks hemlock, preferring to die rather than live in the world the scientists are making. But there's no truth in it. Sokrates died of old age, respected throughout Athens. The whole work is just an embittered polemic, Plato showing his anger at Aristotle and the scientists for taking control of the Akademe and surpassing him in fame."

She nodded slowly. "And Sokrates' last words?"

I smiled and ate a fig. "His real last words were, 'I owe a chicken to Asklepios.' Apparently, he'd forgotten a sacrifice to the god of healing. In the *Apology* he said, 'I cannot live in a world where philosophers have forgotten how to doubt.'"

She cocked an eyebrow. "A strange thing to say."

"Sokrates believed doubt was vital to philosophy. Plato believed that Aristotle's confidence in science was a betrayal of this ideal. Plato never understood that the scientific method is fundamentally based on doubt."

"Thank you," she said. "That was very useful."

I took a sip of wine. "I wish I knew why Ramonojon mentioned it."

"It was a warning," Captain Yellow Hare said.

"If he's a spy, why would he warn me?"

"Even spies have friends," she said, and she looked out through the doorway to make sure he was gone.

I wish I could say that I had heard Ramonojon's words and understood what he was trying to tell me, but I did not. All I could see was the work of Sunthief and the simple understanding of my duty. For my ignorance and my hubris I ask no pardon, for I do not deserve one.

Mihradarius's demonstration was held a few days later. Kleon flew us to a point over the middle of the Atlantic Ocean and by judicious manipulation of the lift and ballast balls kept us stationary above the ocean. Both the sun and moon were on the other side of the earth, but the outer planets and the fixed stars looked down in judgment upon our works.

My Persian subordinate had organized a huge dinner party in the commissary before he showed off his net. Pigs and sheep were roasted. Chickens were baked in herb wrappings. Fresh fruits and fried vegetables filled dozens of serving bowls. There was a table laden with cheeses from all over the League accompanied by dozens of loaves of barley, wheat, and maize bread. To keep our heads clear, the slaves served only fresh fruit juices and very dilute wines.

Mihradarius presented himself in his scholar's robes and even combed his hair in the Athenian style. He went through the crowd of junior scientists, thanking them for their assistance and praising them for guaranteeing the success of our venture. I would never have had the hubris to celebrate before a test, but Mihradarius had never lacked for confidence.

Kleon walked up and down the tables accompanied by a muscular female slave who was carrying a large silver tray. When he saw a bread or vegetable or fruit he liked, Kleon would grab it and put it on the platter. After a quarter hour of this, the tray was laden with enough food for three men. Satisfied, my chief navigator left for his tower to feast in private and prepare for his part of the test.

Ramonojon ate and drank nothing, keeping himself aloof in order to watch Mihradarius's performance.

I ate very little, trying to settle my stomach with bread and sheep's milk cheese. It was concern about the outcome of the test, and the decisions I would have to make if it failed, that suppressed my appetite.

After we had dined, Mihradarius directed us sternward over the gaming field, through the hill country above the laboratories to the groove that held the net trolley. It had been two years since Ramonojon's dynamicists had carved the trench in the body of *Chandra's Tear*. They had cut it with water and polished it with fire and air until it was as smooth as celestial matter that had been touched by the hands of man could be. Then they laid aluminum tracks in the moonstone gully and affixed the copper trolley to them by its air-silver wheels. And there it had sat, waiting with celestial patience for us mere humans to use it.

Mihradarius directed us to the starboard edge of the groove,

where the ten-foot-long, spherical trolley lay waiting. Glimmer-
ing green strands of Aphroditean matter trailed away from the
wheeled ball to the box that held the model net. The box in turn
was connected by a thick tube to a specially designed evac cannon;
the net itself had been threaded through the firing tube and
packed into the belly of the gun, waiting to be shot out.

Just off *Chandra's Tear*'s starboard side one of Kleon's junior
navigators sat on a moon sled, a ten-foot-across disk of gleaming
Selenean matter; its round edge was studded with the fire-gold
knobs of retracted impellers, which could be extended one by one
by pulling on guide wires. Mounted on the sled behind the pilot's
seat was a six-foot cubic fire box that held the simulated sun fragment.

Mihradarius walked over to the evac cannon and waved us to
silence. "Commander Aias, Commander Aeson, and you, my colleagues. Let me say at the outset that I did not plan on doing this
test. Some of you know why it was necessary; the rest do not need
to know. But though I was initially reluctant, over the last three
weeks I have become enthusiastic. You are about to witness the
actual usage of the device we have all been working for. This will
be a foretaste of what we will accomplish when we reach the sun
and steal the true fire of 'Elios."

He looked over at me. "May I proceed, Commander?"

My voice carried clearly through the crisp night air. "Proceed,
Senior Ouranologist."

Mihradarius picked up a torch and waved it toward the moon
sled. The navigator raised his hand in an acknowledging salute
and pulled on a handful of his control wires. Six impellers came
out from the starboard edge of the disk. The air on that side rarefied, brightening the silver glow of the sled. There was a momentary pause, and then the moon sled flew away from us, skipping
over the rarefied air like a silver coin across a choppy lake.

We watched it as it receded from us, bouncing through the
sky; it did not stop until it had flown two miles from the ship.

One minute later, a red-and-gold orb of flame emerged from
atop the disk, flying skyward in a graceful arc, and expanding as
it rose. The fireball momentarily washed the sled's silver light

into the darkness of a new moon. The burning globe passed away from the moon sled and over us. Mihradarius waited until the now hundred-yard-wide ball was half a mile above the stern of *Chandra's Tear*, granting us a taste of daylight. Then he pulled the lever that fired the cannon. The sun net whooshed out, spinning two parallel lines of gleaming filament into the sky.

The strands of brown, green, and silver celestial matter spiraled upward through space until they flanked the blob of simulated sun fire. Then they twisted together, braiding themselves around the sphere. The orb continued to fly, but its motion was now chained in an orbit around *Chandra's Tear*. The trolley jerked to port, pulled along its track by the false fireball.

The pseudo sun fragment circled once, twice, thrice around us, taking a minute for each orbit. I held my breath, waiting for the keening scream of injury to rise up from my ship, but there was nary a murmur, and not even the slightest tremble in our flight.

Mihradarius signaled the navigation tower to start us moving. Kleon pulled in the ballast and lift balls and deployed the small tertiary forward impellers. Freed from this midair anchoring, my ship sailed gracefully toward Atlantea. We flew smoothly, almost as if we were not dragging around a ball of fire that had its own ideas about the natural path it should follow.

Applause rang out from the scientists and soldiers; libations were poured to Athena and Aristotle. I myself picked up a bowl of wine and carried it to Mihradarius. "Well done, Senior Ouranologist," I said, giving him wine to drink with my own hands. "You may proceed with sun net Delta."

"Thank you, Commander," he said, and drained the bowl.

I walked over to Ramonojon and raised an eyebrow. "Well?" I said.

"It's Maia," he murmured. "It's all illusion."

"What do you mean?" I said.

"I mean what you have just seen is impossible."

He turned from me and plunged into the crowd.

The sun net was reeled in after an hour; the celestial matter was extracted from the fireball and the terrestrial fire dispersed into the sky. The dangerous work was done, and the party became even more festive, with the slaves now handing around bowls of undiluted wine.

Four hours of celebration later we were leisurely chasing nighttime across North Atlantea. Aeson, Yellow Hare, and I had drifted away from the crowd and were camping on the sternward slope of the hill. Aeson and I were sitting and drinking. Yellow Hare stood guard, smoking her long pipe.

Not a word passed between us until a spot of silver appeared in the sky, flying toward us from the north. "Get down!" my bodyguard yelled, and I ducked behind her.

Yellow Hare and Aeson drew their throwers and waited. They relaxed a few minutes later, when the spot resolved itself into a moon sled. It descended, skimming twenty feet above the surface of my ship, flying directly toward the hill. As it approached I saw that the gleaming disk was manned not only by a celestial navigator but by a dozen soldiers as well. Crowded flying conditions to say the least.

The moon sled landed a few feet from us. The curtain of guards parted, and the navigator stepped off and came toward us carrying a scroll sealed in a bronze tube. She was dressed in a dark red, open-shouldered tunic with iron disks on her shoulders, the uniform of the Archons' personal messengers.

She saluted Aeson and myself, and handed me the scroll. I broke the double seal carefully, unrolled it, and moved it close to my eyes so I could read Kroisos's flowing handwriting in the ship's moonlight.

"What is it?" Aeson asked.

I read the message twice, then spoke hesitantly, hoping I was hallucinating. "You and I are ordered to accompany this messenger to Delos immediately. The Archons wish to personally give us our final briefing before we leave for the sun."

"We're not ready to leave yet," Aeson said.

"I know. I just hope we can convince Kroisos and Miltiades of that."

"We had better call the senior staff together and tell them we're leav—"

Yellow Hare was suddenly running down the hill. "Stop!" she shouted ahead of her, and, "Guard Commander Aias!" she yelled back at the soldiers.

Aeson and I exchanged quick glances and pursued her, followed closely by the guards.

Yellow Hare ran straight for the net launcher. When we caught up with her, she was holding Ramonojon up in the air by scruff of his neck.

"Put him down!" I shouted.

She shook her head and pointed to a small pile of broken wood on the ground beside the cannon. "He was trying to throw this over the side."

I knelt down and sifted the cherry wood splinters carefully with my fingers. My fingers touched metal and I pulled up two wood chips with straight gold needles sticking out of them and two others with twisted silver needles.

I looked up at Aeson. "This appears to be the remains of a Taoist weapon."

Aeson growled. "Senior Dynamicist Ramonojon, you are under arrest. Captain Yellow Hare, place him in the brig in the cell next to the Middler doctor. We'll settle this when Aias and I return from Delos."

Ramonojon went limp in Yellow Hare's grip, and his face became a gloomy blank.

"It's not true, is it? You can't be a spy," I said in his native tongue.

He looked at me with his sad brown eyes glowing in the washed-out silver light, but said nothing.

"I swear by the waters of the Styx that I will believe you," I said.

"No, Aias," he said. "I'm not a spy, but I can't prove it."

"Then I will," I said.

ζ

With the sole exception of riding a camel bareback over broken ground during a sandstorm, moon sleds are the least comfortable way man has ever found to travel. The spin of the lunar motion coupled with the interminable skip-skipping over waves of rarefied air battered our backsides and bruised our legs. Every cloud and every air current we hopped over added another injury to my body and drew forth from my lips another blessing on the designers of *Chandra's Tear* who had made it large enough to ignore such indignities.

The crowding on the sled added to the discomfort, for even though we were strapped into seated positions, we were so tightly packed that every pitch and roll of the sled knocked me sideways into Aeson, Yellow Hare, or one of the Archons' soldiers.

The only justification for moon sleds is their speed. Their small size and large impeller array makes them fly faster than anything terrestrial or any larger celestial ship. It took us a mere three hours to cross half of North Atlantea and traverse the entire Atlantic Ocean, three hours in which we passed from midnight to a cloud-reddened dawn. So it was that when we reached Europe, it was out of a clear morning sky that we dove down toward the military port at the Pillars of 'Erakles.

Below us a fleet was streaming westward through the gateway that connected the Mediterranean and the Atlantic. Seven warships of the same class as the *Lysander*, escorted by thirty-five smaller picket ships, passed slowly under the massed guns of the overlooking rock. Salutes were fired from the hundred-gun cannonade of 'Erakles, shooting flaming spheres into the air to honor the ships as they left for the wars.

Our navigator angled the moon sled and we descended, flying toward the array of six multitined sky docks that rose up from the Pillars like a half dozen of Poseidon's favorite tridents. When we reached a height of two miles, three armed sleds flew up from one of the docks to greet us. They surrounded us and escorted us down to the ground level of the port. Fifty-foot-across shelves had been cut into the sides of the Pillars, making the ancient stones look like South Atlantean step-pyramids. The escort sleds shepherded us toward one of these ledges, where we landed. A squadron of slaves rushed out and chained the moon sled down with steel chains moored deep in the ground.

"Will we be here long?" I asked the navigator, hoping to stretch my aching legs.

"No, Commander," she said. "As soon as we have been cleared by the port general, we'll be departing. Normally, we would not even have to stop here, but for reasons I do not know, security in the Mediterranean was recently tightened."

Yellow Hare, Aeson, and I kept silent. If the Archons had chosen not to inform their own messengers about the battle kite that had breached the center of the League, we were not going to do so.

Our sled's pilot showed her messenger's staff to an officer of the port, and we were given a flight path to follow while we were in the Mediterranean. We were warned that deviation from the path would result in our being fired on by any naval vessel or celestial ship that spied us.

We took off and ascended to ten miles, then skimmed along the coast of North Africa, catching fleeting glimpses of squat Carthage. Then we sailed over Sicily and suffered a short delay while the celestial ship *Horn of Hathor* sailed into the sky dock of Syrakuse.

Following our flight path we stopped at Sparta to join the daily caravan of a dozen messenger sleds that carried orders and information back and forth between Delos and the military heart of the League.

O, Sparta, city of the Lakedaimonoi, of Aeson and Yellow Hare, of my father and my paternal ancestors going back to before recorded history, Oh city most beloved of 'Era, city of Lykurgus the lawgiver, what shall I say of you? That you of all the cities of the League shun adornment, that your homes are plain stone, your gates are solid doors of steel, and even your temples are unpainted marble. Only to the statues of the gods do you give anything of beauty, and to them you give all. How shall I describe your strength and untempered power, how can I, who was not accepted inside your bosom, tell anyone of your spirit?

Let it suffice, I pray, to declare that as we flew over your walls toward the bristling column of your sky dock, Aeson and Yellow Hare became filled with you, and grew larger with the presence of the gods, so that we who companioned them seemed to be men of the age of stone next to men of the age of gold; that the force of their purity overwhelmed my thoughts, taking from me, for the first time since I had set foot in Athens, the doubting spirit taught in the Akademe.

I can only account it a mercy that we did not stay long; for if we had, I do not know what would have been left of my spirit.

But it took only a brief check of our credentials at the sky dock and we were directed to a line of twelve floating moon sleds waiting to depart for Delos. Thankfully, we were the last sled expected, so the convoy left only a few minutes after we joined it.

Only ten minutes from Sparta, a glint appeared on the horizon and quickly grew into the silver-laced steel dome that covered the whole of the tiny island of Delos. Swivel-mounted cannons tracked our approach until we flew down to water level and floated under the bronze canopy that projected out like a bird's bill from the southern end of the island, a quarter mile of brazen shield, covering the water, protecting the harbor from air attack.

We flew under this aegis and made for the crescent-shaped dock of Delos, where a hundred soldiers waited to defend the Archons. Twenty of them patrolled along the shoreline in squads of five; the other eighty sat inside armored boxes, pointing short-barreled, wide-mouthed cannons out over the water. The caravan of moon sleds halted under the canopy and waited to be invited to land by the soldiers.

After that rapid journey across half the world it seemed ridiculous to sit for an hour on a bobbing sled waiting for our turn to dock, but wait we did. Finally, we were waved forward. Our pilot flew the moon sled into one of the alcoves lining the thick limestone walls at the rear of the covered harbor. Slaves chained the sled to the ground, and guards checked our papers carefully. They politely but firmly required Aeson and Yellow Hare to surrender their weapons, then permitted us to disembark.

I stepped off the moon sled and stretched three hours of aches out of my muscles. I took a deep breath and regretted it immediately; the water-laden air of the island saturated my lungs and dulled my mind just when I most needed to be thinking clearly.

"May I escort you in, Commander?" the messenger asked politely.

I nodded and she led us to the centerpoint of the crescent, where stood the twenty-foot-high iron double doors that formed the last barrier between the Archons and the world.

The door wardens, two beefy slaves dressed only in loincloths, opened the gateway, and the messenger guided us briskly into the tunnel that connected the harbor to the main island. The passage was wide enough for six men to walk abreast, but the low ceiling and the guards stationed every seven feet made the way seem cramped and oppressive, or perhaps that was the heaviness of the air in my lungs or my worries about the upcoming meeting or about Ramonojon. I cannot truthfully account for the feeling of being pressed down on, but feel it I did.

The two guards at the far door checked our credentials again, then ushered us through the thick bronze portals onto the island of Delos. We emerged into a paradise of architecture and greenery, lit by hundreds of fixed-fire globes on pylons of spun glass.

The dome overhead had been painted with scenes of Olympos, showing the war between the gods and the Titans and the eventual triumph of the gods. Elsewhere, I knew, there were scenes of Zeus holding court, of the Elysian fields, of the Trojan War, and of the foundings of most of the ancient cities of the 'Ellenes. Yellow Hare gasped momentarily at the splendor around her; it warmed my heart to know that my stoic bodyguard was not immune to the beauty of Delos.

"I must return to my duties," the messenger said. "You are expected in the Purple Courtyard; it lies about half a mile down this path."

She pointed the way and then disappeared over a grassy hillock.

We wandered slowly across the marble-paved walkway, past blue-domed temples and hanging gardens of rose and hyacinth. We crossed large open courtyards filled with scroll shelves and writing tables, surrounded by vineyards rich with plump grapes. Along the way we came across many statues of past Archons that stared down at us with carved expressions of stern benevolence. Every man who had ever been an Archon of the League was displayed in painted marble somewhere on the island. Those Archons who had been made heroes after their deaths had taller statues painted blue or black to distinguish them from their flesh-toned mortal colleagues.

The only things disrupting this tranquil scene were the bureaucrats and military clerks running hither and yon, fulfilling the Archons' orders and trying desperately to look important so they wouldn't be demoted and sent back to Athens or Sparta, or, Zeus protect them, to the provinces.

The first time I came to Delos I was shocked by the number of people inhabiting the island. Most citizens of the Delian League believed their Archons lived apart from the rough-and-tumble of League politics so they could devote themselves to making those broad decisions necessary to preserving the people's welfare. That was the reason the Archons had originally been placed on this small island that had once held the League's treasury, rather than being housed in Athens with the bureaucracy or billeted in Sparta with the general staff. But over the centuries the governance of the League had grown so complex and the speed of travel so fast that it had become both necessary and easy for certain small but crucial problems to be handed over from the lesser functionaries in Athens and Sparta to the two executives on Delos. As a result the Archons had amassed a staff that continued to grow year by year.

A nervous bureaucrat wearing the green robe of a lower functionary intercepted us in our wanderings.

"Welcome to Delos, Commander Aias, Commander Aeson, Captain Yellow Hare," he said. "If you will come this way, the others are already assembled."

"What others?" I asked.

"The other commanders of the Prometheus Projects," he said, and he led us down a long, narcissus-lined path to an open courtyard surrounded by a purple colonnade. Eight walnut wood couches, richly decorated with Tyrian purple cushions, were arrayed in a semicircle. Four of the seats were occupied by men, and two young, athletic-looking soldiers stood behind them, eyeing our approach with the proper caution of guards. It seemed that only Aeson had dared ask for a Spartan officer to serve as bodyguard. Several tripods had been set out with platters of finger food. Our guide waved us over and disappeared back the way we had come.

I knew three of the seated men. Aegistus of Myteline, one of the most self-deluded scholars the Akademe had ever produced, and Philates, one of the most credulous officers ever to leave Sparta; they were respectively scientific and military commander of Project Forethought. The two of them reclined and whispered to each other. No doubt Aegistus was reassuring Philates that their spurious project was progressing brilliantly.

Across from them, wearing the traditional armor of an Egyptian general, sat Ptah-Ka-Xu, the fifty-year-old veteran who commanded the military side of Project Manmaker. He looked up at us and nodded a greeting, then returned to glaring at Aegistus and Philates with contempt.

Next to Ptah-Ka-Xu, almost hiding in his shadow, was the

man I did not know, a nervous-faced Aethiopian, no more than thirty years old. He was dressed in scholar's robes, and his hair was combed in the Athenian style, but his furtive glances from side to side made it clear that he was unused to the courtyards of power.

Aegistus looked up and waved us over as if he had just become aware of our presence. "Have you heard the wonderful news?" he asked.

Aeson and I exchanged glances. For different reasons, neither of us was fond of Aegistus. I did not like the dignity his field, the blasphemous pseudoscience of mantikology, was afforded in the Akademe; Aeson, like any sensible Spartan, objected to anyone who claimed to be able to create omens that would determine when to carry out a military action. If anyone needs any further proof that something has gone horribly wrong in the history of science, he need look no further than that man's hubristic belief that humans could constrain the gods and compel them to speak the future on command.

"What news?" I asked, turning away from him to peruse a platter of foodstuffs. I selected a strip of mutton wrapped in phyllo crust, chewed it lightly, and swallowed.

Aegistus waited until I had finished eating and had turned back to face him. No doubt he wanted to see the expression on my face. "Our part of Prometheus is a success," he said like a parent boasting of a child's achievements. "Our most capable seer has determined the precise day and hour when you should leave for the sun."

The light pastry in my stomach turned into a clay brick. The reason for our summons was now clear; we were being sent off far too early because of Kroisos's obsession with Project Forethought. I started to sputter my usual objections but Ptah-Ka-Xu interrupted me, standing up between me and my "colleague."

"Aias, Aeson, may I present Kunati, the new scientific commander of Project Manmaker."

I turned away from Aegistus and nodded to the Aethiopian. He nodded back, clearly grateful for any sign of friendliness amid the bickering. "Congratulations," I said. "I am sorry your promotion came under these sad circumstances."

"Thank you." He twisted his hands around the scroll he was carrying. "I hope I'll be able to complete the project."

"You will, young man, you will!" a stentorian voice thundered through the courtyard like the laughter of Zeus. Kroisos and Miltiades strode into the courtyard, setting a furious pace for men in their seventies. Their coterie of scroll-bearing, anxious bureaucrats could barely keep up with them.

Kroisos walked through the arched gateway between the columns and we all stepped forward to greet him. He favored each scholar with a firm arm-clasp, a flash of a smile, and a wordless expression of confidence. By force of personality alone he filled me with renewed faith that despite all difficulties Sunthief would succeed, but then I looked at Aegistus and doubt reentered my mind.

Miltiades followed his more boisterous comrade. The old soldier wore full armor and an expression of iron sternness unmatched by any Spartan except Yellow Hare. Unlike Kroisos's flowing gray locks, the military Archon's hair was still the black of his youth. The only sign of age about him was his face, lined and broken like an ancient cliff blessed by Poseidon the Earthshaker.

The Archon of Sparta waved us back to our seats. Slaves brought brightly painted drinking bowls decorated with figures of the three Fates spinning the short golden lives of heroes and filled them with diluted Samothracian wine, very watery but wonderfully mellow in flavor. Yellow Hare left me to join the other two guards, who seemed astonished to have a Spartan captain as a comrade. Miltiades nodded to her and smiled paternally, an expression his face was clearly unaccustomed to. She smiled in return, and though the expression was directed at the old man, I drew confidence from it.

The two Archons sat down. Miltiades took a bowl of wine. Kroisos buried his nose in a scroll and waved away the slave who brought him drink.

A minute later, the Archon of Athens looked up and rerolled

the scroll with the carelessness of long practice. "This will be the final briefing for the Prometheus Projects."

From a fold in his robes, he pulled out three long strips of papyrus, and handed one to me, one to Aegistus, and one to Kunati. "These are your final operation schedules. They are to be committed to memory now and then returned to me. No written record of this schedule is to be made. All orders to your subordinates will be oral."

I studied the sheet of block printing, carefully memorizing dates and times. Halfway down, I stopped and reread a line three times before looking up. "Archon, my ship cannot reach the sun and return in only four months."

Kroisos's eyes narrowed, and he leaned forward like a snake eyeing a bird. "Your navigator said he could do it, if I gave him the Ares impellers."

My stomach knotted. Kleon would never lie about something like that. It would violate his Pythagorean oaths. But he might not have made allowance for the comfort of the crew during such a flight, and he would certainly be willing to take risks with our lives if it meant cutting down the travel time.

"Archon," I said, "my navigator has not yet finished calculating his flight path and I have not had time to review it. I cannot at this moment guarantee with my oath what our travel time will be."

Kunati chirped a nervous "Excuse me," which immediately drew Kroisos's hawklike gaze toward him.

"Archon," the trembling young man said, "Project Manmaker is . . . technically a success. We have spontaneously generated fully grown pseudomen in the lab, but our prototype warrior has not been perfected. And I don't know if we'll be able to perfect them, and assemble five hundred thousand generation packets, and plant them on the Middle Kingdom border in the two months this schedule gives us. Sir, I only recently took over the project, and—"

Kroisos brushed that aside with an airy wave. His beak darted around. "Aegistus, explain the situation to them."

The mantikologist pulled a folded piece of papyrus from his

sleeve. He opened it, revealing a three-foot square covered with strange, handwritten symbols, including an inaccurate chart of the planets. "According to our Delphic resonators, the time for the attack must be four months from tomorrow. We have tested this hypothesis with six different prognostication methods and all of them produced the same date."

Kroisos smiled and nodded like a puppy. As if that settled the matter.

O ye gods, when the time comes to judge Kroisos, recall the bravery of his youth, remember his ascent to the moon, pay heed to his work in dynamics and Ouranology that led to the creation of fleets of celestial ships and the exploration of the spheres. Pay great attention to his efforts in leading the League through trying times, but forgive him his folly. All of the greatest heroes have suffered blindness in one way or another. Forgive Kroisos because he thought the future could be seen by science without the intervention of the gods.

"Sir," I said to him, hoping that practicalities could dissuade him where I knew theology would fail. "We do not have the materials to make the sun net. For that matter, we don't even have supplies to feed ourselves for that long a trip."

"Already attended. Food and spon-gen supplies await you on the moon. I've also arranged for the celestial matter you need to be refined on 'Ermes and Aphrodite. You can pick them up on the way out and build the net as you go."

I looked to Aeson for help. He had steepled his hands and was staring up at the dome. The picture overhead showed Zeus pulling Orion up from the earth and placing him among the constellations on the sphere of fixed stars. I could feel the longing in Aeson, the desire deep in his heart to travel out through the spheres. But he was too great a Spartan to put his command at risk to fulfill that dream. He looked momentarily at Kroisos, then turned away and stared directly at Miltiades in that practical Spartan way that had many times cut down a rarefied Athenian debate.

"Sir," he said, "I cannot permit *Chandra's Tear* to leave Earth yet. We have serious security problems. It is even possible that one of the senior scientific personnel is a traitor."

Miltiades frowned, thrusting out his jutting chin. He turned to Kroisos. "Security takes precedence over the timetable."

"You can't do that!" Aegistus cried.

The cold gray eyes of the Delian League's military commander in chief turned on him. "Can't?"

Aegistus lowered his head and his voice, wilting into himself like a flower. "We'd have to wait nine years for another day this auspicious."

"Then we will attack on an inauspicious day," the Archon said coldly. "If you had spent your time studying the battles of the past, instead of the entrails of goats, you'd know that as many battles were won when the omens were bad as when they were good. The favor of the gods is not as easy to divine as you believe, and no man has succeeded in stealing the knowledge of the future from them."

Aegistus shook his head, more in sorrow than in anger, and shared a glance of Athenian confidence with Kroisos before turning back to Miltiades. "Archon, those ancient prognostications were crude, unscientific predictions. Project Forethought is the scientific study of the future. It is a thousand times more accurate than the ramblings of those bay-sniffing madwomen."

I held my tongue and wondered when Apollo would avenge himself on this atheist for blaspheming his oracle.

"It is my decision that they wait," the Archon of Sparta said.

"And mine that they depart," said the Archon of Athens.

Miltiades and Kroisos stared at each other for a full minute. The inevitable had happened, as it had to Aeson and myself and to every other pair of leaders in the League. The two Archons were taking opposite views, and one of them would have to give way.

At last Kroisos reached into his robes and pulled out a scroll sealed with the iron peacock of Sparta. Then he slipped a hand into a small fur pouch tied to his belt and removed two cubical dice carved from bone. He laid them down on Miltiades' couch. The Spartan Archon stared at them for several seconds. Finally he swept them up in his huge hand and placed them inside his armor.

Then he stood up and looked at the six of us. "You will try your best to follow the timetable, but leeway will be given.

Kunati, the military will plant the manmaker packages ten days' march closer to the border. Aias, Aeson, you have an extra ten days in which to travel to the sun and return. I hope that will be enough to permit you to solve your security problems."

It wasn't much but I thanked him for it.

"This briefing is ended," Kroisos said. He walked off, followed by the swarm of bureaucrats. The commanders of Manmaker and Forethought left, accompanied by their bodyguards, but Miltiades signaled for Aeson and me to stay. He also waved Yellow Hare over.

Miltiades gripped Aeson's arm in a gesture of farewell. "I regret that was all the time I could give you."

Aeson withdrew his arm and saluted formally. He held his hand over his heart and stared Miltiades in the eyes. By tradition, any graduate of the Spartan war college could ask any other his reasons for a military decision so that the wisdom of experienced commanders would be passed down to their juniors.

"Sir, why could you not give us the time to make sure of Sunthief's security? Surely it had nothing to do with Aegistus's foolishness."

Miltiades broke the seal on the scroll that Kroisos had given him and handed it to Aeson. My co-commander read it and reread it with deliberation. "I was not aware that the war was going this badly."

The Archon nodded. "The Middlers have made a recent breakthrough in miniaturization." He turned to me. "The weapon used on you by that assassin seems to be a man-portable Xi lance, apparently capable of disrupting the balance of bodily humours in the same way that a large Xi lance disrupts the flow of air or water."

I drew this piece of information into my heart and tried to make sense of it. How could the tides or air currents have anything to do with the humours? I tried to fit it in with all the other incomprehensible pieces of Middler science I had read over the years, but I could not put them together into a coherent whole. I sighed out my frustration and the spirit of the Akademe sighed with me.

Miltiades took the scroll and rerolled it. "The Middlers have been arming their commandos with these weapons and sending them to assassinate our governors, our scientists, and our generals. In the last three months we have lost the governors of eight North Atlantean city-states; also the crown prince of the Olmeks; General Tydeus, commander of the armies invading Tibet; and six of our top scientists. If this continues we will be leaderless, and the Middle Kingdom will be able to conquer us easily.

"Kroisos and I concluded that only a quick, decisive large-scale strike on our part can break the back of their strategy. Project Sunthief is our best hope to do that. If you destroy 'AngXou then they, not we, will be leaderless, and our army, aided by Manmaker's pseudomen, will finally be able to end the war."

There was fire in his eyes. "But we must act soon, before we lose too many irreplaceable people. Kroisos laid down those dice to remind me that the time has come when we must take great risks if we wish to survive."

"Then Forethought?" I said.

"Reassures Kroisos that he is doing the right thing," Miltiades said. "But in truth, it is you we are relying on."

I raised my hand to my heart and gave him the Spartan salute.


We flew back to *Chandra's Tear* on the same moon sled with the same navigator and the same guards, but a weightier silence. We traveled mostly in darkness, catching up to night over the mid-Atlantic, then flying over the black expanse of Atlantea. We reached my ship and the return of sunlight high over the Western Ocean. A thousand miles below us lay the island territories indisputably held by the Middle Kingdom; ahead lay Asia and the homelands of the enemy.

Looking at the sunrise from a thousand miles above the half of the world we did not control, breathing in the clarifying upper air, I ruminated on the events on Delos. The Archons had placed their trust in me, and it was my duty sworn before Athena and Zeus to carry out that trust. But Ramonojon had also placed his trust in me, and it was equally my sworn duty to aid him. I hoped that I would not have to choose between them.

We flew in from above and began to descend toward *Chandra's Tear*; I leaned over the side of the sled to watch the small drop of pearl resolve itself into the gleaming silver of my ship. I expected to see that the usual bustle of shipboard activity; I did not expect to see units of guards marching all across the ship, walking to fore and aft, port and starboard, some going into caves, some emerging. It looked as if every single one of Aeson's soldiers was on patrol.

On my instructions the pilot landed the sled near the navigation tower, where more than a dozen soldiers were patrolling the tip end of the ship. Aeson, Yellow Hare, and I unstrapped and stepped from one piece of the moon to another. The sled vanished into sky, while Aeson called over the guards and demanded to know where Anaxamander was.

"On the hill, sir." The man's eyes drooped as if he had not slept during the two days we had been away.

We quick-marched aft, passing several more patrols. They saluted us vigorously, and I detected more than one grateful gaze directed toward Aeson. We reached the command courtyard and found the security chief standing in the shade of Alexander's statue, reading through a sheaf of papers.

"Report!" Aeson ordered.

Anaxamander snapped to attention and saluted. "Full security lockdown has been implemented, Commander. Quadruple guard contingents deployed at all times. All spare men are on random patrols."

So great was his confidence in his bold, dramatic procedures that he did not see that they would only result in exhausted soldiers and decreased efficiency for the crew.

Aeson took a deep breath, and I could feel his annoyance at Anaxamander's overzealousness radiating outward like heat from a fire.

"Tell the men to stand down," Aeson said. "Reduce the guard to double status, cut down the random patrols to once every four hours."

"Yes, Commander."

"Anything else to report?"

"Yes, sir," Anaxamander said. "The prisoner Ramonojon's quarters have been sealed, but I have not searched them yet. I assumed you would want to attend to that yourself."

Aeson stroked his thin beard. "Quite correct, Security Chief. I will do so now." He turned to me. "Aias, what do you—"

"I'm coming with you," I said.

Aeson led me over to the statue of Aristotle and spoke to me in low tones, so Anaxamander would not overhear. Over my head the model of the universe in the hero's hand continued its inexorable turning, marking out the passage of time. "Aias, you have too much to do to waste your time on this. We need to be ready to depart within the next week if we have any hope of meeting the schedule."

"Aeson of Sparta," I said in the formal voice of commander speaking to commander, "do not try to tell me my duty. If Ramonojon is guilty then all the work he has done on this ship will need to be reviewed by the other dynamicists and the ship altered to undo whatever damage he has done. If he is not, I want him freed immediately to finish his work."

"Aias of Athens, do you not trust me to do my duty in conducting this search?" he asked, returning challenge for challenge.

"I trust you, Aeson," I said, softening my tone to one of friendship. "But you don't know Ramonojon as well as I do, nor are you necessarily knowledgeable enough about science to interpret what you find there."

He stared at me for a moment, then gripped my elbow. "I will be grateful for your assistance in this search," he said. "But remember, this is primarily a military, not a scientific, matter."

"Agreed," I said, gripping his elbow in return.

So it was that all four of us—myself, Aeson, Anaxamander, and Yellow Hare—walked down the port side of the hill, toward the circle of brass domes that held the senior staff quarters, through the curtain of Ramonojon's antechamber, and down into the cave where my friend and subordinate lived.

I had not been in Ramonojon's home since before our vacation, and was stunned by the changes he had made since our return. Instead of the rich tapestries depicting scenes from the *Ma'abarata*, the walls were covered with plain linen night blankets. Instead of the thick gold carpet embroidered with complex interleavings of black, red, and blue that seemed to hint of some subtle, unknown structure, there was a brown mat woven of undyed papyrus reeds. Even the soft swan's down pillows on which we had often reclined were absent; in their place was a simple cot.

But most startling by their absence were the four dozen statues of major Hindu gods with which Ramonojon had divinely populated his cave.

Lined up along the fore wall, where there had once been an altar to Shiva, were three large but unadorned oaken chests. On the aft wall, where formerly a series of statues depicting Vishnu as god and each of his avatar forms had stood, was an unpainted pine writing table.

Aeson and Anaxamander opened the chests and began to root through them systematically. They pulled out clothing, scrolls, ink pots, quill pens, brushes, all the usual paraphernalia of the scholar. Meanwhile, Captain Yellow Hare methodically ran her hands along the drapes, feeling for anything hidden.

I watched them for a while, trying to get a sense for what had happened to this room. This was not the home of the Ramonojon I had known. That man had had an eye for beauty and a deep love for the art of his homeland. He had reverently collected and publicly displayed many statues of the Hindu gods. Why had he rid himself of them? And how had he disposed of them without anybody noticing?

"Security Chief?" I said, pulling Anaxamander away from rummaging through a pile of yellow tunics.

"Yes, Commander?"

"Were your men watching Ramonojon after he returned from vacation?"

His face twisted slightly into a wry smile as if he had always known Ramonojon was a spy and was just waiting for the rest of us to catch up with him. "Off and on."

"Was he ever seen tossing anything over the side of the ship?"

Anaxamander took a thick scroll out from a case tied to his belt. He unrolled it, and read it all the way through to himself before answering. "It's possible, Commander. Chief Dynamicist Ramonojon was reported to have spent several nights staring over the port side during the time when you were confined to the hospital. But my men did not approach closely, nor did they keep constant watch over him."

"Thank you." I could hardly imagine Ramonojon doing something as blasphemous as throwing his gods down from the ship to Earth, but that was the only explanation I could think of.

Anaxamander returned to the clothes. With nothing better to do, I opened the drawers of the desk and started skimming through Ramonojon's scrolls, sorting the scientific from the personal.

"I have found it," Yellow Hare said. We all turned to look. From behind one of the drapes she pulled out a small wooden box with silver and gold needles sticking out of one end. It certainly looked like the personal Xi lance that had been used against me, but who could tell with Middler technology?

"There is our proof," Anaxamander said, writing it down on his surveillance scroll with the succinct pleasure of a job well done.

"Do not be swift in judgment," I snapped. "Ramonojon's been under arrest for two days. Anyone could have planted that in here."

"Security was perfect," Anaxamander said coldly.

"Keep searching!" Aeson growled. The two officers followed their commander's order instantly.

I returned to the scrolls, unrolling each one in turn, reading a little and then returning it to the desk; I stopped when I found Ramonojon's copy of the *Ramayana*. I had borrowed the epic many times and knew the feel of this particular scroll. It was heavier than the last time I had held it.

I unrolled the scroll carefully, idly skimming the familiar, block-printed Sanskrit words. A few feet into the document, I came upon another piece of paper rolled up inside the scroll. A broken lead seal with two fish biting each other's tails adorned one end of the paper.

This scroll was also in Sanskrit, but had not been printed; it was in Ramonojon's handwriting, the painstaking pen strokes he used when he wanted to copy something exactly. I read the first few lines and blanched at the contents.

The changes to Ramonojon's room and his questions about ethics finally made sense to me. This scroll proved he was not the spy, but it was also solid evidence that he had committed a different offense the League would not forgive.

I almost opened my mouth to declare what I had found. I wonder now what would have happened had I done so. Would I now not be submitting myself for judgment if I had spoken then? I cannot say. I do know that I made my decision without any god's prompting. Perhaps it was spun into the thread of my fate, but I prefer to take the blame myself. For at that moment when duty to state and duty to friend came into opposition, I chose to balance both of them, to remember both my oaths and do all within my power to keep them.

I rolled the scroll up and slipped it into my robes. Thank 'Ermes, patron of thieves, that the others were still too busy searching to notice what I had done. I looked at the three soldiers methodically tearing Ramonojon's room apart, wondering if any of them could help me with this. I knew Anaxamander was too ambitious. I thought Yellow Hare too Spartan. My eyes lingered on Aeson; he was my friend, but he too placed duty to the state above all else. I concluded, erroneously as it turned out, that I would have to handle the matter alone.

They finished the search soon thereafter.

"We have all the evidence we need," Anaxamander said, holding up the Taoist weapon as if it were a torch shedding light on my friend's guilt. "We must send Ramonojon to Sparta for trial."

Aeson was about to assent to this when I interrupted.

"Commander Aeson," I said formally. "As your co-commander I demand to speak to my subordinate in private in order to learn the truth."

Aeson looked at me with pity. I glared back. I could feel Athena place the mantle of her presence on my back, and Aeson's expression changed to an introspective frown.

"Do you really believe Ramonojon to be innocent?" he asked.

"I do," I said. "And you cannot refuse my demand."

He nodded.

"But I can," Yellow Hare said. "It is against my orders to leave you alone with a potential spy."

"Captain Yellow Hare . . . ," I said, but my voice faded. There was no denying the implacable tone of her voice, and no contravening her orders from the Archons. "Very well," I said at last. "But you will be in attendance only as my bodyguard."

"Of course."

"Then it does not matter to you whether or not you understand the language we are speaking." I expected her to object to this subterfuge, but she surprised me.

"Not at all, Commander," she said. "I will be there solely to protect your life."

The brig on *Chandra's Tear* consisted of five small caves under the hill, connected to the surface by a long tunnel only wide enough for one man to walk through. There was a locked steel door on each cave and another at the tunnel exit. Two guards were stationed up top and two more patrolled the hallway outside the cells. Until we picked up the Middler doctor, the brig had only been used to punish minor infractions by the soldiers, so I had never had occasion to go down into the oppressive, narrow cavern.

Yellow Hare accompanied me into Ramonojon's cell, a bare cave ten feet on a side. The floors and walls had leather straps to tie down prisoners when the ship was moving, but there were no night blankets to mute the ship's silver light. I hoped Ramonojon had managed to sleep through the glare.

We found him sitting cross-legged on the floor. His eyes were shut and his hands lay on his knees, palms curled upward.

"Ramonojon."

His eyes snapped open.

"It's time we talked."

"Yes, Aias, I suppose it is."

I turned to Yellow Hare. "Do you speak Hindi?"

She nodded.

"Pharsi? Etruscan? Egyptian? Phoenician? 'Ebreu?" I ran through the dozen languages Ramonojon and I shared in common, finally finding out that she did not speak Assyrian. That was a relief; otherwise I'd have to talk to Ramonojon in the 'Unan dialect of the Middle Kingdom. I did not think Captain Yellow Hare would be pleased to hear me speaking to a spy in the enemy's tongue.

"I found the Diamond Sutra among your scrolls," I said to Ramonojon. "I can understand why you did not want to tell me you'd become a Buddhist."

"The League does not like us," he said with quiet understatement. "You should turn me in. Otherwise they'll execute you, too, for harboring Buddhist sympathies."

I felt a flush of pride that no part of me intended to turn my friend over to the Spartans for practicing the only religion proscribed in the League. One century ago Buddhism had grown so popular in India that it spread pacifism across the eastern edge of the League and the western edge of the Middle Kingdom. Both the League and the Kingdom had cracked down, executing thousands of Buddhist teachers and monks. Possession of the Diamond Sutra or any other Buddhist tract merited execution in the eyes of Sparta.

But despite their illegality, the fact is that the Buddhists opposed the war. None of them would spy for the Middlers, and none of them could be a party to assassination. That was how I knew Ramonojon to be innocent of the charges against him; but he could hardly use that as a defense. The only result would be in his execution for one crime instead of the other.

"Why did you convert?" I asked.

"That is hard to explain," he said. "I never told you how troubled I had become about my work over the last few years. All the ships I've carved, all the deaths they've caused. I told myself it was my dharma to do this work. But for the last three years, working on Sunthief, I've been haunted by the vision of 'AngXou burning, and then over this vacation . . ."

He paused, uncrossed his legs, and bowed his head between them. "Let me start again. Do you know about Xan Buddhism?"

"No," I said. Xan was not a sect I had ever heard of.

"It was founded about five hundred years ago by Buddhists and Taoists in the border states between India and the Middle Kingdom."

"Taoists? What does Buddhism have to do with Middler science?"

"Mountain Taoists," he said. "They're philosophers, not scientists. The Middle Kingdom has as much use for them as the League does for Platonists. When I was home on vacation, I met a childhood friend whom I had not seen for years; I didn't know at the time that he had been in Tibet learning the eightfold path. I told him about my work and my worries, and he introduced me to a Xan teacher. Instead of beginning with Buddhism, he began with the Tao. He made me see the folly of Sunthief by showing me that we were breaking the balance of yin and yang."

"I've seen those words in captured Taoist science texts. What do they mean?"

"Yin and yang are seemingly opposed . . . forces is the best word for them, though that's far from accurate. The important thing is that their opposition is an illusion. In fact they work together. When they are in balance, the Tao, that is, the way, is followed. When the Tao is not followed, destruction comes for everyone. Sunthief is part of that destruction."

I did not understand anything he had said, but it was clearly important to him. One thing troubled me, though. "If you felt that you couldn't work on Sunthief anymore, why did you come back?"

"My junior dynamicists could carry on the work without me. My hope in returning was to convince you to abandon Sunthief. It was the only way to undo the damage I had already done, the only way to stop you from killing those people. But you returned with assassins after you, a Spartan as your constant bodyguard, and a spirit of suspicion. How could I then speak to you about stopping the work without being thought of as a Middle Kingdom spy?"

"So you changed your tactics," I said. "You tried to slow down the work by convincing me that Mihradarius's net design was flawed?"

A glint of fire returned to his dulled eyes. "It is flawed. If you use that net, you'll wreck this ship."

"Wouldn't that fit in with your plans?"

"No," he said. "It's not just the killing that must be ended, it's the decision to kill. Don't you see, if I said nothing about Mihradarius's error, I would be responsible for your death and the deaths of everyone on this ship."

I believed most of what he was saying, but not his convenient claim that there was something wrong with the net. It seemed to me that the wisest thing for Ramonojon to do to further his ends was make me doubt Mihradarius, because without the Persian, Sunthief would have to be scrapped.

"I will do what I can to free you," I said. "But I have to carry out Sunthief; it's my duty, my dharma."

"I understand," he said. "But I still hope to change your mind."

I turned to Yellow Hare. "Let us go," I said to her in 'Ellenic. She nodded and followed me through the steel door. We walked slowly up the passage and onto the surface, then back up the hill to my office. I expected her to ask me what Ramonojon and I had discussed, but she held silent.

I sat down at my desk and stared up at the ceiling while I tried to digest the interview. Yellow Hare assumed her customary place next to the door, still and holy as a statue.

A few minutes' contemplation led me to conclude that I had to prevent Ramonojon being sent back to Earth for trial while the rest of us journeyed to the sun. That was the only option that would give me time to prove his innocence and see Sunthief through to its conclusion.

"Captain," I said to Yellow Hare, "would you please dispatch a messenger to ask Aeson and Anaxamander to join me here."

"Yes, Commander," she said. She opened the door and waved

over one of the messenger slaves waiting in the library.

Aeson arrived immediately. I asked him to wait until the security chief appeared. Anaxamander took several minutes, explaining that he had been reviewing the troops.

"I have come to a decision concerning Ramonojon," I said, keeping my gaze fixed firmly on Aeson. "I know that he is not the spy, but cannot provide any evidence for this."

None of them spoke, so I continued. "I refuse to let you send him down to Earth for trial."

"Refuse?" Anaxamander said. "Commander Aias, this is a military matter. You cannot countermand this order."

I turned to Aeson. "But you can," I said.

"True," Aeson said. "But I must have a reason."

"I cannot give you one," I said. "But I swear by Athena that if you do not do as I ask, then I will resign my command and Sunthief will never be completed."

Ares rose up behind my co-commander's eyes, and the anger of war was in his voice. "Aias! How can you say that after—" He cut himself off, not wanting to let Anaxamander hear what the Archons had told us. "Aias of Athens, you have a sworn duty."

"I have two sworn duties," I said. "To the state and to my friend."

Aeson scowled at me, but I held my ground and gradually his features softened, as Athena replaced Ares in his mind. "I can't let Ramonojon out of the brig without proof," he said.

"Agreed," I said. "But you will keep him on this ship."

"Very well."

"Security Chief," I said to Anaxamander, "your men will keep searching. There is still a spy on this ship. I want him found quickly. We leave for the sun in a matter of days."

"But . . . I thought . . ."

"That will be all, Security Chief."

"Yes, . . . Commander."

η

_____

For the next several days sleep was a precious rarity as Aeson and I struggled to make the ship and crew ready for departure. He relied on Spartan discipline to keep awake; I needed twice daily injections of Choleric Humour, which had the unfortunate effect of giving me a short temper.

My staff were treated to a side of me they had never seen before, and assuredly did not like. Instead of discussion they were treated to blunt orders, instead of questions, demands, and instead of explanations they received silence.

My first act was to call Mihradarius and Kleon into my office and tell them about our new departure date.

"Why are the Archons doing this?" Mihradarius said.

"That's no concern of yours," I snapped. "All you have to do is make sure your subordinates do their work."

"But, Aias—"

"There will be no argument," I said. "Just go do it."

He pulled up the hem of his robes, showing me his scholar's blue border. I knew I had committed an offense against his dignity as a graduate of the Akademe, but the humour had filled my blood with the fire of Ares, giving me freedom from the cares of Akademic propriety. Athena tried to call my attention to something, but I could not hear her over her brother's battle cries.

I turned to Kleon, leaving Mihradarius to fume. "Finalize the flight path," I said. "Make your last corrections and show them to me."

Kleon darted out to complete his assignment. Mihradarius followed slowly, favoring me with a questioning glance just before he stepped out the door.

I felt a momentary flush of guilt. "Choleric Humour," I said. He nodded and closed the door quietly behind him.

After they had gone, I sent a messenger to Anaxamander reminding him to report on his search for the real spy. It was not until much later that I learned that he did not do so.

From that point onward my memories are blurred. Papers crossed my desk; people came to me, mostly panicking about one thing or another. My reading was cursory, my responses short. But I know that things happened during those days that came to matter a great deal. Therefore, I must crave a moment's indulgence; permit me to ask for the blessings of Themis and Mnemosyne, that my own thought and memory might be retrieved from that fog of sleeplessness and anger.

Two important events present themselves to the mirror of my mind.

One of Ramonojon's subordinates, Balance Manager Roxana, the cautious, middle-aged Persian woman whose duty was to check the results of all reshapings in order to ensure the stability of the ship, came to see me sometime during the third day of preparations.

"Commander," she said, after hesitantly entering. "There's a slight discrepancy in the balance of the ship. I wanted to ask Ramonojon about it, but . . ." She paused for a moment, staring at my scowl. An unaccustomed resoluteness came over her normally timid face. "Commander, I've worked under him for over seven years. I can't believe he's a spy."

"He isn't," I said. Gratitude that someone else shared my opinion threatened to drive the humour from my blood, but the injection was too recent for self-created emotion to overwhelm it.

"Can you get him out of the brig, sir?" she asked.

"Don't you think I would if I could?"

She jumped back, almost colliding with Yellow Hare. "Yes, of course, I'm sorry, Commander."

"Scientific command does not extend to security matters," I explained, restraining the false anger. "Now, tell me about this balance problem; I don't have much time to spare."

"That's just it, sir, it's not a problem; the ship is flying too well."

"Too well?" Ares rose up in my mind. How could she come and bother me about things working when all my thoughts needed to be directed toward solving problems? But the calming hand of Athena stopped me from shouting. I still could not hear what the goddess of wisdom had to say, but she managed to restrain me from an outburst. She was right to do so, of course. The dynamicists had been thrown into confusion by Ramonojon's arrest; the last thing they needed was fury from me.

"Thank you for the information," I said. "Once we're under way, detail some people to find the cause. But for the next few days only come to me with bad news."

"Yes, Commander," she said, slipping out the door. "Sorry to trouble you."

The other memory is vaguer. Mihradarius and Kleon had joined me for dinner in my office; we were to have a brief discussion and then I was to take the three hours' sleep I needed to keep from being driven to mania by the injections.

I remember eating fried goose liver and barley bread, but what were we talking about? Oh, yes, we were making preliminary plans for our actual approach to the sun. Mihradarius needed to know approximately how close we would come to 'Elios himself so that he could make the final adjustments to the net design.

The Persian was remarkably quiet during the meeting, making only a few comments as Kleon and I plotted the approach and concluded that *Chandra's Tear* could safely stand two miles off the sun, provided we were on the inner side of the crystal sphere of 'Elios. I remember Kleon staring at the maps of the heavens and singing to himself, and I remember that neither of them met my eyes once during the meeting. But most of all, I remember feeling Ramonojon's absence.

The days of anger finally ended when I crossed the final problem off my list and went to the hospital for a blissful twenty-four hours of dreamless sleep under Euripos's watchful eyes. I awoke feeling my own emotions for the first time in days and vowed never to subject myself to that rage again.

While I had slept, *Chandra's Tear* had docked one final time at the Pillars of 'Erakles to let off those crew members who would not be needed for the long journey: about thirty scientists whose work was already complete were shipped down to Earth, along with several dozen excess slaves.

When I returned to my office, I found the final crew roster on my desk. Sixty-eight slaves, mostly working in the spon-gen farm and the storage cavern, one hundred soldiers including twenty-two gunners, seven scientists who were directly responsible to me, four navigators and six engineers working for Kleon, twenty-five workers given to Mihradarius to weave the net, and twenty-two dynamicists without an overseer. I hoped Ramonojon would be free so they could receive proper guidance.

Aeson joined me as I was reviewing the list.

"Are we ready?" I asked.

He covered a yawn with his hand and blinked his bloodshot eyes. "As best we are able."

He looked at me expectantly. I turned to Yellow Hare. "Captain, would you call in two messengers?"

"Yes, Commander."

A pair of lithe youths clad in short red tunics with leather message pouches on baldrics entered my office. "Announce a general inspection," I told the first, "and tell the crew to assemble in the amphitheater for the departure ceremony."

The lad bowed and darted away. I turned to the second. "Tell Clovix to bring the sacrificial regalia and the animals to the amphitheater in two hours."

He also bowed and left.

"We should prepare ourselves as well," Aeson said as he

turned to go. "I'll join you at the stern cannon battery in one hour."

Yellow Hare and I returned to my quarters; slaves washed and oiled me, then dressed me in my purple ceremonial robes, put a wreath of laurel leaves on my head, and pinned a golden owl-badge on my left shoulder. Thus arrayed for my priestly duties, I could feel the gods and heroes gather around me waiting for the homage of sacrifice.

While I was being prepared my bodyguard cleaned her armor and donned a necklace of iron beads carved into little masks of Ares and Athena. The gods of battle stood behind her, raising her up above the human. I saw the greatness of her warrior's soul and felt more keenly than ever before the honor her service bestowed on me.

"With your permission," I said to her, "we should join Aeson."

"As you command," she replied.

Aeson was waiting for us at the aft end of the ship. He was dressed exactly as I was except that his badge was an iron peacock, and his robes bulged oddly on his chest and hips, betraying the breastplate and sword he wore under them.

"Hail to you, brother, in Athena's name," I said, touching the owl lightly with my fingertips.

"Hail to you, brother, in 'Era's name," he answered, clasping his fist over the peacock.

With slow formality we traversed the surface and the underground of *Chandra's Tear* from stern to stem, asking the gods to bless the ship in each of its parts and as a whole. But also with our expert mortal eyes we checked each place to make sure all was in order. The net assembly was ready to receive the sun net when it was knitted. The labs were orderly, though there were signs of last-minute panicked cleaning in the dynamicist's laboratory. The gaming fields, commissary, and command hill were festooned with blue and red ribbons as befitted the celebration. The hospital, storage caves, and spontaneous-generation farm were only adequately clean, but no more than that could be expected. The barracks, arsenal, and cannon batteries were deemed satisfactory by my two Spartan companions. We passed by the amphitheater, where the crew awaited us, and the navigation tower, which Kleon had personally blessed with Pythagorean rites. We stopped when we reached the point of the teardrop, the fore end of my ship.

The sky below us was cloudless and we could see the blue waters, rocky islands, and ragged coasts of the Mediterranean stretched out five hundred miles below us.

"Poseidon, though we do not sail on your ocean, give us your blessings," I said to the waters. "For we are sailors with the same fears as those who go across your seas. Bless this ship that she may sail across the skies without mishap, and bless her sailors that they may return home safely."

I felt no touch of acknowledgment from the deity so I looked down, hoping to see some omen in the waters, but they were too far below to make out any details.

We turned our backs on the world and processed solemnly to the stage of the amphitheater. The crew were assembled on the benches, senior staff at the bottom, their juniors above them, and so on upward to the higher tiers occupied by the lowest-ranking soldiers.

On the stage was a red marble altar filigreed with gold, and on that were a blazing fire, a golden bowl, and a sharp steel knife with a handle of chalcedony. Beside the altar, tethered by ropes were a bull, three white sheep, and three black lambs.

Aeson held the bull while I slit its throat with the knife, then roasted it on the fire, offering its life to Father Zeus with prayers for our success. I felt the touch of that greatest of gods and his appreciation of the honor. Then I sacrificed one of the sheep to Athena and felt her familiar presence reassuring me. Aeson burned the second sheep to 'Era. I do not know what passed between him and the queen of heaven, but I saw his face grow stern and grim. Then we both gave the last of the snowy flock to 'Ephaistos, praying that the device on which our success depended would succeed. Aeson and I leaned close to read the flames, but neither of us saw any omens therein.

Then in quick succession we gave the blood of the three black lambs to Aristotle, Alexander, and Daidalos, patron hero of celestial navigation. I could feel the heroes drawing life and presence from the drafts of blood, but when they had drunk their fill they departed in silence.

We spoke no words to the crew; they knew what the ceremony meant, they knew what was to happen, and they knew that all our fates rested in the laps of the gods. Aeson, Yellow Hare, and I waited in silence on the stage as the crew filed out slowly to take up their flight stations. As they passed some raised their hands in salute, but many walked by without acknowledging us, their thoughts intertwined with the gods.

When the last man had left, slaves entered and began to clear the stage and clean away the blood while we left to change from priestly garb to the robes of command.

Half an hour later, Yellow Hare, Aeson, and I met again at the base of the navigation tower. The divine presence of the ceremony had not left us and we could find nothing to say to one another. We climbed the spiral stairs in silence and entered the control room.

Kleon was carrying the scroll with the initial flight path over to the rostrum next to the control seat.

"Come in, come in," he said. "Strap down and we'll be under way."

Yellow Hare, Aeson, and I carefully tied ourselves to the cushioned marble couches riveted to the rear wall of the control tower.

"We are ready," I said to Kleon. My words sounded distant to my ears, as if I had been pulled back from my body and the world around it.

"Excellent." He sat down before the control panel and secured his chest and legs to the floor with half a dozen padded leather thongs.

"Brace for lift!" he called into the speaking tube in front of the control panel. His voice reverberated slowly through the artificially dense air which filled the tube, deepening the timbre of his words, giving them bass overtones he could never have sung himself. A few seconds later the words emerged from the megaphone on top of the tower and echoed across *Chandra's Tear* for all the crew to hear.

Kleon rubbed his hands together and his fingers twitched like a musician eager to play. He pulled down, one after another in rapid succession, the twenty short levers above his head. I heard the tooth-grinding sound of gears turning in the belly of the ship as the ballast spheres that had been hanging down below its centerline were pulled up into the underside of *Chandra's Tear*. Then, a sloshing noise as they emptied their cargo of water into the ship's reservoir. No longer weighted down by the natural heaviness of the water, *Chandra's Tear* began to rise slowly into the sky.

Kleon leaned forward and pulled twenty levers sticking up near his feet. There was an audible hiss that whispered like a west wind across the ship, and a gleam appeared from the window as the twenty fire-gold lift balls were pushed up on their pillars out of the containment pits on the rim of the ship and up to fifty feet above the surface. There was a sudden pull upward as the twenty-foot-across orbs rarefied the air above us. We began to rise faster, but still no swifter than a climbing hawk.

Kleon did nothing for several minutes but rock back and forth on his stool like a rower on a galley, keeping time to the Pythagorean rhythms of flight.

"Now," he whispered. "Brace for speed!" he shouted into the speaking tube, and his voice boomed like war drums across the sky.

Kleon pushed four of the control levers to his right. "Tertiary impellers deployed."

A line of gold rods emerged from the bow like the spears of a phalanx. *Chandra's Tear* tilted upward ever so slightly, and the air around the bow became bright and clear, sharpening my vision. A whine rose up from the bow as fire burned water out of the air.

Kleon pushed the four levers to his left, and a longer row of gleaming spikes joined the first. We were pushed back onto our couches as the ship rose faster into the welcoming sky. The force of the backpush yanked my soul completely into my body and away from the realm of the gods. "Secondary impellers deployed."

Kleon sang a hymn of praise to Pythagoras and pushed the four long levers directly in front of him. Poles a quarter mile long emerged from the bow. Their fire-gold shafts glinted brighter than the ship, brighter than the sun. The sky became the rich yellow of mead, precious, glorious, intoxicating. The whine grew into a scream. "Primary impellers deployed."

The air became as transparent as the crystal spheres themselves, and as the ship angled away from the earth I saw the heavens laid out before me in perfect clarity, the planets dancing in the eternal chorus laid down by the Prime Mover when the world was made. I blessed Ouranos, grandfather of the gods, and praised Zeus, lord of the sky.

The staid natural speed of *Chandra's Tear* was multiplied a hundred times by the thinness of the air created by the Ares impellers, yanking us away from the earth in a swiftly climbing spiral.

"At last," Aeson whispered. The air was pushed from my lungs and my back was slammed down into the couch as we rushed toward the celestial spheres. Day succeeded night succeeded day in cycles of five minutes as we whirled upward in a rising orbit toward the moon.

We flew like that for two breathless hours, until a glint appeared before us, turning rapidly into a transparent wall that filled the sky as we neared the unbreakable crystal sphere that held the moon in place.

"Retracting starboard impellers," Kleon said as he pulled two levers from each group of impeller controls.

The right side of our bow lost its fiery glint and the air over it hazed up in a sudden return of density. We banked sharply, turning parallel to the equator of the sphere that held the moon in place. A mere thousand miles ahead of us, I could see the orb of Selene itself.

"Brace for catching orbit," Kleon called. He retracted the primary and secondary impellers on both sides and redeployed the starboard tertiary impellers. We plowed into suddenly dense air and shed our excess speed. In a matter of seconds we had slowed down to a mere five times the natural orbital speed of the moon.

I sucked in air, grateful to be able to fill my lungs completely. " 'Ermes, lord of messengers, protect us from such speed," I prayed. Then I sat up and addressed the navigator. "Kleon, the crew won't be able to tolerate that speed for long."

Kleon smiled. "I know, Commander. That's why I've scheduled only four hours of flight each day. Two blocks of two hours each."

"Well done," I said.

"But I think I might be able to do better," he said.

Before he could elaborate on that remark, the scarred silver ball of the moon appeared in front of us.

"Brace for stop!" Kleon called as he retracted the tertiary impeller array, and slid us into the five-mile gap between the moon and the crystal sphere that gripped it with the unknown power of its natural motion. Kleon let *Chandra's Tear* assume an orbit just behind the body from which it had been carved.

"Well done, Kleon," I said as I unstrapped myself from the couch and stretched the muscles in my bruised back.

"Thank you, Commander," he said. "I'll see what I can do about minimizing the actual flying time."

"Very good," I said.

Aeson and Yellow Hare extricated themselves from their couches and the three of us left Kleon behind to muse over his lyre and his calculations.

Signal fires were lit on the ship, and in response, the crates of supplies Kroisos had promised were already being ferried up from the carved-out caves of the moon base on dozens of sleds. The guards at the base of the navigation tower told us that Anaxamander was on his way to the reception area with two dozen guards to inspect the cargo; Aeson went to join him.

Yellow Hare insisted that I stay away from the sleds and the crate inspections. She wanted me to go to my cave, but some god, perhaps Selene herself, commanded me to go to the edge of the ship and forced me to look across at the cratered body of the moon.

When Yellow Hare and I reached the port-side railing I caught sight of a gleam of bronze sticking up from the lunar surface. Though I could not make out the details, I knew it had to be the two-hundred-foot-tall statue of Artemis that marked the exact spot where Kroisos and Miltiades had landed on the moon in the year of my birth.

The divinity touched my thoughts and pulled out a memory: my mother telling me that on the first full moon after my birth she had taken me to the courtyard of Ishtar's temple and showed me to the moon; she had looked up and prayed to that flawless pearl for a good life for her son. She talked reverently of the unmarked beauty of that celestial gem.

Now I was looking down, not at the perfect pearl of my childhood, but at a pockmarked hunk of pumice. So many sleds and ships had been mined that the untouched maiden Selene who had greeted me with her silver light had been aged to the life-ravaged hag, 'Ekate. I wanted to look away but the god or goddess would not let me until Yellow Hare tapped me on the shoulder.

"Aias, what are you looking at?"

The deity left, giving me back my mind.

"A casualty of war," I said to Yellow Hare.

"There have been many of those," she said.

"I know, but this one can never be replaced. I wonder if we'll have to carve up all the planets before the end."

"Not if the Archons are right," she said. "If Sunthief wins us the war, there will be no need for more celestial ships. The matter lies in your hands."

"Thank you, Captain," I said, grateful for the reminder that I had the power to change this.

The delivery and checking of supplies took five hours, after which we slipped through the gap in the crystal sphere and entered the translunar heavens. A large escort of ships and sleds saw us away from the moon, and a fusillade of message flares lit a beacon of farewell as we shot out beyond the first sphere of heaven toward the domain of the Prime Mover.

As we flew, the Sun passed behind Earth, darkening a broad cone of space with us in it. The outer planets gleamed in the sudden starlight. I made out bloodred Ares and purple Zeus, and caught a glimpse of sea-green Aphrodite far to starboard. But orange-brown 'Ermes, our next goal, was unseen, hidden like a thief behind the cover of Earth.

\*  \*  \*

The next day, Aeson and I met in my office over a light breakfast of curried lamb; the last few days on Earth we had been fully consumed with making sure the ship was prepared for the journey. Now we had to settle certain matters related to the flight itself.

The first thing Aeson did was hand me a scroll. "Anaxamander's report. He's searched the ship from stem to stern and found no evidence of a spy."

Neither of us knew then that Anaxamander had done no such thing. And here I must enter a plea for Aeson. My co-commander had little regard for his security chief either as a man or as an officer. But whenever Anaxamander had been given an order, he had carried it out meticulously. True, he often failed to exercise common sense in his obedience, but nevertheless he had never disobeyed before. Therefore, though Aeson blames himself for dereliction, I say on his behalf that he had no way of knowing what would come from believing Anaxamander.

But to return to the meeting. I read the report quickly, then tossed it onto my desk. "Aeson, I give you my word that Ramonojon is not the spy."

"Aias," he said, "your loyalty does you honor, but our first duty is to the League. We must see to the welfare of this ship."

"Will you permit me to carry out my own search?" I said, knowing I would not be able to get more than that from him.

"Yes if you must. Now, may we turn to other matters?"

"Yes, of course, and thank you."

First we checked Kleon's timetable: one week to reach 'Ermes, another three weeks to Aphrodite, one month to go from there to the sun, and a further two months to return, dragging the sun fragment with us. Based on that, we spent an hour making up crew rosters, planning emergency drills, setting meal schedules, and so on. Eventually, we came to the last item: bolstering crew morale, sorely needed after the attempts on my life, the attack on the ship, Ramonojon's imprisonment, and our sudden unexplained departure from Earth.

We decided to hold weekly games for the soldiers, weekly debates for the scholars, and biweekly plays for all the crew. After the meeting we had announcements posted in the barracks and the dormitories asking for actors and play suggestions. I cannot say how well these activities worked to improve morale, but they kept the crew busy in their off-duty hours, so that they had less time to worry.

I was not so fortunate. I wanted to devote myself to finding the spy, but it took me the next three days, half of our travel time to 'Ermes, to clear away my other duties and give me time to deal with the problem of Ramonojon. It would have been only two days, but Kleon kept interrupting me with suggestions for how to shave a few hours off our travel time. Some of his maneuvers I approved, others sounded too risky. I always gave quick, peremptory answers, not wanting to be caught up in the minutiae of celestial navigation. I should have noticed the fire in Kleon's eyes as he declaimed the wonderful advantages of some minor course correction or other.

As it was, I did not realize that something was wrong with my chief navigator until just after lunch on the third day, when he burst unannounced into my office and narrowly avoided being killed by my bodyguard for not knocking.

"I've done it," Kleon said, oblivious of Yellow Hare holstering her evac thrower. "I can cut two days off our journey to Aphrodite without increasing the time we spend at speed."

I looked up from a maintenance report on the trolley. "That's quite impressive," I said. "How will you do it?"

"It's so simple." He was capering around the room like a child. "All we have to do is flip the ship on its side so *Chandra's Tear* cuts a sharper corridor through the air."

"Are you mad? We'll all fall off the ship," I said, stunned at having to remind him of basic terrestrial mechanics. "We'll plummet toward the earth and turn into pasty smears when we strike one of the crystal spheres."

He clapped his hands together in a strangely uncoordinated way that produced hollow thuds instead of sharp rapping sounds. "But if we strap everybody down!"

"What about the livestock? What about the water in the reservoir?"

He started to answer; no doubt he had thought of a way to handle that as well, but I cut him off.

"Kleon, stop!" I said. "We have settled the timetable. We do not need any more speed."

"But we can cut down the time," he said, ignoring my attempts at rationality.

"No, Kleon, we will not. I don't want you working on this anymore."

His face contorted into a Fury's mask; he tried to leap across my desk to grab me, but Yellow Hare plucked him out of the air and secured his hands behind his back.

"I have to finish it." His eyes burned with rage and his heavy, sobbing breath stank of choler.

I realized what had happened to him. "Yellow Hare, we have to take him to the hospital."

My bodyguard dragged the navigator, screaming and cursing, down to the hospital caves where I told one of the orderly-slaves to summon Euripos.

"What's wrong?" the old doctor asked when he emerged from the lying-in cave.

"Hyperclarity of Pneuma," I said. "At least I think that's what it is."

"Really?" Euripos beckoned to the orderly. "Fetch me a bag of water-heavy air."

"Yes, Doctor," the slave said, and he darted down the tunnel to the dispensary. He was back a minute later with a large leather sack coated in wax.

"Let me go," Kleon said, struggling to get out of Yellow Hare's steel solid grip. "I have to do my calculations."

Euripos held the bag up to the navigator's mouth and forced him to inhale the contents.

Kleon sucked in the heavy air in harsh, ragged gasps. After a few breaths his eyes dulled and he fell limp in Yellow Hare's arms.

"Captain, please, put him on the examining couch," Euripos

said, motioning toward the oaken bed at the back of the room.

Yellow Hare did so, then walked back to me. "What happened to him? I've never heard of, what was it, Hyperclarity of Pneuma."

"It's the air," I said. "It made his mind so clear that he could only concentrate on one thing. It became a mania to him, his every thought was focused on refining our course. But . . ."

"But what?"

I took a hesitant breath to clear my own mind. "But it's a very rare condition, and the Celestial Navigator's Guild checks its members to make sure they're not susceptible before they let them fly ships. Kleon's been tested repeatedly and always passed."

Euripos came back from examining Kleon. "He'll be well after a few hours' rest and a dose of Sanguine Humour."

"Can he still carry out his duties?" I asked. Without Kleon's brilliant piloting, there was little chance of Sunthief succeeding. None of his juniors was able enough to fly the ship that close to the sun.

"He should be," Euripos said, "but I'll want to give him a heavy-air bag to breath from just in case. And there should be someone watching him at all times."

"Poor Kleon. When the guild finds out they'll never let him fly a celestial ship again."

Yellow Hare turned to stare at the couch. "What are you thinking?" I asked.

"That too many things are going wrong here."

"What do you mean?"

"I am wondering if the Middler weapon that made you sick could have induced this condition in your navigator."

"If so," I said, seizing the opportunity, "someone used it on Kleon recently. Whoever that is is the real spy."

Yellow Hare slowly nodded. "How can we find out if the weapon could do that?" she asked.

"We can ask," I said, and my heart was lifted. Captain Yellow Hare, my perfect Spartan bodyguard, was going to help me find the spy. "Come with me to the brig."

The Middler doctor's name was Zi Lan-Xo. He had been

locked in his silver bright cell since he saved my life. He had been given food and water, but no one had spoken to him.

He looked up at me with sad eyes gleaming from many light-induced tears. His old face was crisscrossed with lines of worry and pain; he reminded me of friezes I had seen of those who suffer punishment in 'Ades for offending the gods.

"What do you with this poor prisoner want?" he asked in slow 'Ellenic.

"I have questions for the honorable doctor," I responded in 'Unan. His eyes widened in astonishment; then he shut them against the glare.

Captain Yellow Hare tapped me on the shoulder and motioned me to the side of the cell. "You didn't tell me you spoke Middler," she whispered in Xeroki.

"Some Akademics learn it," I said. "Those of us trying to understand the enemy's science."

"I thought the Akademe had no success understanding Middler technology."

"True," I said, "but we keep trying. No Athenian likes to admit he can't comprehend something."

I returned to Doctor Zi.

"What does my captor wish of this degraded prisoner?" he answered in rustic 'Unan.

I leaned against the cave wall and stroked my beard. The doctor's gaze turned longingly toward the wavering shadow my body cast on the floor. I wondered how long he had been kept under the glare of the silver walls, away from the peace of darkness.

"The illness you cured me of," I said. "The weapon that brought it on, could it make someone sick from the clarity of the air?"

"What do you mean?" He arched his eyebrows in bewilderment. "How can one be sick from pure air?"

I described Kleon's illness.

"There is no such disease," he said, sitting erect and stern like an Akademe lecturer. "Your barbarian doctors are fools to believe in such a thing."

"Then how do you account for it?"

"Your pilot is a madman; he must have been cursed by a spirit."

"Ridiculous. Kleon is a devout Pythagorean; the spirits would never harm him. This is not a matter of divine action, but human assault."

"If my honored captor says so . . . ," Doctor Zi replied, letting the sentence dangle.

I concluded that this discussion was a waste of time, so I started to turn around to leave. But Athena gripped me, forcing me to look back on the prisoner, who was staring desperately at the patch of darkness I was casting. She whispered that there was much to be gained from this man even if he knew nothing about Kleon's illness.

"There is a spy aboard this ship," I said. "What do you know about him?"

"What could this unworthy prisoner know? Dragged here from a prison camp to heal his estimable captor, and paid with imprisonment in this glowing stone monstrosity in which it is impossible to sleep."

"Help me catch the spy and I will have blankets put up to cover the walls."

"How could this worthless prisoner aid his captor?"

"I do not know," I said. "But if you can I will get you the sleep you need."

Let me say that I did not relish asking this old man to relinquish his honor. But both my duties to the state and to my friend required it of me.

The doctor stared at my shadow, then at the glowing wall. He had been down here for weeks surrounded by silver light. Doctor Zi was a tired, aged man who would never see his home again, and I was offering him a little comfort in his exile. Trembling, he bowed his head.

He spoke haltingly, almost crying as the words came out. "I have heard that a spy would have a . . ." Then he said something I did not understand.

"What does that word mean?"

"It is a contrivance for communicating over long distances."

We knew the Middlers had such a thing, but, as usual, we had no idea what it looked like or how it worked. But I was surprised that a common town doctor captured in a raid on the borders of the Middle Kingdom would know about such a thing.

"There are two pieces to the device," he went on. "A sender and a receiver. The receiver is . . . it looks like a four-inch block of silver with twelve gold needles stuck into it. The needles are arranged in two columns, making six lines of two needles each. A strip of cinnabar paint joins each pair."

"And the sending device?"

He hesitated, then drew a ragged breath and continued. "The sender is a block of glass three feet on a side. It has two columns like the receiver, but instead of gold needles there are silver spikes, and there are no paint lines."

His voice deadened into that of a technical lecturer. "The sender is placed into a Xi flow. Then six lines of cinnabar dust are laid down between the spike pairs. Each line is either solid or has a gap, thus producing a hexagram. The Xi flow is slightly changed by the hexagram. Any receiver lying in the same Xi flow will pick up the change, and its paint lines will develop gaps if there are gaps in the corresponding sender line."

The description of the device seemed clear enough, but how it worked and what a Xi flow was I did not know.

"Why does an ordinary doctor know about this?" I asked.

"Medicine is the foundation of science." he said in the same mechanical way I might recite Aristotle's laws of motion.

I had seen that sentence in several texts on Taoist science but had never believed they meant it. To our science, medicine was an offshoot of zeology, the study of life, and anthropology, the study of man. No Academic could believe that such a minor offshoot subject could be the cornerstone from which an understanding of the world could be built.

"Guard," I called through the door. One of the soldiers opened the heavy steel barrier.

"Commander?"

"Have slaves fetch night blankets for this cell."

"But Commander," he said, "the Security Chief wants the prisoners kept in the light so we can see them."

"That was an order," I said; but both he and I knew that my authority did not extend down into the cells. "If you wish I will have Commander Aeson come down here personally to ratify it."

"Yes, Commander," he said, not wanting to suffer Aeson's displeasure. "I am sorry, Commander. I'll have it done at once."

Yellow Hare and I left as the slaves were hanging darkness in the cell and the doctor was lying down for his first good sleep in weeks.

As we climbed up the tunnel I told my bodyguard about the communications device.

"Will you help me look for it?" I asked.

"Of course, Commander," she said.

"I thank you."

"It is my duty," she replied, but despite the impersonal words, the tone of her voice, or maybe it was a hint of softness in her gleaming gold eyes, I do not know, but there was something that made me believe she appreciated my gratitude.

"Where on *Chandra's Tear* would you hide a three-foot piece of glass?" I asked, drawing on her knowledge of spies and spying.

"Only two places have enough room, protection, and hiding places for an object that large and fragile," she said. "The storage cavern and the spontaneous-generation farm."

We checked storage first, in order to put off the stink of the spon-gen caves for as long as possible. The huge stores cavern had more than a dozen entrance tunnels scattered around the ship. Fortunately one of them was next to the brig access tunnel, so we did not have far to go.

Slaves pushing laden float carts nodded their heads humbly but said nothing as we walked down the echoing tunnel into the perfectly square (Ramonojon had made sure of that), half-mile-on-a-side cavern.

I listened to the hum and bustle of the slaves who lived and worked down there and surveyed the rows and rows of large wooden boxes strapped to the ground by steel bands. A perfect ordering of cubes, arranged in flawless phalanxes around the circular well in the center of the cave that afforded access to the ship's massive reservoir.

Clovix was standing near the entrance, talking to a blond female slave who was balancing two heavy wooden boxes on her shoulders with surprising ease. They stopped speaking as we approached.

"What can we do to serve you, Commander?" the chief slave said in that Gaulish accent that can make even the most humble statement sound like an insult.

"We need to search the stores," I said.

"Commander," he said, "we have over two thousand crates in here. Most of them are sealed until needed. Do you wish us to suspend all our normal work to open them for you?"

"We will do the best we can."

"Should I come with you, perhaps, to help you find what you need."

"No, Clovix, return to your duties."

"Um, yes, Commander."

"He's hiding something," Yellow Hare said to me in Xeroki as we passed into the cave proper.

I laughed. She looked at me in surprise.

"Of course he's hiding something," I said. "Clovix is one of the most corrupt slaves in the Delian League. He makes a great deal of money smuggling little luxury goods into the stores and selling them to my underlings."

"Why don't you stop him?"

I smiled at her Spartan propriety. "I learned a long time ago that it does subordinates good to think they can get away with little indiscretions," I said. "It improves morale."

"That is not true in the army," she said.

"But it is in the Akademe," I replied. We reached a five-foot crate with stenciled writing on the side that claimed it held sacks of flour. A quick search revealed that it contained sacks of flour.

We spent five hours walking from aft end to fore end, searching the open crates and checking the sealed ones for signs of tampering. We found nothing apart from a small cache of South Atlantean kaufi and koka beans hidden under a shipment of dried dates. No doubt Clovix was selling the roasted beans to my underlings for their stimulant qualities.

We stopped searching when the deepened voice of Pandenos, one of Kleon's junior navigators, reverberated from a speaking tube into the cave. "Brace for speed."

The slaves quickly strapped themselves to walls and floors, and we joined them, waiting out two painful hours tied to bare moonrock while Pandenos pushed us nearer to 'Ermes.

After we unstrapped, Yellow Hare and I marched to the fore end of the cavern and into the tunnel that led to the spon-gen farm. We passed through a pair of heavy limestone double doors that had been plastered over and washed clean of any dust. Two lab assistants draped gray linen sheets around our clothes and made us rub a sticky coagulating oil on our hands and faces to prevent us from perspiring, a necessary precaution since just a few drops of human sweat accidentally dripped into a spontaneous-generation mixture could change an embryonic pig into a writhing mass of dragonfly nymphs.

The assistants escorted us through a second set of double doors and closed them behind us. We were instantly assaulted by a cacophony of rank odors, as if a herd of sweating horses had stampeded through a field of wildflowers, then smashed through a tannery, and finally collapsed in exhaustion over a battlefield filled with putrefying corpses.

I held the sheet over my mouth, inhaling its clean smell. Yellow Hare looked around, grimly unaffected by the miasma of the room.

The low-ceilinged cavern contained two hundred steel-buttressed glass boxes in which the farmer slaves grew livestock. Many of the boxes had gray-brown mixtures of slop which had not yet sprouted. In others fetal animals could be seen forming. And in a few, full-grown cows, pigs, sheep, goats, and chickens scratched the walls, waiting to be released.

Between the cases were piles of manure, the primary component of life, and stacks of boxes filled with the odd ingredients I had requisitioned. Captain Yellow Hare and I spent three hours searching through that reeking environment under the watchful eyes of spon-gen farmers and partially made animals. We found nothing.

Tired and reeking of the stench, we returned to my cave. After being washed and oiled clean, I went immediately to sleep, not wanting to eat any food after being that close to seeing it made.

The next day, I went to visit Kleon in the hospital. He had spent the night in the lying-in cave and was breakfasting listlessly on bread and pears when I came in.

"Commander," he said, "I must resign my position. But with your permission I will help train Pandenos for the circumsolar maneuvers."

"Nonsense," I said. "I want you back in the tower flying this ship for the next speed period."

"I can't do it, Aias," he said. "If I catch the Pneuma while flying, I might never slow down. It's too dangerous."

"I've taken care of that," I said. "Someone will be watching you at all times."

"But, Aias—"

"Furthermore, your illness was induced."

"What?"

I told him Yellow Hare's theory, though I did not mention Doctor Zi's denial. The important thing to me was getting Kleon back to work.

"They tried to pull me from the sky!" Kleon's normally smiling face became filled with the rage of Ares. "I'll burn 'AngXou to the ground for this."

"Calm your heart," I said. "Remember who you are. Remembers the purity of Pythagoras. Remember the harmony of the heavens."

Kleon shut his eyes and began to hum for a few moments. Gradually, the rage left him.

"Aias," he said. "Can you have someone bring me my lyre?

Give me an hour with the music and I will be ready to fly again."

Kleon was as good as his word. His juniors told me there was no sign of returned obsession and Euripos said his breath and humour balance were perfectly normal. I hoped we had scared the spy away from making attempts on Kleon. And I hoped that we would catch him before he did something else to jeopardize the ship.

For the four days it took *Chandra's Tear* to reach 'Ermes, Yellow Hare and I continued to search for the communicator. I wandered all around the ship, checking the barracks, the dormitories, and the labs, as well as conducting more haphazard inspections of the storage cave. We found nothing, but I learned later that there were whisperings among the crew about my odd behavior.

Kleon took a cautious approach to the planet of the god of messengers, carefully maneuvering the ship between the main crystal sphere and the smaller epicyclic spheres that gave 'Ermes his few eccentricities of orbit. But after two careful hours sliding through the two-mile gaps between the spheres we reached the orange-red orb itself.

Unlike the pockmarked surface of Selene, 'Ermes has only a single scar on its body, a five-mile-long gash that leads into the League's underground base. Six years previously I spent a year in that cavern complex studying the properties of 'Ermean matter and watching the dynamicists carve out the high-speed celestial ships used for flying low over the Middle Kingdom and spying out their military bases.

Aeson, who had never been farther out than the moon before, drank in the sight of the planet and offered a small libation at one of the 'Erms, thanking the god for the sight.

Soon after we took up orbit, the celestial ships *Mercury's Sandal* and *Rod of Thoth*, the two ruddy, quarter-mile-long swift arrows permanently stationed at the base, flew up from the caves in their planet of origin to deliver the 'Ermean matter we needed for the net. Both ships were slimmer, more maneuverable craft than *Chandra's Tear*, though, as Kleon jealously pointed out, with our Ares impellers they could not match our speed.

Mihradarius took charge of the boxes of 'Ermean matter and set his knitters to work on weaving the second segment of the net. He promised to have the work finished before we reached Aphrodite and obtained the final consignment of celestial matter.

# θ

B eyond the sphere of 'Ermes we lost the comforting uniform-
ity of day and night. The earth so rarely occluded the sun
that we had almost perpetual daylight, but we saw nuances
and distinctions of brightness unknown on Earth. When
*Chandra's Tear* and the sun were in the same quarter of the sky,
the light of 'Elios was so bright that we had to wear cloth over our
eyes to keep from going blind. But when sun and ship were on
opposite sides of the earth, occupying opposite quadrants of the
heavenly circle, we enjoyed stretches of peaceful twilight that
would last for hours. For want of a more original phrase, we came
to call these extended periods of star-filled, dark orange sky the
"long evenings."

Aeson and I reworked the crew schedule so that most of the
staff would be free for at least part of those pastoral spans. Many
times when the heavens tantalized us with the approach of short
night, Yellow Hare and I would find Aeson sitting on the side of
the hill, squinting out through the dregs of light to glimpse the
outer planets and the sphere of fixed stars beyond them. He talked
about the heavens as if they were a magical place, beyond the

touch of man. It was soothing to let his romanticism wash away the cold facts of Ouranology, to forget orbits, epicycles, and lumps of celestial stone, to see with him the royal jewels of the gods adorning the crown of the sky.

Those evenings revitalized me, giving me something to think about apart from Ramonojon's plight and the spy aboard ship; for those problems occupied my thoughts all the remaining hours of the day. My searches of the ship had been fruitless, and as the first week of our flight to Aphrodite waned, I came to realize that I would not be able to find what I was seeking by the systematic methods beloved of the Akademe.

I turned therefore to the gods for inspiration. One by one I consulted them in the manners laid down since man's creation. Athena I entreated first, offering a libation before her statues, but Wisdom, though my patroness, remained aloof. Then I supplicated Apollo, inhaling the burning fumes of bay leaves, but no oracle came to me. To 'Ermes, I gave a black rooster and a necklace of gold during one of the ship's dark periods, but the Lord of Language said nothing. Finally, I turned to the most dangerous source of divine assistance, Dionysos.

We were seven days out from 'Ermes, and *Chandra's Tear* was bathed in one of its rare hours of complete darkness. I was sitting on the floor of my cave, alone with Yellow Hare. The night blankets were down, cutting off the silver glow. The only light came from four beeswax candles sitting on my desk. I had eaten no food and drunk neither water nor wine for twelve hours. I had dressed myself in a handmade tunic of untanned leather; on my lap lay a thursis, a wooden staff wrapped with grape vines, and in front of me sat a large clay jar on which was painted the story of Dionysos's birth and his subjugation of Thebes. The vessel was filled to the brim with unmixed wine, so thick it was almost jelled.

"Lord of the vine," I said, bowing my head to the image of the god on the jar. "Leader of the Bakkhai, holy child born from the thigh of Zeus, grant me the power of your divine mania, bless me with the wisdom of your frenzy."

I lifted the heavy round jar and poured the fire of Dionysos into my mind.

The taste of grape in my mouth became the scent of maple in the forests of North Atlantea. I was a wolf running through the woods, hunting something just out of reach; I knew it was there, but I could not smell it for the heady odor of bleeding sap. I became a dolphin swimming through the oceans, feeling the currents as I fled from a shark. I became a leopard, white against the snowcapped mountains, darting through the new-fallen powder, chasing the white hare. Then I found it, a tiny rabbit cowering against a rock, shivering in fear and cold. I leaped to tear its throat out; but it sprang on me, and with its fragile forepaws blocked the curved blades of my ivory claws and with its back legs kicked hard against the sharp points of my fangs.

"Aias!" The iron-sure heel of Yellow Hare's hand slapped against my cheek, pulling me from the divine vision, but not from the Bakkhanate madness.

I slashed at her again, trying to rake her with my claws, lunging with my hands to scrape across her armored chest, but she was no longer there. Yellow Hare had darted around behind me. As I turned to face her, she grabbed my arms and threw me to the floor. I roared and spit like an angry cat, trying to push her off me, but she had become immovable as Olympos; for half an hour she held me down until the god left my mind and I became human again.

"You can let me up, Yellow Hare," I said through a throat grown dry with snarling.

She released her iron grip, and I stood up, taking care not to move my aching head too quickly.

"My thanks, Captain," I said.

"I was honored to serve as your warden," she said. "Did the god bless you with any understanding?"

"I think so," I said. "I did not comprehend all of the vision, but Dionysos definitely implied that I should seek assistance from you."

A wave of dizziness came over me and my knees buckled, but Yellow Hare caught me before I collapsed. With a gentle, firm grip on my shoulders, she took me over to my couch and helped me lie down.

"Commander," she said, keeping her words mercifully quiet, "I have assisted you in your searches as you asked me to."

"But have you done so with your whole heart?" I took a sip of water from the bowl beside my sleeping couch. It did not clear my thoughts, but it soothed my throat. I had roared for a long time while I was a leopard.

Yellow Hare said nothing for several minutes as I lay with my eyes shut, feeling my pulse course through my temples like the ocean tides through rocky straits.

At last she spoke. "No, Aias, I have not committed the whole of my heart to your search for another spy."

"Another spy?"

"I still believe Ramonojon is an agent of the Middle Kingdom," she said. "Celestial Navigator Kleon's illness only demonstrates that there is another."

"Why can't you believe it's just one spy?" I said, and instantly regretted the vehemence of my words. "Why must you persist in believing Ramonojon guilty?"

"The evidence against him still remains."

"And if there were another explanation of the evidence?" I asked, tentatively.

"Tell me what it is," she said.

And there lay my dilemma. I could not tell her why Ramonojon was innocent; but the god had implied that I needed her assistance to prove his innocence.

Then Athena whispered to me through the fog of Dionysos. The goddess reminded me that there were things that would convince so pure a Spartan as Yellow Hare that would not sway a lesser soul.

My legs nearly gave out from under me as I stood up into the most erect posture I could manage. Then with careful movements I covered my heart with both hands. "I, Aias of Athens, swear before almighty Zeus that I possess evidence exonerating Ramonojon from the charge of spying."

Yellow Hare stared at me with a frown of mingled respect and concern. "Why have you not shown this evidence to Aeson?"

"As Military Commander of this ship," I said, "Aeson has duties he would feel obligated to carry out even if he personally disagreed with them."

Yellow Hare leaned forward, her bright eyes burning with understanding.

"What crime has Ramonojon committed?"

"I cannot tell you that," I said, pleased at the quickness of her mind. "But I swear that his offense will not prevent Sunthief from succeeding. I swear to you before the Styx that in trying to help Ramonojon, I have sought to fulfill all of my own duties."

"Aias of Athens," Yellow Hare said, drawing her sword and holding it point up in front of her face, "I place myself under your command in this matter and will obey your orders so long as they do not put your life at risk."

I reached out and wrapped my hands around hers and the hilt of her sword. "Yellow Hare of Sparta, I accept you into my command."

I released my grip and she sheathed her sword. The last dregs of strength fled my muscles and I collapsed onto the couch. Yellow Hare walked over to my table to extinguish the candles. Full darkness came and soothed the throbbing of my head as I faded off to sleep. That night I dreamed of dolphins and the deep currents of the ocean.

The next morning, I went down to the hospital cave for an injection of Jovial Humour to clear away my hangover. Euripos stuck the quill into my arm, but instead of giving me the usual warnings about giving in to the artificial sense of elation, he muttered curses under his breath in a bad caricature of a Middler accent.

"What in 'Ermes' name are you doing?" I asked when my head had cleared.

A yellowed grin broke the network of lines on his face. "I have a part in an upcoming comedy. I play a Middler alchemist intent on developing a new explosive."

I raised one eyebrow. "Somehow, I can't imagine you in a comedy."

"Don't sound so surprised," he said. "There was a period in

my youth when I did a lot of acting. I think you were about two years old at the time, living with your mother in Tyre. Your father's army was stationed on garrison duty near the upper end of the east bank of the Mississipp. The terrain was swampy, and as company physician I saw a lot of unpleasant diseases. You wouldn't believe the variety of illnesses that bad swamp air produces."

"What about the acting?" I said, not having the mental stamina to sit through another war story about my father.

"Well, the duty was very boring; your father instituted athletics, of course, but there comes a time when even the most dedicated soldier needs something to exercise his mind. So he grudgingly permitted us to put on plays."

"Comedies?"

"Of course. Your father didn't like it, but he knew it was good for morale. At one point, I actually had the part of Sokrates in Aristophanes' the *Clouds.*"

"Please don't mention that play," I said. No Akademic likes to be reminded of that particular piece of slander.

"My apologies, Commander." The old man fell silent. It always bothered him to be reminded that the child who had once ransacked his medicine bag out of pure curiosity now outranked him.

"I look forward to your performance," I said to mollify him, and I was rewarded with a thankful smile. As I walked out of the cave, I realized much to my surprise that I was indeed looking forward to his play. My mind had been freed of the burden of constant worrying by Yellow Hare's gift of her service. Not only had she freed me to think about other things, she had reinvigorated my hope that I would be able to exonerate Ramonojon, guide Sunthief to success, and from thence carry out the Archons' plans to win the war.

Flushed with this feeling of success, I decided to seek out more allies. I took Yellow Hare and went to see Mihradarius.

We found the brilliant Persian in his lab seated at his writing table, staring at the figure of Alexander that glowed on his wall. Mihradarius was tapping the back end of his quill so hard against a parchment full of calculations that the tufts of the feather were flying loose.

I coughed, and he nearly jumped off his stool. "Commander, it's you. You startled me. I'm sorry, I haven't finished these solar drag calculations; I hope you don't need the figures immediately?"

"No, Mihradarius," I said. "I didn't come for your work. I want to talk to you about Ramonojon."

The Persian offered me a stool and a bowl of wine. I accepted the former but declined the latter.

"What about Ramonojon?" Mihradarius asked.

I tapped my lips with my fingertips, hoping to discern Mihradarius's attitudes in his face, and failing. "He's not a spy."

Mihradarius twisted his mouth into a wry grimace and barked out two sharp laughs. "That is the worst-kept secret on this ship." He looked over my shoulder at Yellow Hare and lowered his voice. "Only the military would be stupid enough to think Ramonojon could be an assassin."

The hackles on the back of my neck rose at the insult to my bodyguard, but I kept my peace, wanting to gain Mihradarius's aid rather than argue with him.

"Then who do you think the spy is?" I asked.

"I don't think there is one," he said, taking a sip from his bowl. "I think the Middlers have developed a device that allows them to watch us at long range. Such an instrument would permit them to stage both the raids on this ship and the specific attempts on your life."

"No," Yellow Hare said.

Mihradarius and I both turned sharply to look at her. That blunt, unvarnished word "No" without any accompanying explanation was quite contrary to Akademe manners. The Persian cocked an eyebrow in my bodyguard's direction as if to ask what this rude Spartan was doing interrupting an Athenian discourse.

"Clarify that statement, Captain," I said.

"If the Middlers had such a device," she said, "they would use it to stage ambushes of our armies, or attacks on our undefended cities, not assassinations of our leaders."

"In any case," I said, "such a device would not account for the pieces of Middler technology found on this ship, nor does it explain Kleon's sickness."

"Explain it?" Mihradarius said. "Why does Hyperclarity of Pneuma need explaining?"

I related Yellow Hare's theory about the source of the illness, emphasizing that it was her idea.

Mihradarius threw up his arms hopelessly. "Maybe the captain is right, but who can tell? Speculating about Taoist science is fruitless."

"I know," I said. "But we have so little to go on." I paused for a few seconds but he said nothing, so I continued. "Mihradarius, I would like your assistance in this matter."

"Commander," he said, straightening his sleeves. "Ramonojon and I have never been very amicable, but if there is anything I can do to help you, I give you my word as an Athenian that I will do so."

"Thank you, Chief Ouranologist," I said. "I want you to speak to your staff, find out if they have noticed any hints of strange activities on this ship."

"Right away, Commander," he said, and ushered us out of his laboratory.

I spent the next several days talking to scientists, soldiers, and slaves about Ramonojon, seeking information and allies. Those who knew him well thought it impossible for him to be a spy, but all conceded that he had been behaving strangely; the rest of the crew were so grateful that the unknown menace in their midst had been captured that they did not want to believe a mistake had been made. I gained no useful assistance from either group of people, nor did any of them report any nontrivial peculiarities.

At the end of these interviews, my hope had dwindled from a gleaming fire to a few sad embers. My sadness must have been obvious since Yellow Hare spoke to me about it.

"Commander," she said. "I have learned a great deal about our hidden spy."

"And what have you learned?" I asked.

"That he is sufficiently well placed on *Chandra's Tear* to be able to misdirect and distract the entire crew up to and including the ship's commanders."

"You mean the spy is a member of senior staff."

"Not necessarily," she said. "A well-placed slave could do the same; so could some of the army officers, either of the guard captains, even a well-connected file clerk could do so. But the more we learn the closer I come to finding out who it is."

"Thank you, Captain," I said, pleased at the solidity of her reasoning. "A succinct analysis."

That evening the plays were to be performed and I went to watch with my spirit buoyed by Yellow Hare's words and presence.

The performance took the classical form of a three-part tragedy followed by a one-act comedy. The dramatic trilogy was a two-hundred-year-old work entitled *The Siege of Persepolis*, which recounted in semimythical form an event that happened some three centuries before it was written.

The tragedy had been innocently selected by one of the guard captains for its stirring Spartan "We who are about to die shall go bravely, giving our all for our people!" message, but my historian's eyes saw the performance rather differently. Indeed, as the play progressed I began to realize that the work is a subtly veiled attack on the nobility of soldiers. The muttered growling to my left made me realize that Captain Yellow Hare saw the same thing; once again I was impressed by the clarity of her awareness of all things military.

My suspicions of irony were first aroused in an early scene in the first part of the trilogy. Xanthippos, the Spartan military governor of Persepolis, leaves the city to parlay with T'Sao T'Sao, the Middler general, whose capture of that city launched him on the road to becoming Son of Heaven. Most 'Ellenic plays about T'Sao T'Sao portray him as a monster whose evil was beyond the comprehension of men, but this play paints a very human portrait.

During the parlay Xanthippos tries to convince T'Sao T'Sao to abandon the siege. The debate between the two generals quickly turns into an exchange of quotations from Alexander. The governor finds himself unable to reply when T'Sao T'Sao states word for word Alexander's justifications to the last Persian emperor when our hero had conquered his country. Phrases like "the inevitability of fate," "the clear favor of the gods," and "the glory of victory" resounded through the amphitheater from the yellow-masked actor portraying the future emperor of the Middle Kingdom.

The second play consists almost entirely of a series of arguments between the Spartan Xanthippos and the Athenian governor of the city, whose name has not been remembered. The debates become ever more heated as it becomes clear to both of them that Persepolis will be taken. Halfway through, the Athenian implores the Spartan to permit surrender, but Xanthippos makes repeated reference to Leonidas and the Three Hundred at Thermopylae. The general's lines were written so broadly as to make him seem like a fool blinded by Ate rather than a brave man accepting death in the finest traditions of his homeland.

The trilogy ends with a man-to-man duel between T'Sao T'Sao and the military governor that results in the Spartan's death. Stabbed through the chest, Xanthippos kneels on the stage gasping out his final monologue for nearly five minutes. His soliloquy expresses his firm confidence that letting the city be sacked and the citizens killed assures him a place as a hero on Olympos. T'Sao T'Sao orders his body exposed for the birds to tear at, then commands his own doctors to attend to the survivors on both sides.

The general had, of course, been declared a hero; he had held T'Sao T'Sao in place for that yearlong siege, and by so doing had slowed the Middler general enough to keep him from reaching the Peloponnese itself before he had to turn back in order to take the throne of the Middle Kingdom.

After this veiled dramatic sarcasm, we were treated to the comedy Euripos was acting in. It was a short piece with only two major characters, a pair of Taoist alchemists. The work was a pleasantly crude comedy with a lot of onstage explosions as the pair tried to out do each other in creating bombs to wreak havoc on offstage 'Ellenic soldiers. The play ended with a massive display of pyrotechnics in which the alchemists blew each other up into the heavens. There they were joined by a generic Middler god who offered to show them how to make really large explosions.

Yellow Hare refused to be cheered up by this humorous display, and grumbled all the way back to my cave.

"For whatever the opinion of an Athenian on military matters is worth," I said as we settled in to sleep, me on my couch and her on the floor blankets, "I do not believe that Xanthippos's bravery was really stupidity."

She turned the twin suns of her eyes to me and smiled. "Thank you, Aias. And I do not think the intelligence of the Athenian governor was really cowardice."


Four days later we reached the sphere of Aphrodite and slowed to a crawl as we neared the gray-green planet. Aeson and I watched the approach from the top of the hill, offering libations of honey wine to the goddess of love.

Kleon brought us carefully through the network of Aphrodite's epicycles toward our scheduled rendezvous with *Ishtar's Necklace*, the mining ship that held our consignment of Aphroditean matter for the net.

After an hour's maneuvering we slipped inside the crystal sphere and reached the far side of Aphrodite. There, on the planet's equator, was a tiny scar carved into her body and hidden from earthly view with maidenly modesty. Two miles above that point the ship sliced from the scar was supposed to be waiting.

But instead of a celestial ship, we found seven jagged pieces of green rock floating in perfect synchronicity with the planet below.

"They've been attacked," Yellow Hare said.

"Impossible," I said. "There must have been an accident. The Middlers have never traveled farther out than Selene."

But then a huge silk shadow darted out from behind one of the fragments, giving the lie to my confident pronouncement. It was the largest battle kite I'd ever seen, a two-hundred-yard-long wingless dragon with silver Xi lance spines up and down its water blue back, and a vicious red mouth filled with impossibly liquid fire. Its outline flickered strangely in the mixture of green light from the planet and silver glow from *Chandra's Tear*. The shimmer made it hard to tell exactly where the kite was, but it was definitely coming toward us.

"Down!" Yellow Hare shouted, shoving me behind the statue of Alexander. She and Aeson dove behind the statue, flanking me, and drew their throwers.

Our topside cannon batteries opened fire, spraying a barrage of tetras through columns of rarefied air into the body of the dragon kite. Dozens of holes appeared in the enemy craft, but it flew on. The silken underside of the dragon split open to reveal the bamboo skeleton underneath. Hanging from the arched wooden bones of the kite were dozens of green bundles; in the shimmering haze they resembled eight-foot-long, rolled-up scrolls. The bundles fell out of the dragon and each unfurled into a one-man kite shaped like a jade bat. The swarms of aircraft swooped over our port side, firing their Xi lances in unison at our cannon batteries. The metal cylinders began to coil and twist as if huge invisible hands were wringing them.

The tail of the main kite opened like a flower and from it squadrons of men dropped down, falling impossibly slowly toward the center of *Chandra's Tear*. As they descended they threw small metal stars that flew too fast and cut through our soldiers' armor like scythes through wheat. Huge balls of flame vomited from the dragon's mouth and exploded on our port side, melting the twisted evac cannons into slags of gold and steel.

Our soldiers ran up the hill to reinforce Aeson and Yellow Hare just as the first Middlers touched down in the courtyard. Both sides opened fire at once, filling the air with stars and tetras. Yellow Hare killed four of the enemy with her thrower before they reached her, then she drew her sword and engaged them hand to hand.

She stabbed one man through the throat and fell back to keep between me and the other three. Aeson paralleled her, shooting down the enemy with Spartan calm and accuracy.

One of the Middlers shouted a single word in their language. "Blood!"

Four warriors who had held themselves at a distance threw four large steel stars toward Aeson. My co-commander saw them coming, dove to the ground, and started to roll away, but the Middler who had given the order pointed a handheld Xi lance at the flying stars. As they were about to pass harmlessly over him, the projectiles turned impossibly in midair and spun downward, piercing Aeson's head and chest.

I screamed Aeson's name and started to run across the courtyard toward the Middler who had given the orders, but Yellow Hare pushed me aside and shot the man through the heart. He fell as noiselessly as Aeson had.

Reinforcements arrived—our reinforcements, thank Ares and Athena. They pushed the Middlers off the hill with a coordinated barrage of tetras. I ran over to Aeson and knelt down. He was still breathing, but his eyes were closed and his heartbeat was ragged. Yellow Hare ordered the soldiers to form a perimeter around the hilltop. Then she methodically removed Aeson's helmet and armor, pulled the stars from his body, and bound his wounds.

Forcing myself to remember my duty, I turned away from Aeson to survey the battle. The dragon had made its way to the bow of the ship, curling and darting to avoid the barrage from the forward cannons. The kite's head spat fire again and the amphitheater exploded. As if that were a signal to them, the squadrons of bats left their single assaults and turned to follow their mother's lead, converging on the navigation tower.

"Protect the tower!" I shouted over the hill to our soldiers. "Save Kleon!"

But I need not have bothered. As I was yelling my orders, a line of gold light appeared, clarifying the air to our right as the primary starboard impellers were deployed. A yellow halo rose to cover the starboard edge of the ship as ten lift balls emerged from the right-side rim. Kleon's voice boomed across the ship. "Hang on."

"Yellow Hare, bring Aeson!" I shouted as I realized what

Kleon was doing. She and I grabbed the base of Aristotle's statue and clutched my co-commander's body close to ours.

Pulled by the imbalance of rarefied air, *Chandra's Tear* spun a swift quarter circle, until the deck was perpendicular rather than parallel to the earth's surface. The turning ship swatted down the small kites like so many flies and slammed our port edge into the head of the dragon. The bamboo skeleton of the dragon shattered under the force of spinning moonstone.

Without the mass of moon rock to hold them up, dozens of crewmen were caught out in the open, unable to grab on to some support. For a second they hovered stationary in the air; then they were gripped by their natural earthward motion and fell off the ship. A few moments later their bodies smashed into the sphere of Aphrodite, staining the purity of the goddess.

I screamed at the strain of holding on against nature, but Yellow Hare pulled me up, her strength sufficing for the three of us.

For one long moment the corpse of the dragon kite was frozen in space, still held up by the mysterious power that permitted it to fly in defiance of all known laws of physics, but then that power failed and the splintered body plummeted down through the rarefied air, snapping off half of our starboard impellers before joining its children as celestial jetsam.

The enemy gone, Kleon pulled back the starboard lift balls and the remaining impellers while simultaneously deploying their port-side counterparts. The ship rocked again and righted itself. Kleon quickly withdrew all the balls and rods into the body of *Chandra's Tear* before the ship tipped to the other side.

Yellow Hare and I let go of the statue and carried Aeson to Euripos's hospital across a silver field littered with scraps of steel, silk, blood, and bone. The tunnel down to the hospital was filled with injured soldiers being tended by the doctors and the hospital slaves. Yellow Hare and I wended our way through the crowded cavern until we reached the surgery cave.

"Euripos!" I shouted.

The doctor came running out of the ward.

"Tend to Aeson," I said.

"Yes, Commander."

The old Roman doctor had Aeson taken down to the private ward and set grimly to work. He had seen too many battles to waste his time on words.

He laid Aeson down on a slab of marble covered with a thick woolen cloth. Then Euripos injected him with a quill full of Sanguine Humour and waited for his breathing to become regular. Then he pulled two long rubber tubes with fire-gold tips out of a panel in the side of the slab, unwrapped the makeshift bandages Yellow Hare had tied around Aeson's chest, and cauterized the wounds with quick jabs of the needles; blood-scented smoke rose up from the table.

Euripos sewed spontaneously generated human skin over the holes in Aeson's flesh and poured Sanguine on the joins to speed up healing.

He unwrapped the bandages and studied the punctures in Aeson's skull.

"How is it?" I asked, unable to bear the unknowing silence.

"It does not look good," he said. "Please leave so I can work."

Yellow Hare and I worked our way up to the surface of the ship. As we passed through the wards, those soldiers who were conscious all asked the same question, no matter what their own injuries. "How is the commander?"

"Alive," I said, hoping he would remain so.

By the time we managed to reach the surface, the dynamicists and engineers had taken the heavy cranes and ground graders from storage and were using them to clear away the debris and fix the cracks in the buildings. The amphitheater was a total loss, but I didn't think anyone would be in the mood for plays anymore.

Two trains of thought warred for my attention. Was Aeson going to live, and how did a battle kite get out here through the patrolled spheres of Selene and 'Ermes? But I had little time to think about these questions as person after person came to me for orders. What should be fixed first? Batteries and impellers. What should be done with the remaining bodies? Place them in the storage cave; we'll hold funeral games once we know the full complement of the dead, and so on.

Anaxamander and Kleon found me by the statue of Aristotle,

surveying the damage to the hill. The security chief's armor had two gashes in it where stars had nearly cut him. His helmet was gone, and his sword had snapped in two. Kleon's robes were torn and there were bruises visible on his arms and chest.

Kleon ran up to me wringing his hands. "Alas, I swear to you it was my only option to protect the ship. I'm sorry about the soldiers. I don't think the mania took me again. It was the only thing I could do."

"You've done well, Kleon," I said. "You saved *Chandra's Tear*, you did the right thing."

"Thank you, Aias."

I turned to Anaxamander. "What's the damage, Security Chief?"

"Half the soldiers are dead. Most of the others are injured. Seven scientists and about twenty slaves went over the side as well."

"What about structural damage?"

Anaxamander checked one of his lists. "Port-side battery's gone. We'll have to move some of the cannons around to compensate. We've lost a quarter of the primary impellers—"

"We can fix that," Kleon said.

"See to it, Chief Navigator," I said.

"Yes, Commander," he said.

Anaxamander continued. "Stores suffered only minor damage, but half of the animals in spon gen were killed. Mihradarius says the net came through without a tear, and he's sent out some of our moon sleds to retrieve the Aphroditean matter from the wreckage of *Ishtar's Necklace*."

"What about Ramonojon?"

Anaxamander snarled. "The traitor suffered a few minor bruises, nothing more. But one of the enemy soldiers broke into the other cell and killed that Middler doctor."

He paused, and looked down from the hill to the hospital cave. "How is the commander?"

I put on my best mock Spartan face, not wanting to show my sadness or rage to Anaxamander. "Euripos is still operating, but he wasn't confident."

Anaxamander straightened up and threw back his shoulders. His eyes gleamed with confidence as he looked over our heads toward the sun. "Commander Aias," he said. "As Aeson's second in line, I herewith assume the position of military commander of *Chandra's Tear.*"

ᘄ

naxamander strode off, bellowing orders. At that moment,
I made a critical mistake. I assumed that the rank-and-file
troops would see the great difference between their old
commander and their new one, that they would understand Anaxamander as Yellow Hare and I did. But I did not comprehend how
much the unexpected attack, coupled with the lack of command,
terrified the soldiers. I failed to see that their need for military
leadership far outweighed their ability to judge the worth of a
leader.

Yellow Hare knew, of course, but I did not talk to her about it,
and she could not bring herself to say anything that would under-
mine the discipline of the army.

Thus it was that instead of seizing the moment when I might
have managed, in contravention of all Delian tradition, to cross
the chasm that separated military from scientific authority and
taken full control of *Chandra's Tear*, I stayed on my side of the
division of duty and waited for news of Aeson.

I stood in the middle of the courtyard, watching crews of men
and machines clear away the debris of flesh and stone. I gave no

orders during the hours I waited, but several times I caught the glance of an engineer or dynamicist indolently checking the structural integrity of a column or numbly directing slaves to remove the shattered remnants of a crewman. At those moments, a memory of Aeson would rise up in my thoughts, and, through the light that passed between my eyes and the woe-stricken worker, I would send a little of my injured friend's spirit of Spartan resolution. Then the man's eyes would brighten, not with cheer but with determination, and he would return to his task with renewed vigor.

Sometime during my vigil the sun passed directly overhead, and for the first time in my life, I saw 'Elios alone amid the mead bright sky. Nothing lay between me and the celestial fire but eighty thousand miles of empty air; no crystal spheres stood in the way to shield me from the rain of light and heat.

The sun god pulled at my eyes, wanted me to stare up at him as he burned me with his spear shafts; he wanted to remind me of the hubris of Prometheus, of the penalty inflicted on one who would try to steal fire from heaven. But I had long ago prepared for this moment. I ordered those slaves who were not cleaning the ship to distribute solar protective gear to the crew. Clovix himself brought Yellow Hare and me green smoked-glass goggles to protect our eyes from the overwhelming glare of the universal luminary and burnooses that had been laced with air-silver wires to keep our bodies cool from the bombardment of atomic fire.

Thus protected by the contrivances of man, I turned to face the sun.

"You are not the god," I said to the shimmering orb, and gazed directly into its muted fires, dulled by the glass from pure yellow to a dull green-orange. "You are matter, not spirit. You are not holy. There is no sacrilege in taking from you."

But even as I spoke those words, knowing they were meant to reassure me, my mind filled with the vision of scar-covered Selene, and my voice faltered. Was he not 'Elios, was the sun not the body of the god? Questions never asked in the Akademe, never touched upon in all the studies of Ouranology, came to me, and for the first time I thought of ordering Kleon to sail the ship home to Earth.

But then I looked at Yellow Hare, staring not defiantly but confidently up at the sun. And I knew that if she felt it her duty to storm Olympos itself, she would do so. And I could do no less.

I was about to speak to her when Euripos's voice entered my muffled ears from behind; "Aeson will live."

All my concerns about gods and men vanished in the relief I felt in hearing those words. I turned to look at the old Roman doctor. Through the wrappings and goggles, I could not see his expression. But I could see that his white tunic was stained with his own dried sweat and Aeson's blood; he must have been operating for all the time I had stood mute in the courtyard.

"May Apollo bless you, old man," I said, and reached out to take his hands in thanks, but he shied away from my grasp.

"When can I talk to Aeson?" I asked.

Euripos stared down at the ground, where the silver of the ship had been washed away to the total darkness of the new moon by the glare of the sun. "I said he'd live, but, Aias, Aeon is in a coma. We can keep him supplied with Sanguine and force-feed him so he won't starve, but it might be weeks before he wakes up. If he wakes up. We know so little about comas. . . ."

"Do what you can for him, Euripos," I said. "We need him back."

"Yes, Commander . . . Aias . . . I . . ." He looked up at me. I don't know what that old man who had known me from birth saw through the linen and glass mask on my face, but whatever it was frightened him. "Permission to return to the hospital, sir?"

"Granted," I said, and he hurried back down into his cave.

A coma, not alive, not speaking or commanding, not able to touch me with his voice. And not dead, not mourned, not praised with funeral games, not able to come and give warnings in the Khthonian ceremonies. But completely out of reach of my body or spirit.

One of the work slaves came up to me. The loinclothed man wiped his dirtied hands on his burnoose and bowed quickly.

"Commander," he said, averting his eyes from mine, "we have a problem. The statues of divine Athena at the hill gates. All three of them were damaged in the attack. The engineers said they'll fall over the first time the ship goes fast. But—"

"I understand," I said, raising a hand to silence him. "Send someone for my priest's robes, a cloth of virgin wool, and a jar of pure water."

"Yes, Commander."

"Aias?" Yellow Hare said, in a strangely tentative voice.

"Yes?"

"Can you deconsecrate the statues alone?"

Alone. Without Aeson, without my brother in priestly duties. But what other options did I have? The proper thing to do would have been to enlist his successor's help. But—

"I won't have that fool Anaxamander wiping away Wisdom's eyes," I said out loud.

"Could anyone else help you?" Yellow Hare asked.

"What about you?" I asked. The prospect of divine service with Yellow Hare at my side filled me with the first joy I had felt since the attack.

But she shook her head. "I have never undertaken the duties of a priest," she said.

"What?" I said. "A Spartan officer, not doing priest work? That's unheard of."

"I cannot have a second way to be close to the gods," she said, and I saw the gods of war rise up in battle array behind her, defending the purity of her contact with them. Then I comprehended; for her to pick up the knife of sacrifice, to speak the ritual prayers, to call the gods to her, she would first have to move away from them and see them in priestly light rather than feel them in her warrior's heart. And though most men would regard such a change of view as a blessing, Yellow Hare saw it as a denial of her duty to the gods.

"I understand," I said.

"You do?"

"Yes. You honor the gods more with your devotion than you would with a thousand ceremonies."

"No one has ever known what I meant before," she said. We both fell silent for a time. And in the depths of our shared quiet something began to sing in my thoughts, something large and broad and older than the gods. For the first time in my life, I heard the distant wings of Eros, beating in time to the barely audible music of the spheres.

Yellow Hare reached out and touched my arm. "Is there anyone else on the ship who can help you perform the ceremony?"

In that touch and that reminder of duty, she shared with me her pure Spartan vision of the world, letting me inside the walls of the city that had been shut to me in youth.

"Mihradarius can," I said. But in the distant music I heard a chord of mournful threnody. "No, I will perform the ceremony myself."

"Yes, Aias," Yellow Hare said.

I waited until 'Elios had orbited far enough from the ship that the sky was only as bright as a harsh hot noon. Then I shed the coverings of head and eye and once again saw the world without the mediation of distorting glass. I donned my purple robes of priesthood and walked to each of the gates in turn to perform the most painful ceremony it had ever been my duty to enact.

I wet the virgin cloth with water and wiped the paint away from the goddesses' eyes until they were sightless sockets of white marble. As each statue in turn went blind, I could feel Athena's presence withdraw from the courtyard and from the ship. But, to my great relief, I could still feel the blessed goddess in my heart. At the end of the ceremony I burned the cloth in a fire newly kindled from olive wood. Only when the last ember of that flame had fallen to ashes did I let the slaves uproot the statues and cart them down to the storage cave, where they would be packed in crates until we could take them back to Earth and properly bury them.

The engineers came to me soon thereafter with the report that my office was in danger of collapse and that most of the documents in the library had fallen from the ship. I blame the Fates for the unpleasant irony that the only safe structure remaining on the hill was Aeson's office, now occupied by Anaxamander. I ordered the slaves to bring the scrolls from my office to my cave, and had a messenger inform the security chief that I would be working down there from now on.

Yellow Hare and I returned to my home, which had suffered some damage in the battle. Furniture had been toppled. All the papers had fallen out of their pigeonholes and were strewn about the floor. My stool and sleeping couch were both splintered. We waited in silence while the slaves finished cleaning up, replacing the broken furniture and bringing down my office supplies.

I wanted to speak to Yellow Hare, but Athena required my attention, filling my heart with her presence and my thoughts with the memory of her vanishing eyes. The goddess did not leave me until I fell asleep exhausted from the strain of worship. That night I dreamed again of being a dolphin swimming in the deep ocean tides.

I woke to the sharp taste of rarefied air and a slight shuddering in the floor that meant the ship was flying under the tertiary impellers, not very fast but enough to make walking about the ship difficult.

"How long have we been under way?" I asked Yellow Hare, who, of course, was awake, armored, and watching me from beside the stairway.

"Kleon called 'brace for speed' two hours ago," she said. "I thought about waking you, but you were thrashing in your sleep as if you were in the grip of a god, and I did not want to disturb your communion."

"You honor me," I said as I sat up, and I could tell from the bow of her head and the slight smile on her lips that she had heard all the meanings I put into those words.

She handed me my command robes, which I donned, and we walked carefully out onto the injured surface of *Chandra's Tear* and bowward toward Kleon's tower. The ship rocked and skipped irregularly as it flew across the sky, making it necessary to step gingerly.

As we rounded the fore-edge of the hill, I saw to my amazement and horror that a crew of engineers and slaves was carving up the ruins of the amphitheater and carrying away the debris on float carts. Agile men, used to handling the twisting bulk of heavy water drills and the burning edges of unwieldy fire planes in dangerous conditions, teetered on unsteady feet as they cut away sections of the stage.

"Stop work!" I shouted. "Put down your tools and move away from there."

The foreman turned to look, saw that I was the one giving the orders, and pulled his crew out of the crumbling edifice. Just in time. One of the high tiers of seats, weakened by the dragon's fire and the high-pressure water of the stone carvers, fell over and shattered into a cascade of rocks that bombarded the stage where the men had been working.

"Who ordered you to do this?" I asked.

"We thought you had, sir," the foreman said. "Kleon said he was relaying the commander's instructions."

Anaxamander! I thought.

"No repairs are to be done at speed," I said. "Is that clear?"

"Clear, sir! Should we relay that order to the other crews?"

"What other crews?"

"The ones working on the impellers."

"The impellers! Get those men back on the ship!"

"Yes, sir!"

The crew dispersed to convey my orders, and Yellow Hare and I continued our frustratingly slow walk to Kleon's tower. The guards at the base saluted hesitantly and asked if there was any new word about Aeson. I shook my head and passed into the navigator's sanctum.

Yellow Hare and I found Kleon seated in the control chair. He was staring out over the bow of *Chandra's Tear* at the gleaming phalanx of tertiary impellers and whistling the Pythagorean scales over and over again.

"Kleon! Why are we at speed?"

"Aias! What? I thought you had approved . . . I mean . . . Mihradarius found the Aphroditean matter for the net in the wreckage. He said there was no need to stay. Then Anaxamander came to see me. He told me to cast off and make for 'Elios. He said we had to get away from Aphrodite quickly. I thought that you had to have ratified the orders before he gave them to me."

I took a deep breath of clarifying air and pulled the fangs of anger from my voice.

"Kleon," I said, "I would never give an order to fly and repair the ship at the same time."

"I didn't think you would," he said. "But Anaxamander asked me if it was possible. I had to tell him we could do it."

"Did you tell him how many men would be injured or killed clearing away the debris and fixing the impellers?"

"Yes, but he said this was a military operation and fatalities were to be expected. I didn't know what to do. I thought you had approved."

"I didn't," I said. "And from now on, I want you to double-check Anaxamander's orders with me."

"Yes, Aias," he said. "What should I do now?"

"Stop the ship, then send out the repair crews."

"Thank you, Commander," he said. Kleon turned to the speaking tube and called, "Brace for stop."

He retracted the tertiary impellers, and the ship slowed into a lazy orbit a few hundred miles above the sphere of Aphrodite.

"Aias," Kleon said, hesitantly. "What do I say to Anaxamander if he comes around with more orders?"

"Tell him that you are not in his line of command!"

"Yes, Aias," Kleon said, but I could hear his fear of the security chief.

Yellow Hare and I left the tower and walked aft. The unaugmented natural motion of the ship caressed my feet, soothing me. A growl in my stomach reminded me that I had not eaten since before the attack, so we bypassed the hill and made for the commissary.

The slaves were very slow serving us, but extremely apologetic about it. Several of them had been injured in the battle, and the tunnel from the storage cavern to the kitchens had suffered a minor cave-in. I settled for a loaf of day-old bread, a cold chicken, and some dried figs. Yellow Hare ate cold venison and fresh squash.

We reclined on slightly battered couches and ate in silence while slaves ran in and out, taking meals to the now safely working repair crews. But halfway through our meal a soldier ran into the commissary from the direction of the hill, came over to my couch, and started talking without even a salute.

"Commander Anaxamander wants to see you now!"

Commander Anaxamander? "Tell Security Chief Anaxamander I'll be with him presently," I said.

"Now!" The man paused for a moment. "Sir," he added.

Yellow Hare put down her knife and plate and stepped between my couch and the soldier. The man turned pale and took a pace backward.

"Commander Aias said he would be along presently," she said in a voice that could have frozen fire.

Sweat broke out on the man's forehead. "My orders are to bring him immediately."

"There's no need to chastise the soldier, Captain Yellow Hare," I said, emphasizing her rank. "He is just doing his duty."

I waved to one of the slaves, who brought me a bowl of water in which I washed my hands. The soldier grew increasingly nervous as I took my time to clean up. But he did not dare say a word with Yellow Hare's piercing gold eyes fixed on him.

"We will now leave," I said at last. "I think it is time Anaxamander learned the limits of his command."

Yellow Hare and I accompanied the soldier to the hilltop. Most of the debris had been cleared away, but no one was working to repair the library or my office.

Anaxamander was sitting in Aeson's plain granite office, on Aeson's plain oak stool, in front of Aeson's plain pine writing table, drinking from Aeson's black-figure wine bowl decorated with the marriage of Gaea and Ouranous.

"You are dismissed, Captain Yellow Hare," Anaxamander said without looking up or acknowledging my presence.

"No," she said.

Now he looked up, an expression of disbelief at her disobedience carved onto his aquiline face. "As military commander of *Chandra's Tear*, I gave you an order, Captain."

"Acting Commander Anaxamander," she said. "I am not part of this ship's chain of command. If I were, then as the only active Spartan officer remaining I would be sitting behind that desk, not you. My orders come directly from the Archons and only they can countermand them."

At the cold reminder that he was no Spartan, Anaxamander's face soured. He turned away from Yellow Hare to face me. He started to speak, but I interrupted.

"Anaxamander, I know you've never held a command before, so I thought I should clear away some of your misconceptions. Kleon is one of my subordinates; you are not to give him orders. Furthermore, I decide when this ship flies, and I decide when repairs are done."

"We were attacked," the Security Chief said. "We needed to leave Aphrodite quickly."

"Then you should have talked to me about it!" I said. "That is how dual command works and has worked since the Delian League was founded." He was about to respond but I did not give him time to even draw breath. "Another thing, Acting Commander. Protocol dictates that if you wish to ask me to a meeting, you send a messenger slave with a request, not a soldier with an order. Now, what was it you wanted to speak to me about?"

"A military matter," he said.

"Very well," I said, I sat down on the stool in front of the desk. "Now, what is this military matter?"

He shoved a sheet of papyrus across the desk. "Sign this and affix your seal."

I looked over the paper, rolled it up, and tossed it on the floor. "You are not going to execute Ramonojon," I said.

"Too many of our soldiers have died because of that spy."

"Ramonojon had nothing to do with this," I said, holding my voice steady. "He was in the brig when the ship was attacked."

The Security Chief leaned back and studied me with angry

eyes. "Why are you still defending that traitor Ramonojon?" he asked.

"I regret that you do not understand," I said. "This meeting is concluded."

I stood up and left, followed by Yellow Hare.

"Now what?" my bodyguard asked.

"I have to talk to Mihradarius."

We found the Persian by the sun net assembly. He was watching his staff as they loaded the bales of spun Aphroditean matter into the hopper of the knitting machines, where the threads would be woven together and coiled into the strands of the sun net. As the first green cords emerged from the far end of the long bronze extruding tube, Mihradarius instructed the twenty knitters in how to draw out the cables and then join them to the already completed Selenean and 'Ermean sections stowed in the large containment box next to the trolley.

"Come with me," I said to Mihradarius when he had finished his explanation.

"Can it wait, Commander? I have to make sure this is working."

"Now!"

He turned to face me, his thick eyebrows raised in surprise. "Yes, Commander."

We stepped aside, letting the wind cover the sound of our voices so the straining ears of his workers would not be able to overhear us.

"Mihradarius," I said, "you're my second in line. Why didn't you intervene when Anaxamander started ordering Kleon around?"

"I'm sorry, Aias, I thought the Security Chief had your consent."

"Did you actually think I would do something as foolish as order repairs while we were flying?"

He looked down, not wanting to meet my gaze. "To be honest, Aias, I didn't think about it."

"Mihradarius, Anaxamander is a power-hungry idiot. He has

just proven that as long as he is military commander of this ship, he will continually try to steal my authority. I am counting on your assistance in stopping him."

"Yes, Commander," he said. "Is there anything else you want from me?"

"Yes. No battle kite has ever reached this sphere before; they were always stopped by our patrols around Selene. Turn that brilliant mind of yours toward finding out how they did it."

Mihradarius sputtered in disbelief. "How am I supposed to know how the Middlers do anything?"

"Calm yourself," I said. "I don't expect a definite answer, just some guesses based on what we know of their technical capacities."

"That I can do," he said. "Thank you for your confidence, Aias."

"You are most welcome, Mihradarius. Now, if you will excuse me, I have to return to work."

"Yes, Commander."


I spent the next few days making clear to Anaxamander where his authority ended and mine began. In response to this clear delineation, he began to show off his own power. He tightened security to a ridiculous extent, knowing that I could do nothing to stop him. Guards patrolled continuously, and a constant escort of moon sleds flew patrols around the ship to make sure no more battle kites caught us unawares. Fatigue took hold of the overworked soldiers and their morale deteriorated.

Helpless to affect this terrible style of military command, Yellow Hare and I found ourselves mingling talk of Aeson in with the rest of our conversation, hoping by our memories of him to sway the Fates that they might restore him to health.

Over dinner one evening after a long day spent countermanding Anaxamander's encroachment on the repair work, we sat leaning against the aft wall of my cabin drinking bowls of honeyed rose water. I told her about my early days on the ship and how my friendship with Aeson grew from his gently helping me learn how to command, and my long lectures to him about the planets and the harmony of their movements. Yellow Hare seemed quite pleased with these stories, and related to me her meeting with Aeson at the Olympics and the mutual respect they gained for one another both in practice bouts and strategic discussions.

"It's strange," I said. "For all the good Aeson has done for me during my early days on the ship, the most important thing Aeson did for me was very recent."

"What did he do?" Yellow Hare asked as she lit her pipe and sucked in the aromatic smoke.

"He gave me a new perspective on Sparta."

"What perspective is that?"

"That you are the true Spartan, not my father."

"I thank you and Aeson for the honor, but I do not understand what you mean."

I told her the story of my failure at the Spartan military college and how my father turned away from me because of it.

"Your father did what?" Yellow Hare clenched her fist; the divine fires returned to her eyes and the mantle of the gods fell across her shoulders. "How dare he offend against the honor of the city like that!"

I was stunned by her vehemence, but family duty required me to respond. "Offend against Sparta? My father?"

"Aeson was too gentle in his condemnation," she said. "Your father's actions are nothing short of sacrilege."

"But—"

"Spartan training is for those destined to lead in war. There is no disgrace in failing our tests. It only means that the Fates have not given you the soul of a born warrior. We do not expect everyone to succeed, and we are not so foolish as to demand that the Fates bestow similar souls on our sons and daughters."

"But—"

"No, Aias," Yellow Hare said, and I could hear 'Era, goddess of Sparta, speaking through her. "Aeson spoke the truth. It is your father, not you, who fails to live up to the standards of my city."

Her words and the divine blessing that lay within them filled me with a sudden awareness of the greatness of Sparta's spirit, the holiness of the Spartans' single purpose, and the glory they gave to heaven's queen on the field of battle.

I bowed my head to both woman and goddess, and handed them a bowl full of libation.

The repair work took a total of eight days, during which the debris was cleared up, cannon batteries were redistributed, and remaining primary impellers were evenly divided between the port and starboard arrays. Only when I had formally sealed the last repair report did I gave Kleon permission to begin flying us toward the sun. With only half the proper number of primaries, we flew considerably slower than before, but still far faster than we would have without the Ares impellers. Kleon proposed a schedule of four hours of speed out of every twelve, which I reluctantly agreed to. It was much more stressful than our earlier schedule, but we would reach 'Elios only five days behind schedule.

Two days after we set off, my work was disturbed by an unexpected visit from Clovix, the chief slave.

"Commander, I have some information you might be interested in," he said.

"Might be?"

"Unofficially interested." His eyes fixed on the floor of my cave with seeming fascination. "You see, sir, if it became official it would be a security matter, but Commander Anaxamander's official interest might not be as great as your unofficial interest."

Yellow Hare cocked an eyebrow at this convoluted speech, but I understood what the Gaul meant. I dug a purse out of one of my trunks and counted twenty silver drachmas onto my writing table. Clovix stroked his long red mustache for a second as if deliberating the value of his information. Then he picked the coins up and stuck them into a leather pouch concealed within the sleeve of his tunic.

"During the repairs," he said, "one of the slave maintenance crews found a crack inside the well shaft. It's about forty feet down from the storage cavern, ten feet above the waterline of the reservoir. One of the repair slaves thought he saw a small dark cave through the crack. He could not swear to that, of course."

Yellow Hare and I exchanged glances. "Thank you, Clovix," I said. "You may go. Don't mention this to anyone."

"Of course, Commander," he said as he climbed the stairs out of my cave.

I turned a bitter smile to Yellow Hare. "As I said, there are advantages to having the most corrupt slave in the League."

"The proper thing to do," she said, her voice as emotionless as the day I met her, "is to pass this information on to Security."

"Security is Anaxamander," I said, discomforted by her sudden withdrawal. "He'll find some way to twist this into proof of Ramonojon's guilt. I have two duties, Yellow Hare. I must fulfill them both."

"Then what do you wish to do, Commander?"

I gripped my hands together and cracked my knuckles, preparing them for unaccustomed physical effort. "Search that cave. It must be where the transmitter is hidden."

She said nothing.

"Yellow Hare," I said, "I must do this. It is my duty."

She nodded slowly, and I felt some return of the spirit that had grown between us.

"But," I said, "you will not let me search that cave alone, will you?"

"No," she said.

"Then the matter is yours to decide. If your duty requires that I pass this on to Anaxamander, I will."

"No, Aias," she said after considering the matter for some moments. "I have sworn to obey you in your search for the spy. If you can reconcile this act with your duties as commander, then I will follow you."

"You honor me," I said.

Without another word, we went to the storage cave. A few more coins slipped to Clovix bought us some privacy as he sent the slaves scurrying about a variety of not-really-necessary tasks, away from where we were working. From an equipment crate

Yellow Hare took several ropes and some grapples while I searched a box of spare dynamicists' gear until I found a long evacuated hose with a sharpened iron tip.

"What is that?" Yellow Hare asked.

"A handheld water drill."

Yellow Hare and I lowered ourselves down the side of the wet, silvery well, having secured the ropes to the grapples and the grapples to two of the bronze rings embedded in the granite lip for the convenience of repair workers. The descent was easy for Yellow Hare, and I had done enough mountain climbing as a youth in India to follow her without too much trouble.

Forty feet down we found the crack, an inch-wide scar in the gleaming moon rock. And, as reported, there was a dark cave beyond it. I could see the slight wavering of night blankets and a hint of silver sheen behind them, but I could not make out any details.

"Hold me steady," I told Yellow Hare. She braced her legs against the far side of the well and gripped me tightly around the waist. I dropped the intake end of the hose into the well. There was a splash, and a moment later, water sucked out of the reservoir through the rarefied air in the tube started gushing out the iron tip in a sharp thin stream. Armed with water and metal, I began to methodically enlarge the crack into a hole.

I was not used to that kind of work, but still, after half an hour, I had managed to excavate a hole large enough for us to clamber through.

Yellow Hare crawled in first, unhooking herself from the rope, then slipping through the gap like an eel through coral. I climbed after her, but I did not untie myself until I was standing on solid ground. As I stepped through the opening, Yellow Hare tore down one of the night blankets, flooding the cramped den with silver light. It was a rough-hewn cave eight feet long, seven feet wide, and five feet high. The floor was uneven, and bits of rough rock jutted out from the walls and ceiling. It was all too crude to have been carved by a professional dynamicist.

The only furnishings were rolled-up bolsters of cloth, no doubt stolen from our stores, strewn about the floor to give the occupants some protection from the ship's speed.

Yellow Hare told me to stand in a corner while she searched the cave.

"Two people have been living in this cave for at least a month," she announced after a few minutes of poring over the carpets, the bolsters, and the blankets. "But there is no sign of them having eaten anything."

Two stowaways on my ship? Under the nose of our so-called Security Chief. "They must have been Middlers," I said, restraining my anger, "living off alchemical food pills."

Yellow Hare nodded absently and started walking around the perimeter of the cave, tapping the walls gently with the pommel of her sword. There was a hollow clang halfway along the port wall. She stopped and with the blade of her knife pried out a thin piece of moon rock six inches high and two feet long. Behind this false panel was a niche lined with wadded-up cloth, and nestled in it was a block of glass that exactly matched Doctor Z's description of a transmitter.

"Got them," I said.

Yellow Hare shook her head. "They left this room about four hours ago."

"How did they leave? I don't see any doors."

She continued wall tapping and behind another false panel found a concealed tunnel. This passage was also rudely carved and a mere two feet across, uncomfortable to crawl through to say the least.

"Follow me," Yellow Hare said. "And be careful."

We crawled through the narrow, straight tunnel, scraping hands and knees on the ragged moonstone. After several minutes we reached a dead end. Yellow Hare pushed on the cul-de-sac until the stone blocking the exit gave way.

We emerged into a square pit that contained a wide steel pole, perched on top of which was a large golden sphere. The air around the ball was clear and bright; it had to be made of fire-gold. It took me only a second to realize I was looking at one of the ship's lift balls, and we were in the bottom of its holding pit.

"Climb out of there," a voice called from above. I nodded to

Yellow Hare, and she preceded me up the maintenance stairs that had been cut in an ascending spiral in the walls of the pit.

We stepped out onto the surface of *Chandra's Tear*. I stretched my back muscles and heard a harsh creak in my spine. I turned to the voice that had called us up and was surprised to see, not an individual soldier or even a squad of four, but a dozen of Anaxamander's personal security guards, their throwers drawn and pointed at me and Yellow Hare. Behind this armed phalanx stood Anaxamander and, to my astonishment, Mihradarius.

Anaxamander pointed at us and orated to the invisible audience he always seemed to be speaking to. "Aias of Tyre. Yellow Hare of the Xeroki. I arrest you on charges of treason."

"That is a ridiculous accusation," I said.

"I suspected you from the first moment you defended Ramonojon," he said. "And now we have found the place where you hid your equipment. That is all the evidence we need."

"Aias, you are hereby relieved of command." The Security Chief turned to his left. "Mihradarius, you will take scientific command of this project."

To my amazement, instead of protesting this absurdity, the Persian merely nodded, his face as placid as a statue of a god receiving a sacrifice. In that instant I realized who the spy was, and what a monumental act of folly I had committed in trusting him.

Yellow Hare, meanwhile, had been studying the postures of the guards, and was bracing herself to leap forward. In a flash I realized she was about to lay down her life to give me a chance to escape. I grabbed her arm. "No Spartan self-sacrifice," I whispered. "I need you alive!"

She looked at me with those cat's eyes of hers. I could feel the waves of her anger at the affront Anaxamander was committing against both of us and the honor of the League. I knew she wanted to kill him, and I was confident that she could have reached him through that line of defenders; but she would not survive for long after he was dead.

"I need you alive," I repeated.

Slowly, she nodded. "I accept your command," she said.

She turned toward the line of soldiers and favored them with a glance that must have filled their souls with terror. She reached across her back for her thrower. The barrels of their weapons wavered; but instead of drawing, Yellow Hare slipped off her weapon strap and placed her thrower on the ground. Then with disinterested grace she divested herself of sword and dagger as if it did not matter to her whether or not she was armed.

The relieved guards led us away and locked us in the same cell with Ramonojon.

When we entered, Ramonojon opened his eyes and looked up from his cross-legged posture. "What has happened?" he asked.

The door slammed behind us and the key turned in the lock. I smiled wanly and sat down next to Ramonojon while Yellow Hare prowled near the doorway. "Anaxamander has decided that we are also spies."

"Ah. I see." Ramonojon closed his eyes.

# K

From the new perspective born of my sudden imprisonment, it was easy to see the errors I had made; trusting Mihradarius because he was an Athenian; believing that there were limits to Anaxamander's ambition because of the narrowness of his mind; and the most grievous error of all, thinking that *Chandra's Tear* was my ship given to me by the Archons and that only they could take it away from me. I had relied too much on my position and too little upon my mind.

But throughout my self-castigation, Athena whispered condolence and hinted that perhaps there was some wisdom to be gleaned from my situation. I had just begun to contemplate what that wisdom might be when Ramonojon's curiosity overwhelmed his new-learned Buddhist restraint and he broke the quiet with a question.

"Why did Anaxamander arrest you?" he asked. "Could anyone, even he, believe that you two are traitors?"

"To one like him," Yellow Hare said, keeping her gaze fixed rigidly on the iron door, "the truth does not matter. All he sees is the chance for glory."

"I don't understand," Ramonojon said.

"That is because you are not a Spartan," she said. Her words carried no rebuke; instead they held the offer of her divinely won understanding to those of us not so blessed.

"But Anaxamander isn't a Spartan either," I said.

"True," she said. "But he thinks he should be one, and he thinks he knows what being Spartan is."

"Say on," I said, feeling Athena's prompting.

"All men know that the gods reward doers of great deeds with glory and the place of heroes."

"Of course," I said.

"In Sparta we are made capable of doing great deeds in war; therefore, many of us have received those divine rewards."

She stood up and ran her hands along the door and the moon rock wall in which its hinges were buried. A god moved across her face, one I had never seen in her countenance before. 'Ermes, god of thieves, was whispering to my Yellow Hare and she, warrior pure, was listening to that must subtle of divinities.

After a few moments of communion, the god left her and she resumed speaking as if there had been no interruption.

"Many soldiers who are not of Sparta reverse the divine course; they seek to do great deeds for the sake of the reward of glory rather than for the greatness of the deeds themselves. Such men are not given positions of command because they are a danger to their missions and their underlings. Anaxamander is such a man."

"So, when Aeson was wounded," I said, "Anaxamander saw the only opportunity he would be given to earn the seat of glory. And to do that he tried to take complete control of the ship. And when that failed . . ."

"He removed what he believed were the only two obstacles to his desire," she said. "You and me."

"But isn't he worried about the real spies?" Ramonojon asked.

I looked up to see what she had to say about that. Yellow Hare shook her head sadly at Ramonojon. "He believes that he has the real spy," she said. "He thinks that with you in prison all will go well with Sunthief, and that once we return to Earth, he will be able to simply hand you over for trial and have Aias and myself released. He thinks the glory for Sunthief will go to him and that his indiscretions will be pardoned. His thoughts are filled with a single image: a hero's nine-foot-tall blue statue standing in the main square of Sparta next to Lykurgus, Leonidas, and Alexander, facing the gates of the military college."

She drummed her fingers idly against her empty scabbard. "He is wrong, of course. When we return, the Archons will commit him to death for usurpation and his name will be wiped from the rolls of the army."

"There is one thing you omitted from your admirable analysis," I said.

"What is that?"

"That Anaxamander did not think of this all on his own. He is being advised by the real spy, Mihradarius."

My words pulled her out of her reverent awareness of Spartan spirit. "An Athenian scholar?" she said.

"I believe Aias is right," Ramonojon said. "It is much more likely that Mihradarius colluded in falsifying the demonstration of the sun net than that he would make an error on a matter of Ouranology."

"How did he falsify the test?" Yellow Hare asked Ramonojon.

"Middler technology, I suppose," Ramonojon said. "He must have used that equipment you found me with when you arrested me. But I have no idea how Mihradarius learned to use it."

"He did not have to," I said, and told him about the stowaways.

"But why falsify the test?" Yellow Hare asked.

"In order to destroy the ship with a dangerous sun net," Ramononojon said.

I nodded my concurrence. "The attacks and assassination attempts were meant to distract us while Mihradarius built the means of our destruction in plain sight."

"I see," Yellow Hare said. She steepled her hands together, shut her eyes and resumed her impersonation of Athena Nike. "If that be the case, Commander, we must escape."

"Agreed," I said. I stood up straight and spoke with the breath of command. "Captain Yellow Hare."

My bodyguard faced me and saluted.

"The rescue of prisoners is a military matter. As the senior Spartan officer present, I charge you with the duty of effecting our liberation. Chief Dynamicist Ramonojon and I place our skills and knowledge at your disposal for this mission."

"I am honored, Commander Aias," she said. "I swear before 'Era that I shall carry out the orders you have given me."

For the next two days Yellow Hare had us save most of the water the guards gave us with our meager meals. We stored the collected water in her empty scabbard, which she had been permitted to keep by our unwise captors.

"In a Spartan jail," she said, "they would have stripped us naked and poured water down to us through a small hole in the roof. Much more difficult to escape from."

"Could you?" I asked.

"No one leaves commando school without doing so," she said, and her golden eyes locked with mine and filled my heart with confidence.

During the days of our imprisonment the guards never opened the cell door, not daring to face the danger of a captured Spartan; instead, they slipped plain wooden bowls of food and water under a lockable flap in the iron barrier. I tried to talk to the guards several times, trying to find a crack in Anaxamander's command structure. But those assigned to watch our cell were always security staff, those with a personal loyalty to Anaxamander. I suspected that he was keeping away from me all those soldiers whose allegiance he could not rely on. And I began to wonder how secure his control of the ship was.

When her scabbard was full, Yellow Hare set in motion the plan she had devised with the aid of 'Ermes. First she took the small fire box she used to light her pipe out of her pouch, extinguished the flame, and removed the thin square of fire-gold from the lid of the box.

With laboratory precision, Yellow Hare tore a strip of leather from her greaves, rolled it into a hollow tube, and glued the long edges together with gum extracted from the seals in her sandals. Then she placed the fire-gold inside the tube and waited for the air within to rarefy.

"A water drill?" I asked.

She nodded. "It is an axiom of my city that anything Athens creates, Sparta can turn to war."

For the first time in my life I was pleased by that saying.

"Now," she whispered, "I need you two to start a loud argument. One of those noisy debates Akademics are so fond of."

And for the first time in days, Ramonojon and I smiled.

We began quietly enough, discussing abstruse points of celestial dynamics, then gradually raised our voices until we were shouting formulas back and forth.

Meanwhile, Yellow Hare knelt next to the door and poured the contents of her scabbard through her improvised drill. A stream of high-pressure water gushed out and struck the rock that covered the door hinges. Chips of gleaming moonstone flew from the wall and circled the room like a spiral of snowflakes. Ramonojon and I continued our shouting until both of the steel hinges were exposed. Yellow Hare put down the drill and set to work silently removing the pins from the hinges.

When she was done, Ramonojon and I wound down our argument, finally coming to an agreement on a matter of complete indifference to both of us.

Yellow Hare motioned us over to the holes she had dug in the wall. "Take hold of the lower hinge and pull it out while I do the same with the top."

Together Ramonojon and I managed to exert as much strength as Yellow Hare did on her own. The three of us pulled in unison and the heavy iron door wobbled on its base, then crashed inward, clanging like a bell against the floor of our prison. The two guards stationed outside barely had time to be shocked before Yellow Hare had leaped on them and knocked them unconscious.

My bodyguard quickly relieved the soldiers of their throwers, swords, knives, and keys to the brig doors. Then she bound and gagged them with their armor straps and locked them in an unoccupied cell.

"Stay here," she said, and ran noiselessly up the tunnel. A few minutes later she came back and waved us to follow her onto the surface of the ship.

It was late evening, and the summer constellations looked down upon us from the distant Sphere of Fixed Stars. Overhead the purple orb of Zeus occluded the heart of the Scorpion, while Ares and Khronos conferred secretly in the arms of the Kentaur. *Chandra's Tear* glowed bright defiance against the darkness of the goddess Night, but I did not welcome the revealing light of my ship, for she was showing me to my enemies.

"We need a base of operations," I said to Yellow Hare, who was stooped over the insensate bodies of the three guards assigned to the brig tunnel exit, methodically stripping them of their weapons. "Where would you suggest we secrete ourselves?"

"The storage cavern," she replied as she relieved the last soldier of his sword.

But fifty yards of brightly glowing open space stood between us and the nearest tunnel down into the cavern, and four soldiers guarded that entrance. We hid from their view around the side of the hillock in which lay the door down to the brig, but the moment we started toward them they would see us.

Yellow Hare drew one of the throwers she had taken from the guards and aimed; I hoped she was not going to shoot the soldiers, who were only doing their duty. I should not have worried. She set her sights on the top of the hill, aiming toward the back wall of Aeson's office, and fired a spray of tetras that ricocheted off the marble colonnade. The sounds of the shots rang through the clear air, and just as they struck, Yellow Hare screamed out a frighteningly real cry of agony that echoed piercingly across the ship.

Two of the guards ran for where the shots hit. The other two remained behind; they drew their throwers and faced away from each other. Neither was looking at the entrance they were supposed to be guarding.

Yellow Hare fired again. This time she aimed over the heads of the guards so her shot would fly into the cave. The clangs of metal on moon rock resounded through the underground, multiplying through echoes into the report of a thousand throwers. The two remaining guards spun around and darted down toward the storage cavern. We ran across the now unwatched open space and reached the tunnel. Yellow Hare pulled us into one of the heavy-equipment niches carved into the sides of the passage. This particular alcove held a moon sled chained to the floor. At my bodyguard's direction we crouched up against the wall, hiding behind the floating disk.

For two hours, guards ran back and forth, looking for whatever saboteur was in the storage caverns. Each time a patrol passed us we changed hiding places, ducking behind the fire box of a road grader, then under a float cart, and finally secreting ourselves inside the empty reservoir of a large water drill. Eventually, when the exhausted and confused men returned to their stations, we slipped down the tunnel, past the unwatchful eyes of the slaves, and hid inside a large empty crate that had once held stonecutting tools.

"Where do we go from here?" I asked Yellow Hare.

"We stay," she said. "This is the safest place from which to act."

I surveyed our empty wooden cell. "We'll need cushioning," I said.

Yellow Hare ducked out and returned a few minutes later with several bolts of wool cloth, which we laid on the floor of the bulky pine box.

Ramonojon and I waited in silence while over the course of an hour Yellow Hare went on foray after foray, stealing food, water, ammunition, and light sources.

Her final trip provided us with a couple of jars of wine and some medical supplies. She laid them carefully in the corner, then with my permission, she curled up to sleep.

Ramonojon leaned back on a bale of cotton linen. "I do not think my teachers would approve of what we are doing."

"What do you mean?" I asked. I opened a bag of figs Yellow Hare had obtained and ate one.

"I cannot seem to cultivate the proper Buddhist detachment."

"Explain," I said, handing him the bag. He took a fig and ate it. His face brightened as he savored the flavor; then he shook his head and resumed chewing with a forced disinterest.

"If I cannot resist the desire for fruit," he said, sighing, "how can I possibly overcome the greater desires?"

I handed him a bag of water and he drank a little. Then, unprompted, he began to talk about Buddhism; how it had begun in India three centuries before Alexander conquered that country; how it took hold in many parts of India, Tibet, and the Middle Kingdom as well as the various smaller lands around that region; and how it was mostly ignored by both empires until a popular form of the religion began to preach pacifism throughout the eastern part of the Delian League and the western lands of the Middle Kingdom.

"This part I know," I said. "Both the League and the Kingdom outlawed the practice of Buddhism and executed anybody found practicing it."

"But Buddhism didn't die," Ramonojon said. "Its monasteries were burned, many of its teachers and adherents killed, and the wearing of a saffron robe was proscribed in both empires. But Buddhism does not need all that ritual. It became a secret religion, still attracting new disciples who felt the futility of the war."

"Are you saying the Buddhist Rebellion is still going on covertly?"

"There never was a Buddhist Rebellion," he said. "There was only a purely passive attempt to try to stop the war by making the people lay down their arms and refuse to fight."

"Most people would regard that as rebellion," I said, keeping a stern neutrality in my voice.

"Whatever you choose to call it," he said, "preaching or rebellion, it failed. My teachers in Xan say that was because the other Buddhist sects do not follow the Tao."

"What does the Tao have to do with this?" I asked. "The Middler science texts all talk about it as some sort of progression of natural actions. How can a natural course relate to the success or failure of a rebellion?"

"The scientific definition is too narrow," he said. "Tao means 'the Way,' the natural process of all things. My sect joined the philosophy of the Tao to that of the Buddha."

"So you understand the meaning of Tao?"

"A little, and not at all the way the Taoist technologists do; my teachers were philosophers, not scientists. They could no more explain the working of a Xi lance than Plato could understand the design of *Chandra's Tear*."

"Philosophers?"

"Yes," Ramonojon said. "Taoist philosophy did not vanish the way Platonism did. When the first 'An emperor drafted the practical Taoists to make weapons, the real Taoists fled into the mountains of Tibet to hide. After the 'rebellion' they encountered some Buddhists who were also hiding, and Xan was born."

"So that is the crime you were concealing," Yellow Hare said, uncoiling from where she slept. She turned her golden eyes toward me and I felt the wrath of the Spartan spirit stab through my heart. "Aias," she said, with a voice as cold as the touch of marble in winter, "how could you defend a Buddhist, a profaner of the gods?"

"Out of friendship," I said quietly, facing her spirit with my own. Slowly, she lowered her gaze, accepting the answer.

"We do not profane," Ramonojon said.

"You deny the divinity of war," she replied.

"No," he said. "We deny the rightness of war; we deny that the soul is made greater by battle."

"That is sacrilege," she said, and laid her hand on the knife that hung from a strap around her neck.

"Enough!" I said. "Yellow Hare, Ramonojon's offenses lie between him and the gods and he will answer for them in a greater tribunal than we can convene. Anaxamander and Mihradarius's crimes are our immediate concern."

Yellow Hare deliberated with herself for a few seconds, then said, "What are your orders, Commander?"

Her question paralyzed me for a moment. For the past two days I had been so intent on escape that I had given no thought to what should be done once we were free. Anaxamander and Mihradarius had to be stopped, of course, but . . .

"The first thing we have to do is get Aeson to safety," I said.

"Why?" Ramonojon asked.

"Now that we're out of the brig, anything the stowaways do will be blamed on us. Killing Aeson would consolidate Anaxamander's control over the ship, which is just what Mihradarius wants."

"Then we should go now," Yellow Hare said. She offered swords and throwers to me and Ramonojon. I took them, but he refused.

"I will not harm anyone," he said.

Yellow Hare glared at him contemptuously, then turned away and noiselessly opened the side of the huge crate. We emerged from our hiding place and slowly made our way aft, creeping low to the ground and darting from crate to crate so none of the slaves would see us. Yellow Hare directed our steps, showing us how to move quietly through the maze of boxes so that we reached the tunnel that led up to the hospital without being heard.

Yellow Hare slipped quietly up the curving passageway to take care of any guards Anaxamander might have posted in the wards. She returned in less than a minute. "Someone has killed the soldiers," she said. "Follow me, but be careful."

We ran up the ramp past four armored corpses, their hearts gashed open by throwing stars.

In the hospital's dispensary we found two doctors and seven orderly-slaves lying on the ground, breathing irregularly. The air was laden with a heavy smell of jasmine and honey; sickly sweet, but alluring like a dewy glade on a summer's day; some sort of alchemical gas. I ran over to a bolt of linen bandages in the far corner, tore off three strips, clamped one over my mouth, and gave the others to Yellow Hare and Ramonojon.

"Take short breaths," I said in a muffled voice.

Yellow Hare wrapped the gauze around her mouth as she darted through the short, arched tunnel that led through the public ward and into the private; Ramonojon and I ran after her, holding our breaths until we needed to gasp in enough air to keep going. In the large circular lying-in area we found doctors, patients, guards, and slaves strewn across the couches and floor. Some of the patients had fallen off their couches as if they had been struggling to rise when the drug-filled air overcame them.

Yellow Hare did not pause to look at this scene, but ran directly into Aeson's room. Ramonojon wanted to help the fallen, but I pulled him along after me into the private ward.

Aeson lay strapped down on the marble operating slab in the center of the room. His eyes were shut and his arms drooped at his sides as if he were dead, but his chest rose and fell with the gentle rhythms of sleep. But Aeson could never have slept through the battle going on right next to him.

To the left of the slab stood Euripos wearing a linen mask across his nose and mouth. In each hand the doctor held a long injection quill dripping with a pale green liquid. The old Roman was using the poisoned feathers to fend off a young Nipponian man in a gray silk gi armed with a curved steel sword and a miniature Xi lance. I would have thought the battle hopeless for Euripos, but the spirit of his city and the warrior-hero Romulos who founded it stood over him, guiding his aged hands as he fought to keep the attacker at bay.

Sword first, Yellow Hare leaped at the assassin. He whirled to meet her, parrying her wide, thick blade with his thin, angled one. She blocked his counterstroke and rolled past him to place herself between him and Euripos. Time froze as the two combatants eyed each other like Akhilleus and 'Ektor across the plains of Troy. Then they jumped toward each other, slicing through space with their swords, two whirlwinds weaving the formerly still air into a storm of iron.

Euripos fell back to give Yellow Hare room to fight, and as he did so the Roman spirit left him and the hero who had saved his commander's life became again a frail old man.

Yellow Hare froze momentarily into stillness; the Nipponian slashed crosswise to decapitate her, but she ducked into a squat and cut upward, sliced into her opponent's left hand, making him drop the lance at his feet. He took a step back, and she swept her leg sideways, kicking the weapon over to me. I grabbed the small wooden box and thrust it into the folds of my robe.

The assassin's black eyes flicked from Yellow Hare to me to Aeson's helpless form, then back to his opponent. He stood frozen in inaction. Yellow Hare sprang into midair and sliced downward with her blade. He turned to parry her, continued his turn, and ran from the battle directly toward me. But instead of cutting me down, he leaped straight over my head. I stabbed upward and felt my sword cut silk and possibly skin. But wounded or not, the assassin landed gracefully and ran out through the public ward.

Yellow Hare ran after him, calling to Euripos as she did so, "Tell Anaxamander there's a Nipponian commando after Aeson."

Ramonojon and I followed her.

"Mars and Romulos go with you," Euripos called after us, gasping out his words through the pungent air.

We chased the assassin out through the curtains of the hospital onto the sunlit surface of the ship. The ship's surface light was overwhelmed by the sun; *Chandra's Tear's* glow had dimmed from glorious silver to bland tin. 'Elios was directly overhead, blinding my ungoggled eyes. I threw my arm above my head to shield myself from the spears of the burning god.

I shielded my eyes as best I could and managed to make out the shape of Yellow Hare chasing the gray-clad man, who wore neither mask nor goggles, but seemed to suffer neither from his own poisoned air nor 'Elios's raging heat. Ramonojon and I charged after them, but we had no hope of catching those running gazelles as they sped sternward. For every step Ramonojon and I took, they took two. I was about to tell Ramonojon to give up the chase when a spray of tetras flew over our heads, followed by a shout from behind us. "Stop!"

"Keep going!" I yelled, grabbing Ramonojon's hand. We turned to port and ran low over the gaming fields, dodging and ducking the shots of guards we did not dare stop to look at. Ramonojon's breathing was ragged. He was too old for this. So was I. After an eternity of running through the heat, we reached the hill and ducked to port of it, into the shadow it now cast from the sun's obscuring light.

Ramonojon and I stood, shaking and wobbly, trying to catch our breaths. The heat was too much for him and he collapsed to the ground. It would not be long before the guards caught us.

A glance aft showed me that Yellow Hare and the assassin had reached the hill country above the laboratories. The Nipponian dove into one of the tunnels and Yellow Hare followed him. That gave me an idea.

"In here," I said, pulling Ramonojon after me. We ran into the now deserted brig tunnel and hid in an empty cell.

We waited silently for hours, listening to the echo of soldiers searching above us. The noise finally died down, and we crept cautiously up the cramped tunnel. Halfway up we found Yellow Hare crouching against the wall.

"What happened to the Nipponian?" I asked.

"He eluded me in the laboratory warren," she said, and I heard the self-accusation in her words. She would accept no excuses for herself, not her lack of protection from the sun, nor the toll the gas must have taken on her. "What are your orders, Commander?"

"Back to our hiding place," I said. "Anaxamander now knows there is a threat to Aeson. He'll have to guard him if he wants to keep the army's loyalty."

Return was uneventful. The storage guards were elsewhere, looking for us or the assassin, so we had only to evade the slaves, who were not at all vigilant.

"Rest," Yellow Hare said to me when we were safely ensconced in our padded crate. "You look exhausted."

That was a suggestion I gratefully accepted. I drank a little water, ate a crust of bread, and curled up to sleep on the linen padding.

An hour or so later, I was awakened by Kleon's voice echoing through the storage cavern. "Brace for speed. Brace for speed. Everyone be in your quarters, strapped in. Oh, and make sure you have enough food and water. Repeat, brace for speed. Commander, wherever you are, I am doing this under Anaxamander's orders."

Anaxamander threatening my navigator? Make sure you have enough food and water? What in Athena's name was going on? Then the ship lurched and we tumbled against the aft wall. My shoulder twisted. I put my hand in my mouth and bit hard on my knuckles to keep from screaming.

It took us ten painful minutes to get into speed positions, braced up against the wall with blankets under us for cushioning. We waited out the usual four hours, during which the pain in my shoulder subsided to a dull throb. But the ship did not slow down. We waited longer, managing to eat a little bread and drink a little water, but the speed and the pressure did not go away.

The constant pain made it impossible to sleep and barely possible to eat. I had no way of telling how long the relentless push of high speed remained pressing my body down. But some time during the flight Mania gripped my mind with perverse, lying visions. I saw myself as Prometheus chained to the cliff. Zeus was interrogating me in Anaxamander's voice, demanding to know who the spy was and why I thought man deserved the gift of fire. I could not answer him; the eagle had torn out my throat.

Then we lurched to a stop and my mind came back to the world. Kleon's voice boomed through my head like the thunderbolt of Zeus. "Solar orbit. Repeat, we have reached the sun. Do not go out onto the ship's surface without protective clothing and goggles. And as for you, Anaxamander, I've done what you wanted, now take your cursed soldiers from my tower."

The sun? Already? "How long were we flying?" I asked through a throat dry and ragged.

"Six days," Yellow Hare said, standing up slowly. She stretched her arms, touched them nimbly to her toes, then straightened up and shook off that weeklong torture.

Ramonojon and I supported each other as we stood. He could barely walk. I had a raging thirst which I tried to quench with water, but it would not go away.

Six days under speed. It made a certain twisted sense. No one on the ship would be able to move under those conditions; not us, not the Middler spies, no one. Anaxamander would be able to use the sun net without anyone having an opportunity to sabotage it.

The one problem with Anaxamander's surprisingly intelligent stratagem was that the net was the only thing on the ship the Middlers would not want to sabotage.

"We have to stop the launch," I said, then gulped down more water.

Yellow Hare nodded grimly. "Wait here. I'll find some cloaks and goggles."

Ramonojon and I nodded gratefully and sank back to the floor. "We don't have much time," I said. My throat felt cracked and dry, and no amount of drink could take away its aridity.

Ramonojon nodded and took a small bite of bread. He chewed painfully through bleeding gums.

Yellow Hare returned in a few minutes. She had three sets of goggles and three hooded cloaks lined with a cooling mesh of airsilver.

"Make for the aft exit," I said after we had donned the protective gear. "Don't bother to hide. We can't worry about whether or not the slaves see us."

Fortunately, the slaves were too busy unstrapping themselves from the walls to care about three people running through the storage cavern. We passed Clovix on our way out the tunnel, but he seemed too bewildered to say anything.

We stepped out onto the surface of *Chandra's Tear* to face a sky filled from horizon to horizon with red-gold fire. So fierce and terrible was its color that it overwhelmed the green filter that covered my face. The light of the sun pierced my eyes and entered my heart, carrying the sun god's voice to my mind. 'Elios spoke to me, as he had been trying to speak since first we set off from Earth, but I had refused to listen until that moment, when I stood a mere two miles from his surface and could no longer ignore him.

He spoke of hubris and até, of the follies of those who had tried to be heroes in defiance of the gods. Bellerophon had only wanted to fly to Olympos, Phaethon had only attempted to guide the path of the sun for one day, Orpheus had only tried to charm the lord of all the dead. But I, who had thought myself reverent, I who had known that the Akademe had turned a blind eye to many affronts to the gods, I had planned to snatch the eternal fire and bring it to Earth to be used as a weapon.

"But my duty to the League," I whispered to him. He brushed that aside with a wave of his fiery hands. Then he spoke again, and his words were sharp and clear; he burned a thought into my heart, carved it with a blade of burning steel, and sealed it with the red-hot point of his spear: Your first duty is to the Good!

"Drop your weapons!" somebody barked. Yellow Hare spun me away from the vision of the sun, but the blessed thought remained, scorching the embers of my heart.

"Aias," Yellow Hare said. "Aias, come back." She pulled my mind once again into the world and I saw in front of me ten guards with evac throwers leveled at us.

"You were right," one of the soldiers said to a man behind them. "They were after the sun net."

Mihradarius strode forward. "The soldier said to drop your weapons."

I looked at Yellow Hare. She slowly put her thrower and her sword on the ground. I dropped my sword as well. Mihradarius told the guards to take us up the hill. We went quietly, but I could see Yellow Hare's brow furrowed in concentration. She looked the guards over one at a time. I could see her deciding not to fight, at least not yet.

At the top of the hill we found Anaxamander talking to a yawning, angry Kleon.

"Caught again, Captain Yellow Hare?" the security chief said. "What would the Spartan war college have to say?"

Yellow Hare looked over at me, forcing Anaxamander to follow her gaze.

"We came to prevent you from launching the net," I said.

"Admission of treason, excellent," Anaxamander said. He gazed up at the sun and spread his arms wide as if to grasp that wall of flame and draw it into himself. But I saw as he obviously did not that 'Elios was poised to spear him.

"You fool," I said. "Mihradarius is the traitor."

"Mihradarius? Sunthief is his crowning glory."

"Sunthief is my crowning folly!" I said. "I bear the responsibility for it. I will answer to the Archons and the gods for its results. But it is not too late for you, Anaxamander. If you launch the net *Chandra's Tear* will shatter, and you will go down in history as Anaxamander the Simpleton. Comedies will be written about your foolishness, and no father will ever name a son Anaxamander again. But if you release us and turn this ship around for Earth, you will be its savior and paeans of praise will be sung to you for preventing Aias's folly."

"Do not seek to save yourself with these useless lies," Anaxamander said. "You will stay here and witness the failure of your treason."

"Aias?" Kleon said. "Is it true?"

"Yes," I said. "The ship will be destroyed."

"Silence!" Anaxamander shouted. He drew his sword and held it to Kleon's back. "You will pilot this ship," he said, and with his free hand he shoved the frightened navigator toward the tower.

Mihradarius watched them go. Then he turned to stare at the statue of Alexander, and mouthed the name of the Zoroastrian Adversary, "Ahriman."

That single word revealed to me in a flash of clarity why he was doing this, showed me the fanatic who had been hiding for years under the mask of Athenian propriety and using his native genius to rise to a high enough place from which to strike. I leaped for him, but four guards grabbed me. "Stop him!" I shouted. "I order you to stop him!" But they were unmoved.

Mihradarius waved to me and walked down the hill toward the sun net. I struggled against the guards but they held me fast.

Six moon sleds specially equipped with thirty-foot-long poles of fire-gold took off from the stern of *Chandra's Tear*, flying sunward. The sleds lined themselves up in two columns like an honor guard, poles pointed inward, creating a corridor of rarefied air that joined my ship to the sun. The golden light glared even brighter, and 'Elios raised his spear to cast it through that lane.

There was a muffled whoosh and two long strands of celestial rope shot out from the net cannon, laced together by thick terrestrial cable. The ropes followed the corridor of air straight and sure toward the sun. The lines reached out like two spreading claws, then pulled inward, striking through the fire into the sun. Their terrestrial components flared away into nothingness, but the indestructible celestial matter plunged through the heart of 'Elios. But the sun god did not scream; instead, he drew back his arm to throw the spear of retribution.

Their mission accomplished, the sleds darted back toward the supposed safety of my doomed ship.

A minute passed as the four-mile-long claws spun themselves into a net, twirled through the guts of 'Elios, and arced out, dragging a half-mile-wide sphere of Olympian fire. For a moment there was a hole in the sun; then the remaining flame flowed back to heal the gash.

The net and its cargo twirled in space, the multitude of motions adding together into an angry dance. First it pulled away, then it doubled back and flew over *Chandra's Tear*, scorching our marble rooftops from a mile up. As the fireball was about to turn again, the trolley was released along its track, pulling the sun fragment into a sedate orbit around our moon fragment.

For one brief moment everything was going as I had originally conceived of it, and I dared to hope that despite all that had happened Sunthief might yet succeed. For that hope I ask the forgiveness of 'Elios.

Then the god let his javelin fly. The ball of fire ceased its natural orbit; it turned in midair and flew straight away from the stern of the ship, nearly pulling the trolley out of its tracks.

*Chandra's Tear* bucked; her aft end was pulled upward toward the sun by the confused motions of the net and the fragment. The force threw us over on our backs as the fragment made anther pass overhead, pulling the ship around and about. The ball of celestial flame was a wild horse, dragging my ship like a hapless chariot that had been foolishly yoked to a steed untamable.

# λ

The sun fragment twirled across the fire-painted sky like a bull dancer in a ring. *Chandra's Tear* flew after it, pulled helplessly toward blazing oblivion as the ball of celestial flame tried to reunite with 'Elios. The guards, unprepared for the sudden shock of unexpected movement, tumbled into a heap at the base of Alexander's statue. No longer constrained to stand under the weapons of the soldiers, I ducked down and rolled across the shaking hill until I reached the circle of couches. Ramonojon and Yellow Hare followed my example. My bodyguard and I slid under one couch and huddled together clutching the hot marble legs. Ramonojon dove under the next couch and copied our actions.

In the crimson sky ahead of us, the fireball made a sudden turn downward, twirling *Chandra's Tear* about its central axis until our bow pointed upward. The pointed tip of my teardrop ship became a spearpoint aimed at the heart of the sun, while her broad, arced stern looked down through the spheres, down toward the tiny dot of Earth that lay at the center of the universe, tugging inexorably at our terrestrial bodies, calling us home. A score of crewmen who had assembled at the trolley to watch the triumph of Sunthief heeded that call and fell screaming off the ship. The lucky ones flew into the sun fragment and burned up instantly; the rest tumbled helplessly through space down the eighty-thousand-mile stretch of emptiness that lay between the spheres of 'Elios and Aphrodite.

The fragment made a right angle turn to port, violating all the laws of celestial motion. The impossible motion pulled *Chandra's Tear* toward the blade-thin edge of the crystal sphere that held 'Elios in his orbit. I offered what I was sure would be a final prayer for forgiveness to the sun god as my ship hurtled toward the celestial knife of sacrifice.

Then the sky grew sharp and bright as two lines of gold spears appeared across our bow, thrusting out into space: the secondary and tertiary impellers. Kleon's voice echoed through the ship. "Brace for speed."

"Daidalos bless you, Kleon," I whispered.

A moment later, Kleon deployed the port ballast and starboard lift balls; the ship rolled onto its side, so that instead of our stern, our broad-bottomed keel faced the sphere's edge. There was a jarring scrape, and a noise like chalk on slate reverberated through the underside of the ship. Shards of moon rock were carved away from our bottom as we turned away from the edge of indestructible crystal and began to fly sideways toward the sun, fleeing Skylla to be caught by Kharybdis.

But Kleon had not saved us from one death to commit us to another. He retracted the starboard phalanx of impellers, trying to pull us away from 'Elios and face us toward the inner spheres. But the sun fragment turned again; now leaping upward toward the stars, it pulled us stern first past the sun and through the gap in the crystal sphere.

More gold appeared on the bow as Kleon deployed the primary impellers, trying to oppose the force of the fragment and pull the ship back down toward Earth. Drawn upward by the fragment and down by Kleon, my ship screamed like a man being torn apart by wild horses. *Chandra's Tear* sang out her agony, chorusing the Pythagorean chord of the moon, the high unwavering howl of a terrified child torn from its mother.

The scream shook the ground like the wrath of Poseidon, bringing forth a wave that ripped like an earthquake from fore to aft across *Chandra's Tear*. The quake shook the navigation tower, splintered what was left of the amphitheater, then shattered barracks and dormitories and cannonades as it passed sternward.

"Hold on!" I shouted as the wave came up the fore end of the hill, but whether I was warning Yellow Hare, Ramonojon, or myself, I could not say.

The shaking moon rock exploded the colonnade as if the marble columns were hot glass suddenly immersed in freezing water. A cloud of marble dust rose up, crowning the brow of the hill in a fog of stone chips. Then the harmonic reached the circle of couches. The solid marble legs took in the shock and transmitted it to my body. My hands lost their purchase, and I tumbled away toward the front of the hill, clutching to no avail at the angry smoothness of the ground.

But a strong hand grabbed my left wrist and yanked me backward. I could feel a tracery of scars in the palm that held me in an iron grip. It pulled me up and helped me grasp again the legs of the couch.

"I have you," Yellow Hare said into my ear. I wiped the dust from my goggles, then blinked to clear away the stinging pain of the light. I saw a wavering movement out of the corner of my eye, and shouted, "Run!" to Ramonojon.

He scrambled out from under his sanctuary just as the statue of Aristotle toppled from its pedestal, smashing down on the marble couch. The scholar's statue broke into a dozen pieces; his head splintered into dust. The little globe model of the universe he had so proudly carried flew off into space, freed from its terrestrial constraints. But his left shoulder and right leg hit Ramonojon from behind. My poor friend collapsed under the weight, screaming, his arm pinned under Aristotle's shoulder.

"Stay here!" Yellow Hare said as she ducked from our place of safety.

"No!" I followed her onto the rocking ground. Yellow Hare ran forward, keeping her footing despite the random tilting of the ship. Knowing I could never match her agile gait, I crawled after her across the few feet that separated me from where Ramonojon lay pinned, howling in inarticulate pain.

Yellow Hare knelt down beside Ramonojon, bracing herself between Aristotle's errant leg and torso.

"Take hold of him," she said as I arrived. "I'll move the statue."

Ramonojon was breathing raggedly. His trapped arm was bent in ways it had never been meant to turn. I reached around his waist and leaned back, ready to pull. Then Yellow Hare heaved the stone, rolling the old scholar's remnants off the hill.

I pulled Ramonojon out, and he cried out again, his voice mingling with the ship's harmonic keening. As if in answer to the screams of its creator, *Chandra's Tear* howled a deep note of suffering, then spun around again, pulling our fore end downward to the sun. The three of us tumbled backward. Yellow Hare grabbed hold of a couch leg and pulled Ramonojon and me to safety.

The line of gold on our fore end dimmed and I realized that Kleon had angled the impellers down toward the underside of the ship, turning the ship upside down. An inverted eagle, we swooped upward, climbing once again away from the sun. It seemed that Ikaros's fate was not to be ours.

But that last abrupt maneuver was too much for my poor ship. The scream of *Chandra's Tear* rose to an agonized pitch. The surface of the ship split at the fore end of the hill. And through the spreading crack, I saw the storage cavern below. I saw Clovix run beneath the fracture, pushing his underlings out of the way. For one brief second he met my eyes and I felt his spirit reaching out, imploring me to do something. Then the crack widened and Clovix ran aft to escape the swiftly spinning shards of moon rock.

The ship climbed away from the sun, the impellers straining against the natural pull of the sun fragment. And as we rose the crack grew wider and wider, deeper and deeper. Then Kleon turned to port, trying to right us, and *Chandra's Tear*, my ship, my home, broke in twain, singing out its death song, one pure clear note more beautiful than any mortal poet could pluck from a lyre, a paean so sad that only blessed Orpheus or Apollo of the musicians could have sung it.

The aft end to which we three clung tightly was jerked upward by the sun fragment, while the fore end with the navigation tower leaped away from us, orbiting in a wild spiral. Half of the impellers snapped off, leaving that broken triangle of moonstone helpless to control its flight. It tumbled wildly through a mass of partially rarefied air until the sharp half of the silver tear fell blackened into the sun.

"Kleon," I screamed, but for once that poor brilliant navigator could not save his ship. The fore end of *Chandra's Tear* flew downward through the great light of heaven; the impellers vanished as the celestial fire consumed them; then the navigation tower exploded from the heat, taking the life of the greatest pilot ever to fly through the heavens. May his soul be well received by the judges of the dead, and his Pythagorean purity grant him a good life beyond life.

A minute later the forward half of *Chandra's Tear* emerged from the body of 'Elios, a perfect triangle of moonstone, seemingly untouched by the flames. All things terrestrial had been burned away and there was no sign that humans had ever lived on it.

O, ye gods, ye all-knowing Fates, tell me, did so many men have to die for your purposes to be accomplished? No, forgive my plaint. The lives of my crew were spun out and cut short; that I must accept. Permit me to continue speaking that the gallant dead who died in those fires will be properly remembered in song and thought.

When the last man had fallen I heard a gurgling sound from within the remaining half of the ship. At the ragged fore edge of the hill, a waterfall had formed. The reservoir water poured out into the sun, trying futilely to extinguish that divine fire. Crates of stores tumbled out, followed by farmers from the spon-gen labs, filling the air with the screams of beast and man.

Pulled by the drunken flight of the sun fragment, the aft end of the ship spun in wild circles. The waterfall became a twisting helix, spilling the lifeblood of my dying ship into empty space.

Yellow Hare, Ramonojon, and I clung to one another and the still-rooted couch. My muscles strained against the unfamiliar pain, but Yellow Hare held me tight.

Then, as the fragment was turning to pull us upward again, the trolley jammed in its tracks, and the fireball, unable to orbit us and following whatever impossible dictates of motion were constraining it, took up a straight-line flight, dragging us up away from 'Elios faster than *Chandra's Tear* had ever flown.

As the ship skipped across open space like a moon sled through the air, Yellow Hare pulled Ramonojon and me out of our place of safety.

"What are you doing?" I yelled, clutching the leg of the couch.

"We have to reach the brig," she shouted over the rushing air. "It's the only safe place."

Yellow Hare and I crawled aft across the hilltop, pulling Ramonojon after us. We managed, the gods alone know how, to roll down over the side into the brig tunnel with only a few bruises and abrasions. Ramonojon's arm was black and blue and bleeding. His eyes watered and there was blood on his lips, as if he'd bitten his tongue.

Yellow Hare in the lead, we crawled down the steps of that narrow passageway until we reached the cell without a door. The ship spun again and I was slammed up against the ceiling and then back to the floor, but I managed to stay conscious and tie myself to the starboard wall with the long leather securing straps. Ramonojon fainted as Yellow Hare lashed him in to the aft wall before securing herself to the port side. She kept up her calm Spartan exterior, but I could see her grit her teeth against the cuts and bruises on her body, and lean on her left leg because she had somehow injured her right.

Tied to the walls, we were carried along through that whirlwind ride. Direction lost any meaning as the ship twirled through space. My ears rang, and I screamed in pain as we spun and spun and spun. I do not know when I blacked out, but I thank the gods most humbly for granting me that respite of oblivion.

\* \* \*

I lurched forward onto twisted leather straps and choked myself awake. The ship had stopped moving. At first I wondered if this strange stillness was a momentary respite amid the wild careering of sun fragment and moon fragment, so I hung there on the wall for a time, waiting for the next turn or pull; but no new motion occurred.

"I think it's safe to remove the straps," I said to Yellow Hare, who had just shaken herself back to consciousness.

She nodded and untied herself. My restraints had become knotted during the flight and she had to cut me down. I came down off the wall and tested the feel of the ground with my feet. There was a slight aftward tilt in the angle of the ship, as if whatever was holding us steady had altered the normal direction of down a few degrees.

Ramonojon, unconscious and delirious from the pain in his broken arm, also needed assistance to be freed. Yellow Hare picked up Ramonojon's unresisting body and carried him up the stairs; she looked very haggard, and leaned heavily on her left leg as she negotiated the steps with her moaning burden. I followed her, but slowly. My head spun with dizziness, my stomach had the hollow feeling that comes after a long fast, and each muscle in my body ached with a signature pain that made me feel every movement I took.

The steel door at the top of the brig tunnel had been crumpled downward during the flight, embedding itself halfway into the ground, and Yellow Hare had to force her way through the opening on top and then drag Ramonojon and me after her.

We emerged onto a bleak silver landscape. All the buildings, columns, and statues that had lined the hill had been stripped away during our wild flight. The port and starboard cannon batteries were crushed into lumps of iron. But, through the hillocks of the laboratory warren, I could see that the rear cannon battery looked remarkably intact.

I took a deep breath of fresh air and the dizziness and nausea vanished. I still felt the aches and pains of bruised muscles, but they no longer concerned me. My mind began to fill with one pure question: Where were we?

I breathed in more and that query became the only idea in my head. I had to know the answer; nothing else mattered. I looked around, seeking understanding. To port I saw a dull yellow glow, like a distant lantern seen on a faraway hilltop at night. I knew immediately that it was 'Elios and that we had flown a long long way from him.

Yellow Hare said something to me, but I paid her no attention. I needed to know exactly where we were. Ignoring the pains in my legs, I ran up the hill until I could see all the way aft and over all the sides of the ship.

Sternward I saw the trolley still jammed in its tracks, having somehow survived the pulling battle between sun and moon. The sun net itself was stretched over the port side and seemed to be curving downward.

I looked to port and saw a mere hundred miles below us a bloodred orb the size of the earth. Above it the sun fragment was dangling helplessly in midair, flopping around like a netted fish; the net trailed behind it and seemed to have looped itself around some invisible ball, tethering the ship and the stolen celestial fire to empty space.

For a minute the strange tableau overwhelmed my thoughts. But then long-known theoretical understanding connected with the facts before my eyes. I realized where we were and the need that had come over me was satisfied. My joy at having realized the answer to that one simple question was greater than any happiness I had ever felt save when the gods themselves had elevated me with their presence.

"Ares!" I cried aloud, and the word was an ecstatic release.

I ran back to Yellow Hare. "Ares," I said.

Yellow Hare looked up from examining Ramonojon's injuries. "What?" she said.

"That planet is Ares," I said. "And the net is wound around one of the war god's epicycles."

She stood up and stared at me with her piercing eyes, but the ecstasy I was feeling allowed me to ignore even her eagle's gaze. I went on babbling to her about the celestial mechanics of the globe off our port bow.

"Of all the planets in the universe," I said, "Ares has the most complex orbit, for within the gap in the huge crystal sphere lie half a dozen small spheres, each connected to the planet and to the outer sphere. They turn like a mass of gears, each adding its own circular motion to the war god's world."

The complex equations that governed Ares' eccentric orbit filled my mind, vying for space with the realization that we were the first people ever to reach this sphere.

I kept on and on, until Yellow Hare slapped my face. "Aias!" she said.

In that momentary flash of pain, I realized with perfect clarity what had happened to me.

"Don't breathe deeply," I said. "The air's too pure for human minds."

"I understand," she said, and the gods of Sparta wrapped themselves around her, protecting her purity from that of the celestial winds. "We need to take Ramonojon to the hospital cave. I only hope enough medical supplies survived to save his arm."

The upper building of the hospital had shattered and been blown away during the flight, and the tunnel that led to the wards and dispensary was exposed to the cold air of the outer spheres. The smell of rotting meat assailed us as we made our way down the cracked passageway, and I held my nose rather than risk too deep a breath.

Most of the couches in the public ward had been uprooted and smashed against the walls, and a jumble of shattered and twisted corpses lay on the floor, too broken and bloody for me to recognize the men and women whose souls had flown and now waited on the shores of the river Styx. From the corpses flies had already spontaneously generated and were buzzing lazily around the room.

"Euripos!" I yelled, but no answer came; I hoped that he was not among the indiscernible bodies.

Yellow Hare salvaged some cushions from the broken

couches, piled them against a wall, and laid Ramonojon down on them. I went down the tunnel into the dispensary to find supplies. Smashed urns and boxes were strewn across the floor. The walls had been stained with a variety of medicines, painting a bizarre multicolored pattern across the silver cave. I managed to find bandages, two dozen injection quills, a large bronze amphora full of water, a few splints, and a padded case filled with jars of the various humours.

Yellow Hare made a sling for Ramonojon's arm and injected him with Sanguine Humour to speed the healing process and Jovial to cut the pain. He thrashed about for a few minutes as the liquids settled into his blood; then he seemed to relax and fall into natural sleep.

While we watched him, Yellow Hare treated me for cuts and bruises and I wrapped her injured ankle in gauze. I was tempted to stay and wait for Ramonojon to wake up, but it was my duty as commander of that sad, wrecked vessel to see if any of my crew had survived and to do death rites for those that had not.

"Where do we go first?" Yellow Hare asked.

"Through there," I said, pointing toward the private ward. "Paeans should be sung to Aeson, coins put over his eyes, and the Khthonian gods propitiated."

We walked through the ragged curtain, heads bowed like mourners. But Aeson was not dead. He lay securely strapped down on his slab, just as he had been the last time I had seen him. The flight had taken its toll on his body in the form of welts and cuts from where the tightening leather had dug into his flesh, but his Spartan soul still dwelled in its mortal vessel. I reached out and tentatively squeezed Aeson's arm. There was no response; he was still in a coma, oblivious of the fate of his ship and his command.

I turned to say something to Yellow Hare and caught a glimpse of a torn, black-fringed robe buried under a fallen medicine cabinet in the corner. I ran over to it and heaved away the tumbled oaken chest to reveal Euripos's body. He had obviously died quickly when the heavy cupboard fell on him.

I knelt down and prayed. But my prayers then were formed from my childhood remembrances of that old man. Therefore let me now give my proper respects to Euripos of the Claudian gens, a Roman patrician who did honor to his city by service in battle, a doctor who never shrank from his duty to save the lives of his comrades, and a man who served under my father and myself with the greatest personal loyalty that any commander could ask for.

Yellow Hare gripped my shoulder, gently pulling me from my mourning. "What do you want done now, Commander?" she said.

"We should survey the rest of the damage," I said, accepting her gentle reminder of my duty to the living. "And search for more survivors."

"And we need food and water," Yellow Hare added.

"Agreed," I said. "We should search the storage cavern first. Then we can see if anything or anyone is in the labs."

We went through the dispensary and down the tunnel to the half of the storage cavern that remained after the sundering of the ship. The crimson glare of the war god flowed in from the open fore end of the cave, illuminating the corpses of slaves splattered against boxes and walls.

Many of the crates in the aft end were still secured. There might be enough grains, vegetables, and dried meats to keep us alive for a time. But one look at the dry moon rock at the bottom of the well told me that water was our greatest need.

Then I heard a low moan echoing through the cavern.

"Is that sobbing?" I asked.

Yellow Hare cocked an ear. "This way."

We followed the sound to the starboard aft corner of the cavern, where we found Clovix tied to the wall, crying aloud and cursing in his native language. Hanging next to him was the body of a young Pridaenean slave. Her safety thongs had cut into her throat during flight and strangled her.

Yellow Hare cut Clovix down, but he did not notice his freedom. His thoughts had focused on one thing alone, and his relentless cursing of Anaxamander told me what that thing was.

"Clovix!" I said. But he did not hear me. The veneer of civilization which Clovix had long cultivated and which had earned him the position of chief slave had vanished as he wailed out the names of every slave on the ship and told their ghosts to hunt down the security chief to avenge their deaths. Clovix's rage opened my eyes. He who I had always seen as corrupt and indifferent, as a slave whose heart was empty of virtue, he had seen himself as commander of our slaves, as responsible for their lives and spirits. His anger was my anger, the wildfire wrath of a chief betrayed.

In the knowledge of our oneness, I found the words that would draw him back from the grip of Mania.

"Anaxamander is already dead, Clovix!" I said, though I had not seen him die.

At those words he looked up at me, and his blue eyes glowed with bloodlust. "Where is his body? I want to watch the crows pluck out his eyes. I want to drink mead from his skull."

"He must have fallen from the ship," I said.

"I'll hunt him down in the dead lands," he said. "I'll chase his spirit with my hounds. I'll—"

He fell to weeping again, but the hyperclarity seemed to have left him, so we waited for his angry passion to abate. At last he ceased his wailing and looked at me, this time with recognition in his reddened eyes.

"Commander?" he said. "You're alive!"

"Yes, Clovix."

"Commander—" He gripped the edge of my robe to make sure I was not a ghost. "My people are dead."

"As are mine, Clovix," I said and helped him to stand. "But we are not."

"Everyone is dead?"

"Not everyone," I said. "Ramonojon is in the hospital ward. And Aeson survived."

"You and Commander Aeson are both alive," he said slowly. A spirit of relief settled on his shoulders. I could not understand why he who had shown us nothing but disdain would be grateful for our survival. But then Athena touched me with realization. Clovix had always relied on us; he had been corrupt because we had made it safe for him to be so. I could not let him sink back into that relaxed weakness.

"Clovix," I said. "We need your knowledge of this ship and its cargo if we are to survive and avenge the deaths of our people."

Clovix stared at me, unable to comprehend what I was saying, but then the breath of the upper spheres cleared his mind. I could see his eyes begin to gleam again; a new purpose was rising in him to fill his aching thoughts.

"What do you require of me, Commander?" he said, and he sounded not like the most corrupt slave in the Delian League, but like a soldier seeking to do his duty.

"I need you to attend to Ramonojon and then go look for water."

"Water?"

"The reservoir was destroyed in the wreck. We found a jar of water in the hospital, but we will need a great deal more."

"Yes, sir," he said, and walked off toward the dispensary tunnel, back straight, breath and soul filled with a fresh resolve.

Yellow Hare and I left the cavern and went aft to survey the laboratories. Ramonojon's lab was completely destroyed. Tables had toppled every which way. The materials cabinet had fallen over and the floor was pitted with fragments of metal, stone, and wood. A huge splatter of ink had dried into a spiral pattern on the same spot in the ceiling where Ramonojon's model of the ship had crashed.

We walked back to the surface, then down the stairs to Mihradarius's lab. Halfway to the bottom Yellow Hare stopped and waved me to silence. Voices drifted up from the laboratory—three people conversing in the Kanton dialect of the Middle Kingdom.

"He failed," one voice said in an accent I did not recognize.

"I did not," Mihradarius said. Yellow Hare's eyes squinted and her lips broke into a savage smile. I saw the Persian's death in her eyes and I nodded my official sanction to her desire.

Mihradarius continued speaking, unaware of how close the gates of 'Ades were. "Sunthief is no more. 'AngXou is safe."

"Perhaps," the third voice said in a very cultured Middler accent. "But we are left here to starve. This is not the death I had planned for myself."

"One—no, two people are on the stairs," the oddly accented voice said. "Come down!" he called to us in 'Ellenic.

I looked at Yellow Hare and pointed down the stairs. She nodded and preceded me through the passage and into the remains of the Ouranology lab, which had fared much better than any other part of the ship. The walls with their gleaming frieze had survived, undamaged, the tables had been secured to the floor by iron stakes, and the three people inside were clean and well dressed. For the first time I became conscious of how disheveled Yellow Hare and I were. My robes of command were torn, stained with sweat, and covered with white marble dust and silver moondust. Yellow Hare's armor was battered and dented, the sleeves of her tunic were torn, and the Spartan brassard she wore around her neck dangled by a thin ragged edge of leather strap.

The three people we saw inside were Mihradarius, a Nipponian who I suspected was the assassin Yellow Hare had fought earlier, and an old Middler man dressed in a green silk gown decorated with blue oceans and covered with a multitude of pockets. He tapped long fingernails against his wispy beard and studied us as if we were laboratory samples.

Mihradarius glowered at us. The Nipponian bowed slightly to Yellow Hare. She returned the gesture.

"Who are these?" the old Middler asked Mihradarius.

The Persian traitor pointed at me. "Aias of Tyre, the man who originally conceived and then served as Scientific Commander of this mission of Ahriman."

The Middler bowed to me and I to him.

"The Atlantean," Mihradarius went on, "is Captain Yellow Hare, a Xeroki corrupted by the Spartans."

"Introduce your stowaways, Mihradarius," I said in my most cultured Persian.

Mihradarius pointed to the old Middler. "This is Phan Xu-Tzu. A scientist from 'AngXou." He nodded to the Nipponian. "And this is Miiama Shizumi, a commando. They wish to thank you for your hospitality. They have been on *Chandra's Tear* since the attack that put you in the hospital."

I switched to Kanton and addressed the old man with as much

irony as I could muster. "I wish you had informed us of your presence. We would have treated you more appropriately."

He cocked an eyebrow at me, then smiled and inclined his head slightly.

"Your failures increase," Miiama said to Mihradarius. "These at least I can correct."

He drew his sword and leaped for me. Yellow Hare was between us before I had a chance to blink. She was unarmed, but seemed to have no trouble dodging the Nipponian's sword or striking at him with her bare hands.

The two warriors sparred like angry gods while we scientists looked on. Then Phan spoke. "Miiama, stop!" he said in harsh Kanton. The commando stepped out of the fray, blocking Yellow Hare's kick with the flat of his blade. She also stepped back.

"My orders—," Miiama said, keeping his eyes fixed firmly on my bodyguard.

Phan cut him off. "Your orders are to obey me. Only two more people need to die in order to complete our mission, and those only at the proper time."

I raised my eyebrow at this statement. "And who might they be?" I asked in Kanton.

Phan clacked his fingernails together in a quiet staccato. "Miiama and myself," he answered in 'Ellenic. "We were supposed to die with this ship, but our Persian accomplice failed to complete the destruction of this vessel."

Mihradarius shrugged. "I have struck a great blow against the 'Ellenes."

"Why did you do this, traitor?" Yellow Hare said. "You were held in high honor by the Akademe; you could have joined the immortal heroes for serving the League."

A spirit crossed Mihradarius's face; a Fury from the world below looked out from his eyes.

"He wants no honor from us," I said. I pointed to the frieze of the last emperor of Persia surrendering to Alexander. "Mihradarius is a Zoroastrian fanatic. He is trying single-handedly to defeat the invaders who conquered his people and assimilated his religion a thousand years ago."

"And I have done so," Mihradarius said in the blood-slaked voice of the vengeful Fury.

I nodded to Yellow Hare, meaning to have her carry out the death sentence on Mihradarius, but she was paying attention to something else.

"Six men are on the stairs," she said.

We turned to look, and six of Anaxamander's soldiers wearing battered steel armor stepped into the laboratory. Through the visors of their helmets I could see their eyes glowing from Hyperclear Pneuma. They leveled their throwers at us and their leader spoke.

"Stand still, traitors! We have orders to bring you to Commander Anaxamander." He turned to the other five guards. "Take them to the navigation tower."

The soldiers advanced, intent on bringing us to a place that the anger of 'Elios had already destroyed.

# μ

Yellow Hare spun around and kicked the thrower out of the grip of the leftmost guard just as the soldier slammed his hand into the ammunition bag; a spray of tetras flew from the mouth of the thrower, striking the ceiling. At same instant, Miiama leaped at the rightmost guard, sword upraised, and cut him down with a single swipe of blade across throat. The other soldiers wheeled drunkenly to fire at the two commandos, but they were far too slow.

The orderly line of guards dissolved into chaos as Spartan and Nipponian bore down on those maddened men. With perfect efficiency Yellow Hare disarmed them and knocked them senseless. Miiama simply killed them. In a matter of seconds three guards were dead, three disabled, and neither Yellow Hare nor Miiama had been so much as touched.

The Nipponian stepped over to one of the unconscious guards and raised his sword to decapitate him. Yellow Hare grabbed the defenseless man's sword and prepared to defend the life of the soldier she had just rendered helpless.

"Miiama, you have done enough," Phan said, much to my surprise.

"But Master Phan, the mission—," the Nipponian began to object.

"Is under my command," the old man said quietly. "You will kill no one else without my express instructions."

"Yes, Master Phan," the Nipponian said. He stepped back from Yellow Hare and without taking his eyes off my bodyguard sheathed his sword in one smooth motion. Yellow Hare held her blade in front of her and flicked a look in my direction. I shook my head. Obeying my implicit command, she sheathed her captured sword in her too-long-empty scabbard.

I tore the night blanket from the roller on the port wall and wrapped up the bodies of the dead in that shroud of black linen. I promised their bewildered spirits that time would be found to mourn them properly along with the rest of the dead crewmen. While I attended to their deceased comrades-in-arms, Yellow Hare relieved the three living guards of their weapons and tied them up with straps from their own armor.

"I wonder if there are any more soldiers alive on the ship," I said after covering the face of Miiama's last victim.

Mihradarius laughed, profaning the sadness of the place and time. "Why? Are you worried about dodging Anaxamander's guards for your last few days of life?"

"No," I said. "I will need all the help I can get in order to ensure our survival."

Mihradarius snorted like a contemptuous stallion. Yellow Hare nodded to me, and I saw a gleam of pride in her golden eyes. Phan turned to face me. "You believe survival is possible?"

"Whether it is or not," I said, "it is my duty to keep the remnants of my crew alive."

At those words, Miiama's hand drifted toward the hilt of his sword, lightly touching the red wingless dragon that stretched from pommel to guard. Yellow Hare saw him and interposed herself between me and the assassin. The Nipponian's eyes flicked down toward my bodyguard's limping leg, and I could see him deciding that this was his best chance to kill her. His hand gripped the hilt of his sword and he tensed, ready to draw.

"Miiama," Phan said, "I told you, no."

"Master Phan," Miiama said, "he threatens the mission."

"That is still for me to decide."

The Nipponian stood frozen for a moment, paralyzed by the order; then, one by one, his fingers released their grip on the carved lacquer hilt of his weapon.

"What now?" Yellow Hare asked me. Her eyes flicked toward Mihradarius, requesting my assent to his death.

"I see no reason to stay here," I said, firmly nodding toward the staircase. I did not know if Miiama would defend the Persian, and injured as she was I did not want Yellow Hare to risk her life in another duel with the Nipponian.

"I will join you," Phan said. "I would like to see this sun net of yours."

I turned to look at him, to study the face of the man who had overseen the destruction of all my works. He now seemed strangely reticent about finishing the task he had been set, and was apparently curious about the project itself. His reluctance struck me as very odd, and I wondered if he had some hidden motive, something he wished to learn before setting his assassin on me.

But then Athena tapped me on the shoulder and whispered a question into my ear. How would I act in Phan's place? she wanted to know. If my duty seemed accomplished would I not let my curiosity have its head, like a horse given the leisure to graze in a field after a long day spent pulling a chariot through a hard-won battle.

I acknowledged the goddess's point but said back to her that were I in Phan's place, I would yoke that horse again to its chariot if my enemies showed any sign of rising from defeat. Athena said nothing in response, but she hovered nearby, protecting my thoughts with her presence.

Yellow Hare and I preceded the others up the winding staircase and out the hillock at the top onto the surface of the ship.

Then we walked slowly over to the port edge of the ship, from which we could gaze on Ares, the sun net, and the still-dangling fragment of celestial fire.

For several minutes Phan stared in silence at the sun net, and with his fingers traced its taut arc over the side of the ship and around the epicycle that imprisoned it.

"Amazing," he said at last. "When the Son of Heaven first told me of this plan and sent me to sabotage it, I thought I would be going to my death for nothing."

"What do you mean?" I said.

"I thought it would be impossible, even for your incomprehensible science, to steal fire from the sun. And yet, there it is."

"And all for nothing," I said, turning away from the sight of my greatest error. I found myself staring into Mihradarius's hateful smile.

"You admit the folly of Sunthief," he said.

"Oh, yes," I replied. "It was sacrilegious of me to steal fire from 'Elios. I should have devised some other invention for the good of the League."

The Persian spat on the ground in front of me. "Ahura Mazda will curse you in the life behind."

"Will he?" I said. "And how will your god of truth feel about the lie your life has been?"

Mihradarius's face flushed with my accusation. He turned away. "I look forward to your lingering death from thirst."

"Death can always be quick," Miiama said. He drew his sword and turned to Phan. "Ours are long overdue."

The old man looked around him, surveying the silver ruins of *Chandra's Tear*. Then he turned to stare again over the side at Ares and the sun fragment. His voice was subdued, but it carried through the dry, thin air. "Not just yet, Miiama. Our deaths are assured. I want to study this part of heaven before I die."

The Nipponian stared at the Middler through cold eyes, as if he were contemplating defiance. Then he bowed from the neck and sheathed his sword.

Phan sat down on the ground near the port edge; the wind of the outer spheres tightened his robes about his body, showing a frail, bony form. From the voluminous pockets of his silk gown he removed a hand-sized block of camphorwood that had six spiraling golden wires depending from it, a roll of rice paper, two small clay pots of black ink, and a horsehair calligraphy brush.

The Taoist scientist dangled the gleaming metal wires over the side of the ship. He began to stare intently at the block. I looked over his shoulder and, to my amazement, I saw that the grain of the wood was changing before my eyes, as if the camphor was not solid wood, but water flowing in a river. After a while Phan put down the block and began to draw strange twisty spirals on the paper.

"What are you doing?" I asked.

"Charting the Xi flows around this planet," he said. "I've never seen heavenly patterns this complex."

I had never watched a Taoist working before, and I found myself fascinated by what he was doing. My thoughts began to fixate on the question of what was causing the wood grain to change. Hypotheses appeared in my mind. Some mysterious force unknown to 'Ellenic science? Something about the particular properties of camphor? Perhaps the wires were responsible. But before I fell into that maelstrom of inquiry, Yellow Hare pulled me away from the edge of the ship and put her hand in front of my mouth, stopping me from breathing.

I choked and tried to fight back, but then I saw the look of concern in her eyes and I realized how close I had come to another attack of Hyperclear Pneuma. I ceased struggling and she took her hand away.

"Thank you," I said.

Mihradarius laughed like a barking coyote, drawing a glare of cold hatred from Yellow Hare. "Aias, if you have that little mental discipline," the Persian traitor said, "you won't live long out here. I look forward to watching your bodyguard kill you."

Yellow Hare turned to look at him and opened her mouth to speak. Ares moved across her face, filling her words with the power of divine pronouncement.

"You will die before anyone else here," she said, and the gold of her eyes seemed bloodred under the light and spirit of Ares.

Mihradarius glared at her, defying both the woman and the god within her. The cold wind of the outer spheres picked up abruptly and swept his matted hair into his face.

"I have destroyed Aias's lifework," he said, and a spirit rose in him as well, a creature barking and yapping with divine madness. "It does not matter whether I precede him into the world beyond. He will never be honored as a hero by the 'Ellenes, but when the Delian League is destroyed and the Empire of Persia revenged, my name and story will be carved on the ruins of the emperor's palace and I will be remembered forever."

I said nothing to this boast, but in my heart I swore by the waters of the Styx that I would bring this ship back to Earth, that the full tale of Sunthief would be told, and that Mihradarius's name would be scraped from the rolls of the Akademe.

At that moment I caught a glimpse of some movement near the hill. Clovix emerged from the storage cave escorting Ramonojon, who was unsteady on his feet, but, thank Apollo the Healer, he was walking.

Miiama's scowl clearly declared his displeasure at the sight of more survivors. Mihradarius also seemed furious, particularly at the sight of Ramonojon.

"The Chief Dynamicist insisted on coming, Commander," Clovix said when they reached us. He looked at Phan and Miiama. "Sir, who are—?"

I explained about our stowaways.

"You mean they wrecked the ship? They killed my people!" Clovix said. The light of rage returned to his bloodshot eyes; he let go of Ramonojon, who tottered on his feet for a moment, then quickly settled himself on the ground. Clovix turned to face the Nipponian. Miiama waited impassively, as if he felt no threat from the redheaded giant towering over him.

"Clovix, did you carry out my orders?" I said, trying to pull the slave away from the growing anger that threatened to overwhelm his mind.

Clovix ignored me and took a step toward Miiama.

"The commander asked you a question," Yellow Hare said, filling her voice with Spartan authority.

"C-Commander." Clovix faltered; he took a hesitant step toward Miiama, then almost against his will the slave chief turned to face me.

"Commander," he said, trying to put back his mask of civility. He enunciated each syllable of his words with great care, like a student unfamiliar with the language he is speaking. "I have not yet had a chance to inspect the storage cave thoroughly. But after a cursory search, I can tell you that our situation is serious. All the heavy equipment is gone, the cranes, the graders, all the dynamicists' carving machines. The moon sleds apparently broke their moorings during the flight; they are probably orbiting far below us. I checked the Ouranology supplies as well. There are no more than ten pounds of fire-gold left. I understand little science, Commander, but that isn't enough to get us home, is it?"

"No, Clovix," I said. "It is far from enough."

He bowed his head and resumed his recitation. "We have plenty of food, Commander, mostly grains and dried fruits and vegetables. But the only drinkables left are olive oil and undiluted wine."

Unquenchable thirst stared at me from Clovix's barely controlled countenance and became the face of Thanatos, the visage of unavoidable death. My mind was suddenly gripped by the god who touches the life of every man. Thanatos opened wide his black robes and two hundred ghosts flew from the shadowy emptiness of his body. Every man and woman who had died in my service on this ship cried to me that it was my duty to avenge their deaths.

My eyes opened of their own accord and I stared through the red rage of Ares at the men who bore the blame for this disaster: Mihradarius, Miiama, and Phan. None of them seemed to have noticed my reaction. Mihradarius was too intent on exchanging angry glares with Ramonojon, Miiama's eyes were fixed on Clovix, and Phan was still studying the planet Ares, not knowing how near to him the god of that orb was.

"Give me a thrower, Yellow Hare," I hissed in Xeroki.

"No, Commander," she said. She turned to face me with Athena in her eyes. My patron goddess reached through those golden orbs to touch my heart. The host of the dead retreated from that divine presence and their cries for vengeance were muted. Ares exchanged words with his sister, but she showed him the Aigis she carried in their father's name and he too departed, leaving an aching hole in my heart.

"Why do you stop me?" I asked Yellow Hare.

"Because you think too much," she said, and her spirit reached out to me and I knew those words were no rebuke.

"What does that mean?" I asked.

"Those who think about everything do not make good soldiers. When they take lives, their minds become filled with the contemplation of death. Their hearts become filled with the Khthonian realm. Black bile dominates their humours. They either come to love the act of killing or come to hate it. But whichever happens, they are no longer capable of doing their duty."

"And what makes you Spartans different?" I said, asking the question my father had always answered with contemptuous silence.

"Our souls are filled with war, not death. We kill and die as needed for our victories, and that is where it ends. You are commander here. If you believe the traitor and the spies should die for the good of the League, then I will kill them, and having done my duty I will spare no more thought for them thereafter. That is the mind of a Spartan."

"Thank you, Yellow Hare," I said. I looked again at the three men, and Athena looked with me and whispered wisdom in my ears. Mihradarius would die whether we returned to Earth or not; I saw no need to order his execution. Miiama and Phan were dangerous, but both of them had been doing their duty to their empire. It would have been right for them to die in battle, but there was no need to execute them either unless they acted to prevent our return. It was a dangerous gamble to take, leaving the Nipponian alive, but I knew that had I ordered his death then and there, he would not have died alone, and I needed the help of all my people. The unrevenged ghosts of the dead I would appease with the proper sacrifices when I was able.

"No deaths," I said to Yellow Hare. And she acquiesced as soldier to commander.

Ramonojon had been sitting a few feet away, staring intently at me. He did not speak Xeroki, but he asked me a question that told me he had understood as friend to friend what had just happened to me.

"You have decided that we will live?" he said.

"Yes." And I realized that I had so decided.

"Is there anything I can do to help?" he said.

"We need water," I said. "Do you have any ideas on how some can be obtained, Chief Dynamicist?"

Ramonojon was momentarily startled at the title, but he recovered quickly and composed himself to think. After a few minutes of introspection he spoke. "We could make a desert-water collector as they do in Iudea and Sa'ara. We need to put a porous blanket over a barrel and cover that with a grate of fire-gold. Water will drip out of the air the fire-gold rarefies and seep through the blanket into the barrel."

"That will not work this far away from Earth," I said. "The air is too dry."

But then Athena struck me with an idea. "Packing crates!" I said.

"What?" Ramonojon said.

"Wooden packing crates! There is a great deal of water in wood. All we have to do is remove the earth from it. We can use air-silver and fire-gold for that. Clovix!"

"Yes, Commander?" he said.

"Get all the fire-gold we have out of storage. And remove the air-silver lining from some solar protector cloaks. Then bring up a wool blanket, a large empty barrel, and some wood from the broken crates."

"We'll have water, Commander?" he said, his eyes lighting up with the thought of life. "We'll live?"

"Yes," I said.

"No," Miiama said, cutting the air with one syllable of the Middle Kingdom tongue.

"Miiama!" Phan looked up from his work. "Leave them to their work. Water will only prolong their lives a short time."

The Nipponian looked at the old Taoist scientist. Something cold descended onto the commando's shoulders. He stood poised for a moment, balancing on the edge of a decision, but at last he bowed his head and walked portward around the edge of the hill.

Yellow Hare looked at me inquiringly.

"Keep track of him," I said. "But do not attack."

"I am doing so," she said, cocking her head to listen.

I turned to Clovix. "Do as I said."

Clovix bowed quickly and darted off through the laboratory hillocks and down a tunnel into the storage cave. A few minutes later he returned carrying a large oaken barrel under his right arm and clutching a dozen cracked pine boards under his left. He put the barrel down in front of me and pulled a blanket, several one-foot-long rods of fire-gold, and six hastily extracted webs of air-silver mesh out of it.

"Well done, Clovix," I said.

"Thank you, Commander," he replied.

It took Ramonojon and me an hour to arrange the fire-gold and air-silver rods on top of the blanket, which covered the barrel in such a way as to force the water out of the wooden planks without setting them on fire.

Sometime during all this preparation, Phan finished his drawings and came over to watch. His eyes gleamed with interest as we placed the first bits of wood on top of the metal gridwork and the first curlicues of steam began to rise. A moment later dew began to form on the upper lip of the barrel and the air filled with the unmistakable scent of wet wool.

"How does this work?" Phan asked.

"The fire and air force the water from the wood," I said. "We use the wool blanket to soak it up before it has a chance to evaporate into the air. When the blanket's completely sodden, we'll squeeze the water out and drink it."

Phan frowned. "More of your incomprehensible science. Why does turning wood into earth produce water?"

"We are not turning wood into earth," I said. "That would be impossible. We are extracting water from wood, leaving a residue of earth."

His brows knit in puzzlement. "Wood is wood, earth is earth. One changes into the other. Why should anything remain?"

I considered giving up on the conversation, but I had never had the opportunity to speak to a Taoist scientist before and my curiosity was too strong. But before continuing the discussion I spoke to Yellow Hare. "Watch me," I said. "And stop the conversation if I show any signs of hyperclarity."

"Yes, Aias," she said.

"We seem to be having a language problem," I said to Phan. "Let us start from first principles. You know the atomic theory, of course."

"I have seen that phrase in your books, but I have never understood it."

"Atomic theory says that everything in the terrestrial world is made of minute pieces of earth, air, fire, and water. The material properties of an object can be changed by modifying the amount of each element it contains."

Phan shook his head. "Anything can be in a state of earth, air, fire, water, or wood," he said. "The ten thousand things are changed into one another by the natural flow of transformation."

We continued to argue about basics for half an hour. I explained that matter and form were fundamental to the behavior of objects. He declared them to be accidents, saying that the flow and transformation of things lay at the heart of all science. At the end of that time we had found no common ground, but we were both very thirsty. Thankfully, the blanket was soaked through with water. We squeezed the liquid out into a large bronze bowl Clovix had found and took turns drinking. The water was brackish; it smelled of pine and tasted of wool, but my parched throat took it in as eagerly as if I were drinking the first sweet wine pressed from springtime grapes.

Yellow Hare and Ramonojon came forward to quench their thirsts, as did Clovix. I looked around for the others, but could not see them.

"Where are Mihradarius and Miiama?" I asked Yellow Hare.

"They walked to the port side of the hill," she said, taking only a sip from the bowl. "I can hear them from here. They've been discussing our chances for survival and considering whether it would be better to try and kill us now or wait. I decided it was better to let them plot where I could hear them rather than let them sit here and scheme in silence."

"Very wise," I said.

Phan crinkled his nose in disgust as he swallowed some more gray water. Then he took a small packet wrapped in dried green lotus leaves from one of his pockets and unwrapped it. Inside were a dozen orange-gold pills about the size of ripe grapes. "Not many left," he said as he ate one.

"Middler food pills?" Yellow Hare asked.

"Hmm?" He looked at her curiously. "Survival pills, actually. They keep one awake and alert for days as well as satisfying the need for food. Water, however, is still necessary."

He started to put them away, then looked at my bedraggled appearance and tired, red eyes. A gentle spirit entered him and he held the pills out to me. "Would you like one?"

I took one of the pills and studied it.

"Aias, don't take it," Yellow Hare said. "It could be poison."

"I'll take the risk," I said, "if it can increase our chance for survival."

"Commander, as your bodyguard I should test it."

"No, Yellow Hare," I said. "If you die, there will be no one to protect Ramonojon or Clovix from Miiama."

"Commander, I insist—"

But I swallowed the pill. It tasted like a lump of dried clay, but the moment the pill was in my stomach the aches I had been trying to ignore went away, my eyes stopped straining, my hunger disappeared, and the niggling desire to yawn vanished. My muscles, which had been through days of pain, stopped groaning. But most amazing, my mind felt released to range freely rather than to focus on one thing at a time to the exclusion of all others. The threat of hyperclarity went away, yet the sharpness of thought bestowed on me by the upper air remained.

"Amazing," I said to Phan.

"They are common pharmaceuticals," he said.

I was tempted to ask him how they worked, but did not, at that point, desire another confusing conversation. Instead I turned to my bodyguard. "I believe the pills are safe."

Ramonojon, Clovix, and Yellow Hare each took one after that. My bodyguard glared at me balefully for the risk I had taken, but I felt a spirit of compassion behind her anger.

"I will have to make some more soon," Phan said, staring down at the seven pills remaining in the crackling bundle of lotus leaves.

"How long do they last?"

"One week," he said.

"A week without sleep or food?" I said in amazement.

Phan did not even notice my surprise. He seemed lost in thought. "Miiama will not be happy about my giving them to you. But I doubt we will live long enough for him to report my indiscretion."

Yellow Hare cocked a puzzled eyebrow. "Is not Miiama your subordinate?"

"And my jailer," Phan said.

"Your jailer?" I said in 'Unan, sure that Phan was mistaken in the 'Ellenic word he had just spoken.

"That is correct," he said in his native language. "This unworthy one is here to redeem his family from his disgrace."

"What do you mean?" I asked.

"Two years ago," he said, his eyes losing focus and staring off into the past, "I designed a fire tamer."

"A what?" I said.

"A device that controls the Xi flows that govern the way a fire spreads. The device worked perfectly in the laboratory, and the Son of Heaven himself congratulated me and gave me a position in the main laboratories in 'AngXou. My fire tamer was given to an army in the land you call North Atlantea. They planned to use it to burn down one of the great eastern forests, depriving your city-states there of materials and protection. But I had made an error."

"The fire tamer did not work," I said.

"It worked perfectly, except that the Xi that governs the wind can overpower the Xi that governs the motion of fire. The battle kites that flew above the army need to control the Xi of the wind in order to fly. The wind Xi forced the fire to go one way, and my fire tamer forced it to go in another direction. A tornado of flame rose up and burned half the army to death."

Phan took another sip from the bronze bowl and wiped the residue of wool from his lips with his sleeve.

"The Son of Heaven ordered my execution and that of my three groups of relatives, but the Minister of Celestial Affairs intervened. He offered me the chance to save my family by aiding in the destruction of your ship. My death, of course, was inevitable."

"What does that have to do with Miiama?" Yellow Hare asked.

The old man half smiled out of the left side of his mouth. "The plan, as I said, required that no matter what else happened, I was to die, so they gave me Miiama as assassin, guardian, and warden."

Phan crossed his hands in his lap and clacked his long fingernails together. "But I am not as staunch as I should be in my acceptance of death. I was willing to die in the fires of the sun, but I find it harder to starve to death out here or to throw myself off and shatter against the lower spheres. Miiama would kill me if I asked him to, but I cannot bring myself to do so. I do not know how long he will be patient with me."

He took another drink of water. "No doubt Miiama will choose his moment."

Then he stood up, bowed to all of us, and went back to the edge of the ship to continue his drawings.

I stared at him for a time while Kleio and Athena whispered to each other in the back of my mind. At last I turned to Yellow Hare.

"Would you give someone in disgrace such an important assignment?"

"Of course not," she replied. "I would give it to someone willing to die in the full knowledge that he would be acknowledged a hero for his acts."

"As would I," I said. "And would you assign someone else to make sure such a man died?"

"That would be an insult to the honor of whomever I had given the assignment," she said. "What are you thinking, Aias?"

"I don't know," I said. "Kleo and Athena are whispering to me, but I do not yet understand enough to comprehend what the blessed goddesses are trying to say to me."

"The water barrel is full," Ramonojon said, interjecting a note of practicality. "What should we do now?"

I considered his question for a while. With food, water, and Phan's survival pills, we would be able to live, at least for a time. I turned my thoughts toward finding a means by which we could return to Earth.

To move we needed impellers. And to make impellers we needed fire-gold, of which our stores held only ten pounds. The ship did not have much raw gold on board, nor did we have a foundry by which we could turn gold into fire-gold. That meant we would have to scrounge material for impellers from the only source left on the ship, the evac cannons.

The forward, port, and starboard batteries had departed with the front half of *Chandra's Tear*. That left only the rear cannon battery.

Yellow Hare objected when I explained my idea. "The aft cannons are intact. If you take the fire-gold from them this ship will be defenseless."

"We don't have enough gunners to shoot the cannons," I said. "We might as well use the fire-gold for movement."

"If that is your decision, Commander," she said.

"It is." I turned to Clovix. "Fetch some long pry bars."

"Yes, Commander," he said.

The rear cannon battery jutted defiantly upward, pointing its metal spear shafts toward the planet of the war god. In the red light of Ares, the bronze-and-steel cylinders glowed like a clouded sunset. At the base of each cannon near the gunner's seat was a series of levers that rotated the artillery piece in any direction. One by one Yellow Hare worked the gears to rotate the cannons until they lay flat across the surface of the ship. Then Clovix crawled inside the barrels and pried out the hand-span-around hemispheres of fire-gold that rarefied the air inside the cannons.

Ramonojon and I piled the gleaming yellow metal into a mound and kept a running tally of how much of the precious substance we had amassed.

At some point Phan joined us. He seemed fascinated with the fire-gold, picking up the nodules and studying them with an intent eye.

"We have never understood this substance," he said. "I have experimented on captured pieces of it time and again. All I have gotten from my studies is a terrible smell and a light-headed feeling. I did transmute it into fire once; that was remarkably easy and remarkably bad for my laboratory."

I laughed, remembering the play Euripos had been in with its wide array of explosions. Old man, I thought, may you join the chorus of actors in 'Ades and perform the greatest comedies before the lord and lady of that realm.

I took a deep breath; my mind cleared and I returned to thinking like a scientist. "Fire-gold is just metal impregnated with as much fire as it can hold," I said to Phan.

"That makes no sense," he said, turning the nodule around and watching the air clarify around it.

I tried the atomic theory one more time. "Metal is earth mixed with fire."

"Metal is metal, fire is fire, earth is earth," he said.

"I do not think we will make any progress arguing basic principles," I said.

Phan cocked his head to the side and thought for a minute. "Very well," he said. "Of what practical use is this fire-gold?"

"It pushes the earthly impurities out of the nearby air, rarefying it."

"So?"

"The thinner the air, the faster objects can move through it."

"Objects move as Xi directs them," he said, returning to basics.

I looked over at Ramonojon for assistance. He shrugged his

shoulders helplessly. I sighed and gave up the debate. I had what I thought were more important issues to occupy my mind.

Over the next several hours we gathered all the fire-gold, amassing nearly two hundred pounds of the precious metal.

"Ramonojon," I said, "is this enough to get us home?"

He sat down with a ragged piece of papyrus and a charcoal stick salvaged from the labs and started scribbling. He stopped half an hour later and frowned at his calculations. "We do not have the equipment to improve the dynamics of the ship, so those are fixed. But we can make new ballast balls and install some crude controls for new impellers. If we did all that, we might reach 'Ermes in one hundred and forty-seven years."

"One hundred and forty-seven years?"

He nodded. "I concerned myself only with flight time. There is also the problem of maneuvering the ship out of this maze of epicycles we are trapped in, not to mention the difficulty of flying past the sun without a professional navigator. I am also assuming that we will jettison the net. There is no way we could make it back with the fragment pulling us randomly through space."

"We need to find another way," I said.

"I have a thought," Ramonojon said. "We could do nothing."

"Nothing?" Yellow Hare said.

"We can wait until the *Spear of Ares* arrives," Ramonojon said. "They are supposed to depart for this planet in two months."

I shook my head. "After Kleon stole their impellers, they had to commission new ones which will not be ready for at least eighteen months. And their expected flight time is another six. We could not extract enough water for all that time, and I doubt very much that Phan could make enough survival pills for such a stay."

We lapsed into silent contemplation for a time. As we sat alone with our thoughts and our gods, Ares rolled inexorably in his epicyclic orbit, dipping below the horizon of the ship and dragging the sun fragment with it. The sky became dark and the stars came out for that brief nighttime. We were closer to the Sphere of Fixed Stars than any men had ever been, and all we wanted to do was return to Earth.

"I wish Aeson were awake," I said, thinking of my friend's romantic love for the stars. "Without him, I can only half command."

"Excuse me," Phan said. "But is someone asleep?"

"Aeson is in a . . ." I stopped and turned to Ramonojon. "What's the 'Unan word for coma?"

He scratched his head. "I don't know."

I turned back to Phan. "Aeson is in a sleep from which he does not wake."

"Ah, yes, the man Miiama failed to kill," Phan said. He stroked the side of his beard and raised an eyebrow. "Why does he not wake?"

"He was injured."

"Are his wounds healed?"

"Yes."

Phan's fingernails did a dance on his cheek. "Does he breathe regularly? Is his pulse calm?"

"Yes."

"So wake him up."

"We don't know how!" I said.

The Middler threw up his hands in disbelief. "That is ridiculous. Bring me to this man. I will wake him."

"Are you a doctor?" I said, recalling Dr. Zi's peculiar claim of a connection between the whole of Middler science and their medicine.

Phan's face wrinkled in contempt. "Certainly not."

"Then how will you cure him?"

He switched to 'Ellenic. "I know medicine."

"But you said you weren't a doctor," I said in 'Unan.

Phan's black eyes lit with sudden understanding. "A doctor knows only medicine. A scientist must go beyond that simple beginning. Medicine is the foundation stone of alchemy, and alchemy is the foundation stone of science."

I turned to Ramonojon. "Does that make sense to you with what you know of the Tao?"

"I told you, Aias," he said, "my teachers are philosophers, not scientists."

"Teachers?" Phan said.

"In Xan Buddhism," Ramonojon said, no longer caring who knew.

Phan snorted contemptuously. "Those empty-headed, ragged mountain men know nothing of the Tao."

Ramonojon eyed him calmly. "They say the same of you narrow-minded, laboratory-bound city alchemists."

They seemed about to launch into a pointless argument so I interrupted. "Phan Xu-Tzu, do you claim to be able to heal Aeson?"

"I would have to examine him first," the Middler said, "but I believe so."

"Then do so," I said.

We stopped in Mihradarius's lab to retrieve a heavy blue silk bag of equipment Phan said he needed, then went to Aeson's private ward in the hospital.

My co-commander lay as we had left him, eyes closed to the destruction around him. At Phan's direction Yellow Hare removed Aeson's restraints.

"If you injure him, Middler," she said after loosing the last strap, "I will do to you what neither the shipwreck nor your Nipponian has done."

"I understand, Captain," he said, and his voice was calm, but not with the flat calm of a man resigned to death; it was the calm confidence of a scientist who knows his field.

"Yellow Hare, let him work," I said.

Phan went to work examining Aeson. Over the course of an hour he cautiously prodded my co-commander with gold needles and traced mysterious lines across his chest with thin blocks of balsa wood.

"It should take no more than five minutes longer to waken him," Phan said at last. My heart leaped with relief. Yellow Hare narrowed her eyes and put her hand on her sword.

Phan placed a survival pill under Aeson's tongue, then stuck long gold needles into my friend's wrists and ankles. Then he leaned up against the side of the slab, cradled Aeson's head in his hands, and felt his pulse in his throat for five minutes.

"Now," he said, and gently poked a silver needle into the back of Aeson's neck.

Aeson's eyes flashed open. He looked into Phan's placid gaze and smiled; a second later the smile grew into a tiger's hungry grin. Aeson grabbed Phan by the front of his robe and threw the old Middler scientist to the floor. My co-commander let out a wild beast's scream no Spartan warrior in his right mind would let leave his lips as he jumped from the slab onto Phan. The old man struggled to escape, but Aeson grabbed him by the throat and started to choke the breath of life from him.

# ν

han tried to push Aeson off of him, but the feeble old Middler had no hope against a Spartan warrior, even one who
had lain inactive for weeks. Aeson tightened his grip around
the old man's throat, clutching the fragile neck with hands hard as
tiger's jaws, ready to rip flesh. My co-commander threw back his
head, shaking his mane of unkempt hair. A feline roar came from
Aeson's mouth, and a cry of crimson bloodlust echoed through
the silver caverns, calling forth the thirsty spirits of the dead.

Yellow Hare leaped from my side and kicked Aeson's left arm,
forcing him to release the old man's neck. Aeson howled in animal
pain and ducked behind the operating slab. Phan curled into a ball
and gasped raggedly into his shaking hands.

Aeson sprang up onto the balls of his feet, arms wide, ready to
wrestle. The gold needles popped out of his limbs and neck and
clattered to the floor. His eyes glowed bloodred, his pupils
dilated, and his head jerked from side to side as if he could not see
what was right in front of him.

Yellow Hare circled around the slab, cautiously approaching
her opponent. Her hands were held up in front of her armored

chest, a boxer's posture. Aeson roared again and leaped through the air over the marble block. He landed a few inches in front of her and swung his massive arms to crush her like a bear. Yellow Hare ducked the blow, stuck out a foot, and swept his legs from under him. As Aeson fell he reached out and grabbed her injured leg, pulling her off balance. As he struck the moon rock deck, Aeson rolled portward and threw my bodyguard toward the wall. Yellow Hare twisted in midair and hit the port side of the cavern feetfirst. Yellow Hare gritted her teeth to stifle the pain of impact as she rolled off the wall to stand on the ground.

I started to run across the room to help her, but a single piercing glare from her golden eyes held me back. Two Spartans were fighting; I had no power to take part. Instead I pulled Phan away from the fray, over to the safety of the starboard wall, while the warriors continued their battle.

Aeson charged toward Yellow Hare. She leaped into the air on one foot, kicked off from the wall, and spun in flight to meet his charge. Aeson reached out to pluck her from midair. He grasped her right arm and yanked her closer, but she gathered in this gift of impetus to add force to her kick. Her steel-shod feet slammed into Aeson's bearlike chest. Ribs cracked, blood and breath blew out of his mouth. Aeson gasped once; then like a mighty tower he tumbled to the floor and lay still, gasping for air.

Yellow Hare fell upon him, rolled him over onto his chest and twisted his arms behind his back.

"Straps," she said tossing me a knife. "Quickly."

I cut the leather restraints off of the operating slab. She used them to tie Aeson up and then bandaged his ribs. While she attended to that I walked over to the starboard wall, where Phan sat massaging his throat.

"What is wrong with Aeson?" I said, reaching down to grab him by his robes. "What did you do to him?"

The Middler coughed, then cleared his throat. "I do not know. No one has ever reacted this way before. What were your doctors doing to keep him alive?"

"Injections of Sanguine."

"You mean blood?"

"Purified blood without any of the other Humours," I said. "Surely you must know about it."

"Only from your medical texts," he said, standing up slowly. He kept his eyes fixed on mine. "I know nothing about its properties."

"You mean you don't know what will happen to him." I pulled him closer to me and the old man shrank back in momentary fear.

"The survival pill should flush out whatever drugs you've given him," he said in a hurried voice. "He should recover within two hours."

"If he does not," Yellow Hare said, standing up from the trussed form of my co-commander, "you will escort him into the world below."

"I understand," Phan said. I released him and he bowed from the waist to Yellow Hare and then to me. "May I sit down while we wait?" he said.

I nodded and stepped aside; Phan walked over to the operating slab, seated himself in a cross-legged posture on top of it, and fixed his gaze on Aeson.

Yellow Hare methodically set the fracture in her foot and then stood guard over Aeson. For one and a half hours we waited while my friend slavered and writhed in his bonds like a trussed lion. I watched and prayed to Apollo for Aeson's recovery. The god gave me no reassurance and I had begun to despair when without any warning Aeson doubled over and started to groan.

He lay howling for a minute, then began to thrash crazily, tightening the leather restraints around him. Blood vomited from his throat, drying instantly into a black stain on the floor. Yellow Hare's sword point was suddenly an inch from Phan's throat.

"No!" said the Middler. "He is not dying. He is recovering."

The sharp point of steel stayed where it was while we watched.

The spasms ended as abruptly as they had begun and Aeson lay still, gasping for air. A moment later his eyes flashed open— clear dark eyes, untouched by madness. He blinked twice, then focused on me.

"Aias," he croaked. "I need water."

Yellow Hare ran out to the dispensary and was back in minutes with a bowl filled with the last clear water remaining on the ship. I held the bowl to Aeson's mouth and he drank it eagerly. Yellow Hare cut away the bonds while Phan felt Aeson's pulse in his wrists, then his neck, then his ankles.

"As I thought," Phan said. "He will recover completely if you do not give him any more of your medicines."

Aeson finished the lost drop of water and sat up slowly. His eyes fixed on the Middler. "You are not Doctor Zi." Aeson turned to me. "Aias, who is this Middler, and what is he doing on our ship?"

"It is a long story," I said. I sat down on the floor next to my friend and stared directly into his eyes, letting the full spirit of the disaster flow out to him through the light from my eyes. "And a sad story."

Aeson listened to my detailed account of all that had passed while he slept. Fury grew in his heart, painting his face with red rage as I told him of the actions Anaxamander took in the name of his position. When I related our arrest, Aeson actually cursed his Security Chief's name and prayed earnestly that the judges of the dead would condemn him to torment. When I described the wreck of the ship, my co-commander grasped my arm in sympathy; but even as I cataloged the difficulties of our situation I could see the spirit of Spartan defiance rising in him, and I knew that if a way could be found for us to return home, Aeson and I, reunited in command, would find it.

"So," Aeson said when I had finished the tale. "Our ship's complement consists of you, me, Yellow Hare, Ramonojon who is not a traitor, Mihradarius who is, three guards you have tied up, Clovix, and two Middler spies."

I nodded.

"The ghosts of our crew lie unmourned," he said. "But we will have to wait before we do them honor. For now we must concern ourselves with the living."

"Agreed," I said.

"Well," Aeson said, standing up slowly on legs unused to walking, "the first thing to do is free those three soldiers."

Aeson's iron practicality was taking over, filling the gaps in my own leadership. A little peace came into my soul; it seemed to me that for the first time in weeks, I would be able to concern myself only with that half of command which was my duty.

Aeson took a few tentative steps, slowly regaining his familiarity with his legs. When he was ready we walked out of the hospital and up onto the surface of the ship.

Ares floated above us, raining down the red light of battle on our crippled vessel. As we walked out of the cave, Aeson stopped to stare at the planet, and his eyes gleamed with his old accustomed joy in the heavens. He permitted himself a single minute of divine communion before he looked away, recalling himself to duty. Eyes fixed straight ahead of him, Aeson marched to Mihradarius's lab, where we had left the bound soldiers.

The angry guards sat up against the aft wall, below the part of Mihradarius's frieze that showed Alexander besieging the high turreted walls of Susa, Persia's ancient capital. Steam-powered evac cannons shot primitive spherical balls of iron at the guard towers while the soldiers on the walls looked on in horror at the new terror weapons Aristotle had created for his pupil.

The living guards tied up below that scene looked at Yellow Hare and me with the same fear the ancient Persians had shown, but when they saw Aeson their expressions changed into the blissful acceptance that comes over men blessed by the presence of the gods. The madness left their eyes as they stared in wonder at their leader returned to them.

Aeson nodded to Yellow Hare, and she cut their bonds.

The soldiers stood to attention, eyes fixed on their commander. Aeson stepped in front of them and they saluted him with their hands over their hearts.

"Xenophanes, 'Eraklites, Solon," Aeson said, addressing each man by his name. "You have done your best to fulfill your duties under trying circumstances. Anaxamander, however, did not do so; his violation of duty will be judged in 'Ades. His orders to you are rescinded. In particular, you are to know that Commander Aias and Captain Yellow Hare are not traitors. Is that understood?"

"Yes, Commander," they said.

"Excellent. Now, here are your new assignments." He pointed to the first one. "Xenophanes, you will stand guard over the traitor Mihradarius. Make sure I am informed of everything he does. Solon, you will stand guard over the Middler scientist." He turned to the third man. " 'Eraklites, your assignment is more difficult. You are to watch the Nipponian, but not to approach him. If he tries to do anything that you feel might endanger any of our lives let me or Captain Yellow Hare know about it. Do not attempt to fight him yourself."

They saluted again and marched in newly restored order out of the laboratory to take up their proper duties.

"Now, Aias," Aeson said after the guards were gone, "we need a planning meeting."

"Agreed," I said. "Yellow Hare and I will find Ramonojon and Clovix, and we will join you on top of the hill in twenty minutes."

Aeson nodded.

"Aeson," I said. "There is something more I must tell you."

"Yes?"

"When you see the hill, I want you to know that I closed the eyes of Athena's statues, but Alexander and Aristotle were taken from us without due ceremony."

"You closed her eyes alone?" he said.

"Better that than to let Anaxamander defile Wisdom with his fool's hand," I said as we left the traitor's cave.

Yellow Hare and I went to the water extractor to tell Ramonojon and Clovix about the meeting. We found Ramonojon bent over two barrels. One was the original water extractor, the other one a plain barrel covered with several layers of gray, sludgy cheesecloth. Ramonojon was slowly ladling the brackish water we had extracted from the first barrel into the second.

"Filtering the water?" I asked.

"Yes," he said. "Where have you been?"

We told him about Aeson's recovery.

"Phan cured Aeson?" Ramonojon said after a moment's silent thought.

"Yes."

"Why?"

"I do not know," I said. "But I suspect that old Middler wants to live. Strange considering that he came here to die."

Ramonojon closed his eyes and began to speak in the Kanton dialect. I could tell he was quoting but I did not know the source. "Heaven endures," he said. "Earth survives. The reason Heaven and Earth can endure and survive is that they do not live for themselves. Therefore they can endure forever.' "

He opened his eyes. "Lao-tzu, the *Canon of Way and Virtue.*"

"Thank you," I said, feeling something not yet born stir in my heart.

Ramonojon smiled and turned back to his work. He pulled the cheesecloth away from the second barrel, dipped in a clean bowl, and handed it to me. My reflection stared up at me from the clear water. I drank eagerly, savoring the sweet, cold taste, then handed the bowl to Yellow Hare, who drank the remainder.

"Well done," I said to Ramonojon. "But you will have to wait until after the meeting to finish this."

"Meeting?" he said.

I explained. "Would you find Clovix and inform him?" I said.

"Yes, Commander," Ramonojon said.

A quarter of an hour later, the five of us assembled in the stumps of ruins that dotted the top of the hill. We sat cross-legged on the bare moon rock in the place where the couches had been. Ares was high above us, shedding harsh red light down to mingle with the cold silver of the ground. The twisting of the crystal epicycles had brought the sun fragment up over the starboard side, adding 'Elios's yellow to the harmony of illuminations.

The wind whipped coldly through me, biting into my wool robes, but whatever was in Phan's pills kept me comfortable no matter the temperature. The pure waterless air had dried my skin to cracking, but that did not hurt either. The only pain I felt was that of loss as I sat amid the ruins of work and beauty.

I had set myself down next to Aeson. Yellow Hare was to my left and Ramonojon next to her. Clovix sat down among us, but he showed not the former arrogance of the slave, but the pride of a man fulfilling his duties.

Uninvited, Phan, Miiama, and Mihradarius came together at

the base of the hill. The old Taoist, I knew, had been resting from his ordeal. As to the traitor and the assassin, Yellow Hare informed me that they had been conducting a private survey of the ship, no doubt looking to reassure themselves that there was no chance of our survival. Their guards had formed themselves into a short phalanx a little way up the slope of the hill, interposing themselves between those three and us.

Aeson and I opened the meeting with a single prayer to Zeus. "Father of gods and men," we prayed. "We cannot offer you proper sacrifice. We cannot give you the honor you are due. We can only lay ourselves before you as supplicants and humbly ask for your favor."

Something stirred in my mind, something large and awesome like a distant thunderstorm preparing to approach. I looked over at Aeson and saw a gray cloud in his eyes. I nodded to him and he leaned forward to speak.

"Our task is to survive," Aeson said, "and to return to Earth. Are we all agreed?"

All on top of the hill gave their assent.

Aeson stood up. All his Spartan grace had returned to him. He strode over to the remnants of Alexander's statue, drawing our gazes along with him. Half of the pedestal and one of the conqueror's legs were all that remained, but when Aeson approached I felt the hero-general's presence return to the ruined statue.

"Since I woke," Aeson said, "I have been praying to the gods and the heroes to furnish me with a means of survival. As I waited here on top of the hill for the rest of you to join me, the hero Alexander came to me with that means."

Elation filled my heart at those words, but distant thunder rumbled again, muting my joy.

"When he was a young man," Aeson said, "Alexander brought his army to the city of Gordius. The hero had been told a legend about a temple in that city. In that temple was a knotted rope; it was said that he who untied that knot would conquer the whole world."

Aeson paused. The hackles on the back of my neck rose. In a formerly quiet corner of my heart there was a clap of thunder and a flash of lightning. In that sudden burst of luminescence I saw Athena and Kleio together holding up a globe of the earth for Father Zeus to study.

"Alexander went to look at the knot. He saw a mass of thongs twisted and tied around seven pieces of wood. One of his generals suggested he cut it with his sword. Alexander refused, saying, 'Not every problem is solved by the blade.' He sent back to his camp for Aristotle, who was traveling with him in order to watch his protégé carve his way through the world.

"Aristotle studied the knot for an hour, and then quickly untied it. Seven planks of wood clattered to the floor of the temple and the scientist handed a single uncut leather cord to his student. Alexander turned to the general who had wanted to sever the knot and said, 'The right man is greater than the right sword.' "

Aeson paused again. Yellow Hare's eyes were fixed on him and a flash of understanding passed between them, a spirit wholly Spartan but strangely unwarlike.

"Alexander's message to me was clear. Our survival is a scientific, not a military problem," Aeson said. "Therefore, I am turning complete control of this ship over to Commander Aias. All his instructions will be obeyed to the letter. I am vesting all my authority in him, including the traditional military duties to discipline the crew and to try and sentence traitors and spies."

He walked over to me; the spirit of honor that lay across his shoulders drew me up to a standing posture. He delivered a full Spartan salute, then sat down at my feet. "We await your orders, Commander."

I was stunned by this violation of protocol, this abrogation of duty on Aeson's part, but deep within me I knew that he had done the right thing.

"You do me honor," I said, and Athena and Kleio rose up in my mind, filling me with a great light. "If it be within my power, I will not disappoint you."

The thunder cracked again, this time nearer to me. The great presence filled me with a vision of the universe. I rose up from the surface of Earth through the spheres, touching each of the gods in turn, until I reached the Sphere of Fixed Stars. I laid my hands upon that ebon ball with its glistening fires and felt the engine of the universe, the Prime Mover, rumbling behind it, giving impetus to all existence. Pure motion passed through my hand, filling my mind with a power that needed to be transmitted. I turned away from the sphere and descended again to Earth to bring that movement to the world of man.

The vision left me and I looked up into the concerned eyes of my comrades.

"I would like to speak with Aeson alone," I said. Ramonojon and Clovix bowed to me and left, but Yellow Hare remained behind. I looked at her.

"Alone," I said.

"Not out of my sight," she said.

I nodded my agreement. She walked down the hill and joined the guards.

"Aeson," I said, "I know that you did the right thing. But I do not know why it was right. Why did you, of all people, violate the rule of dual command?"

In the air he sketched a sign from the Orphic Mystery. I responded automatically with the countersign. "We are Eurydice trapped in 'Ades," he said. "Only you can take the role of Orpheus and find the song that will lead us out."

"How do you come to that comparison?"

"When I woke from my coma," he said, "everything had changed. I felt not as if I were once again alive, but that I had finally died. That I stood upon the threshold of 'Ades confronted with the problem of Orpheus."

"I understand," I said. "But still, to give up dual command, the thing that has sustained the League through nine long centuries."

"Aias, if by some strange spinning of the Fates the two of us found ourselves in the heart of the Middle Kingdom, surrounded by their armies and with no clear chance to survive, would you not feel as I do now?"

"What do you mean?" I said.

"Would you not, if prompted by a divinity, pass over to me

your authority, believing that I had the only hope of finding a way for us to escape?"

"Yes, Aeson, I would," I said, bowing my head. "Please leave me and give me time to think."

"Yes, Commander," he said. He walked down the hill, past the guards, and entered into some heated argument with Mihradarius which I could not overhear.

I walked to the edge of the hill where the ship had split in two and stared over the ragged edge with its myriad of irregular facets all gleaming a cold silver. Three hundred thousand miles straight down lay the earth, a longer journey than even Orpheus had taken back from 'Ades, and I lacked the power of his voice to charm the universe. All I had was my mind and the impetus given me by Father Zeus.

I stared down that great fall and waited for that raw interior motion to turn into a coherent idea. But the only thought that came to me was the one 'Elios had burned into my mind when he pointed out my hubris. Your duty is to the Good.

"But what is the Good, here?" I said, calling down through the heavens to the sun god.

"To survive," Yellow Hare said from behind me. "And to bring back to the League that which will aid our cause upon the earth."

I turned around. Yellow Hare stood on top of the hill, the highest point in existence presently occupied by man. The glow of Ares had washed her steel armor into bronze, but the war god's mantle did not lie across her shoulders. The divinity that set her golden eyes to glowing was Sparta's patron, 'Era, queen of heaven.

"And what could we bring back to the League from this debacle?" I asked.

"I do not know," Yellow Hare said while 'Era kept divine silence. "Aeson gave you his authority because only you can answer that question."

I walked up the hill and joined Yellow Hare at the heights of humanity. "And have the Fates given me the power to answer it?" I said.

"They have," 'Era said through her, "and you shall."

Thunder filled my heart; I leaned forward and kissed Yellow Hare gently on the lips. Breath joined with breath and god with god. There was a moment when Zeus and 'Era spoke to one another through our mingled Pneuma. Then the gods were gone and only Yellow Hare and I remained. I stepped back from the embrace and looked into her golden eyes.

"You do me honor," I said.

"As do you to me," she replied.

We stood for a time in silent communion, exchanging wordless thoughts in light and breath; then we turned and walked in unison back down the hill.

All the survivors of the vessel were assembled at the base of the slope looking upward; even Mihradarius, Miiama, and Phan sat among the others. They had all been waiting for us, or rather for me, to come down with my judgment.

I looked over at Mihradarius. "Despite your actions, we will live and return to Earth," I said. Then I turned to Miiama. "I am not ordering your executions now, for two reasons. First, it would put my soldiers' lives at risk, and second, when we return to Earth, you will be taken prisoner and your actions dealt with in accord with the customs of war prisoners. Understand, however, that while you are on my ship you will be watched constantly. Any attempt to interfere with what we are doing and you will be killed before you succeed in any act of sabotage. You will live only so long as you keep still."

"I am not concerned," Mihradarius said. "There is no way to bring this wreckage back to Earth."

"And how do you know that?" I said.

"Because I cannot think of any such way," he replied. "And your mind was never a match for mine."

"It is true," I said, "that you are more blessed by the scientific Muses than I am. But there are other, greater sources of inspiration."

Mihradarius shook his head as if shrugging off the insults of a madman.

Miiama had eyes only for Yellow Hare and Aeson; it was clear that he regarded me as no obstacle to his work. Only the Spartans were dangerous to him. Death lay on his shoulders, both ours and his, but Death did not come out of him, for on our side War opposed it. The spirits stared at each other through human eyes, then gradually subsided. Miiama would not kill unless he could kill us all, and neither Yellow Hare nor Aeson would attack without my orders.

I turned to look at Phan. He stared up into my eyes impassively. No words passed between us, but he slowly bowed his head.

"Very well," I said. "Now as to how we shall survive. To begin with, our resources are: half of *Chandra's Tear*, two hundred pounds of fire-gold, the net, and the sun fragment."

Ramonojon looked up. "The fragment is a problem, not a resource."

I shook my head, suddenly realizing what I had been saying. Athena and Ourania blessed me with the light of inspiration. "No, Ramonojon, the sun fragment is the only thing we have that is fast enough to bring us back to Earth. If we can guide it, it could pull us home like a horse pulls a chariot. The question is how we can control it."

Phan stared at me quizzically. "I do not understand your problem," he said. "Why would it be difficult to guide the fireball down to the earth?"

"Celestial matter moves in circles; that is its nature. How could we constrain it to a linear motion?"

He scratched his beard and nodded slowly. "The Xi flows that guide the planets are circular. Is that what you mean?"

"Perhaps," I said, focusing my clarified mind on the strange concepts of Taoist science. "Since I do not understand the meaning of the word *Xi*, I cannot answer your question. Regardless, we have to find a way to force the sun fragment to draw us down to Earth."

"No," Phan said. "All you have to do is strengthen the proper Xi flow and the fireball will follow it as a matter of course."

Athena struck me with sudden realization. "Are you saying that we can use your technology to return to Earth?"

"Say nothing!" Miiama said in a voice cold enough to shatter steel.

"Be quiet," Yellow Hare said to the Nipponian; she and Aeson drew their swords and signaled for the guards to do the same.

The soldiers waited for my command. I was sorely tempted to order Miiama's death then and there, but though I was certain Yellow Hare and Aeson could kill the Nipponian, I was equally certain that one or both of them would die in the process. I also knew looking at Miiama that he would not act until he was sure both Phan and I would die in his attack. He would not die uselessly, and I would not throw away the lives needed to kill him. In my heart grew the strange realization that the best thing I could do to further my purposes was nothing.

And with that realization, I remembered the incomprehensible references in Taoist texts to action through inaction.

I turned back to Phan, thinking I would have to encourage him to continue, but much to my surprise, the old man answered my question without any further prompting. "In theory it could be done. In practice . . . I do not know. Battle kites are easy to fly. This piece of the moon, I do not know."

"How do the kites fly?" I asked.

Phan shut his eyes and massaged his temples. He seemed to be struggling for the right 'Ellenic words. "We have mapped the Xi flows of the atmosphere. Our kites use Xi enhancers to strengthen the flows so the natural motions of the universe can support the heaviness of the kites. Once that is done our kites travel along the strengthened flows as easily as birds through the air."

"Are there Xi flows here in the outer spheres?" I asked.

Phan gave out a strangely musical laugh that reminded me momentarily of Kleon. "Xi is the movement of existence; it flows everywhere."

He pulled the rice paper scroll he had been drawing on previously from a pocket and unrolled it. On it were eight small circles arranged in a line. Each circle had a single Middler character inscribed in it. The first had the character for Earth, the second for the moon, and so on out to Khronos. I realized immediately that it was a map of the heavens, but instead of the planets being embedded in the celestial spheres, as we would draw them, they were surrounded by carefully inked wavy lines that resembled the ocean currents on a terrestrial pilot's map.

"This is how you represent the universe?" I asked.

"Of course," Phan said. He pointed to sets of wavy lines that connected each planet to the one directly above it. "There are major Xi flows between each pair of adjacent planets, including this one." Here he pointed to Ares. I noticed that the war god's world was surrounded by a confusing multitude of eddies and crosscurrents.

"What are those?" I asked.

"The tides that make this planet's orbit so eccentric."

"You mean those are the epicyclic crystal spheres?"

"There seems to be some connection between the flows and the matter," he said. "Our heaven theorists have never understood the spheres or why the Architect of Heaven rooted the planets in them. According to our theories, if the spheres were gone the planets would still orbit in the same way as they do now. Of course, we cannot prove that.

"But here are the long flows," he said, returning to his map and pointing out two sets of parallel lines extending from Ares, one of which led outward toward Zeus, the other inward toward 'Elios.

I stared at it squint-eyed, trying to think like a sailor. "So," I said at last, "if we could reach this inward flow, you could guide us down it to the Sun, then from the Sun to Aphrodite, and so on down to Earth?"

He shook his head. "If this ship were a battle kite I could do so, but the flows that control celestial objects are more complicated; our science cannot truly predict how this piece of moon rock will fly. That is why the first expedition to the Moon crashed trying to return to Earth."

Yellow Hare cocked an eyebrow. "What is he talking about? Kroisos and Miltiades landed safely."

"Two Middlers reached the moon before Kroisos and Miltiades," I said, "but they did not make it back alive. Their kite crashed in Gaul. Some pieces of Selenean matter were found in a box that survived the crash, and those samples prompted the League's first expedition to the moon."

"Why have I never heard of this?" she said.

"The Archons of that time restricted that information to Ouranologists," Aeson said. "Later the knowledge was given to all commanders of celestial ships as well. Had I not been placed in command of *Chandra's Tear*, I would never have heard of it either."

"I see," she said. But I saw a hint of troubled thought cloud her sunlike eyes.

"The moon pieces were responsible for the crash," Phan said. "The circular movement of the samples pulled the kite out of the Xi flow between Earth and the Moon."

His hands described an elegant crash landing.

"So you cannot guide us down," I said, preparing to abandon this line of inquiry and search for others.

"I cannot keep celestial matter aligned with the inward flows for long periods of time," Phan said.

"How long?" I asked, a possibility forming in my mind.

"No more than twenty minutes," he said.

"And we would be flying at the natural speed of the Sun for that period?" I said.

"Yes," he replied.

"Aias, what are you thinking?" Ramonojon said.

But I did not answer him. My mind had become filled with a storm of calculations.

"I think we can do it," I said at last.

I picked up a quill and quickly sketched my idea on a sheet of virgin papyrus. "We can use the fire-gold we have to make small impellers that we can use as reins to guide the sun fragment toward the Xi flow. Phan, you can then fly the ship down the flow until the fragment's natural motion orbits it away from the current. We then do nothing at all, while the fragment pulls us in a vast circular path around Earth and eventually back to the flow, where we repeat the process."

"What?" Aeson said.

"It's simple," I said. "We will enter the flow, descend, orbit, enter, descend, and so step by step we will reach Earth."

"But, Aias," Yellow Hare said, "the last time the fragment pulled the ship, we did not fly in a circular orbit. There was no regularity at all."

I looked at her for a moment and smiled. "That," I said, "is because Phan was disrupting the normal motion. Were you not?"

The old Middler bowed his head. "Yes," he said. "I strengthened the eddies around the Sun and let them drag the fragment wildly."

"Now you will help us tame it?" I said.

"Yes," he said. "Might I have the paper and pen, Commander Aias?"

Phan took the sheet and the quill and began draw a picture of the ship next to my calculations. "If we could build functional wings for this piece of moon rock, and if I can build a large enough Xi enhancer, it might work."

I looked over at Ramonojon. "Chief Dynamicist?" I said.

"What kind of wings do you need?" he asked Phan.

The three of us sat down to calculate. Ramonojon sketched a redesign of *Chandra's Tear* with cloth wings added while Phan and I discussed the two different guidance systems we would be using, where they would have to be placed, and what material we would need to make them.

We sent Clovix to the storage cave to find steel rods and as many bolts of cloth as we had, in order to make the wings. We also needed silver and gold to make the Xi devices, and we needed to make guide wires for the sun fragment. Staring at the design, I wished Kleon were alive. I knew a little about celestial navigation, but Daidalos himself would have been hard put to fly this hybrid bird we were building.

Three hours later, we knew the thing could be done. I folded the sheet of papyrus and looked up at Aeson, who had stood guard over us while we worked.

"Now we can mourn our dead," I said to him.

We held the ceremony on the playing fields. The 'Erms were gone but we offered wine to 'Ermes Psychopompos, asking him to guide the souls of our ship's ghosts down the long ways to the courts of 'Ades. We had no black-wooled sheep to give blood to the dead, but we did have a small stock of silver coins, most of which Clovix donated from his hoard; these we gave so that the dead might pay the fare to Kharon the ferryman and so cross over the river Styx. We had no one to sing the songs of mourning but we swore to remember the dead and bring their names and fates back to their families. And we had too few people for funeral games, but we promised to deliver the roll of honor to Olympia and entreat the overseers to include our crew among those praised at the next games.

When the ceremony ended, I made silent conference with Kleon's ghost, saying that I would fly this vessel in his name. I knew that no sacrifice of blood or wine would do more honor to that greatest of celestial navigators.

Over the next few days we worked to make reality from my vision. We had no cranes, so Aeson and the guards had to assemble the wing struts by hand. A steel framework was laid over the middle of the port and starboard edges of the ship, secured by bronze spikes to the corpse of *Chandra's Tear*. The guards had to crawl out over the side to join one steel rod to the next with the silver rivets Phan insisted were necessary for proper Xi control. Meanwhile Clovix and Ramonojon sewed the wings themselves out of every scrap of cloth we could scrounge from the ship's night blankets, from bolts of linen used for making clothes, from the thick cotton used to pad the insides of armor—every piece of fabric on the ship except the clothes we were wearing was stitched into those patchwork wings.

Ramonojon secured the trolley in place by roughening the

groove, breaking the wheels, and wedging all the marble we had into the channel itself. It took him a week, but he was finally satisfied that when the fragment moved it would pull the ship after it without dislodging the trolley and returning to orbit the ship.

Meanwhile, I formed our precious reserves of fire-gold into small nodules. These I attached to four long, silver guide wires I planned to use as reins for our horse of the sun. When I had finished them Aeson himself, clad in protective clothing, crawled along the sun net and around the epicycle that tethered it to Ares in order to interleave the wires with the twisted strands of celestial thread.

The skeleton of a huge bird gradually grew up from the remains of *Chandra's Tear*. The truncated fore end had become the bird's tail, and the port and starboard sides became shoulders. The net was the neck, and the sun fragment itself was the head.

Throughout this time, Yellow Hare watched Miiama and Mihradarius, making sure that they did nothing. As we progressed she reported to me that the Persian was becoming sullen and seemed to be spending most of his time in nervous prayer to his gods. But the Nipponian was studying everything we were doing with great care.

"Aias," Yellow Hare said. "He is going to attempt sabotage soon. Give the order for his execution."

"Can you guarantee your survival in a fight with him?" I said. "Even with Aeson's help, can you promise me that with both of you still recovering from injuries that you can kill him without either of you dying?"

"No," she said. "I cannot swear to that."

"Then I will not give the order," I replied. For fear of being overheard I did not tell her that I thought the matter would be taken care of without any of us being put at risk. For I had been watching Phan carefully over the past few days; in the old Taoist's eyes I had seen the dawning realization that the ship we were building might actually work to fly us home. I had taken Phan's measure; I had seen the desire for life grow in him until it was ready to burst out. And I had seen Phan cast his gaze at Miiama and realize that the Nipponian was the only thing that stood in the way of survival. But Phan could not act swiftly; as long as he believed other possibilities lay open to him, he would not act against Miiama. But if my assessments were accurate, he would soon come to realize that all other choices were gone.

Later that day Phan came to see me. "I need to make more survival pills," he said. In a catch in his voice, I heard the spirit of realization stirring in his heart.

"What do you need?" I said, breathing out reassurance in my words. He handed me a piece of rice paper with a list of ingredients even more esoteric than those required by the spon-gen farms.

I called Clovix away from making the wings and told him to assist Phan in searching the stores for what he needed. They returned an hour later.

"Some substitutions were necessary," Phan said. "I will not be able to make pills as good as those we have been using. But I will do what I can."

Phan seemed to be having difficulty meeting my gaze, and I began to grow suspicious, wondering if his cooperation had been a means of concealing something. But then 'Ermes entered my heart and I realized the source of Phan's nervousness.

"Do your best," I said. "I have every confidence in you."

Three hours later Phan announced that the pills were ready. The entire ship's complement assembled at the water distiller. Phan handed around the pills and I took mine with a nod. These new tablets had an ugly purple-gray mottling and a slightly burned taste, but I swallowed mine with confidence and felt the return of a tirelessness that I had not realized had been waning.

Phan put away his alchemical supplies and he, Ramonojon, and I settled down to review our schedule. The wings would take at least two more weeks to complete, and I would need that time to brush up my celestial navigation and do my best to calculate flight paths, given the impossible mode of transport.

Phan only half paid attention to our talk. He kept looking to port and then to starboard, following the course of the sun as it came around for its daily trip under us. 'Elios fell directly beneath us, and the sky grew dark with the eclipse of Ares. The stars blinked down on us, and I looked up to the sky with the tentative hope that I would again see the heavens from the earth.

Then it happened. Mihradarius screamed and clutched at his throat. Saliva dribbled down his lips, and he collapsed to the ground. Miiama jumped up and ran toward Phan. Yellow Hare tried to grab him, but he fell over on his own before she could reach him. The Nipponian clawed at his throat until blood poured out of his neck.

Mihradarius's eyes flashed open, but he was not gazing on this world. A god I had never felt before touched my heart with a pure drop of truth to show me what the Persian was seeing. He approached the bridge to the afterworld of Ahura Mazda. But it was not the broad bridge of a soul judged good, but the sword's edge pathway that an evil man must tread. Upon the bridge stood Mihradarius's second soul, not the maiden shape of a blessed spirit but the withered, twisted hag form of one who had done Ahriman's bidding.

Mihradarius screamed and fell dead. Miiama crawled a few inches toward Phan and tugged at his sword; then he too collapsed, his soul fleeing the world, for what strange afterlife I did not know.

"I had to poison their pills," Phan said; his hands shook like autumn leaves about to fall from a tree. "I had to. I waited as long as I could. But the work was becoming dangerous. I knew Miiama would find a way to arrange an accident. I had no choices left, no options."

"I know, Phan," I said. "You have done well."

After a stunned moment in which nobody moved, two guards rushed over and grabbed Phan by his trembling arms.

"Let him go!" I said stepping forward. "He was doing what I wanted."

All heads turned to look at me. The soldiers released the old man, but did not step away from him until I walked over and escorted Phan to a seat near the barrel of clean water.

I filled a small brass bowl from the barrel and gave it to Phan to drink.

"You did well," I said to the old man.

"I had no choice," he said as he stared hard at his reflection in the bowl.

"Aias," Yellow Hare said, and I heard the echo of divine sternness in her voice. I looked over at her, standing tall and solid, grave as a mountain. The wind whipped through her braids and her eyes flashed in the gleaming light of Ares. "Did you order Phan to poison them?"

I stepped forward to meet her; my eyes drank in the fiery gold light of her eyes and the questioning spirit they carried. In my heart I understood her anger. Why had I not trusted her who was sworn to me in so many ways to carry out this task?

"I did not give the command," I said. "But I surmised what he had planned to do and I approved. Had I told you of it, you would have disapproved. You would have prevented me from taking the gamble, fearing that Phan was going to poison us and not them. As commander, I took that risk."

"But poison?" she said. "Why did you not let me execute them properly?"

"I judged that the taking of their lives was not worth the risk of losing yours," I said. I turned to Aeson. "Is it not a commander's duty to choose when to place his soldiers' lives in peril and when to keep them safe?"

Aeson nodded, and slowly Yellow Hare bent her head in acknowledgment.

But while my words satisfied the Spartans, they did not do so for the Buddhist. "But how could you add to the deaths?" Ramonojon asked.

"Because Phan is correct," I said. "Eventually, they would have tried to kill us. In my heart I had already condemned them. It was only a question of finding the opportunity. Phan provided it."

"I could not think of another way," the old man said. "I tried my best, but there was no choice. No choice."

"But, Aias," Aeson said. "To trust a Middler."

"Those who dwell in 'Ades," I said, "are equally dead."

Aeson bowed.

Phan looked up into my eyes and I could feel him still turning the possibilities over in his mind, still looking for another way to have solved the problem, and though he could find no such answer, his own mind forced him to continue the search.

"He thinks too much," Yellow Hare whispered to me, and I finally understood what those words had meant so long ago. Had it been my hand, not just my desire, that had taken the lives of Mihradarius and Miiama, had I actually been the conduit of Thanatos, I would be suffering the same confusion as Phan. The Spartan testers had been right to cast me out from their city of war. But though I had sympathy for Phan Xu-Tzu, there was nothing I could say that could help him.

Ramonojon, however, did know words of comfort that could aid an old Middler scientist.

"Still your thoughts," Ramonojon said, sitting down next to Phan. "Rest in the Tao."

Phan turned an angry gaze on Ramonojon. I could see his lips poised to emit an insult, but in my friend's eyes he saw a gentle spirit that could not be abused by words. "I have never learned how to stand upon the Way," the Taoist said. "The Tao outside of me I know well, but the Tao within I do not."

"I have been told that they are the same," Ramonojon said. "But I do not understand it either, and my teachers are too far away to offer help."

Athena stirred in my heart and I saw a vast chasm between myself and Phan, wide as the gulf between Earth and the Fixed Stars, deep as Tartaros itself. The goddess told me that somewhere along its rocky rim there was a bridge to be found or built.

ξ

---

For the good of our souls and our bodies we spent the next three weeks concentrating solely on the work of remaking the ship. In that time the soldiers finished the skeleton and tacked the cloth over the bones of steel and silver to make the wings. The work was more difficult than before because the new survival pills were not as good as the old ones. We needed some food and some sleep, and we felt the aches and pains of strained muscles. The guards did not complain, but I could see their haggard faces when they came back onto the body of the ship after unrolling and riveting down the black-wing sails. Aeson worked alongside them and the three guards drew great comfort from his presence. When he stepped fearlessly onto the fluttering patchwork of linen that stretched out over the side of the ship and crawled across the sheets billowing in the wild crosswinds of Ares, the men took heart and confidently followed him to do their work above the vast emptiness of the upper air.

While the soldiers did the work of sailwrights, I took up the post of charioteer, designing reins for the horse that would be pulling us and trying to teach myself how to guide that heavenly steed. I may say truthfully that I am an excellent Ouranologist; I can calculate to the inch the position of any planet at any time and plot a course from Earth out to the Fixed Stars, but my hands had little practical experience in celestial navigation. The only time I had ever piloted a celestial ship was when I had been stationed on 'Ermes. I had learned to control the medium-sized vessels that did the day labor around that orb. Those were the easiest ships to control, not wild and bucking like a moon sled, and not slow to turn like *Chandra's Tear*. Just simple, easy flying, a pull here, a tug there, a reliance on natural motions; that was all I had to do. That free and easy flight hardly compared to the job of controlling this new, untested vessel that even we, its designers, barely understood.

To try and make up for my lack of experience I made the controls as simple as possible to operate, and prayed that Daidalos the hero or perhaps the ghost of Kleon would help guide my hands as they piloted the ship through the shoals of heaven.

The controls I created consisted of a simple arrangement of four reins, silver guide wires that were interlaced with the strands of the sun net itself. The wires ran up the outside of the net, one on the port meridian, one on starboard, one on top of the net, and one on the bottom. Strung along each wire like drops of dew on a spiderweb were thumb-sized nodules of fire-gold. When a rein was pulled, the line connected to it would tighten and the nodules would rise up along that edge of the net. A thin column of rarefied air would be created and the net itself would be pulled in that direction; the sun fragment would follow the net, a horse following the guide of its reins, and the ship, chariotlike, would turn to follow the steed pulling it.

One week after I began work making these reins, Ramonojon presented me with a coiled strand of wire that glowed with the silver of Selene.

"What is this?" I said, holding the rope in my hands, feeling it slowly roll of its own accord through my fingers.

"I managed to take some of the moon rock that broke from the walls during the long flight and draw it out into a wire. Unlike your other reins, this one is unbreakable. It is to be laced through the center, in a spiral. When you pull on it, it will compress the net itself and draw the sun fragment toward the ship. That should slow us down momentarily if you need to. Don't overuse it; this ship cannot take much more strain."

"Thank you, Chief Dynamicist," I said.

Ramonojon bowed and left, and I returned to preparing the ship.

I needed a sheltered place from which to fly the vessel, so the guards built me a makeshift control cabin out of one of the storage crates. The large pine box was hauled out of the storage cavern, leaned up against one of the laboratory hillocks, and lashed to the body of the ship with steel bands and spikes. A door was cut in the starboard side and a window in the front, from which I could see the now solidly anchored trolley, the sun net, and my fiery horse. The four silver and one Selenean control wires were strung through the cabin's window and tied to hempen pull ropes that hung down from pulleys on the ceiling. I glued my charts of the spheres and epicycles to the walls of the cabin and put rolled-up carpets on the floor as a pilot's seat. It was not Kleon's navigation tower, but it would serve.

While I did all this, Phan prepared the controls he would need for his half of the piloting duties. Each day he wandered seemingly aimlessly across the ship, nailing gold and silver spikes into various places: seven of each on top of the hill, over twenty next to each wing, one at each of the cracks and turnings in the ragged tail of our bird. Then he took a large vat of vermilion paint and, with a horsehair calligraphy brush, painted lines of red between selected pairs of spikes. Three times he did something with a mesh of woven gold laid on the ground that made the lines of paint skitter across our surface, rearranging themselves into strange patterns that drew the eye to follow them. The curves of crimson flowed into graceful arc from wing across hill to wing, from tail to tip and back again. After the third such action, Phan pronounced himself satisfied.

"What have you done?" I asked.

"I have healed the body of this ship," he said. "It should now be able to survive the rigors of flight."

In response to this Ramonojon dug out the few dynamicist's tools he had remaining and, tapping the ground with a hollow hammer, calculated the solidity of *Chandra's Tear*.

"Many of the stress fractures are gone," Ramonojon reported to me when he had finished the survey. "Somehow, Phan has caused the Selenean matter to heal itself as if it were the flesh of a living being."

"That makes no sense," I said.

"Yes, it does," Ramonojon replied. "It accords with the Tao."

"Are you saying you now understand Taoist science?" I asked.

"No," Ramonojon replied. "I can only accept it by ignoring my own training. If I think about Selenean matter, if I concentrate on the dynamic form of the ship, all I can see is a block of stone to be carved into the right shape. But if I apply all the mental disciplines I learned from Xan and breathe deeply of the clear air to push out of my mind what I know to be true, then, for a brief moment, I can accept that one could treat this ship as an injured animal and try to cure it."

"Interesting," I said. "Tell me if any more of what Phan does begins to make sense to you."

"Yes, Aias," Ramonojon said.

Phan had the guards haul two three-foot-cubic bundles of bamboo lashed together with golden wire, each studded on one side with exactly one hundred silver nails, from a secret cave in Mihradarius's lab. Under the old man's direction, the soldiers secured these wooden sheaves to what had been the aft end of *Chandra's Tear*, but had now become the fore end of our as yet unnamed new ship. The blocks were placed equidistant from the midpoint of the ship's long edge, the spiked ends pointed out across empty space toward the sun net. Phan painted more cinnabar lines across the surface of the ship to connect these blocks to the makeshift cabin he had set up at the base of the hill a quarter of a mile directly behind mine.

"What are those bamboo sheaves?" I asked.

"Xi strengtheners," he said. "I used them to increase the fragment's wild flight when you first captured it. They were supposed to ensure the ship's destruction, but I think they were responsible for bringing us to Ares on the long Xi flow."

"How did you smuggle them onto my ship?"

"Mihradarius had the raw materials brought on during your absence, before anyone on *Chandra's Tear* knew of oncoming danger. I assembled the devices myself once I had been smuggled aboard."

"But why are you mounting these weapons here?"

"They are not weapons," he said. "They make the power of a given Xi flow stronger. Using them, I will be able to guide the fragment down the descending currents from planet to planet. I am also going to use them to slow the fragment down when we are orbiting so that we will be able to move about safely on the ship's surface."

"Are you finished with your preparations?" I said.

"Yes," Phan replied. "We can attempt to leave this orb whenever you give the order."

"First we must pray," I said.

I gathered the crew together on the playing fields next to the fluttering left wing of our new-made bird. I had timed the ceremony so that 'Elios, Ares, and the sun fragment were all beneath our keel, so the only light came from the stars and the body of the ship itself.

I dressed myself in my purple robes and stood in the mingled light of above and below. In my hands I held a plain bronze bowl filled with unmixed wine.

"The time of preparing is done," I said. "When Ares rises in four hours we will cast ourselves before the knees of the gods and try to escape this trap of the heavens."

I paused and raised the bowl up in front of me.

"Zeus, lord of the sky, bless our undertaking." I poured purple wine upon the silver ship. Thunder rumbled in my heart.

"'Era, queen of heaven, bless our undertaking." More wine poured on the ground, and that goddess descended onto Yellow Hare's shoulders.

"Athena, guide our thoughts. 'Ermes, guide our hands. 'Elios and Selene, forgive our thefts. Ares, let us flee from your snare." With each god's name I spilled more wine and felt the touch of the divine presence invoked. The assembled divinities waited in my heart, filling me with strength. The stars grew bright, and overhead the gleaming purple orb of Zeus passed in his majestic orbit around the earth.

"The omens are good," I said, and laid down the empty bowl.

"Phan Xu-Tzu," I said, turning to the old man, "is there any ceremony you wish to perform?"

"No, Aias," he said. "There is no proper li, no ritual for this place and time."

Athena touched me gently, whispering in my ear. "Very well," I said to Phan. "Then I give to you the honor of naming our new ship."

Phan turned in a slow circle, studying the bird with wings of night and head of fire, body of the moon and will of the sun, that we would soon be riding to life or death.

The old man raised his arms and his silken work robes glistened in the moonlight. "I name this vessel *Rebuke of the Phoenix*," he said; then he turned and walked to his control cabin in silence.

"A strange name," Yellow Hare said. "I wonder why he chose it."

"I do not think he did," I said. "I think he answered the prompting of a spirit."

We separated then, each to his own meditations. Yellow Hare and I went to the top of the hill and spoke together for a time. What passed between us then was as between man and woman, and thus I will leave it as private.

When Ares rose across the bow of our new ship trailing the sun fragment behind it, I left Yellow Hare to go to my control cabin while she joined the rest of the crew in the brig cells, the safest place for them to be during the flight. Yellow Hare protested at being separated, but I pointed out that there was nothing she could do to help me if some piloting disaster occurred, but she might be of help to those down below in case any of them were injured during the flight.

In my cabin, I leaned back against the hard wooden wall and strapped myself to the carpeted floor with long cords of twisted hide wrapped in spun cotton. The leather handgrips of the five pull ropes dangled down in front of my face. The port and up reins were to my left, starboard, and down to my right, and Ramonojon's gift, the emergency rein, hung directly before my eyes.

I waited for Ares to turn and pull *Rebuke of the Phoenix* toward the inner side of the war god's crystal sphere, so that we would not have to negotiate our way through the whole gear work of epicycles.

The red glare of Ares faded as he set under us, spinning eccentrically downward; then he rose again to port, pulling us after him. I tightened my grip on the guide wires and held my breath. The light of the sun glittered up through half a dozen of Ares' interlaced epicycles. I waited as the obstacle spheres spun away one at a time until, according to my calculations, only two invisible orbs, one of which tethered the sun net, lay between the *Rebuke* and the open skies.

I pulled the handle of the up wire. The rope strung across the ceiling became taut, pulling on the silver cord. Through the window I saw a gleam of gold rise up along one edge of the net, and I saw the sky become clear and sharp along that gleam. The air rarefied in an arc, pulling the net away from the sphere that trapped it, sliding off like a ring from a finger; then, like a knot untying itself, the sun fragment pulled the net behind it, freeing the ship from its moorings.

The sun fragment, like a racehorse let loose from its hobbles, spun up from the capturing epicycle. It tried to swerve and dance through the sky, but the reins held it; the rarefied air pulled the sun net out of its arc into a straight line, and that line of twisted celestial matter pulled the ball of flame after it.

The ship bucked and turned, following the net in a rapid spin. The breath was pushed from my lungs as the ship swayed angrily from side to side. My eyes swam with sudden dizziness.

The fragment swooped down, pulling us toward Ares. I yanked on the handle to the port rein and heard a snap reverberate down the line. The rope that tethered the port guide wire came away in my hand. I grabbed the wire itself and felt the sharp silver bite into my hand; a trickle of blood fell onto my sleeve, staining the blue scholar's fringe student red.

But I had the wire in my hand, I pulled, and a new line of gold sprung up along the net, pulling us to port until we faced the sharp edge of the main crystal sphere. I counted five heartbeats and then felt a humming in my back; Phan had activated his Xi strengtheners right on time. The sun fragment drifted farther to port in a gentle curve, and we turned slowly and gracefully away from the cutting edge of the unbreakable crystal, away from Ares and down toward the sun.

I released the guide wires. The gold shimmers vanished from the net, but the sun fragment continued in its flight downward, down and down, until, like a horse tired of running and wanting to graze, it turned away from its marked-out racecourse and took up an orbit around the earth a few hundred miles below the war god's sphere.

It took me half an hour to untie myself with my one uncut hand and walk across the rocking body of the *Rebuke* to the other control cabin. Phan was already outside, wearing a smile of satisfaction on his face that must have matched mine.

He bowed deeply to me, and I returned the courtesy.

We orbited for two days while Ramonojon, Phan, and I checked the ship to see how well it had survived its first use. Apart from some patching needed on the starboard wing and a stronger pull cord for the port guide wire, *Rebuke of the Phoenix* had come through its maiden flight intact.

Repairs done, we waited until the ship's natural motion pulled it back toward the invisible currents that connected Ares and the Sun. To my mind the next segment of our flight was the real test to see whether or not we would return to Earth. Neither Phan nor I was sure how fast we would be flying. He knew how great a speed a battle kite could attain in this Xi flow, and I knew how fast sun and moon tethered together would fly if no force was applied, but we could not yet add those knowledges together to calculate the speed of *Rebuke of the Phoenix*. We had to rely on experiment.

As we orbited under Ares, we resumed our flight stations,

Phan and I in our cabins, the rest of the crew strapped to the walls of the cells. The war god circled overhead and the sun fell below us. I pulled on the down guide wire and the netted fireball dove like a dolphin into the Xi current. The Xi strengtheners started to hum, sending a tickling shiver up and down my back, and we began to fall toward the sun, drawn down through the currents in the ocean of air toward the fire below.

The speed pushed me back against the hard wooden wall. The straps bit into my arms and legs, but I did not care. Like a Bakkhanate at a revel, I sucked in the same joy of flight that Kleon reveled in. I felt the navigator's ghost rise up laughing in my heart, drinking in the exhilaration like blood at a sacrifice, drawing Kleon back to the world of the living.

The navigator's spirit filled my ears with the sound of blissful harmony that the musical universe sings to the souls of Pythagoreans. And in that ode of the planets I heard, not saw, the Xi flow that gave this rapturous speed to our ship. The song was a duet sung in strophe and antistrophe by Ares and 'Elios in turn. And through my soul and throat Kleon sang with them, raising my untrained voice to match the music played on the lyre of existence.

And then without a warning, without epode, the song stopped and Kleon left me. The fireball had orbited out of the pathway between the planets and the echoes of the song of heaven faded away into the distance.

Dazed by the sounds I had heard, I stumbled from my cabin and surveyed the sky above and below us. Ares was a small red ball hanging high above us and far to port; 'Elios a large golden coin below and to our starboard. Once again they seemed to be mute balls of matter, but I had heard their voices.

Phan joined me to look at the spheres. He looked at each orb in turn as if he had never seen them before.

"Phan Xu-Tzu," I said. "Is Xi a musical harmony?"

"Yes," he said. "Is each planet a single note?"

"Yes," I said.

In my heart Athena raised the Aigis in salute while something that was not a spirit or a god passed through Phan's eyes and gave him a look of pure, quiet comprehension.

During the following week, we took four more rides down the song of the Xi flow and reached an orbit only ten thousand miles from the sun. One more downward plunge and we would return to 'Elios himself, and if we survived passage through the riptides of the sun we would reach the inhabited spheres. I decided we should spend several days just orbiting since I felt we all needed time to clear our thoughts before we attempted passage through the sphere that had wrecked *Chandra's Tear*.

On the second day of rest, the soldier Xenophanes came to my home cave, where Yellow Hare and I were relaxing after a long day's work, she smoking her pipe, I reclining against the cave wall.

Xenophanes saluted. "Commander Aeson requests your presence and that of Captain Yellow Hare, Commander Aias," he said.

"Where does Aeson wish to meet?" I said.

"In the dynamics lab, sir. He is there now with Chief Dynamicist Ramonojon."

"Inform Commander Aeson that we will be along in a moment," I said.

Xenophanes saluted again and walked out.

"Do you have any idea what this is about?" I said to Yellow Hare.

"I have a thought," she said.

"And?"

"And I would prefer that Aeson tell you," she said as she stood up and strapped on her armor and handed me my formal robes of command.

A few minutes later we walked down the steps to Ramonojon's old laboratory. Aeson and Ramonojon were seated on the floor in the center of the room under the ink stain. Aeson was wearing his full formal bronze armor; he had even put on the horsehair-crested helmet, and all had been shined to a sparkle. He sat cross-legged with his sheathed sword lying across his bronze-greaved knees and waited for us to approach and sit down to join them.

From a small pitcher Aeson poured out a bowl of dark red wine and mixed in a little water. He handed me the bowl; I drank a little and waited for him to speak.

"Commander," Aeson said. "Now that our survival seems likely, have you turned your thoughts to what we will do when we return to Earth?"

"Could you be more specific?" I said.

"Do we hand the sun fragment over at Selene," he said, "or try to carry out our mission by personally using it on 'AngXou? The latter seems to me quite difficult since we are neither on schedule nor carrying the armament we would need to reach the heart of the Middle Kingdom."

Ramonojon's face had grown white with horror as he listened to Aeson. "Is that why you called us together?" he said. "How can you even—?"

He took a deep breath to compose himself, then turned to look at me. "Aias, I would not have helped you repair this ship if I had known you were still planning to use the sun fragment as a weapon. And I am certain Phan would not have helped either."

"I have not said that I would still use it," I told him.

Aeson turned to stare at me in surprise. Yellow Hare, however, seemed completely undisturbed by my statement.

"You have put victory back within our grasp, Aias," Aeson said. "Now we must decide how best to achieve it."

"That is not what I have done," I said.

"But—"

"To steal fire from heaven for man's survival may be justified to the gods," I said. "But the words of 'Elios to me before the launching of the sun net were quite clear. That fire is not to be used for mortal wars."

" 'Elios spoke to you?"

I nodded.

"Then what are we to do, Commander?" Aeson said; his Spartan soul would never contradict a pronouncement of the gods.

"I do not know," I said. "I have too many conflicting duties. To the gods, to the League, to Ramonojon and Phan."

"To Phan?" Aeson said. "What duty do you owe him?"

"His life," I said. "Without his aid we would all be dead."

"Without him *Chandra's Tear*, our ship, would not have been destroyed," Aeson said. "We owe no duty to a saboteur."

"I disagree," I said. "The onus for the destruction of our ship lies on Mihradarius for his treason and Anaxamander for his folly. Phan was only doing his duty."

"Aias," Yellow Hare said gently. "You cannot save Phan's life. If we give him to the League they will execute him for sabotage. If we return him to the Kingdom they will execute him for failing in his mission."

"Then why did he help us?" Aeson said. "Why did he not take death when it was offered him?"

"Because a change might come," Phan said. He was standing on the bottom step of the cave entrance, looking around at the wreckage of Ramonojon's workplace. "In the turning of heaven and earth, there is always the hope of something unforeseen arising."

All of us looked up, startled at his entrance, except for Yellow Hare.

"You heard him coming?" I said to Yellow Hare. She nodded curtly.

Phan walked over and sat down next to Ramonojon. The old man sat with his knees bunched up against his chin, hiding his beard behind his now threadbare silks.

"You put your trust in Fortune?" Aeson asked. "She is a most unreliable goddess."

"Not in Fortune, as you think of it," Phan said. "In the certain knowledge that the world changes, and that between heaven and earth new things will come to be. It is a final desperate hope, but hope it is."

Phan looked around at each of us in turn.

"And if nothing comes of the hope," he said, "then perhaps it will not be so bad to be ruled by you."

"What are you talking about?" I said.

"The war," Phan said. "You 'Ellenes are winning the war. The Son of Heaven has lost his mandate. Maybe it is finally time for an outsider to rule All under Heaven."

"What makes you think we are winning?" I asked.

Phan waved for the wine bowl. I gave it to him, and he drank deeply. "Everyone knows it. You have conquered the river Mississipp in Atlantea and begun to spread into the Western Territories. You have made incursions into Xin again. Our kites are no match for your celestial ships, nor our cavalry for your artillery. It is common knowledge around 'AngXou that we are going to lose."

"But—"

"Aias . . . ," Aeson said.

The one word reminded me of the requirement of secrecy, and yet I could not keep still. Athena filled my heart with the need to comprehend.

"I must speak, Aeson," I said. I turned to Phan. "I do not understand this at all. The Archons told us that you were winning the war. They said that you had made new advances in miniaturization."

"Minor tricks," Phan said. "They gave our warriors individual weapons that could cause injuries your doctors cannot heal, but nothing more came of it. It is not sufficient."

"But our governors and generals are being assassinated," I said. "Miltiades told us that Prometheus was our only hope for disrupting the Middler government."

I lapsed into silence. Phan took a long drink, then closed his eyes. "Assassins are the weapons of desperate men deserted by the gods," he said, "not the tools of a Son of Heaven bent on conquest."

Kleio stirred in my heart. "I need to do some studying," I said, and stood up. "We will discuss this matter again."

Yellow Hare and I returned to my cave, each of us in quiet communion with our gods, I with Kleio, Yellow Hare with 'Era.

In my broken and battered home, I rooted around through the smashed furniture and wrecked cases until I found, wrapped in some old robes, the scroll Ramonojon had given me so long ago in the shadow of the Muses on the Acropolis, the scroll Yellow Hare's presence had prevented me from looking at: the *Records of the Historian* by Ssu-ma X'ien.

"Yellow Hare," I said, "I hope you will not think less of me for hiding this from you."

"What is it?" she said.

"Middle Kingdom history. Ramonojon brought it back with him. I assume he obtained it from his Buddhist friends."

"At first you did not know me to trust me," she said. "Then you had Ramonojon to protect. Since then you have had other worries. There is no dishonor in your concealment."

"Thank you," I said.

I slid the rice paper roll out of its plain black lacquer case and began to read an eight-centuries-old account of Alexander's war on the Middle Kingdom and the changes it wrought inside All under Heaven. It was a strange document, unlike the histories written before the Akademe banished Kleio; its chapters were titled with the names of different people involved in that war and in the placing of the first 'An emperor on the throne. Each chapter told the life story of that person and concluded with a brief explanation of Ssu-ma's opinion of his character and how he helped or hindered the cause of the Middle Kingdom. And though it was a tale of men's deeds it was not like reading a chronicle of heroes. There was no sense of worship, no reverence even for the most exalted people. It was more like a list of proofs than a remembrance for the honored dead.

I looked up some time later with an itch in my mind, as if Athena were trying to burst forth from my head. Yellow Hare sat against the wall where the cubbyholes had once hung, quietly smoking her pipe.

"I think I understand how both sides of a war can think they are losing," I said to her.

She extinguished the burning leaves with her hand and stared at me with her wide golden eyes. "Say on."

"What does Sparta teach is the most important element in the waging of successful war?"

"Generals whose souls have been filled with the spirit of war and the favor of the gods."

"So if our side has no such generals we would lose the war."

"Of course."

"The Middlers see it differently. Instead of filling their leaders with the spirit, they choose as their generals those who won battles as captains. They take these earlier victories as proof that these officers wage war in accord with the way of battle."

"I do not understand," she said. "A successful captain may be made general if he shows the proper spirit; if not he would remain captain."

"But to the Middlers war is a way, not a spirit. Spirits may help or hinder battles, and there are gods who oversee the progress of war, but they do not give victory or defeat; it is the way the general wages war that determines success."

Yellow Hare closed her eyes and the mantle of war fell upon her shoulders. The gods of battle clustered around her as she thought upon my words.

"It could be done that way," she said at last. "Without offending the gods, a man could be a general without a warrior's soul. But he could not persevere as a Spartan must. Eventually he would give up the life of war and some other general would take his place."

"And the same applies to their rulers," I said. "We take as leaders those who show the potential to be heroes; they choose those who demonstrate accord with the way of heaven, which can change."

"Our way is clearly better," Yellow Hare said. "We find souls with constancy."

"Is it?" I replied. "Consider Mihradarius."

"What about him?"

"He had great potential, the genius that makes Athenian heroes. If he had not felt the need to stop Sunthief, he might have risen to the post of Archon. Or consider my father."

Yellow Hare growled.

"He was an excellent general who inspired loyalty among his troops and governed cities well, but as you and Aeson have both pointed out, he violated the true essence of Sparta. A Middler general would hold to that essence while he served in war."

"You may be right, Aias," Yellow Hare said. "But how can both sides believe they are losing?"

"Consider what Phan said. He said the Middle Kingdom was losing battles and territory. That proved to him that the Son of Heaven has lost the mandate to rule, so the Middle Kingdom is bound to lose the war unless the Son of Heaven is replaced. They need to buy time for a new emperor to be found, so they engage in the desperate act of killing our leaders. The League's view, on the other hand, is that its leaders are being killed, so we will not have the heroes we need to win victories, so we are bound to lose unless we can strike quickly and decisively."

Her eyes widened, gold reflecting the silver light of the cave. Athena stirred in her mind and the Aigis gleamed through Yellow Hare's eyes. "Both sides believe they are losing," she said, "so as you say, both sides engage in desperate actions. The Middlers assassinate and the League creates the Prometheus Projects. Both sides are taking desperate gambles that are not necessary."

She gripped the hilt of her sword. "Neither side has acted in accord with the proper conduct of war," she said.

"Neither side is acting in accord with the Good," I said, and the words of 'Elios flared again in my heart.

# O

Kleio, I prayed after the revelation of Ssu-ma's writings, you have shown me your mystery, shown me how you can grip the hearts of men and nations and draw them down paths so disparate that the men of one people cannot speak to the men of the other. But goddess of history, inspirer of a lost study, what am I to do with your blessing?

And in the shadows of my heart Kleio and Athena together answered me. History bridged the chasm Wisdom had shown, and a new place grew in my heart near where my understanding of science dwelled. It was a dark cavern, as yet unformed and unfilled with the light of knowledge. But in that umbral grotto I heard a sound, an echoing chord, the song of the Xi flow that spanned the air between Ares and 'Elios.

Then the chord fell silent and a voice resounding with heavenly thunder roared through the darkness: Fill this place!

I will, Father Zeus, I will.

"Yellow Hare," I said, opening my eyes to the sight of the more familiar cave I called home, "would you have one of the guards find Phan and ask him to join me on top of the hill."

"Yes, Aias," she said.

The old Taoist met me half an hour later beside the stumps of Alexander's legs.

"I need to know more about your science," I said to Phan.

"Tell me how to teach you," he said. There was a quiet glow in his dark eyes and something lay on his shoulders that made his seventy-year-old frame look younger and stronger. "If you can learn to learn, then perhaps I can as well."

"What do you mean?" I said.

"I need to know your science, also," he said, and his eyes grew brighter. "But where do we begin?"

"At the weakest point in the barrier between us," I said. "The walls of theory are too high; let us start with practice. Show me your equipment. Pretend that I am not a scientist. Pretend that I am some ignorant bureaucrat who wants an explanation of your work so he can make out reports."

The old man smiled and bowed. "Will you do the same for me?"

"Of course."

Over the next week, Phan and I gave each other basic introductions to the paraphernalia of our sciences. I showed him how we used rare and dense air to create forced motion, and he showed me how gold, silver, and cinnabar placed along Xi flow could modify or control natural motion. Slowly, the dark cavern in my heart began to grow bright with a second vision of the universe, one of change and flow instead of matter and form. And as the light of practical work grew from a flickering candle to a solar beacon, it illuminated the bewildering Taoist texts I had studied over the years but had gained nothing from.

Memories boiled up in my mind of days spent poring over rice paper scrolls with block-printed characters, words in the Middle Kingdom language I had learned but not understood. There had been nights when the pictographs had seemed to dance before my eyes, mocking me with their hidden meanings. In those dark hours I had prayed long and hard to Athena and to 'Ermes, lord of translators, to help me penetrate the enemy's mysteries. And now at last they had answered me, and the texts that I had memorized began to unravel themselves in the light of my new-made mental cavern.

Had I been given the freedom to do so, I would have been content to let *Rebuke of the Phoenix* stay in that orbit, letting the combination of pure air and divine favor fill me up with comprehension, but I had other duties, and I had to carry them out. So Phan and I pulled ourselves away from our learning and teaching. In two languages with two visions we plotted out the ship's passage through the riptides of Xi that flowed out from the body of 'Elios, carried by the light and the atomic fire of the solar wind.

When we were satisfied with our calculations, I went to each of the crew in turn and spoke to them in private. We all knew that the flight through the sphere of 'Elios would be the most difficult test for the ship. If *Rebuke of the Phoenix* survived this leg of the journey we would have no difficulty flying back to Earth.

I spoke to Clovix first, praising him for his service since the disaster, and he bowed to me in thanks.

The soldiers I congratulated on their diligence, and I assured them that they had done honor to the army and the League.

Ramonojon and I shared a brief moment of silence, and let it pass at that.

Aeson and I spoke in quiet whispers of the mystery of Orpheus, then gripped hands and separated.

Of what passed between Yellow Hare and me, let that remain locked in the lips of Aphrodite.

Then Phan and I put on solar protective goggles and cooling cloaks and strapped ourselves into our pilots' compartments, while the rest of the crew went below into the safety of the brig. The ship flew into the Xi flow between Ares and 'Elios; Phan activated the Xi strengtheners and I pulled the reins, banking *Rebuke of the Phoenix* down the paths of heaven toward the fire of the sun.

Out the front window of my cabin I watched 'Elios grow and grow until he filled the sky with spears of red flame, and the words he burned into my heart caught fire once again.

Am I not serving the Good? I prayed. Have I not crossed the chasm?

Not yet! the sun god roared as *Rebuke of the Phoenix* passed through the crystal sphere and bore down on the celestial fire. God of the day, I prayed, let me go; I must steer the ship. 'Elios released my mind to once again calculate and pilot. The currents of Xi flowed out from the sun, invisible spirals pushing the Selenean part of my ship away from the fireball; but there was a single contrary flow that pulled on the sun fragment, trying to draw it back toward the body of fire from which it had been stolen.

It was my task to keep the fireball away from that flow while Phan maneuvered us through the push of the main currents to reach the inner spheres. The Xi strengtheners hummed in a staccato rhythm as we darted from flow to flow, pulled to left and right by the riptides, but Phan's sure hand kept us going downward, always downward. As we approached within five miles of 'Elios, I pulled on the port and up guide wires, drawing the fragment away from the sun, up and leftward. The sun disappeared beneath us, and the sky turned suddenly from the red of sunfire to the gold of sunlight as we flew over 'Elios.

I released the wires and the sun fragment dipped down again, I hoped to pull us past the sun itself; but the fragment continued to dip down farther than I had planned. The inward current had caught hold of the fireball and was trying to drag it under the ship and back around toward the sun. I pulled the central rein, tugging the cord of Selenean wire with all my might to call back the fragment, to hold it for just a few seconds.

I held on with all the strength that lay in my arms and all the will I could muster. I counted the heartbeats—five, ten, twenty—as we flew over the lamp that lit the universe. The ship turned pitch black from the wash of golden gleam that shone up from below. Tongues of fire danced beneath us, and then we were over the top of the sun, and the light shone from behind. The shadow of the hill fell across the bow of *Phoenix*, a long shadow as if the sun were setting directly behind me. We were past 'Elios, past the sphere of the sun god and away from the solar wind and the wild eddies of Xi that railed like the worst sea storms around that ball of celestial flame.

I let go of the wire and the sun fragment resumed its normal pull on the ship. The Xi strengtheners stopped humming and we took up an orbit just a few tens of miles below the crystal sphere that held the sun.

Thank you, lord of the day, I prayed. I give thanks to you, O 'Elios, for the safety of my people.

Not yet! burned the words in my mind. Not yet!

But despite this divine warning, my heart was filled with relief. We had passed through the fire and had entered the inhabited spheres. I left my cabin to join my crew in celebration. When I stepped out onto the surface of the ship, I saw a spot of silver in the sky off our port bow. As I watched, it grew larger and resolved itself into a glowing triangle. Then I realized what it was: the fore end of *Chandra's Tear*, circling lazily in a slightly higher orbit than *Rebuke of the Phoenix*.

Poor ghost ship, I thought, I hope your dead are resting.

As if in answer four small spots of silver flew out from the back end of the broken ship. Moon sleds, but piloted by whom?

Whoever they were, I could not let them find Phan before I had time to explain his presence and our circumstances. Assuming I could explain.

I turned and ran aft toward my copilot's cabin. A hundred yards from my goal, I smelled rarefied air and heard the clear moonstone-on-moonstone clang of a sled landing behind me.

"Aias, halt!" said an all-too-familiar voice.

I stopped and turned around, hardly daring to believe what I had heard. There, dressed in scorched armor and wearing a tattered air-cooling cloak, his skin blistered, scarred, and browner than an Aethiopian's, was Anaxamander, pointing an evac thrower at my chest.

At that moment I cursed the gods and the Fates; I railed against heaven for letting this man survive. For that blasphemy, I beg the forgiveness of the gods.

"Anaxamander," I said, "put down that weapon and surrender yourself. Enough of my crew have died because of you."

He laughed and his pinprick-pupiled eyes gleamed as he raised the thrower. "Did you think you had escaped retribution, traitor?"

"Fool," I replied. "Mihradarius was the traitor, he who advised you and set you on this course to ruin. I say again, put down your weapon."

He stood there waiting, not heeding my words, posed like a military statue. Behind him on the open deck of *Rebuke of the Phoenix* three more moon sleds landed, and two dozen of my old ship's soldiers stepped off. They too showed signs of prolonged exposure to the sun: scorched clothes, darkly tanned skin, and pupils small as the eyes of needles.

"How?" I said. "How did you survive?"

"I prepared," Anaxamander said, looking up toward the heavens. "A true soldier always prepares. I knew that you and Ramonojon might have sabotaged the ship, so I provisioned four moon sleds and detailed my most loyal soldiers to pilot them. I was not on *Chandra's Tear* when your treasonous acts destroyed it. After the disaster I and my surviving crew flew back into the near half of the ship. We have waited weeks for rescue. Then we saw you returning with the prize of your treachery. What was your plan, Aias, to use the sun fragment against Delos? Against Athens? Against Sparta?"

I said nothing, knowing that no reason, no evidence, would penetrate the solid wall of folly in Anaxamander's mind.

"Search this vessel," Anaxamander said as his soldiers gathered around him. "Everyone on board is a traitor. Take prisoners if you can; kill if you have to."

The soldiers broke up into four squads of six. Three of the groups spread out across the ship; one remained as a guard for Anaxamander. I prayed Yellow Hare, Aeson, and our own three soldiers would be able to deal with the small squadrons.

"Now, traitor," the security chief said to me, "what is that?"

He pointed at Phan's control cabin. I said nothing.

"Bring him," Anaxamander growled, and two of the soldiers walked behind me and grabbed my arms, twisting them behind my back. I bit back the pain, not wanting to show any weakness in front of the imbecile who had destroyed my ship. The guards force-marched me after their lunatic leader to the secondary control cabin. Two men went inside and a few moments later dragged Phan out. His face was a mass of bruises, and he stumbled as they pushed him.

He looked up at me with sad, dead eyes and started to speak. Anaxamander hit him on the shoulder with the barrel of his evac thrower. "Silence, Middler!"

Phan groaned and slumped against one of the guards. The soldier pushed him away and watched smiling as the old man fell to the ground, tearing his silk robe at the knees.

"Enough!" I said.

"Be quiet, traitor," Anaxamander said. He slapped me across the face with his gauntleted fist. I felt blood flowing from my cheek, but I bit my lip to keep from making a sound.

The guards pulled Phan to his feet, and we stood waiting at the base of the hill while Anaxamander surveyed our new ship and scowled at us.

A few minutes later, surrounded by six guards, Yellow Hare was escorted up from the brig cells. She had been stripped naked except for a bloodstained linen bandage around her shoulder, but the gods of war had enveloped her in a cloak of dignity and none of the soldiers dared approach or taunt her. She turned her golden eyes toward me and I felt a spirit of quiet confidence grow in my heart. Then she looked at Anaxamander and I saw her swear to deliver his soul to 'Ades. At that moment, naked and injured, with six evac throwers pointed at her, Yellow Hare's glare quelled Anaxamander. The Security Chief turned away. I saw the fear in his eyes, and I knew that he was about to have Yellow Hare shot.

"Do not give that order," I hissed to him. "Naked and dying she would still be able to kill you before the soul left her body."

"I am not afraid of that Xeroki," he said, and in those words I saw how tightly madness had gripped his soul.

"Then you are a greater fool than I thought," I said, hoping that this one truth might reach him. "She is a Spartan, a warrior in body and soul."

"It is of no consequence," he said, blustering for himself and for his guards. "We will bring this traitor back to Sparta and show them that they do not always choose their officers rightly."

He turned to the guards. "Was there anyone else below?"

"Yes, Commander," one of them said.

Four more of Anaxamander's guards emerged from the tunnel, escorting Ramonojon, Clovix, and our three soldiers; there was no sign of Aeson. Ramonojon seemed impassive. Clovix's eyes gleamed as he saw Anaxamander; the slave almost licked his lips. But when the Security Chief's gaze lit on Clovix, the Gaul resumed his long-abandoned servile posture.

"What happened?" I whispered to Yellow Hare as the guards escorted her over to me. "How were you hurt?"

She glowered and adjusted her bandage. "I was careless. They threatened to kill Ramonojon. I interfered. One of them shot me in the shoulder."

"Where is Aeson?" I whispered in Xeroki.

"He left the brig when you and Phan stopped the ship. I do not know where he went."

"Good. Maybe he can do something about . . ." My voice trailed off as I saw six soldiers escorting my co-commander up from the storage cave. Aeson walked with the full solemnity of a Spartan general surrounded by a guard of honor, and the soldiers, basking in the glow of his reflected glory, grew larger than their comrades.

"Security Chief!" Aeson shouted in his best parade ground voice. "What is the meaning of this?"

The blood drained from Anaxamander's sunburned face. "Commander?" he whispered.

Aeson strode forward like Zeus deigning to be seen among mortals. "Security Chief Anaxamander, you are relieved of command. Hand over your weapons."

For a moment, Anaxamander wavered under the pressure of Spartan authority. He looked down, avoiding the gaze of his commander, and his soul balanced on the edge of realization. The colossal error he had committed battered at him. All the self-justification, all the insinuations Mihradarius had poured into his ears, all the evidence he had compounded in his own mind against Ramonojon, Yellow Hare, and myself could not be turned against Aeson, his unsullied superior.

Had Anaxamander possessed a warrior's soul, a true Spartan spirit, he would have surrendered then and there and given himself over for punishment. But he was only a play soldier, a pretend Spartan, all appearance, no spirit. He could not accept that he had brought about the catastrophe that had befallen those under his command.

His spine stiffened by hubris, he raised up eyes blinded by até and spoke: "Aeson of Sparta, I arrest you for the crime of treason against the League."

The madman turned his back on his own commander and on the true way of the warrior. "Guards, put him with the other prisoners."

The soldiers looked first at Aeson, then at Anaxamander. Slowly, tentatively, they raised their throwers and pointed them at Aeson.

Aeson was herded over with the rest of us and forced to sit down on the side of the hill; he did so with quiet dignity. They kept us together in a circle, except for Phan, whom they isolated.

"Why did they obey Anaxamander instead of you?" I whispered to Aeson.

"Survival training," he and Yellow Hare said simultaneously.

I raised a questioning eyebrow.

"It is done," Yellow Hare said, "by sending a group of soldiers and a commander into long-term danger. If the commander keeps the soldiers alive, they learn to obey him instinctively. When they come out they will do anything he asks."

"And these soldiers," Aeson said, "have been trapped orbiting near the sun with meager food and water for weeks. After that long even Anaxamander's blustering manner could raise a man's spirits to the point of loyalty."

The Security Chief walked around the neat little circle of his prisoners like a hen counting her eggs. Then he resumed his heroic posture, looking skyward. "And now, we will fly this ship back to Earth to fulfill our mission." He looked lovingly across the bow at the sun fragment floating in midair. " 'AngXou will burn!"

"And how will you fly this ship to the Middle Kingdom's capital?" I asked.

He pointed his thrower at me. "You will be my pilot."

"Why should I do that?"

His guards pointed their throwers at our little circle of prisoners. "If you do not," Anaxamander said, gesturing theatrically, "you will all die."

Athena touched my heart then, reminding me that given time wisdom would overcome folly. "Very well," I said, "but I cannot fly this ship alone."

He waved his hands around the circle. "You have all the assistance you need."

I pointed at the mournful figure of Phan, sitting isolated a dozen yards away. "I need him."

Anaxamander snorted. "Ridiculous. You are just trying to keep your spy alive."

"I swear by the river Styx that without Phan Xu-Tzu this ship will never reach Earth."

"A blasphemer as well as a traitor," Anaxamander said.

"Nevertheless," I said, "I have sworn, and the gods will not permit me to contravene that oath."

"The gods will already condemn you for your crimes," he said.

"If you will not accept the oath that cannot be broken," I said, "then look around you. This ship uses Middler technology. No Delian scientist understands their equipment. Do you think that I am the only exception?"

Anaxamander stroked his chin and slowly nodded. He was too blind to accept my word, but he could easily believe in my incapability.

"Very well, you shall have your Middler," Anaxamander said, feigning magnanimity. "His death is only delayed."

As is yours, I vowed silently.

"Let me explain the situation to Phan," I said. "I can make him cooperate."

"No one will speak with the Middler," Anaxamander said.

"He will be locked up until you actually need his help flying this ship."

There was no point in arguing further so I nodded my acquiescence.

"We will depart for Earth when this ship is secured!" Anaxamander said to the world around him.

He pointed at Clovix. "Slave! Attend me!"

Anaxamander turned away, and the guards parted to let the chief slave stand. Clovix stepped forward, back bent, walking meekly but quickly behind Anaxamander. The Gaul's posture seemed more subservient than he had ever been, but in that crouch I saw an angry wolf poised to spring. The ghosts of all of *Chandra's Tear*'s dead slaves clustered about Clovix thirsting for Anaxamander's blood. The fires of vengeance gleamed in the Gaul's sharp blue eyes. He stalked forward head bowed until, when he was only a foot behind the Security Chief, the Gaul leaped up, grabbed Anaxamander by the back of the throat, and started to wring his neck.

There was a hail of tetras from the throwers of the guards, and the blond giant's body fell to the ground. His soul departed from his body and joined the throng of spirits. I could feel the touch of his breath upon me, trying to fill me with his need for vengeance, to enrage me as he had been enraged. But the goddess of wisdom shielded me from the throng of spirits.

Return to 'Ades, I said to them. Anaxamander's death will not come today, but I vow to you that it will come.

Anaxamander gasped and choked, holding his throat until he regained his breath.

"A slave revolt as well," Anaxamander said.

"Clovix wanted proper revenge for your actions," I said. "Your foolishness killed those who were under his command."

"Your treason did that," Anaxamander said. He waved a dismissive hand toward the guards. "Lock up the prisoners and throw this slave's body overboard."

The guards took us down to the brig and locked us into the three cells that still had doors. Their former comrades-in-arms Xenophanes, 'Eraklites, and Solon were given a cell. Yellow Hare was put in with Ramonojon. Aeson and I were locked down together.

"Até and hubris," my co-commander said. "The Fates have written Anaxamander's death."

"But why have they done so?" I said. "Why did they preserve him in the first place?"

"Perhaps he is to be the instrument by which the sun fragment is delivered," Aeson said. "Perhaps Anaxamander will be responsible for winning the war."

"No, Aeson, even if 'AngXou burns the war will not be won."

"How can you know that?" Aeson said.

"I have learned a great deal in the last week about the Middle Kingdom," I said. My eyes lost focus. I could no longer see Aeson; rather, my vision was filled with the panorama of men and events Ssu-ma X'ien had painted with his words. "It is true that without their capital the Middle Kingdom will be disorganized. And yes, they will lose a great deal of territory, maybe all of Atlantea, maybe Tibet. But no, we will not defeat them. They will step up their campaign of assassination and in a matter of months they will disorganize the League. Eventually they will choose a new Son of Heaven and a new capital. Eventually they will develop a means of stopping Sunthief. At some point in the future, they will gain scientific superiority again, and Sunthief will become just another in a long series of scientific advances that was of temporary use in the war."

"Aias," Aeson said, "I heard the thunder of Zeus in your voice. What is happening to you?"

"The gods have been trying to tell me something," I said. "And I almost know what it is; but I have not yet heard it all."

Hours later our cell door was opened and two guards motioned me out. "The commander wants you," one of them said.

"Your commander is right there," I replied, pointing to Aeson. The guard pushed me up the stairs.

I was led across the deserted surface of the ship to my control cabin. Anaxamander was inside with two of his soldiers. "The

Middler claimed we could turn inward soon," he said.

I looked out the window. 'Elios was almost directly above us. "Phan is correct," I said.

"Good," Anaxamander said. "I am anxious to return to Earth."

His guards tied me down in the pilot's seat with my own straps, and then they and Anaxamander tied themselves to the walls of the cabin with ropes threaded through knotholes in the boards. All five of them pointed their throwers at my immobile body.

"Is Phan in the other control room?" I asked.

Anaxamander nodded. "The Middler knows his job, and the penalty for failure."

*Rebuke of the Phoenix* entered the Xi flow, and I pulled on the port guide wire, turning our bow downward along the direction by which the current of nature traveled. I was thrown lightly back by the sudden impetus, but once we entered the flow there was no force upon my body; nature carried me along cradled in her arms. No pilot of the Delian League had ever flown so smoothly. Far away I saw the tiny green dot of Aphrodite waiting at the far end of that river of Xi. The familiar hum of the Xi strengtheners started and the ship picked up speed.

Aphrodite was a slim green coin in my forward window as we started to fall. Then she grew, and grew, until when we turned starboard and righted ourselves the goddess of love was a sphere one foot across. We had halved the distance between planets in a handful of minutes.

Anaxamander looked out the window in wonder, and his face lit with ecstasy.

"This ship is a great prize," he said. "Thank you for providing it, Aias."

You will not live to bring it home, I swore silently.

"Take him back to his cell," Anaxamander said to the guards.

"I need pen, ink, and papyrus to make some calculations for the next flight," I said.

"You shall have them," he replied, his eyes fixed firmly on the heavens.

"I need Phan as well."

"No. You will not see the Middler." Anaxamander turned to look at me. "Take him away."

The guards returned me to my cell and gave me the supplies I needed. I sat down on the floor and consulted the two sciences in my heart, and the gods above, to give me aid in planning an accident.

It took me two days to do the theoretical calculations for the Taoist device I wanted to make. No doubt Phan could have done them in a matter of minutes. But those two days of work sharpened my awareness and gave me a feel for the Xi that I had not possessed before.

At the end of that time, Anaxamander brought me out to pilot the ship downward again. Thankfully, we did not quite reach Aphrodite in that fall, but we were sufficiently close that the next time we entered the Xi flow it would carry us all the way to the green sphere. I had no choice, I had to act immediately.

"The guide wires are coming loose," I said to Anaxamander when we emerged from the control cabin. "I have to fix them or they will snap during the next flight."

"What do you have to do?"

I pointed to the twirling, intertwined lines of the sun net. "Climb out along that," I said.

Anaxamander bared his teeth in a parody of a smile. No doubt the prospect of my risking my life to help him appealed to his twisted soul.

The soldiers tethered me to the ship by long hempen ropes tied to my shoulders and waist. I crawled carefully out onto the sun net, followed by two men who did not seem to care how dangerous the trek was.

The spun cords of celestial fibers bit into my leather-gloved hands and stung my legs through the folds of my robes. The wind whipped around me, threatening to pull me off as I climbed across the open space, following the port guide wire until I reached the first of the finger-long impellers that lined the silver cord.

From a pouch tied to a rope belt I had threaded around my waist, I removed two small gold needles, a paintbrush, and a pot of vermilion paint. I tied the needles to the closest impellers on the port and starboard wires. Then carefully crawling backward, I painted a thin line of red down a single strand of 'Ermean matter. That crimson stripe connected the gold needles to the network of red paint lines Phan himself had drawn on the body of the ship.

If I had done the job correctly, then whenever I pulled on the starboard or port guide wires a humming signal would be sent to Phan's control cabin through the Xi strengtheners. I could only hope he would interpret the signals correctly.

The next day, as *Rebuke of the Phoenix* neared the Xi flow, the guards took me from my cell and strapped me down again in my cabin. I sat, hands poised near the pull ropes, and waited to put my plan into action. The ship passed over Aphrodite, eclipsing the goddess of love, and I pulled gently on the port wire to start our maneuvers. The fragment bucked a little to the left, and a tingle ran up and down my arm. The transmitter was working. I hoped that Phan understood my messages. I wished I had been able to devise something to receive responses from him, but Anaxamander had not let me near Phan's cabin.

We turned downward and started to fall toward the sea green orb below. We flew along the last few hundred miles of the Xi flow and entered the calm tidal currents around Aphrodite. I pulled us up ever so slightly. The planet disappeared beneath the prow of the ship. Then I yanked hard on the port wire, turning us sharply to the left and sending a shock up and down my arm. Phan got my message and turned off the port-side Xi strengthener.

The sun fragment reversed itself, turning hard to starboard and pulling *Rebuke of the Phoenix* in a wild spiral.

"Right us!" Anaxamander shouted, leveling his thrower at me.

"I'm trying," I lied. I pulled on the starboard wire. A shock went through my right arm, and the other Xi strengthener turned off. The sun fragment was free of the currents of natural motion; now it was solely under my command. I pulled the down and port wires and the ship stopped tumbling a quarter of a mile above Aphrodite's surface. I did not give Anaxamander time to notice that we were stable. I pulled frantically on the down wire and the ship dove nose first toward the planet below. Then, before we crashed, I pulled hard on the up wire and gently on both port and starboard wires. The hum of control returned; but before we pulled up, *Rebuke of the Phoenix* scraped its underside on the love goddess's skin.

The ship wailed in anger, screaming the note of the moon. I heard a sharp crack and knew our keel had fractured. In my cabin a board broke off the wall and slammed down on the head of one of the guards, knocking him unconscious. I pulled again on the up cord and we sailed through the gap between planet and crystal sphere. We passed inward beyond the green orb and limped into orbit like a wounded horse.

Now only 'Ermes and Selene stood between us and Earth.

"I warned you that I could not fly this ship without consulting Phan," I said to Anaxamander. "Now we will have to repair the keel before we can go on."

"Very well," he said. "We will heave to for repairs."

"I need Phan," I said.

"No, the Middler stays where he is."

"Then at least give me the assistance of a dynamicist; give me Ramonojon."

Anaxamander untied himself from the wall and stalked over to where I was sitting. With his mailed left hand he lifted my head up by the chin and forced me to meet his gaze. I could feel him trying to muster the spirit of a warrior with which to intimidate me, but the gods of war wanted nothing to do with Anaxamander. I stared straight into his eyes, while with 'Ermes' aid I hid my hatred deep inside my heart. "Very well," Anaxamander said. "Take the Indian."

"And I will need Mihradarius's laboratory; it is the only intact work space on the ship."

"Agreed," he said, and walked out onto the ship to stare up at Aphrodite and the Sun beyond her.

Two guards brought Ramonojon to me in Mihradarius's lab and then stationed themselves at the bottom of the staircase. My friend's face was worn and haggard, his pants and shoulder wrap were torn and disheveled, and there were bruises on his neck and arms. I gripped his hand gently and smiled reassuringly at him.

"Aias," he said, "what has been happening?"

"There was an accident," I replied. "We need to repair a crack in the keel. Come help me with the equipment."

We walked over to the corner of the lab behind Mihradarius's old writing table and opened the leather bag in which Phan kept his gear. Ramonojon cast me a quizzical look but I shook my head. I rooted through the bag while giving a very long-winded technical description of the damage.

The guards rapidly lost interest and Ramonojon and I gradually stopped speaking 'Ellenic and started speaking Hindi.

"Is Yellow Hare all right?" I asked.

"She is well. Her shoulder healed quickly thanks to Phan's pills; but she is still pretending to be injured for the sake of the guards." He paused and rubbed his bruised face lightly. "Anaxamander wants me to sign a confession before we reach the moon."

"With Athena's help we will have taken back the ship long before then."

"You have a plan?" he asked, leaning forward to catch my words.

"During the repairs we will be making certain devices." I outlined what I had in mind.

"Can you make such things?" he said.

"When Athena graces my heart," I said, "I can."

Over the next week Ramonojon and I took several moon sled trips to the underside of the ship, accompanied as always by the guards. We laid a huge leather bandage over the twenty-yard-long crack in the ship's underside. I mapped the Xi lines and, using the equipment Phan had employed to heal the ship previously, I made the hole begin to repair itself. To speed the process up we used fire-gold cannibalized from sled impellers to melt the edges of the crack and seal up the damage. The combination of repair techniques worked extremely well; the softened matter, guided by the Xi lines, sealed itself into a silver scar. And as the gap closed in the body of my ship, the chasm in my mind closed with it. Guided by Athena, thoughts leaped across from one science to the other, each side casting light upon its opposite.

The guards watched us carefully; Anaxamander had told them to make sure we did nothing except fix the crack. They were suspicious of us, but that did not disturb me as long as they did not concern themselves with what we did with the leftover scraps of leather and the small flakes of fire-gold we shaved off from the impellers.

Working under their noses was difficult, but we managed with the help of stealthy 'Ermes to cut ten thin leather strips, put silver pins in the ends of each band, carefully paint ruler-straight cinnabar lines down the smooth front of each strip, and cover the rough back sides of the leather with a mesh of fire-gold wires.

When we were finished, I informed Anaxamander that the ship was ready to fly. He had me locked in my cell with Aeson while he and his men did a thorough inspection of the repairs.

That one action, placing me once more with Aeson, proved to me that the gods were guiding Anaxamander to his own destruction. He could not have delivered himself to me more perfectly if he had given me a sword and laid his head down on the chopping block. For in returning me to prison, he allowed me to give one of the leather strips to Aeson.

"What is this?" Aeson asked.

"Put it under your tunic," I said. "The fire-gold side must face outward."

"But what does it do?"

"It should protect you from the guard's throwers."

"What? How can something this thin serve as armor?"

"It is not armor, and do not ask me to explain; it is too technical."

"Very well, Aias," Aeson said, and he slipped the band under his tunic, placing it near his heart.

I had already given Ramonojon the rest of the leather strips, except for one that I had hidden in the folds of my robe. I just had time to explain my plan to Aeson before the guards came to take me to my control cabin. We strapped down as usual, I, Anaxamander, and two blindly loyal guards. The soldiers tied me down, but I managed with a little subtle squirming to slip the knots slightly loose after the soldiers had strapped themselves to the walls.

I steered the ship into the Xi flow connecting Aphrodite and 'Ermes, and we begin to pick up speed. Out the fore window I saw 'Ermes grow larger and larger, and beyond it I saw a little dot of silver, Selene. The Moon was in a straight line with 'Ermes and Aphrodite. At first I thought nothing of that, but as the song of the Xi flow entered my mind, I realized that I was hearing three voices singing, not two.

Too late the thought arose from the cavern of Taoist science that three planets aligned made an immensely stronger flow than just two. We rushed down the river of Xi, faster and faster. I did not know if *Rebuke* could take the stress, especially after her recent injuries. But there was nothing I could do to stop the flight.

The planet of 'Ermes grew from a tiny dot to its full size in mere minutes. We hurtled down toward him, skipping out of the main flow and across the currents around the planet of messengers. In seconds we were bearing down on the red-brown orb itself. I held my breath and pulled gently on the up wire. It lashed back, tearing skin from my hand. I pulled again and the impellers came up in a thin gold line, rarefying the air above the net.

*Rebuke* rose slowly above the horizon of 'Ermes. Four crimson celestial ships flew up from the cave in the planet to meet us, but we rushed past them. 'Elios pulled our chariot and Xi sped us on our way and we could not have slowed to meet those 'Ermean envoys if I had wanted to.

Then we were over 'Ermes and through the crystal sphere. The trio of singers became a duet as Aphrodite's note vanished from the chord. Phan turned off the Xi strengtheners and *Rebuke* orbited out of the flow hundreds of miles below the sphere of 'Ermes. It would be hours before those four ships we passed caught up with us.

Anaxamander and his guards were dazed by the flight. They hung limply from their straps, but they were still conscious and though their aim was very bad they would still be able to shoot me with their throwers. I prayed briefly to 'Ephaistos, god of crafts, that my devices would work while I untied the last of my restraints and stood up.

"Do not move," Anaxamander said. He waved his thrower at me like a drunkard and tried to fumble at his restraints.

My soul composed for death, I walked toward him and grabbed the long metal tube that he held out in front of him. Anaxamander fired at my chest. A spray of tetras rushed forward, coming within an inch of my robes. Then they entered the thin region of slightly rarefied air in front of me. The bronze projectiles swerved to the side and slammed hard against the wall. The guards fired and the same thing happened to their shots. Anaxamander gaped as I took his thrower from him.

"What have you done?" he said, his voice slurred.

I said nothing. Instead I turned the thrower toward the guards.

"Drop your weapons," I said. They did so. Then one by one I knotted their restraining leathers together, securing them to the walls.

"Aias," Anaxamander said, "I will see you in 'Ades for this."

"Security Chief Anaxamander," I said turning to face him. "I, Aias of Athens, sole commander of the vessel *Rebuke of the Phoenix*, do hereby sentence you to death for mutiny. Sentence will be carried out by Captain Yellow Hare of Sparta. When next you see her, she will take your life."

I turned and left the cabin. Then I ran across the open ground to the other control room. I had to reach Phan before his guards realized that something had gone wrong.

Behind us, a dozen small silver globs flew away from the four ships pursuing us. Fast moon sleds. Our lead time had been cut to half an hour at the most.

I ran through the door in Phan's cabin and caught the first guard just as he finished unstrapping himself.

"Sit down!" I said as I leveled the thrower at his face. I tied him and his comrades up and released Phan from his control seat.

There were scars on the old man's face. The sleeves of his silk robes had been torn off, and his arms were covered with burn marks. His eyes were dull with pain, but he managed a weak smile when he saw me. I handed him a strip of leather. "Put this in your robes," I said.

He studied it for a moment with Akademic detachment. "It is a guide to control the movements of small pieces of metal," he said.

"It deflects thrower shots," I said.

"But evac thrower shots are too fast to be controlled by the Xi-flows, unless . . ." He turned the strip over. "You lined it with fire-gold."

He slipped the deflector under his robes.

"Yes," I said. I led him outside, and we ran toward the prison tunnels. I held his arm to steady him as we went. "The fire-gold gives the tetras enough impetus to follow the guideline."

"Amazing," he said, and bowed deeply to me. "Truly Heaven has opened your mind."

I bowed back to him before resuming our dash to the brig. But we had not been needed there. Yellow Hare, Aeson, our three soldiers, and Ramonojon emerged from the tunnels behind a line of four unarmed guards. Aeson and Yellow Hare were both armed and armored and each carried a drawn thrower.

Aeson and Yellow Hare saluted me. A moment later Xenophanes, 'Eraklites, and Solon did the same.

"What is to be done with the prisoners, Commander?" Aeson said.

My answer was cut off as from the storage cave entrance two dozen yards portward the last dozen of Anaxamander's soldiers charged onto the ship's surface, their swords and throwers drawn, and their lips shouting war cries into the crimson skies.

# π

Anaxamander's phalanx fired, filling the air with a shower of sharpened steel tetras that sped toward us like a myriad of angry hornets.

"Stand firm!" I yelled. My crew, obedient and confident, did not move, defiantly standing firm like emplaced targets while the deadly projectiles flew toward us. Then, to the confusion of our enemies, as the shots were about to tear through our clothes and skin, the glinting steel baubles turned and fountained upward into the sky. A few seconds later, the tetras, their impetus spent, fell back down and clattered harmlessly onto the surface of the ship.

"Surrender!" I called across the open space at the base of the hill toward the attacking soldiers. "Your leader, Anaxamander, has been taken. Surrender and your lives will be spared."

Their answer was another useless volley of swift but ineffectual shots.

I nodded to Yellow Hare; she and Aeson leveled their throwers to return fire. They aimed low, and with Spartan accuracy and efficiency fired short bursts of tetras into the legs of our attackers. The pellets cracked through the soldiers' greaves; blood flowed from their calves until their legs could no longer support them. One by one the soldiers crumpled to the deck until Yellow Hare and Aeson had winnowed their numbers from twelve to six. Then their fanaticism finally broke, and the six who could still stand retreated into the storage cave, taking cover inside the arched entryway of the cavern.

"Should we pursue them?" Yellow Hare asked.

I turned to look aft. The convoy of moon sleds was only a few miles behind us. All I had to do was wait for them to arrive and we would have plenty of soldiers to assist us in rounding up the renegades. At that moment I could have done nothing, could have let the squadrons from the ships of 'Ermes come to our assistance. They would have eagerly aided us in quelling the mutiny, and then assisted me in returning to Earth, to the Delian League, to a hero's welcome for a great duty fulfilled.

And yet . . .

A spark flared to sudden life in my mind, a tiny firelight that grew into a flickering torch brand. At first I thought the flame was 'Elios, but the sun god's light would have grown brighter still until it was a blinding crown of fire. This flame was smaller, and there was something comforting and warming about it, like the welcoming crackle of a hearth fire on a winter's night.

Then I saw a hand holding out the torch, offering the flame to me: the hand of Prometheus, creator of humanity, forewarner of mortal and immortal alike, he who had dared the wrath of Zeus himself and suffered, chained to a mountain for the sake of mankind.

Will you give fire to man? the prophetic Titan asked, and my mind filled with visions of battle. Celestial flame scoured the earth, boiled away rivers, scorched fields, burned away the stone walls of cities, consumed steel towers like tallow candles, and in a flash reduced humans in their millions to coils of smoke rising high into the air.

Or will you give fire to man? Prometheus asked. The Titan drew my eyes away from war, but did not give me peace to look at. He showed me something else, something indistinct, complex, subtle, imageless. It was not a picture, though light transmitted it;

it was not breath, though I inhaled it. It was pure, clean Pneuma, the substance of thought, the subtle body of the mind, composed purely of fire and air, unsullied by any touch of earth or water. He showed me and filled me with the atmosphere that lies just inside the Sphere of Fixed Stars. Look up, the Titan said. Bring down the starlight lanterns from the heights of heaven, not the fire that lives only halfway up the ladder of the universe.

My eyes flashed open and I saw the spheres above, I saw the climb that could be made by man, if, if. If the moon sleds just a mile above *Rebuke of the Phoenix* were not permitted to land.

"No, Yellow Hare," I said. "Do not chase them."

I turned to look at the others. "Flight stations, everyone!" I said. "Aeson, have your men drag the wounded soldiers below. Yellow Hare, come with me."

No one questioned my orders. Phan darted around the hill to his cabin. Aeson, Ramonojon, and our soldiers pulled the injured men down the tunnel to the brig while Yellow Hare and I took off at a run toward my control cabin.

The moon sleds came in close, circling the ship cautiously, studying the unexpected configuration of *Rebuke*, then finally drawing up into a line across our stern preparatory to trying to land on the hill.

Yellow Hare and I reached my cabin; I threw open the door. Anaxamander and his two guards were exactly as I had left them, tied to the walls and spitting with fury.

"Kill him," I said to Yellow Hare.

Anaxamander's eyes grew wide and he started to speak, but with one smooth, swift motion Yellow Hare drew her sword and decapitated the security chief before a word could leave his mouth. His men screamed and cursed, but one glare from Yellow Hare quelled them.

As I secured myself to the pilot's chair, my bodyguard cut Anaxamander's corpse loose from the wall and threw his carcass and his severed head out the door onto the surface of *Rebuke of the Phoenix* to fall into empty air when next the ship turned downward toward the earth.

Yellow Hare then strapped herself down on the floor next to me.

I gathered the reins in my hand and, pulling gently on the port and starboard wires, signaled Phan to turn on the Xi strengtheners. The familiar hum started up, sending slight shivers through my back and arms. I pulled the starboard rein and turned the ship around, reversing our course to speed us back toward the Xi line that connected 'Ermes and Selene. Our pursuers were left no doubt gravely confused and wondering just who was piloting this strange vessel.

Before we reached the river of Xi, we passed a mere fifty miles under the four 'Ermean celestial ships which had been following their moon sleds. The four ships stopped in midair and waited for us to rise to meet them, but we continued in our flight, passing swiftly beneath those ruddy orange rods of 'Ermes.

I could imagine the confusion of their commanders and the debates they must have had as to what to do. Long before they came to any decision, we had entered the flow, turned downward, and crossed a thousand miles of space. With only ballast balls and impellers to lend them speed in descent, it would be many hours before they could catch up with us.

I signaled Phan to turn off the Xi strengtheners, and pulled *Rebuke* into a stable orbit.

Only when my hands had left the reins did Yellow Hare ask me the question that had clearly been troubling her.

"What duty are you pursuing, Aias?" she said.

"The duty I owe to the gods," I answered, unstrapping myself. I nodded toward the two guards tied to the wall. "Bring them, please."

"Yes, Commander," Yellow Hare said. She bound the hands of Anaxamander's guards with their own restraints and marched them at sword's point to the base of the hill where the rest of the crew and the six injured guards waited.

"The rest of Anaxamander's men are tied up in the storage cave," Aeson said to me. "We caught them unawares when you slowed the ship."

"Bring them out, please," I said.

Aeson and our three soldiers entered the cavern and emerged leading the last half dozen of the mutineers, unarmored, their hands bound behind them. At my instructions all fourteen of the prisoners were seated in a line at the base of the hill. My crew stood in front of them waiting to hear my words.

"This ship is not returning to the Delian League," I said.

There was a stunned silence, broken only by the mutters of "Traitor" from Anaxamander's soldiers.

"Nor is it going to the Middle Kingdom," I said.

Aeson stepped from the line and walked toward me, his hand on his sword's pommel and his eyes sad with a spirit of unwanted duty. But Yellow Hare stepped between us, blocking his path. She held her hands at her side and met his gray gaze with her gleaming gold eyes.

For a time they stood, unmoving, facing each other like two statues. No words were spoken, but their spirits wrestled in a silent challenge of pure Spartan determination. At last Aeson cast down his gaze and broke the silence, speaking, but to me, not to Yellow Hare.

"Aias of Athens, I require that you justify your orders," my co-commander said.

"If we return to the League," I said, "the Archons will be forced by their own sense of duty and their own awareness of the desperate state of our people to use the sun fragment as a weapon. I cannot permit them to do that."

"But you know that the situation is not desperate," Aeson said.

"But I could not convince them of that," I said. "Kroisos is an Akademic; he will not hear the words of history. And Miltiades can not surrender a weapon once it is in his hands, can he?"

Aeson slowly shook his head. "No Archon of Sparta would so betray his oath."

"The Archons would be trapped by their minds and their duties," I said, "into doing that which the gods would not have done."

"And you?" Aeson said.

"I was offered a choice," I said. "I made it. I will undo the damage of Sunthief and at the same time give the Delian League what it is my duty to give them. But to do that, I must return to Earth with this ship."

Aeson turned back to Yellow Hare. "Why do you support him in this action?" he said.

"For the same reason you gave him your authority to command," she said.

"But we are no longer beyond human reach," Aeson said. "We have returned to civilized space."

"No," said Yellow Hare. "We will not have so returned until Aias says we have. Until then we are still surrounded by obstacles to survival and duty, and it is between Aias and the gods to decide what we must do."

"What have you seen?" Aeson asked, stepping close to her and locking his gaze with hers.

"The face of Zeus through the eyes of 'Era," Yellow Hare replied.

Aeson stepped back and drew his sword with one swift motion. Yellow Hare stepped aside, giving Aeson a clear path to reach me. Phan gasped, but I stood still, waiting for what was to come. Aeson stepped forward and handed me the weapon hilt first. "I remain at your command."

"Thank you, Aeson," I said, handing back the sword. "The first thing we must do is remove our enemies from this ship."

Anaxamander's soldiers looked up at me; some glared with defiance, others sweated in their fear. I walked over to where they sat, fourteen men in a row.

"I am not going to kill you," I said, kneeling down and looking into their worried faces. "You thought you were doing your duty in obeying Anaxamander. You will be set adrift on one of your moon sleds. Our pursuers will find you and pick you up."

I turned to Yellow Hare. "Tie them tightly to the moon sled. I am going to write a message to the Archons and leave it with them."

"What message?" Aeson said.

"A cursory explanation of everything that has happened since our departure from Earth, with particular emphasis on Anaxamander's unlawful takeover of *Chandra's Tear* and his appointment of that traitor Mihradarius as Scientific Commander."

"And will you explain why we are not returning to fulfill our mission?"

"That will have to wait," I said. "But the message will make clear to Kroisos how ill-omened this expedition was, and it will explain to Miltiades why we did not carry out the orders he gave us. The rest of the explanation will follow once we have returned to Earth."

"Why wait?" Aeson said.

"Because the explanation will require compelling evidence which I cannot give from here."

While the others secured the prisoners to the sled, I wrote the message and sealed it with the stamp of my commander's seal. The owl of Athens impressed in black wax on the edge of the paper stared up at me, and I felt Athena's reassuring presence flutter through the dark places of my heart on the wings of night.

The prisoners were strapped down supine in the center of the sled, forced to stare up at the sky. I approached the glowing silver disk and was about to tie the scroll onto one of their chests when Athena gently nudged me.

"Xenophanes, 'Eraklites, Solon," I called out. The three soldiers stepped forward and saluted.

"What is to come is beyond the duties of common soldiers," I said. "Therefore I am ordering you to accompany these prisoners and deliver them to the commanders of whichever celestial ship rescues the sled."

"Yes, Commander," they said. There was a glimmer of relief in their eyes. I had no doubt that the events they had witnessed and taken part in since the wreck of *Chandra's Tear* had been greater trials than they had been trained to endure.

"You will also see to it that this message is delivered to the Archons," I said, handing the scroll to Solon.

"Yes, Commander," the soldier replied. The three of them stepped onto the moon sled and secured themselves amid their comrades turned prisoners.

I turned to the rest of the crew. "Only Phan and I are needed to pilot this ship. Any of you who wishes may go as well."

Yellow Hare said nothing. Her stolid gaze told me what I already knew, that she would stay with me until the day of my death and even beyond if the gods permit.

Ramonojon shook his head with a slight smile. "The Delian League would not welcome me back," he said.

"Aeson?" I said.

"Are your ordering me to go?" he asked.

I hesitated. I knew Aeson would not leave without such a command, and I was tempted to give the order. The testimony of my writing would be greatly enhanced by Aeson's presence, and if he went, he would certainly survive what was to come. But to force him to depart, to give up the last vestige of his command for the sake of his life, was to make him betray the spirit of his city. His Spartan soul could not emerge intact after obeying such an order.

"No, Aeson," I said. "I am not ordering you."

We set the men adrift, knowing that the gleaming silver dot of the moon sled would attract the attention of our pursuers. With their departure, our crew had dwindled to a mere five from the two hundred who once occupied *Chandra's Tear*.

When the sled had dwindled to the size of a coin far aft of us, I said to the four people remaining under my command, "Now we will run the barricade of the moon."

I steered *Rebuke of the Phoenix* into the Xi line connecting 'Ermes and Selene. Phan activated the Xi strengtheners and we began to fall toward the scarred body of the silver moon. In the music of the spheres, the goddess sang a dirge into my soul, calling me down to her with a sad lament of youth lost to the ravages of time and man.

Selene called and my ship answered, crossing the one score thousand miles in an hour's time. I could imagine the reaction on the moon as the patrol ships spotted our approach and the impossibly fast pace we were setting.

As we entered the Xi shoals around Selene, I saw more than twenty celestial ships and over a hundred moon sleds waiting to meet us. If we slowed and greeted them they would have known that all was well. But after I had given one swift tug on the port rein, causing *Rebuke of the Phoenix* to dart deftly around the right edge of their well-ordered battle lines, they had no choice but to adjudge us enemies.

The cannonades of the four nearest ships spat steel into the air; a hail of tetras blanketed the sky before us. I pulled the down rein and *Rebuke* dove toward the surface of the moon, ducking under that wall of flying steel shards.

Ground cannons fired up at us, slamming into our underbelly. Another wall of ships flew up from the caverns of the moon, their forward cannons firing a new fusillade into our underside. I yanked on the reins of our fiery horse, pulling us left and right, trying to dodge as many of the tetras as possible.

The hum of the Xi strengtheners grew louder as Phan fought to hold the ship together against the onslaught.

Then the flagship of the lunar fleet, the battleship *Bow of Artemis*, flew out from the moon's equator; huge and terrible, shaped like an angry eagle with a two-mile wingspan, her forward edge was lined with cannons from one wing tip to the other. She tried to fly above us, but I pulled the up rein and the *Phoenix* rose above the eagle.

Denied the perfect bow shot, she still fired, and half a thousand tetras struck the underside of my ship.

The harmonic of Selene shuddered up my spine as the ship's keel cracked under the force of the barrage. There was a rumbling noise from below, a sound I'd heard before but could not identify.

Then we were through the barricade of Selenean ships, past the moon herself, through the inmost crystal sphere, and flying down from the lowest reaches of heaven toward the earth.

We outdistanced our pursuers easily and took up orbit halfway between the earth and the moon. I left my cabin and joined the crew at the base of the hill.

"The ship has been badly damaged," Yellow Hare said.

"Show me where."

She led me and the rest of the crew down the tunnel to the storage cavern. The once-solid floor of moon rock had been punched through by the repeated artillery barrages, so that through the many holes in the floor the earth could be seen. Most of the large boxes had been splintered by ricocheting tetras and their contents had fallen out of the ship.

"There is no way to repair this much damage," Ramonojon said. "This ship will not be able to fly much longer."

"We have a more serious problem," Yellow Hare said. "Our supplies are gone."

I called Phan over from his survey of the cracks in the hull. "How well are we supplied with survival pills?"

"We have taken the last of them," he said. "They will wear off within two days."

"The omens are clear," I said. "Our journey must end soon."

# ρ

"Where are we to go?" Phan said.

"A mountain on one of the borders where the armies of both the Delian League and the Middle Kingdom can find us," I said.

"You want to be found?" Aeson said.

"Yes," I said, "but not immediately. We must have a few hours on the ground before we are located."

Ramonojon took a deep breath and spoke. "There is a place in Tibet we might land—"

"Tibet?" Phan said in disbelief. "The country is swarming with the Son of Heaven's armies."

"And the armies of the League are permanently camped on Tibet's borders," Yellow Hare said.

Ramonojon nodded and a thin smile broke out on his lips. "And the Tibetans have a myriad of places to hide from both armies. The mountains of Tibet have many hidden communities of Buddhists; one of them is the place where I was taught."

Aeson cocked an eyebrow at Ramonojon. "Whatever Aias's

plan is, it involves both armies finding us. Do you want your teachers killed?"

"They would give up much more than their lives to stop Sun-thief," Ramonojon said.

"But they do not have to," Yellow Hare said. "There are mountains in South Atlantea where we could hide for a few hours."

"Do you know them well?" Ramonojon said. "Can you spot a good hiding place from the air?"

"No," she said. "We would have to search."

"I know how to reach my teachers' refuge," Ramonojon said.

"Ramonojon's idea is the best," I said. "The Buddhists are the only other people on Earth being hunted by both empires. They may be able to give us the aid we need."

"What aid is that?" Aeson said.

Athena opened my mouth and spoke through me. "A mountain peak, a mountain cave, pens, ink, and paper," she said. "Those are the last things you will require."

"My teachers can provide those," Ramonojon said.

"Then there you will go," Wisdom declared.

Yellow Hare and Aeson bowed at the divine voice. Ramonojon covered his face, and Phan stared quizzically into my eyes, then slowly bowed.

From that moment until this, Athena has not left me. She has dwelled in my heart and filled my mind with her wisdom, so that even though we had descended into the heavy air of the earth, my mind remained clear and my purpose never wavered.

The goddess returned my voice to me as she settled herself into the two caverns of science that had grown within my heart.

"We will go to Tibet," I said.

With the underside of the ship badly damaged from the cannonades of the moon, I did not dare let anyone strap down below. We bundled together in the control cabins. Yellow Hare and Ramonojon came into my cabin. Aeson went with Phan to his.

I steered us into the huge Xi flow that joined Selene and Earth, and we fell toward the night-shrouded Pacific Ocean. *Rebuke of the Phoenix* screamed as we plummeted, the now horribly familiar howl of moonstone cracking. There was an angry snap and a large piece of our port side broke off. The gaming fields went spinning off into a silent orbit, carrying half our left wing with them. No more funerals would be held on our ship, and the games of our dead would have to be played on Earth.

The balance of the ship shifted sharply to starboard, and the straps securing me started to loosen. My head slammed into the aft wall, dazing me; Yellow Hare loosened her own straps, freeing her arms but keeping herself securely tied to the floor by her legs. She leaned over and grabbed my shoulders to keep me steady.

The ship continued to dive down toward the moonlit waters of the vast ocean. Out the forward window, I saw dark spots against the waters, islands only a few miles below us. I tried to pull on the starboard wire to drag us out of the Xi flow, but it strained against me; Yellow Hare reached over and took hold of the pull rope, adding the strength of her arms to mine. Phan turned off the strengtheners just as Yellow Hare and I, together, managed to drag the starboard control wire in enough to turn the sun fragment and pull the ship in a wide swoop away from the water.

We took up a swift orbit only two miles above the earth. Groups of islands flashed below us as we flew westward toward the Middle Kingdom and Tibet. In the night sky above us I saw flecks of silver growing larger, celestial ships descending to catch us.

The ship passed from darkness into twilight over the islands of Nippon. Battle kites rose up in their hundreds from that rugged land to meet and challenge us. The air above the mountain air bases of Nippon became thick with strengthened Xi currents, but the currents that buoyed up the silk-skinned bamboo bats and dragons flying toward my ship only gave added speed to *Rebuke of the Phoenix*.

Silver dust and boulders of moon rock spilled from *Rebuke* as she cracked again from the strain of dodging two flotillas.

Phan turned on the Xi strengtheners and I released the reins. Given its head, our horse of fire plowed through the assembled squadrons of aircraft, scattering the Middle Kingdom's wood-and-cloth dragons upward into the sky, where they met the diving moonstone battleships of the Delian League. Evac cannons spat and Xi lances roared as battle was joined between our two pursuers. My people and Phan's turned and met again across the chasm of their sciences and death erupted from that void. Where he and I exchanged words they exchanged fire.

"No longer!" I shouted. "Fight no longer." But the two fleets could not yet hear my words and the thunder of their weapons drowned out the thunder of my voice.

And then we were through the cloud of pursuing dragons. *Rebuke* had been injured; the ship was bleeding a stream of silver moondust to spin and glisten in the sky behind us, leaving a trail for celestial ships and dragon kites to follow.

*Rebuke of the Phoenix* flew past the islands and over the twilight ocean east of the Middle Kingdom. We sped on, following the curve of the earth, until out the forward window, there on the horizon, lay the Kingdom's capital, 'AngXou. Its glittering jade towers sparkled in the sunlight reflected from the lake on its western edge and the ocean on its east.

O, ye gods, I beg that you know how much I was tempted to dive my ship down toward that city, to fulfill the simplest of the duties I had been given. It would have been easy to abandon the commands of the gods for the orders of men to rain down celestial fire and destroy a million lives for the glory of the Delian League. One tug on the downward rein at the right moment and I would have guaranteed my own immortality.

But I held back my hand. Though every battle kite in the capital rose up on silken wings to batter my ship with breaths of fire and twisting currents of Xi, though *Rebuke of the Phoenix* was shaking and cracking as if it would shatter in a moment, and though every lesson my father had ever battered into my heart about duty cried against me, still, with Athena's help and Prometheus's vision, I held my hand.

We flew over the cities, the towns, the farmlands of the Middle Kingdom, no doubt striking terror into the hearts of the people of that land. But we continued on, bleeding silver into the air, until we reached and passed the Kingdom's western border and entered the maze of pinnacles that rise above the clouds, stabbing upward from the mountains of Tibet.

I steered toward those peaks, hoping to reach our goal before *Rebuke of the Phoenix* died, never to rise again.

"Descend, Aias," Ramonojon said. He pointed toward a tall peak that pierced the low-lying clouds, the snow on its cap melding its frozen white with the floating white of the clouds. "That is the mountain we must reach."

I pulled the down rein, and we dropped among the peaks. Snow that had been frozen since the world began melted from the unnatural nearness of the sun fragment.

Like a hunted bird, we dodged and wove between the mountains. Our wing spars cracked against the mountainsides, but we kept flying. A trail of silver marked our path, glittering in the sunlight. With each turn we took to dodge between one mountain and another, *Rebuke of the Phoenix* broke a little more and screamed its suffering in the voice of ravaged Selene.

But, at last, we managed to reach our goal: a cold, peaceful mountain high in the 'Imalaias, desolate and empty, with no sign that anyone had ever lived there.

As we neared the peak, I pulled hard on the starboard guide wire, pulling the sun fragment sharply toward the apex of terraced stone. As I had planned, the net snagged on the jutting pinnacle of the mountain, and the sun fragment, flying in a spiral, wound the net into a tight knot around the jutting spire of stone and snow.

By this means I moored *Rebuke of the Phoenix* to the roof of the world. Then I pulled on all four reins, drawing out the small impellers that lined the net. A column of rarefied air appeared, pointing up from the mountaintop toward the sky. The sun fragment bobbed inside that column, trying to fly upward but held down by the net and the mountain. The fireball became a gleaming beacon that would mark our position clearly for those who hunted us.

The Selenean body of my ship floated a few hundred yards from the peak, orbiting lazily around its mooring.

Yellow Hare, Ramonojon, and I unstrapped and joined Aeson and Phan. We boarded one of the remaining moon sleds, and I piloted it down the side of the mountain until we passed through the water-thick clouds, down into the lower reaches of the mountain.

There on a spar of rock looking up into the sky stood perhaps ten or twelve men, clad from head to toe in heavy furs.

"There," Ramonojon shouted above the blustering Tibetan winds. "Land where they are."

I brought the moon sled in for a soft landing on a snowdrift near the rocky outcropping. Aeson and Yellow Hare secured the sled to a nearby boulder with mooring ropes while the rest of us stepped down onto the solid, unmoving ground of Earth. The cold of winter bit through my sandals into my feet, and I watched in momentary fascination as my breath condensed into a cloud of steam.

The fur-garbed men walked over as we disembarked. They threw back their hoods to reveal a variety of Middler and Tibetan faces, all craggy, all weather-beaten, and all remarkably calm about our presence.

From the center of the group stepped a short, thin Tibetan man with a serene face and gentle brown eyes. There was something lying across his shoulders; it was not a spirit, but it could have been had he wanted it to be. He smiled at me, and I felt the smile pass through my eyes and touch Athena in my heart.

Ramonojon stepped up to him and bowed, grasping the old man's hands warmly.

"Master," my friend said. "We seek assistance."

The Tibetan touched Ramonojon's shoulder and my friend straightened up. "Come with us, Ramonojon. We are leaving this place for a safer one."

"Master," Ramonojon said, "I cannot. The weapon I contributed to making is tethered to this mountain. I have not yet stopped the warriors from using it."

"Ramonojon," I said, "go with your teachers. I promise you that Sunthief will not be used as a weapon."

Everyone turned to look at me.

"Aias," Ramonojon said, "how can you promise that?"

"Because History and Wisdom have told me how it can be done." I took Ramonojon's arm. "Please go," I said. "You have a place of refuge. People who can harbor you. Please go to safety, my friend."

Ramonojon stood still for a while, his eyes shifting back and forth between myself and his master. At last he turned to face the old Tibetan and said, "Master, I must stay with them. I have not gained enough detachment to leave my friend to a fate that should be mine."

The old man shook his head sadly, but said nothing to try and dissuade Ramonojon.

"We need a cave," I said.

"Follow that trail," the Buddhist teacher said, pointing toward a rough-hewn track that ambled down the side of the mountain.

"Yellow Hare, Aeson, Ramonojon," I said. "Find the cave. Phan, you and I must return to *Rebuke of the Phoenix*. We have work to do."

My comrades followed the trail down the mountainside while the Buddhists followed a different path that led them into a deep ravine on the north side of the mountain, where they disappeared from our sight.

Phan and I took the moon sled back to the ragged body of my ship. The sun fragment had melted the permafrost from the peak of the mountain, laying bare the sheets of stone that had not seen daylight since the world was made. The air was filled with heavy trails of steam, thick with mind-dulling water, but Athena kept my thoughts clear and focused on the plan she had inspired in me.

I landed the moon sled near the bow of the ship, beside the laboratory hillocks, and tied it to one of the cave entrances.

"Get your equipment from Mihradarius's lab," I told Phan. "And meet me by the port Xi strengthener."

"Yes, Aias," Phan said.

When we met again, the two of us set to work changing the configurations of the Xi strengtheners by painting a thick line of cinnabar from each of the spiked blocks to the base of the trolley, then another one from Phan's cabin down the ship's axis, over my cabin, and onto the trolley. We finished our task by nailing a dozen silver spikes into the left and right sides of the trolley itself.

I did not tell Phan what we were doing or why we were doing

it; but I knew in my own heart that I did not need to do so. I do not know what god guided him or whether he had truly found the Tao in his heart and was simply doing what needed to be done.

But whatever divinities inspired us, Phan and I worked together swiftly and efficiently as if we had been comrades-in-arms from childhood.

When the last stroke of paint was laid down and the last silver nail hammered, we went to our control rooms but did not strap down. With slow, cautious rein work, I uncoiled the fragment from the mountain peak, freeing *Rebuke of the Phoenix* for its final flight.

The ship twisted to port, and the last vestige of our wings shattered against a mountain. I pulled the up rein and let the fragment pull us above the highest peaks of the 'Imalaias.

Then Phan activated the port and starboard Xi strengtheners at the same time. There was no hum in my cabin because the line we had just drawn connecting the cabins and the trolley dampened the Xi flow in the body of the ship. The port and starboard sides of the vessel came alive with the flow of nature, but the central axis of *Rebuke* was as lifeless as the spine of a corpse.

I pulled back on all five reins. The central cord hauled in the sun fragment, loosening the coils of the net. The other four reins rarefied the air in four small columns, pulling the loosened strands of celestial matter away from one another, undoing the knots Mihradarius had tied. The sun net came apart like a cascade of hair released from a ribbon.

The sun fragment, freed from its net, would have leaped up into the sky, but the Xi strengtheners had created flows that pointed left and right, not upward. Pulled by the opposite natural motions, that perfect sphere of sun fire deformed into an ellipsoid, its long axis stretched across the sky, and in that oblate ball, fire pull against fire, straining to follow two different dictates of nature.

We waited for five tense minutes, watching the fragment strain while the strands of green and brown and silver celestial matter that had comprised the net separated into two bundles of heavenly streamers, flapping upward in the breeze.

The fragment sang its torment, wailing the harmonic of the sun through the mountains of Tibet. Then that song became a cry of freedom as the glowing red ellipsoid tore itself in twain. Two balls of fire shot away from each other, one flying left along that Xi flow, the other flying to the right.

Each of the celestial flames flew into one of the strands of uncoiled net, and when heavenly fire touched heavenly rope, I let the reins go. The strands twisted, but not back into the unified net Mihradarius had designed. Now there were two sun nets, each holding half the fragment.

For a short time, my chariot had not one horse, but two. With reins and Xi strengtheners Phan and I turned those twin steeds around and set them to pull *Rebuke of the Phoenix* down toward the mountains.

*Phoenix* cracked under the strain of that turn. The harmonic of the moon reverberated back and forth through the body of the ship, growing stronger with each echo. It jarred my bones and shook my teeth, but I held on to the reins, steering the ship back to the mountain that had tethered it before. The scream of Selene filled my ears, threatening to blot out all other thoughts, but there, there was the pinnacle. I tugged the port and starboard reins and the twin fragments twisted to left and right, coiling themselves in opposite spirals around the peak and yanking at the ship from opposite directions.

Only when they were solidly moored did I release the reins. Then I ran from my cabin over the straining ground, dodging streams of moon sand and bombards of silver rocks. Phan and I met at the moon sled. I cut the mooring rope with a knife; the two of us dove onto the disk of moon rock, and we flew away from the bucking ship.

Behind us the ship screamed one last time and broke in half along the line of deadness we had drawn down her meridian. There was a blinding hail of silver moondust which splattered the moon sled and dug deep into our robes and skin.

But we had succeeded. All that remained of *Rebuke of the Phoenix* were two huge slabs of moon rock welded to the two halves of the trolley, which in turn hung on to the two sun nets which were wrapped around the mountain. The whole makeshift arrangement chained the sun fragments, like twin Prometheuses, to the rock.

"Well done," I said to Phan, brushing the silver dust off my body and watching it float away in a lazy spiral.

"Well done, indeed," he replied, clearing the gleaming moon sand from his glowing face.

I piloted the moon sled down the trail until I found the Buddhists' cave, a large cavern shielded from view by icy ledges. Inside there were two dozen small circular huts made of stitched white furs thrown over skeletons of lashed-together bamboo. On the back wall had been painted a picture of a serene-faced Indian man holding the world in his open palm and looking down at us with a comforting gaze. The image was roughly drawn and little color had been used, but still it compelled the soul as strongly as Athena's statue in the Parthenon.

"Shakyamuni Buddha," Ramonojon said.

Yellow Hare looked away from the image, but I bowed briefly to our host.

Near the entrance was a vegetable garden planted with rows of cabbages, turnips, and some kind of bean unfamiliar to me. There was also an underground stream that flowed from a break in the cave walls; the water sparkled clear and cold against the rock floor.

Yellow Hare and Aeson were sharpening their swords beside the river. Ramonojon was sitting in the door of one of the huts.

"What now, Aias?" Aeson said.

"Now we will bring our pursuers here and the will of Zeus will be done," I said, and my voice echoed through the cave.

I pointed to Aeson and Ramonojon. "I want you two to take the moon sled and deliver messages to the fleets pursuing us."

"The League or the Middle Kingdom?"

"Both," I said.

"What are we to say?" Aeson asked.

"Tell them that if they will send to me delegations of a dozen men, comprised of both soldiers and scientists, then they can each have one of the fragments. If they refuse, tell them I will sink the celestial fires into the earth, where they will burn through Gaea's body, orbiting inside the body of the world forever."

"Aias," Aeson said, "how can you arm the Middle Kingdom?"

"I am not arming them," I said, "though they will think I am."

Aeson stood up and sheathed his sword. Ramonojon left the hut and walked over to the entrance, where I had tethered the moon sled.

"Tell them to come tomorrow morning three hours after dawn," I said. "Warn them that if they come before the appointed time or take either of you prisoner, I will carry out my threat."

The Buddhist and the Spartan sat down on the disk of moonstone and flew off into the sky to carry my promise and my threat to the empires that ruled the world. I watched them go, following their flight with my prayers.

# σ

I n the icy water of the underground stream, we bathed for the
first time since the wreck of *Chandra's Tear*. The pure, clear
flowing water washed from my body the accumulated dust of
the long weeks of work I had spent toiling to return us to Earth.
With potash soap and a cloth of rough linen I scrubbed off the
moondust that had stuck to my skin, and I watched it float away
through the water, adding a mirror gleam of silver to the transparent stream.

When the celestial accumulations had been washed from my
body, I lay on my back, floating in the ice-cold river. The last
vestiges of the survival pills let me bathe in comfort in that newly
melted snow. I relaxed and listened through the flow of water to
the comforting heartbeat of Gaea, mother of all things; the deep
pulse of the earth washing over my temples welcomed me back to
the folds of her bosom.

A few feet downstream, Yellow Hare methodically scrubbed
her body clean with a bamboo brush she had found in one of the
huts until her skin shone with a red-gold gleam. Then she untied

her braids and washed her hair in the silvered waters until it glowed like ravens' wings in moonlight.

Phan had built a small fire near the rear wall of the cavern, and Yellow Hare and I repaired there to dry ourselves while the old Taoist entered the stream to wash himself. Left alone with Yellow Hare, I leaned close and whispered in her ear.

"There is a secret I must tell you," I said. "You will have need of it in case we do not live out the next day."

She turned her golden gaze on me, and I felt her spirit enter my heart through my eyes and discern the nature of what I wished to tell her. "Aias," she said, her whispered words soft as a breeze but sharp as the bite of winter wind, "will you betray an oath sworn before the gods?"

"No," I said. "I make no betrayal, for we are still in 'Ades and I am duty-bound to help you escape."

She slowly nodded her head and brought her ear to my lips. I whispered to her the secret of the Orphic mysteries, telling she who had guarded my life how to free her soul from the realm of the dead.

I stand before you now and avow that my words to Yellow Hare were no violation of my oath. For it was by the secret of the mystery that Aeson had given me the duty of ensuring our survival, and that duty had not yet been fulfilled when I spoke those words to Yellow Hare, initiating her into the sacred band of those who know the true path of Orpheus. And with that secret handed over I no longer feared whatever might come of my actions. From that point until this, neither I nor any of those who stood with me feared whether life or death would come to us.

A little later, 'Elios set over the range of peaks in the west, but the two sun fragments still gave light to our mountain, twin beacons that guided Aeson and Ramonojon back from their embassies. Cleaned and dressed, Yellow Hare, Phan, and I went out to greet them and help them moor the moon sled to the ledge outside the cave.

"How did you fare?" I asked my messengers once we had stepped back into the shelter of the cavern.

"The Middlers were at first reluctant to send a delegation," Ramonojon said, arching his back and rubbing his shoulders. "It was clear that they suspected some trap. But when I told them that Phan was alive and partially responsible for our safe return, their general decided that they had to come and find out what was worth his risking the lives of his family."

"I do not think he will be disappointed," Phan said. "And if all goes well, I think my family will survive."

I turned to Aeson. He cupped his hand in the river and drank deeply of the silver water. Then he wiped the glow from his lips. "General Antiokles, commander of the squadron of celestial ships pursuing us, will be here. He is eager to find out what cause would turn two Spartan officers and an Athenian scholar away from their obvious duties."

"Well done," I said. "Now, gather around. We have a great deal to do before morning."

At my behest, Ramonojon found us some sheets of rice paper, a few bamboo pens, a dozen sticks of red ink, and a few inkstones that the Buddhists had left behind. Phan and I settled ourselves on the fur-carpeted floor of the largest hut, laid the paper on wooden boards, and began to write.

By the light of the sun fragments gleaming down through the clouds into the cave, we scribed the bridge between our sciences. Phan, used to writing with brushes, stumbled a few times setting down Middle Kingdom characters with pen strokes. And my hand slipped occasionally, as I was unaccustomed to a stick of bamboo in my hand rather than a quill feather. But the problems of our mortal shells were easily swept aside by the understanding that flowed from our souls onto the pages during that long, bright night.

When 'Elios rose in the east to greet his kidnapped children chained to the mountain, I had covered thirty sheets of paper with 'Ellenic text and formulas while Phan had filled five sheets with the more compact Middle Kingdom characters.

"Now we must ready ourselves for our guests," I said.

Aeson and Yellow Hare dressed themselves in their armor, which they had cleaned and burnished during the night. Their

Spartan brassards with the iron badge of 'Era's peacock hung nobly around their necks and the horsehair plumes of their helmets stood straight and firm. During the night Ramonojon had stitched up the holes in Phan's torn silk robes, restoring dignity to the old man's attire. My Indian friend had also washed my scholar's robes, restoring them to whiteness and giving a gleam to the blue Athenian fringe. On my right shoulder I placed my badge of command, proudly displaying the unblinking owl of Athena.

Ramonojon himself donned a simple robe of Buddhist saffron. The yellow garment silently but boldly declared his separation from both the League and the Kingdom.

At the third hour after dawn, we arrayed ourselves to receive visitors. We stood ten yards within the cave and waited facing the cave entrance; Phan and I stood next to each other in the center, Ramonojon behind me to the left, Yellow Hare and Aeson flanking us. The Spartans stood at attention, their flared steel swords held naked in front of them in the traditional stance of an honor guard.

A wind rose in front of the cave, whipping up billows of snow. In my heart a clap of thunder sounded. Something great and terrible rose within me, growing in size until it filled all the caverns of my spirit. The whole of my mind became awash with the sounds and sights of a vast storm, but the tumult in my heart did not disturb me, for by the power of that divinity who rules the heavens I stood above the clash of thunder and beyond the blinding force of the lightning strike.

I turned my head to the right and saw Phan standing amid a quietness, a gentle flow like the zephyr winds of spring, but deep and sonorous like the tides of the ocean deeps. He was gazing at me and through my eyes and through his eyes the greatnesses that stood within us watched each other for a time, then reached out across the streams of Pneuma that bound us light to light and breath to breath, and so they touched.

"Aias," Aeson said from a long way off. "They are here."

I turned to look at the cave entrance. A large moon sled had landed outside. Next to it a dragon kite floated coiled, hovering only three feet above the ground. The delegations stepped from their transports and in two columns entered the cave. On the right came the men of the Delian League led by a Spartan general and an Athenian scholar, both wearing badges of command. I did not know the Spartan, but the Athenian was a sixty-year-old man named Polykrates. We had worked together some years before in the study of Middler science; he was a man of agile mind and great devotion. I could feel that Athena's hand was behind his presence here.

Behind these two leaders came a dozen soldiers in light bronze infantry armor with sheathed swords and throwers, and at the end of the line came two young women dressed in scholar's robes. The general saluted Aeson and Yellow Hare and they returned the gesture. Polykrates stared at me with a quizzical look, as if he hoped to divine the meaning of my actions.

On the left marched ten soldiers of the Middle Kingdom dressed in brown silk armor; they had sheathed swords across their backs and personal Xi lances holstered at their belts. After them came their general, a middle-aged, tall man wearing a light coat of steel that moved like cloth in accord with the motions of his body. Then came two younger men dressed in robes similar to Phan's. They looked uncertainly at my companion, then bowed their heads very slightly.

Phan and I stared at the delegations for a time, letting the spirits within us flow out to touch the hearts of the men who had come to listen. The sound of the wind outside mingled with the thunder that roared out from me, and the wash of the mountain stream joined with the harmony of Xi that flowed out from Phan, filling all those present with the song of Heaven and Earth.

"You have come for the sun fragments," I said, and the thunder rose in my words. "You may take them once your scientists have read these papers."

Yellow Hare stepped forward and gave my writings to Polykrates, while Aeson carried Phan's work to the Middle Kingdom scientists.

The scholars opened the sheaves cautiously. They began to read with mild curiosity which was rapidly replaced by avid fascination.

"Aias!" Polykrates said, looking up at me, his face painted with awe. "Have you truly done this?"

"Read on," I said.

One of his subordinates jabbed at my early pages. "Here is an experiment we could do tonight," she said. "We have all the equipment on the ships."

I smiled slightly. The first few experiments in both Phan's and my papers were designed so that the normal complement of scientists that accompanied any army of either empire could do them. The later experiments we outlined would require the laboratories of Athens or 'AngXou and the attentions of dozens of scientists.

As I knew it would, the animation and wonder of the scientists grew as they read through the works.

Writing the scientific part of the thesis had been simple. It had been much more difficult subtly placing into the pages the historical references that showed how the two empires had come to their eternal conflict, and why both sides thought they were losing the war. Kleio had warned me that no one now alive would understand those words, but if as Athena had promised the science we were giving them would remove the desperation from both the Delian League and the Middle Kingdom, then sometime, perhaps in thirty years, fifty years, or even a century, scholars would arise who would be capable of reading the hidden meanings of my text, and they would step forward to speak history in the grove of Akademe.

Both groups of scholars finished reading at approximately the same time, and both turned to ask us questions. I did not give them the chance.

"Here," I said, handing another sheet of rice paper to Polykrates while Phan did the same to one of the Middle Kingdom scientists. The paper I offered showed how to hitch a sun net to a celestial ship using an arrangement similar to our controls for *Rebuke of the Phoenix*. Phan's diagram showed how to guide a fragment between several battle kites down a corridor of rarefied air laid across a strengthened Xi flow; it also explained how to make the corridor using samples of captured fire-gold.

"These will instruct you in how to recover the sun fragments," I said. "Take them and go."

"But—," Polykrates said.

"Go!" the voice of Zeus roared from my lips.

Both groups retreated from the cave, and the spirit that raised me up went with them to ensure that they would gather up the sun fire and depart, carrying back to their homes the secrets we had imparted. As the thunder left my heart, Athena reappeared and whispered reassurance that there would be no battle today; neither general would risk losing what we had given him for the sake of stopping the enemy.

An hour later the gleam of fire from the mountaintop that had colored the sky a rich golden red diminished and eventually vanished.

"They have taken the sun fragments," I said. "It is accomplished."

"What have you done?" Aeson asked.

"I have changed the war," I said, "from a desperate struggle of two sides that cannot comprehend each other, and so can do nothing but battle, into a conflict between nations that will grow to comprehend each other, and so need not fight over all things and need not treat the whole of the universe as material for their strife."

"I do not see," Aeson said, staring up at the sky and following the path of 'Elios with his romantic's eyes.

"For nine centuries the Akademe has justified to itself its failure in investigating Taoist science by declaring that once the Middle Kingdom was conquered its scholars would be able to learn all the secrets of that study. But by giving them what I had learned of Taoist science, I lit a fire that burned away that excuse, a flame of research that will consume every mind in the Akademe. Nine hundred years of pent-up desire will burst forth, filling every scholar in every field with the need to understand his counterparts in the Middle Kingdom. A new form of glory will rise up in the Akademe; heroes will be made for advances in Taoist science rather than solely for military work."

'Era settled on Yellow Hare's shoulders and her divinity added depth to Yellow Hare's voice. "And Sparta will accept that the nature of this war has changed from eternal conflict to intermittent strife, from continuous battle for a final goal to occasional fights over specific objectives. The glory of war will rise to new heights as well when the heroes of Sparta accomplish great deeds that will not be reversed in a year or a century or a millennium."

"And in the gaps of battle," Ramonojon said, sitting peacefully on the ground in his saffron robes, "both sides will have to speak to each other."

Aeson turned away from his study of the sky. "That I do not see," he said.

"My notes told the Akademe everything I know about Taoist science," I said, "but though the gods themselves aided me in learning it, still I do not know much about the Tao or the flow of Xi and the manner in which it guides nature. Phan's notes are similar in what they tell the Middle Kingdom about Delian science; there are many gaps in his understanding of matter and form, of material and force. Both sides have enough information to start their researches, but progress will be frustratingly slow."

"The Akademe has worked slowly before."

"But they will know that the enemy has the answers to their questions. They will try to use prisoners to get information, but that will not get them far. In the periods of peace when Sparta and the generals of the Middle Kingdom have nothing to fight over, questions will be asked and answered across the no-man's-lands, and scholars who bring back knowledge from such interchanges will rise high in the Akademe."

My throat was suddenly dry from all this talk, and I felt a weariness in my heart, a lethargy that seemed to flow from the core of my being through the whole of my body.

Without being asked Yellow Hare brought me a bowl of water from the icy stream.

As I closed my eyes to drink the cold water of Earth, my heart filled with a vision of Olympos. From the cloud-wrapped heights of the divine mountain, 'Ermes descended on winged sandals and touched me with his serpent-entwined rod. The god of messengers caught up my soul and carried me up the side of the mountain here to the courts of the gods.

O divinities assembled, that is the whole of my tale. I have tried as best my mortal heart could comprehend them to heed the commands and warnings you gave me and have endeavored to carry out the duties you placed upon my shoulders. I lay myself at your feet and clasp your knees in supplication, hoping that I have accomplished your ends. Kleio, I pray that my deeds will lead to the restoration of your worship. Selene, 'Ermes, Aphrodite, 'Elios, may your celestial bodies never again be carved up for the sake of human war. Athena, O my patroness, I pray that I have freed your city from its self-induced blindness. And to you, O Father Zeus and you, 'Era queen of heaven, I give thanks with all my soul for the honor you have shown me, the honor of serving you in the ordering of the world.